Praise for the Sarantine Mosaic

Sailing to Sarantium

"A superb adventure. An extraordinary writer at his best."
—Jack McDevitt, author of *The Devil's Eye*

"Compulsively readable. . . . Once again, Guy Gavriel Kay has taken a period of history and transformed it into something magical, creating a multilayered society you can lose yourself in for days."
—Lisa Goldstein, author of *The Red Magician*

"*Sailing to Sarantium* confirms, yet again, Kay's status as one of our most accomplished and engaging storytellers." —*The Toronto Star*

"Up to Kay's usual high standard." —*Booklist*

"For some time now, Guy Gavriel Kay has been recognized as one of the finest writers of high fantasy in the world. Now he has achieved one of the finest works of historical fantasy . . . in years. Kay has constructed his novel as a literary mosaic of great intricacy and delicacy." —*Edmonton Journal*

"*Sailing to Sarantium* is an intricately plotted, fascinating historical novel and a moving story. Kay's distinctive prose style always flows smoothly and sometimes reaches strikingly beautiful depths." —*Winnipeg Free Press*

"A spellbinding tale . . . the chapters speed by as you lose yourself in passages that are indescribably elegant . . . simply one of the most beautifully written books I have read in ages." —*The Telegram* (Canada)

"An enchanting, colorful fantasy adventure." —*Time Out* (London)

"Kay deftly brings all his characters—be they mosaicists, slave girls, imperial postmen, dancers, charioteers, senators, tribunes, or emperors—to vivid life."
—*Starburst* (UK)

continued . . .

"Reality transformed by sparkling fantasy; buy, read, learn, and enjoy."
—*SFX Magazine* (UK)

"A top-quality romantic adventure." —*Interzone* (UK)

Lord of Emperors

"*Lord of Emperors* is wonderful. I never expect less from Guy Gavriel Kay."
—Robert Jordan

"Gripping . . . a grandly realized and wonderful story." —*The Denver Post*

"A masterful performance . . . his most ambitious work yet . . . powerfully written and compulsively readable. Guy Gavriel Kay is a superb storyteller and a writer who dominates a genre—historical fantasy—he virtually invented. . . . All of Kay's strengths and interests are at work in the Sarantine Mosaic. . . . When it comes to imaginary worlds, Guy Gavriel Kay is the Lord of Emperors."
—*Maclean's*

"Compulsively readable. . . . Kay is a global phenomenon. . . . His prose is sure-footed and poetic. Kay is a storyteller on the grandest scale; his Sarantine empire [is] peopled by prostitutes, charioteers, senators, and slaves, all drawn in fine detail. Yet despite the distance of time and place, his historical characters breathe and bleed; we feel they are our intimates. . . . Kay has complete control of all he creates. . . . His real subject is the power of art to survive and give posterity its version of the world. . . . Mosaic serves as both subject and style; Kay's method is to juxtapose chunks of contrasting tales, breaking and building suspense, inviting parallels between individuals high and low in society. It is fascinating . . . to see how the stories connect." —*Time* (Canada)

"Guy Gavriel Kay has transformed his own array of literary elements into something quite remarkable. . . . Closer to Tolstoy than Tolkien, in the Sarantine Mosaic Kay plumbs his reworkings of history and finds the deeper truths at its heart."
—*Locus*

"Complex and richly textured . . . Kay's characterization is matchless. The two books that comprise the Mosaic contain, in my mind, some of the finest writing to arise in the last decade in any genre." —*The Vancouver Sun*

"Kay is fulfilling the promise of *Sailing to Sarantium* beautifully." —*Booklist*

"His Sarantium (and the road to it) is an intricate and highly detailed creation populated by a legion of memorable and sharply delineated characters. Kay's judicious use of fantasy gives Sarantium a beguiling air of otherworldliness while leaving most events grounded in the engagingly gritty historical realism of chariot races, midnight trysts, and regal feasts." —*The Toronto Star*

"*Lord of Emperors* is the epitome of what a fantasy novel can be. Although the elements which are strictly 'fantastic' are few and far between, Kay's novel presents interesting and real people caught up in epic events against a glorious backdrop. In a world of derivative fantasy novels, *Lord of Emperors* clearly demonstrates itself to be sui generis." —SF Site

"Truly astonishing . . . every aspect of *Lord of Emperors* reveals a master at work. . . . Now complete, the Sarantine Mosaic takes its place as a major historical fantasy, one which redefines the possibilities of and sets new standards for the genre. Simply not to be missed." —*Edmonton Journal*

"Vintage Kay—richly written, exploring themes of art and power, interweaving alternate history and high fantasy to create a strange yet familiar world." —*Winnipeg Free Press*

"Larger than life . . . mesmerizing . . . brilliant. . . . Kay has done what the best writers do, and that is to stake out his territory in the landscape of literature. [His] books ring with authenticity. They are literate and imaginative and work on many levels. History aficionados will delight in the small and telling insights Mr. Kay brings to the era and its cultures, while other readers will simply delight in the grand sweep of the story, the rich characterization, and Mr. Kay's sheer gift with language." —*Ottawa Citizen*

"A complete joy . . . a fascinating story, moving, touched with magic, with characters that intrigue and delight the reader. *Sailing to Sarantium* was a delightful and promising book, but *Lord of Emperors* is more, the fulfillment of that promise, a feast of riches that will be read and reread." —*The StarPhoenix* (Canada)

WORKS BY GUY GAVRIEL KAY

The Fionavar Tapestry
The Summer Tree
The Wandering Fire
The Darkest Road

Tigana

A Song for Arbonne

The Lions of Al-Rassan

The Sarantine Mosaic
Sailing to Sarantium
Lord of Emperors

The Last Light of the Sun

Beyond This Dark House (poetry)

Ysabel

Under Heaven

SAILING TO SARANTIUM

BOOK ONE OF THE SARANTINE MOSAIC

GUY GAVRIEL KAY

A ROC BOOK

ROC
Published by New American Library, a division of
Penguin Group (USA) Inc., 375 Hudson Street,
New York, New York 10014, USA
Penguin Group (Canada), 90 Eglinton Avenue East, Suite 700, Toronto,
Ontario M4P 2Y3, Canada (a division of Pearson Penguin Canada Inc.)
Penguin Books Ltd., 80 Strand, London WC2R 0RL, England
Penguin Ireland, 25 St. Stephen's Green, Dublin 2,
Ireland (a division of Penguin Books Ltd.)
Penguin Group (Australia), 250 Camberwell Road, Camberwell, Victoria 3124,
Australia (a division of Pearson Australia Group Pty. Ltd.)
Penguin Books India Pvt. Ltd., 11 Community Centre, Panchsheel Park,
New Delhi - 110 017, India
Penguin Group (NZ), 67 Apollo Drive, Rosedale, North Shore 0632,
New Zealand (a division of Pearson New Zealand Ltd.)
Penguin Books (South Africa) (Pty.) Ltd., 24 Sturdee Avenue,
Rosebank, Johannesburg 2196, South Africa

Penguin Books Ltd., Registered Offices:
80 Strand, London WC2R 0RL, England

Published by Roc, an imprint of New American Library, a division of Penguin Group (USA) Inc.
Previously published in HarperPrism hardcover and paperback editions.
Published by arrangement with the author.

First Roc Printing, September 2010
10 9 8 7 6 5 4 3 2 1

Library of Congress Cataloging-in-Publication Data

Kay, Guy Gavriel.
Sailing to Sarantium/Guy Gavriel Kay.
p. cm.—(The Sarantine mosaic)
"A ROC book."
ISBN 978-0-451-46351-7
1. Mosaicists—Fiction. I. Title.
PR9199.3.K39S25 2010
813'.54—dc22 2010019383

Set in Adobe Garamond Pro
Designed by Catherine Leonardo

Printed in the United States of America

For my sons,

Samuel Alexander and Matthew Tyler,

with love, as I watch them

". . . fashion everything

From nothing every day, and teach

The morning stars to sing."

ACKNOWLEDGMENTS

I imagine it is obvious from the title of this work, but I owe a debt of inspiration to William Butler Yeats, whose meditations in poetry and prose on the mysteries of Byzantium led me there and gave me a number of underlying motifs along with a sense that imagination and history would be at home together in this milieu.

I have long believed that to do a variation in fiction upon a given period, one must first try to grasp as much as possible about that period. Byzantium is well served by its historians, fractious as they might be amongst each other. I have been deeply enlightened and focused by their writing and—via electronic mail—by personal communications and generous encouragement offered by many scholars. It hardly needs to be stressed, I hope, that those people I name here cannot remotely bear any responsibility for errors or deliberate alterations made in what is essentially a fantasy upon themes of Byzantium.

I am happy to record the great assistance I have received from the work of Alan Cameron on chariot racing and the Hippodrome factions;

Rossi, Nordhagen and L'Orange on mosaics; Lionel Casson on travel in the ancient world; Robert Browning, particularly on Justinian and Theodora; Warren Treadgold on the military; David Talbot Rice, Stephen Runciman, Gervase Mathew and Ernst Kitzinger on Byzantine aesthetics; and the broader histories of Cyril Mango, H. W. Haussig, Mark Whittow, Averil Cameron and G. Ostrogorsky. I should also acknowledge the aid and stimulation I received from participating in the lively and usefully disputatious scholarly mailing lists on the Internet relating to Byzantium and Late Antiquity. My research methods will never be the same.

On a more personal level, Rex Kay remains my first and most astringent reader, Martin Springett brought his considerable skills to preparing the map, and Meg Masters, my Canadian editor, has been a calm, deeply valued presence for four books now. Linda McKnight and Anthea Morton-Saner in Toronto and London are sustaining friends as well as canny agents, and a sometimes demanding author is deeply aware of both of these elements. My mother guided me to books as a child and then to the belief I could write my own. She still does that. And my wife creates a space into which the words and stories can come. If I say I am grateful, it grievously understates the truth.

. . . and we knew not whether we were in heaven or on earth. For on earth there is no such splendour or such beauty, and we were at a loss how to describe it. We know only that God dwells there among men, and their service is fairer than the ceremonies of other nations. For we cannot forget that beauty.

—*Chronicle of the Journey of Vladimir, Grand Prince of Kiev, to Constantinople*

N
W
E
S
KARCH
SAURADIA
Inicii
Tribes
BATIARA
Megarium
Varena
Mylasia
Rhodias
Baiana

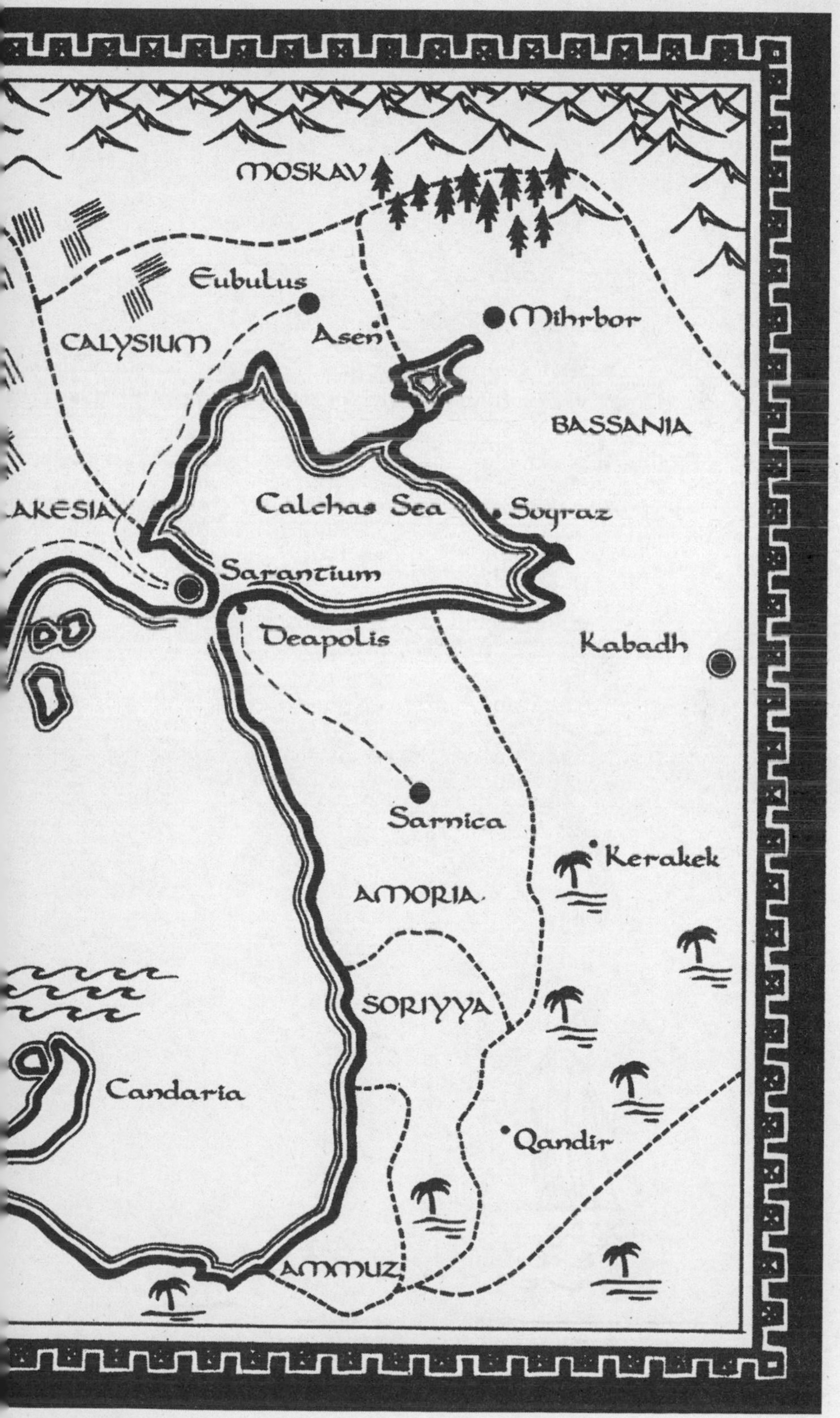

MOSKAV

Eubulus

Mihrbor

Asen

CALYSIUM

BASSANIA

AKESIA

Calchas Sea

Soyraz

Sarantium

Deapolis

Kabadh

Sarnica

Kerakek

AMORIA

SORIYYA

Candaria

Qandir

AMMUZ

PROLOGUE

Thunderstorms were common in Sarantium on midsummer nights, sufficiently so to make plausible the oft-repeated tale that the Emperor Apius passed to the god in the midst of a towering storm, with lightning flashing and rolls of thunder besieging the Holy City. Even Pertennius of Eubulus, writing only twenty years after, told the story this way, adding a statue of the Emperor toppling before the bronze gates to the Imperial Precinct and an oak tree split asunder just outside the landward walls. Writers of history often seek the dramatic over the truth. It is a failing of the profession.

In fact, on the night Apius breathed his last in the Porphyry Room of the Attenine Palace there was no rain in the City. An occasional flash of lightning had been seen and one or two growls of thunder heard earlier in the evening, well north of Sarantium, toward the grainlands of Trakesia. Given the events that followed, that northern direction might have been seen as portent enough.

The Emperor had no living sons, and his three nephews had rather spectacularly failed a test of their worthiness less than a year before and had suffered appropriate consequences. There was, as a result, no Emperor Designate in Sarantium when Apius heard—or did not hear—as the last words of his long life, the inward voice of the god saying to him alone, *"Uncrown, the Lord of Emperors awaits you now."*

The three men who entered the Porphyry Room in the still-cool hour before dawn were each acutely aware of a dangerously unstable situation. Gesius the eunuch, Chancellor of the Imperial Court, pressed his long, thin fingers together piously, and then knelt stiffly to kiss the dead Emperor's bare feet. So, too, after him, did Adrastus, Master of Offices, who commanded the civil service and administration, and Valerius, Count of the Excubitors, the Imperial Guard.

"The Senate must be summoned," murmured Gesius in his papery voice. "They will go into session immediately."

"Immediately," agreed Adrastus, fastidiously straightening the collar of his ankle-length tunic as he rose. "And the Patriarch must begin the Rites of Mourning."

"Order," said Valerius in soldier's tones, "will be preserved in the City. I undertake as much."

The other two looked at him. "Of course," said Adrastus, delicately. He smoothed his neat beard. Preserving order was the only reason Valerius had for being in the room just now, one of the first to learn the lamentable situation. His remarks were . . . a shade emphatic.

The army was primarily east and north at the time, a large element near Eubulus on the current Bassanid border, and another, mostly mercenaries, defending the open spaces of Trakesia from the barbarian incursions of the Karchites and the Vrachae, both of whom had been quiescent of late. The strategos of either military contingent could become a decisive factor—or an Emperor—if the Senate delayed.

The Senate was an ineffectual, dithering body of frightened men. It was likely to delay unless given extremely clear guidance. This, too, the three officials in the room with the dead man knew very well.

"I shall," said Gesius casually, "make arrangements to have the noble families apprised. They will want to pay their respects."

"Naturally," said Adrastus. "Especially the Daleinoi. I understand Flavius Daleinus returned to the City only two days ago."

The eunuch was too experienced a man to actually flush.

Valerius had already turned for the doorway. "Deal with the nobility as you see fit," he said over his shoulder. "But there are five hundred thousand people in the City who will fear the wrath of Holy Jad descending upon a leaderless Empire when they hear of this death. They are my concern. I will send word to the Urban Prefect to ready his own men. Be thankful there was no thunderstorm in the night."

He left the room, hard-striding on the mosaic floors, burly-shouldered, still vigorous in his sixtieth year. The other two looked at each other. Adrastus broke the shared gaze, glancing away at the dead man in the magnificent bed, and at the jeweled bird on its silver bough beside that bed. Neither man spoke.

Outside the Attenine Palace, Valerius paused in the gardens of the Imperial Precinct only long enough to spit into the bushes and note that it was still some time before the sunrise invocation. The white moon was over the water. The dawn wind was west; he could hear the sea, smell salt on the breeze amid the scent of summer flowers and cedars.

He walked away from the water under the late stars, past a jumble of palaces and civil service buildings, three small chapels, the Imperial Silk Guild's hall and workspaces, the playing fields, the goldsmiths' workshops, and the absurdly ornate Baths of Marisian, toward the Excubitors' barracks near the bronze gates that led out to the City.

Young Leontes was waiting outside. Valerius gave the man precise instructions, memorized carefully some time ago in preparation for this day.

His prefect withdrew into the barracks and Valerius heard, a moment later, the sounds of the Excubitors—his men for the last ten years—readying themselves. He drew a deep breath, aware that his heart was pounding, aware of how important it was to conceal any such intensities. He reminded himself to send a man running to inform Petrus, outside the Imperial Precinct, that Jad's Holy Emperor Apius was dead, that the great game had begun. He offered silent thanks to the god that his own sister-son was a better man, by so very much, than Apius's three nephews.

He saw Leontes and the Excubitors emerging from the barracks into the shadows of the predawn hour. His features were impassive, a soldier's.

IT WAS TO BE a race day at the Hippodrome, and Astorgus of the Blues had won the last four races run at the previous meeting. Fotius the sandalmaker had wagered money he couldn't afford to lose that the Blues' principal charioteer would win the first three races today, making a lucky seven in a row. Fotius had dreamt of the number twelve the night before, and three quadriga races meant Astorgus would drive twelve horses, and when the one and the two of twelve were added together . . . why, they made a three again! If he hadn't seen a ghost on the roof of the colonnade across from his shop yesterday afternoon, Fotius would have felt entirely sure of his wager.

He had left his wife and son sleeping in their apartment above the shop and made his way cautiously—the streets of the City were dangerous at night, as he had cause to know—toward the Hippodrome. It was long before sunrise; the white moon, waning, was west toward the sea, floating above the towers and domes of the Imperial Precinct. Fotius couldn't afford to pay for a seat every time he came to the racing, let alone one in the shaded parts of the stands. Only ten thousand places were offered free to citizens on a race day. Those who couldn't buy, waited.

Two or three thousand others were already in the open square when he arrived under the looming dark masonry of the Hippodrome. Just being here excited Fotius, driving away a lingering sleepiness. He hastily took a blue tunic from his satchel and pulled it on in exchange for his ordinary brown one, modesty preserved by darkness and speed. He joined a group of others similarly clad. He had made this one concession to his wife after a beating by Green partisans two years before during a particularly wild summer season: he wore unobtrusive garb until he reached the relative safety of his fellow Blues. He greeted some of the others by name and was welcomed cheerfully. Someone passed him a cup of cheap wine and he took a drink and passed it along.

A tipster walked by selling a list of the day's races and his predictions. Fotius couldn't read, so he wasn't tempted, though he saw others handing over two copper folles for a sheet. Out in the middle of the Hippodrome Forum a Holy Fool, half naked and stinking, had staked a place and was already haranguing the crowd about the evils of racing. The man had a good voice and offered some entertainment . . . if you didn't stand downwind. Street vendors were already selling figs and Candaria melons and grilled lamb. Fotius had packed himself a wedge of cheese and some of the bread ration from the day before. He was too excited to be hungry, in any case.

Not far away, near their own entrance, the Greens were clustered in similar numbers. Fotius didn't see Pappio the glassblower among them, but he knew he'd be there. He'd made his bet with Pappio. As dawn approached, Fotius began—as usual—to wonder if he'd been reckless with his wager. That spirit he'd seen, in broad daylight . . .

It was a mild night for summer, with a sea wind. It would be very hot later, when the racing began. The public baths would be crowded at the midday interval, and the taverns.

Fotius, still thinking about his wager, wondered if he ought to have stopped at a cemetery on the way with a curse-tablet against the principal Green charioteer, Scortius. It was the boy, Scortius, who was likeliest to stand—or drive—today between Astorgus and his seven straight triumphs. He'd bruised his shoulder in a fall in mid-session last time, and hadn't been running when Astorgus won that magnificent four-in-a-row at the end of the day.

It offended Fotius that a dark-skinned, scarcely bearded upstart from the deserts of Ammuz—or wherever he was from—could be such a threat to his beloved Astorgus. He *ought* to have bought the curse-tablet, he thought ruefully. An apprentice in the linen guild had been knifed in a dockside caupona two days before and was newly buried: a perfect chance for those with tablets to seek intercession at the grave of the violently dead. Everyone knew that made the inscribed curses more powerful. Fotius decided he'd have only himself to blame if Astorgus failed today. He had no idea how he'd pay Pappio if he lost. He chose not to think about that, or about his wife's reaction.

"Up the Blues!" he shouted suddenly. A score of men near him roused themselves to echo the cry.

"Up the Blues in their butts!" came the predictable reply from across the way.

"If there were any Greens with balls!" a man beside Fotius yelled back. Fotius laughed in the shadows. The white moon was hidden now, over behind the Imperial Palaces. Dawn was coming, Jad in his chariot riding up in the east from his dark journey under the world.

And then the mortal chariots would run, in the god's glorious name, all through a summer's day in the holy city of Sarantium. And the Blues, Jad willing, would triumph over the stinking Greens, who were no better than barbarians or pagan Bassanids or even Kindath, as everyone knew.

"Look," someone said sharply, and pointed.

Fotius turned. He actually heard the marching footsteps before he saw the soldiers appear, shadows out of the shadows, through the Bronze Gate at the western end of the square.

The Excubitors, hundreds of them, armed and armored beneath their gold-and-red tunics, came into the Hippodrome Forum from the Imperial Precinct. That was unusual enough at this hour to actually be terrifying. There had been two small riots in the past year, when the more rabid partisans of the two colors had come to blows. Knives had appeared, and staves, and the Excubitors had been summoned to help the Urban Prefect's men quell them. Quelling by the Imperial Guard of Sarantium was not a mild process. A score of dead had strewn the stones afterward both times.

Someone else said, "Holy Jad, the pennons!" and Fotius saw, belatedly, that the Excubitors' banners were lowered on their staffs. He felt a cold wind blow through his soul, from no direction in the world.

The Emperor was dead.

Their father, the god's beloved, had left them. Sarantium was bereft, forsaken, open to enemies east and north and west, malevolent and godless. And with Jad's Emperor gone, who knew what daemons or spirits from the half-world might now descend to wreak their havoc among helpless mortal men? Was *this* why he'd seen a ghost? Fotius thought of plague coming again, of war, of famine. In that moment he pictured his child lying dead. Terror pushed him to his knees on the cobbles of the square. He realized that he was weeping for the Emperor he had never seen except as a distant, hieratic figure in the Imperial Box in the Hippodrome.

Then—an ordinary man living his days in the world of ordinary men—Fotius the sandalmaker understood that there would be no racing today. That his reckless wager with the glassblower was nullified. Amid terror and grief, he felt a shaft of relief like a bright spear of sunlight. Three races in a row? It had been a fool's wager, and he was quit of it.

There were many men kneeling now. The Holy Fool, seeing an opportunity, had raised his voice in denunciation—Fotius couldn't make him out over the babble of noise, so he didn't know what the man was decrying now. Godlessness, license, a divided clergy, heretics with Heladikian beliefs. The usual litanies. One of the Excubitors strode over to him and spoke quietly. The holy man ignored the soldier, as they usually did. But then Fotius, astonished, saw the ascetic dealt a slash across the shins with a spear shaft. The ragged man let out a cry—more of surprise than anything else—and fell to his knees, silent.

Over the wailing of the crowd another voice rose then, stern and assured, compelling attention. It helped that the speaker was on horseback, the only mounted man in the forum.

"*Hear me!* No harm will come to anyone here," he said, "if order is preserved. You see our banners. They tell their tale. Our glorious Emperor, Jad's most dearly beloved, his thrice-exalted regent upon earth, has left us to join the god in glory behind the sun. There will be no chariots today, but the Hippodrome gates will be opened for you to take comfort together while the Imperial Senate assembles to proclaim our new Emperor."

A louder murmur of sound. There was no heir; everyone knew it. Fotius saw people streaming into the forum from all directions. News of this sort would take no time at all to travel. He took a breath, struggling to hold down a renewed panic. *The Emperor was dead. There was no Emperor in Sarantium.*

The mounted man again lifted a hand for stillness. He sat his horse straight as a spear, clad as his soldiers were. Only the black horse and a border of silver on his overtunic marked his rank. No pretension here. A peasant from Trakesia, a farmer's son come south as a lad, rising in the army ranks through hard work and no little courage in battle. Everyone knew this tale. A man among men, that was the word on Valerius of Trakesia, Count of the Excubitors.

Who now said, "There will be clerics in all the chapels and sanctuaries of the City, and others will join you here, to lead mourning rites in the Hippodrome under Jad's sun." He made the sign of the sun disk.

"Jad guard *you*, Count Valerius!" someone cried.

The man on the horse appeared not to hear. Bluff and burly, the Trakesian never courted the crowd as others in the Imperial Precinct did. His Excubitors did their duties with efficiency and no evident partisanship, even when men were crippled and sometimes killed by them. Greens and Blues were dealt with alike, and sometimes even men of rank, for many of the wilder partisans were sons of aristocracy. No one even knew which faction Valerius preferred, or what his beliefs were, in the manifold schisms of Jaddite faith, though there was the usual speculation. His nephew was a patron of the Blues, that was known, but families often divided between the factions.

Fotius thought about going home to his wife and son after morning prayers at the little chapel he liked, near the Mezaros Forum. There was a grayness in the eastern sky. He looked over at the Hippodrome and saw that the Excubitors, as promised, were opening the gates.

He hesitated, but then he saw Pappio the glassblower standing a little apart from the other Greens, alone in an empty space. He was crying, tears running into his beard. Fotius, moved by entirely unexpected emotion, walked over to the other man. Pappio saw him and wiped at his eyes. Without a word spoken the two of them walked side by side into the vastness of the Hippodrome as the god's sun rose from the forests and fields east of Sarantium's triple landward walls and the day began.

PLAUTUS BONOSUS HAD NEVER wanted to be a Senator. The appointment, in his fortieth year, had been an irritant more than anything else. Among other things, there was an outrageously antiquated law that

Senators could not charge more than six percent on loans. Members of the "Names"—the aristocratic families entered on the Imperial Records—could charge eight, and everyone else, even pagans and the Kindath, were allowed ten. The numbers were doubled for marine ventures, of course, but only a man possessed by a daemon of madness would venture moneys on a merchant voyage at twelve percent. Bonosus was hardly a madman, but he *was* a frustrated businessman, of late.

Senator of the Sarantine Empire. Such an honor! Even his wife's preening irked him, so little did she understand the way of things. The Senate did what the Emperor told it to do, or what his privy counselors told it; no less, and certainly no more. It was not a place of power or any legitimate prestige. Perhaps once it had been, back in the west, in the earliest days after the founding of Rhodias, when that mighty city first began to grow upon its hill and proud, calm men—pagans though they might have been—debated the best way to shape a realm. But by the time Rhodias in Batiara was the heart and hearth of a world-spanning Empire—four hundred years ago, now—the Senate there was already a compliant tool of the Emperors in their tiered palace by the river.

Those fabled palace gardens were clotted with weeds now, strewn with rubble, the Great Palace sacked and charred by fire a hundred years ago. Sad, shrunken Rhodias was home to a weak High Patriarch of Jad and conquering barbarians from the north and east—the Antae, who still used bear grease in their hair, it was reliably reported.

And the Senate here in Sarantium now—the New Rhodias—was as hollow and complaisant as it had been in the western Empire. It was possible, Bonosus thought grimly, as he looked around the Senate Chamber with its elaborate mosaics on floor and walls and curving across the small, delicate dome, that those same savages who had looted Rhodias—or others worse than them—might soon do the same here where the Emperors now dwelled, the west being lost and sundered. A struggle for succession exposed any empire, considerably so.

Apius had reigned thirty-six years. It was hard to believe. Aged, tired, in the spell of his cheiromancers the last years, he had refused to name an heir after his nephews had failed the test he'd set for them. The three of them were not even a factor now—blind men could not sit the Golden

Throne, nor those visibly maimed. Slit nostrils and gouged eyes ensured that Apius's exiled sister-sons need not be considered by the Senators.

Bonosus shook his head, irked with himself. He was following lines of thought that suggested there was an actual decision to be made by the fifty men in this chamber. In reality, they were simply going to ratify whatever emerged from the intrigues taking place even now within the Imperial Precinct. Gesius the Chancellor, or Adrastus, or Hilarinus, Count of the Imperial Bedchamber, would come soon enough and inform them what they were to wisely decide. It was a pretense, a piece of theater.

And Flavius Daleinus had returned to Sarantium from his family estates across the straits to the south just two days before. Most opportunely.

Bonosus had no quarrel with any of the Daleinoi, or none that he knew of, at any rate. This was good. He didn't much *care* for them, but that was hardly the issue when a merchant of modestly distinguished lineage considered the wealthiest and most illustrious family in the Empire.

Oradius, Master of the Senate, was signaling for the session to begin. He was having little success amid the tumult in the chamber. Bonosus made his way to his bench and sat down, bowing formally to the Master's Seat. Others noticed and followed his example. Eventually there was order. At which point Bonosus became aware of the mob at the doors.

The pounding was heavy, frightening, rocking the doors, and with it came a wild shouting of names. The citizens of Sarantium appeared to have candidates of their own to propose to the distinguished Senators of the Empire.

It sounded as if there was fighting going on. *What a surprise*, Bonosus thought sardonically. As he watched, fascinated, the ornately gilded doors of the Senate Chamber—part of the illusion that matters of moment transpired here—actually began to buckle under the hammering from without. A splendid symbol, Bonosus thought: the doors looked magnificent, but yielded under the least pressure. Someone farther along the bench let out an undignified squeal. Plautus Bonosus, having a whimsical turn of mind, began to laugh.

The doors crashed open. The four guards fell backward. A crowd of citizens—some slaves among them—thrust raucously into the chamber. Then the vanguard stopped, overawed. Mosaics and gold and gems had their uses, Bonosus thought, amused irony still claiming him. The torch-bearing image of Heladikos, riding his chariot toward his father the Sun—an image of no little controversy in the Empire today—looked down from the dome.

No one in the Senate Chamber seemed able to form a response to the intrusion. The crowd milled about, those still outside pushing forward, those in the chamber holding back, unsure of what they wanted to do now that they were here. Both factions—Blues and Greens—were present. Bonosus looked at the Master. Oradius remained bolted to his seat, making no motion at all. Suppressing his amusement, Bonosus gave an inward shrug and stood.

"People of Sarantium," he said gravely, extending both hands, "be welcome! Your aid in our deliberations in this difficult time will be invaluable, I am certain. Will you honor us with those names that commend themselves to you as worthy to sit the Golden Throne, before you withdraw and allow us to seek Jad's holy guidance in our weighty task?"

It took very little time, actually.

Bonosus had the Registrar of the Senate dutifully repeat and record each one of the shouted names. There were few surprises. The obvious strategoi, equally obvious nobility. Holders of Imperial Office. A chariot racer. Bonosus, his outward manner sober and attentive, had this name recorded, as well: Astorgus of the Blues. He could laugh about that afterward.

Oradius, evident danger past, roused himself to a fulsome speech of gratitude in his rich, round tones. It seemed to go over well enough, though Bonosus rather doubted the rabble in the chamber understood half of what was being said to them in the archaic rhetoric. Oradius asked the guards to assist the Empire's loyal citizenry from the chamber. They went—Blues, Greens, shopkeepers, apprentices, guildsmen, beggars, the many-raced sortings of a very large city.

Sarantines weren't especially rebellious, Bonosus thought wryly, so long as you gave them their free bread each day, let them argue about religion, and provided their beloved dancers and actors and charioteers.

Charioteers, indeed. Jad's Most Holy Emperor Astorgus the Charioteer. A wonderful image! He might *whip* the people into line, Bonosus thought, briefly amusing himself again.

His flicker of initiative spent, Plautus Bonosus leaned sideways on his bench, propped on one hand, and waited for the emissaries from the Imperial Precinct to come and tell the Senators what they were about to think.

It turned out to be a little more complex than that, however. Murder, even in Sarantium, could sometimes be a surprise.

IN THE BETTER NEIGHBORHOODS of the City it had become fashionable in the previous generation to add enclosed balconies to the second and third stories of houses or apartments. Reaching out over the narrow streets, these sunrooms now had the ironic, if predictable, effect of almost completely blocking the sunlight, all in the name of status and in order to afford the womenfolk of the better families a chance to view the street life through beaded curtains or sometimes extravagant window openings, without themselves suffering the indignity of being observed.

Under the Emperor Apius, the Urban Prefect had passed an ordinance forbidding such structures to project more than a certain distance from the building walls, and had followed this up by tearing down a number of solaria that violated the new law. Needless to say, this did not happen on the streets where the genuinely wealthy and influential kept their city homes. The power of one patrician to complain tended to be offset by the ability of another to bribe or intimidate. Private measures, of course, could not be entirely forestalled, and some regrettable incidents had unfortunately taken place over the years, even in the best neighborhoods.

IN ONE SUCH STREET, lined with uniformly handsome brick facades and with no shortage of lanterns set in the exterior walls to offer expensive lighting at night, a man now sits in a flagrantly oversized solarium, alternately watching the street below and the exquisitely slow, graceful movements of a woman as she plaits and coils her hair in the bedroom behind him.

Her lack of self-consciousness, he thinks, is an honor of sorts extended to him. Sitting unclothed on the edge of the bed, she displays her body in a sequence of curves and recesses: uplifted arm, smooth hollow of arm, honey-colored amplitude of breast and hip, and the lightly downed place between her thighs where he has been welcomed in the night just past.

The night a messenger came to report an emperor dead.

As it happens, he is wrong about one thing: her absorbed, unembarrassed nakedness has more to do with self-directed ease than any particular emotion or feeling associated with him at this moment. She is not, after all, unused to having her body seen by men. He knows this, but prefers, at times, to forget it.

He watches her, smiling slightly. He has a smooth-shaven, round face with a soft chin and gray, observant eyes. Not a handsome or an arresting man, he projects a genial, uncontentious, open manner. This is, of course, useful.

Her dark brown hair, he notes, has become tinged with red through the course of the summer. He wonders when she's had occasion to be outside enough for that to happen, then realizes the color might be artificial. He doesn't ask. He is not inclined to probe the details of what she does when they are not together in this apartment he has bought for her on a carefully chosen street.

That reminds him of why he is here just now. He looks away from the woman on the bed—her name is Aliana—and back out through the beaded curtains over the street. Some movement, for the morning is advanced and the news will have run through Sarantium by now.

The doorway he is watching remains closed. There are two guards outside it, but there always are. He knows the names of these two, and the others, and their backgrounds. Details of this sort can sometimes matter. Indeed, they *tend* to matter. He is careful in such things, and less genial than might appear to the unsubtle.

A man had entered through that doorway, his bearing urgent with tidings, just before sunrise. He had watched this by the light of the exterior torches, and had noted the livery. He had smiled then. Gesius the Chancellor had chosen to make his move. The game was begun, indeed. The man in the solarium expects to win it but is experienced enough in the ways of power in the world, already, to know that he might not. His name is Petrus.

"You are tired of me," the woman says, ending a silence. Her voice is low, amused. The careful movements of her arms, attending to her hair, do not cease. "Alas, the day has come."

"That day will never come," the man says calmly, also amused. This is a game they play, from within the entirely improbable certainty of their relationship. He does not turn from watching the doorway now, however.

"I will be on the street again, at the mercy of the factions. A toy for the wildest partisans with their barbarian ways. A cast-aside actress, disgraced and abandoned, past my best years."

She was twenty in the year when the Emperor Apius died. The man has seen thirty-one summers; not young, but it was said of him—before and after that year—that he was one of those who had never been young.

"I'd give it two days," he murmurs, "before some infatuated scion of the Names, or a rising merchant in silk or Ispahani spice won your fickle heart with jewelry and a private bathhouse."

"A private bathhouse," she agrees, "would be a *considerable* lure."

He glances over, smiling. She'd known he would, and has managed, not at all by chance, to be posed in profile, both arms uplifted in her hair, her head turned toward him, dark eyes wide. She has been on the stage since she was seven years old. She holds the pose a moment, then laughs.

The soft-featured man, clad only in a dove gray tunic with no undergarments in the aftermath of lovemaking, shakes his head. His own sand-colored hair is thinning a little but not yet gray. "Our beloved Emperor is dead, no heir in sight, Sarantium in mortal peril, and you idly torment a grieving and troubled man."

"May I come and do it some more?" she asks.

She sees him actually hesitate. That surprises and even excites her, in truth: a measure of his need of her, that even on this morning . . .

But in that instant there comes a sequence of sounds from the street below. A lock turning, a heavy door opening and closing, hurried voices, too loud, and then another, flat with command. The man by the beaded curtain turns quickly and looks out again.

The woman pauses then, weighing many things at this moment in her life. But the real decision, in truth, has been made some time ago. She trusts him, and herself, amazingly. She drapes her body—a kind of defending—in the bed linen before saying to his now-intent profile, from which the customary genial expression has entirely gone, *"What is he wearing?"*

He ought not to have been, the man will decide much later, nearly so surprised by the question and what she—very deliberately—revealed with it. Her attraction for him, from the beginning, has resided at least as much in wit and perception as in her beauty and the gifts that drew Sarantines to the theater every night she performed, alternately aroused and then driven to shouts of laughter and applause.

He *is* astonished, though, and surprise is rare for him. He is not a man accustomed to allowing things to disconcert him. This happens to be one matter he has not confided in her, however. And, as it turns out, what the silver-haired man in the still-shaded street has elected to wear as he steps from his home into the view of the world, on a morning fraught with magnitude, matters very much.

Petrus looks back at the woman. Even now he turns away from the street to her, and both of them will remember that, after. He sees that she's covered herself, that she is a little bit afraid, though would surely deny it. Very little escapes him. He is moved, both by the implications of her voicing the question and by the presence of her fear.

"You knew?" he asks quietly.

"You were extremely specific about this apartment," she murmurs, "the requirement of a solarium over this particular street. It was not hard to note which doorways could be watched from here. And the theater or the Blues' banqueting hall are sources of information on Imperial maneuverings as much as the palaces or the barracks are. *What is he wearing, Petrus?*"

She has a habit of lowering her voice for emphasis, not raising it: training on the stage. It is very effective. Many things about her are. He looks out again, and down, through the screening curtain at the cluster of men before the one doorway that matters.

"White," he says, and pauses before adding softly, no more than a breath of his own, "bordered, shoulder to knee, with purple."

"Ah," she says. And rises then, bringing the bedsheet to cover herself as she walks toward him, trailing it behind her. She is not tall but moves as if she were. "He wears porphyry. This morning. And so?"

"And so," he echoes. But not as a question.

Reaching through the beads of the curtain with one hand, he makes a brief, utterly unexceptionable sign of the sun disk for the benefit of the men who have been waiting in the street-level apartment across the way for a long time now. He waits only to see the sign returned from a small, iron-barred guard's portal and then he rises to cross toward the small, quite magnificent woman in the space between room and solarium.

"What happens, Petrus?" she asks. "What happens now?"

He is not a physically impressive man, which makes the sense of composed mastery he can display all the more impressive—and unsettling—at times.

"Idle torment was offered," he murmurs. "Was it not? We have some little leisure now."

She hesitates, then smiles, and the bedsheet, briefly a garment, slips to the floor.

There is a very great tumult in the street below not long after. Screaming, desperately wild shouts, running footsteps. They do not leave the bed this time. At one point, in the midst of lovemaking, he reminds her, a whisper at one ear, of a promise made a little more than a year ago. She has remembered it, of course, but has never quite let herself believe it. Today—this morning—taking his lips with her own, his body within hers again, thinking of an Imperial death in the night just past, and another death now, and the uttermost unlikeliness of love, she does. She actually does believe him now.

Nothing has ever frightened her more, and this is a woman who has already lived a life, young as she is, where great fear has been known and appropriate. But what she says to him, a little later, when space to speak returns to them, as movement and the conjoined spasms pass, is: "Remember, Petrus. A private bath, cold *and* hot water, with steam, or I find myself a spice merchant who knows how to treat a highborn lady."

ALL HE'D EVER WANTED to do was race horses.

From first awareness of being in the world, it seemed to him, his desire had been to move among horses, watch them canter, walk, run; talk to them, talk about them, and about chariots and drivers all the god's day and into starlight. He wanted to tend them, feed them, help them into life, train them to harness, reins, whip, chariot, noise of crowd. And then—by Jad's grace, and in honor of Heladikos, the god's gallant son who died in his chariot bringing fire to men—stand in his own quadriga behind four of them, leaning far forward over their tails, reins wrapped about his body lest they slip through sweaty fingers, knife in belt for a desperate cutting free if he fell, and urge them on to speeds and a taut grace in the turnings that no other man could even imagine.

But hippodromes and chariots were in the wider world and of the world, and nothing in the Sarantine Empire—not even worship of the god—was clean and uncomplicated. It had even become dangerous here in the City to speak too easily of Heladikos. Some years ago the High Patriarch in what remained of ruined Rhodias and the Eastern Patriarch here in Sarantium had issued a rare joint Pronouncement that Holy Jad, the god in the Sun and behind the Sun, had no born children, mortal or otherwise—that *all* men were, in spirit, the sons of the god. That Jad's essence was above and beyond propagation. That to worship, or even honor the idea of, a begotten son was paganism, assailing the pure divinity of the god.

But how else, clerics back in Soriyya and elsewhere had preached in opposition, had the ineffable, blindingly bright Golden Lord of Worlds made himself accessible to lowly mankind? If Jad loved his mortal creation, the sons of his spirit, did it not hold that he would embody a part of himself in mortal guise, to seal the covenant of that love? And that seal was Heladikos, the Charioteer, his child.

Then there were the Antae, who had conquered in Batiara and accepted the worship of Jad—embracing Heladikos with him, but as a demigod himself, not merely a mortal child. *Barbaric paganism*, the orthodox clerics now thundered—except those who lived in Batiara under the Antae. And since the High Patriarch himself lived there at their sufferance in Rhodias, the fulminations against Heladikian heresies were muted in the west.

But here in Sarantium issues of faith were endlessly debated everywhere, in dockfront cauponae, whorehouses, cookshops, the Hippodrome, the theaters. You couldn't buy a brooch to pin your cloak without hearing the vendor's views on Heladikos or the proper liturgy for the sunrise invocations.

There were too many in the Empire—and especially in the City itself—who had thought and worshipped in their own way for too long for the Patriarchs and clerics to persecute aggressively, but the signs of a deepening division were everywhere, and unrest was always present.

In Soriyya, to the south between desert and sea, where Jaddites dwelt perilously near to the Bassanid frontier, and among the Kindath and the grimly silent, nomadic peoples of Ammuz and the deserts beyond, whose faith was fragmented from tribe to tribe and inexplicable, shrines to Heladikos were as common as sanctuaries or chapels built for the god. The courage of the son, his willingness to sacrifice, were virtues exalted by clerics and secular leaders both in lands bordering enemies. The City, behind its massive triple walls and the guarding sea, could afford to think differently, they said in the desert lands. And Rhodias in the far-off west had long since been sacked, so what true guidance could its High Patriarch offer now?

Scortius of Soriyya, youngest lead racer ever to ride for the Greens of Sarantium, who only wanted to drive a chariot and think of nothing but speed and stallions, prayed to Heladikos and his golden chariot in the silence of his soul, being a contained, private young man—half a son of the desert himself. How, he had decided in childhood, could any charioteer do otherwise than honor the Charioteer? Indeed, he was inwardly of the belief—untutored though he might be in such matters—that those he raced against who followed the Patriarchal Pronouncement and denied the god's son were cutting themselves off from a vital source of intervention when they wheeled through the arches onto the dangerous, proving sands of the Hippodrome before eighty thousand screaming citizens.

Their problem, not his.

He was nineteen years old, riding First Chariot for the Greens in the largest stadium in the world, and he had a genuine chance to be the first rider since Ormaez the Esperanan to win his hundred in the City before his twentieth birthday, at the end of the summer.

But the Emperor was dead. There would be no racing today, and for the god knew how many days during the mourning rites. There were twenty thousand people or more in the Hippodrome this morning, spilling out onto the track, but they were murmuring anxiously among themselves, or listening to yellow-robed clerics intone the liturgy, not watching the chariots wheeled out in the Procession. He'd lost half a race day last week to a shoulder injury, and now today was gone, and next week? The week after?

Scortius knew he ought not to be so concerned with his own affairs at a time such as this. The clerics—whether Heladikian or Orthodox—would *all* castigate him for it. On some things the religious agreed.

He saw men weeping in the stands and on the track, others gesturing too broadly, speaking too loudly, fear in their eyes. He had seen that fear when the chariots were running, in other drivers' faces. He couldn't say he had ever felt it himself, except when the Bassanid armies had come raiding across the sands and, standing on their city ramparts, he had looked up and seen his father's eyes. They had surrendered that time, lost their city, their homes—only to regain them four years later in a treaty, following victories on the northern border. Conquests were traded back and forth all the time.

He understood that the Empire might be in danger now. Horses needed a firm hand, and so did an Empire. His problem was that, growing up where he had, he'd seen the eastern armies of Shirvan, King of Kings, too many times to feel remotely as anxious as those he watched now. Life was too rich, too new, too impossibly exciting for his spirits to be dragged downward, even today.

He was nineteen, and a charioteer. In Sarantium.

Horses were his life, as he had dreamed once they might be. These affairs of the larger world . . . Scortius could let others sort them out. Someone would be named Emperor. Someone would sit in the kathisma—the Imperial Box—midway along the Hippodrome's western side one day soon—the god willing!—and drop the white handkerchief to signal the Procession, and the chariots would parade and then run. It didn't much matter to a charioteer, Scortius of Soriyya thought, who the man with the handkerchief was.

He was truly young, in the City less than half a year, recruited by the Greens' factionarius from the small hippodrome in Sarnica, where he'd been driving broken-down horses for the lowly Reds—and winning races. He had a deal of growing up to do and much to learn. He would do it, in fact, and fairly quickly. Men change, sometimes.

Scortius leaned against an archway, shadowed, watching the crowd from a vantage point that led back along a runway to the interior workrooms and animal stalls and the tiny apartments of the Hippodrome staff beneath the stands. A locked door partway along the tunnel led down to the cavernous cisterns where much of the City's water supply was stored. On idle days, the younger riders and grooms sometimes raced small boats among the thousand pillars there in the echoing, watery spaces and faint light.

Scortius wondered if he ought to go outside and across the forum to the Green stables to check on his best team of horses, leaving the clerics to their chanting and the more unruly elements of the citizenry hurling names of Imperial candidates back and forth, even through the holy services.

He recognized, if vaguely, one or two of the names loudly invoked. He hadn't made himself familiar with all the army officers and aristocrats, let alone the stupefying number of palace functionaries in Sarantium. Who could, and still concentrate on what mattered? He had eighty-three wins, and his birthday was the last day of summer. It could be done. He rubbed his bruised shoulder, glancing up. No clouds, the threat of rain had passed away east. It would be a very hot day. Heat was good for him out on the track. Coming from Soriyya, burnt dark by the god's sun, he could cope with the white blazing of summer better than most of the others. This would have been a good day for him, he was sure of it. Lost, now. The Emperor had died.

He suspected that more than words and names would be flying in the Hippodrome before the morning was out. Crowds of this sort were rarely calm for long, and today's circumstances had Greens and Blues mingling much more than was safe. When the weather heated up so did tempers. A hippodrome riot in Sarnica, just before he left, had ended up with half the Kindath quarter of that city burning as the mob boiled out into the streets.

The Excubitors were here this morning, though, armed and watchful, and the mood was more apprehensive than angry. He might be wrong about the violence. Scortius would have been the first to admit he didn't know much about anything but horses. A woman had told him that only two nights ago, but she had sounded languorous as a cat and not displeased. He had discovered, actually, that the same gentling voice that worked with skittish horses was sometimes effective with the women who waited for him after a race day, or sent their servants to wait.

It didn't *always* work, mind you. He'd had an odd sense, partway through the night with that catlike woman, that she might have preferred to be driven or handled the way he drove a quadriga in the hard, lashing run to the finish line. That had been an unsettling thought. He hadn't acted on it, of course. Women were proving difficult to sort out; worth thinking about, though, he had to admit that.

Not nearly so much as horses were, mind you. Nothing was.

"Shoulder mending?"

Scortius glanced back quickly, barely masking surprise. The compact, well-made man who'd asked, who came now to stand companionably beside him in the archway, was not someone he'd have expected to make polite inquiry of him.

"Pretty much," he said briefly to Astorgus of the Blues, the preeminent driver of the day—the man he'd been brought north from Sarnica to challenge. Scortius felt awkward, inept, beside the older man. He'd no idea how to handle a moment such as this. Astorgus had not one but two statues raised in his name already, among the monuments in the spina of the Hippodrome, and one of them was bronze. He had dined in the Attenine Palace half a dozen times, it was reported. The powers of the Imperial Precinct solicited his views on matters within the City.

Astorgus laughed, his features revealing easy amusement. "I mean you no harm, lad. No poisons, no curse-tablets, no footpads in the dark outside a lady's home."

Scortius felt himself flush. "I know that," he mumbled.

Astorgus, his gaze on the crowded track and stands, added, "A rivalry's good for all of us. Keeps people talking about the races. Even when they aren't here. Makes them wager." He leaned against one of the pillars supporting the arch. "Makes them want more race days. They petition the Emperors. Emperors want the citizens happy. They add races to the calendar. That means more purses for all of us, lad. You'll help me retire that much sooner." He turned to Scortius and smiled. He had an amazingly scarred face.

"You want to retire?" Scortius said, astonished.

"I am," said Astorgus, mildly, "thirty-nine years old. Yes, I want to retire."

"They won't let you. The Blue partisans will demand your return."

"And I'll return. Once. Twice. For a price. *Then* I'll let my old bones have their reward and leave the fractures and scars and the tumbling falls to you, or even younger men. Any idea how many riders I've seen die on the track since I started?"

Scortius had seen enough deaths in his own short time not to need an answer to that. Whichever color they raced for, the frenzied partisans of the other faction wished them dead, maimed, broken. People came to the hippodromes to see blood and hear screaming as much as to admire speed. Deadly curses were dropped on wax tablets into graves, wells, cisterns, were buried at crossroads, hurled into the sea by moonlight from the City walls. Alchemists and cheiromancers—real ones and charlatans—were paid to cast ruinous spells against named riders and horses. In the hippodromes of the Empire the charioteers raced with Death—the Ninth Driver—as much as with each other. Heladikos, son of Jad, had died in his chariot, and they were his followers. Or some of them were.

The two racers stood in silence a moment, watching the tumult from the shadowed arch. If the crowd spotted them, Scortius knew, they'd be besieged, on the spot.

They weren't seen. Instead, Astorgus said very softly, after a silence, "That man. The group just there. All the Blues? He isn't. He isn't a Blue, I know him. I wonder what he's doing?"

Scortius, only mildly interested, glanced over in time to see the man indicated cup hands to mouth and shout, in a patrician, carrying voice: *"Daleinus to the Golden Throne! The Blues for Flavius Daleinus!"*

"Oh, my," said Astorgus, First Chariot of the Blues, almost to himself. "Here too? What a clever, clever bastard he is." Scortius had no idea what the other man was talking about.

Only long afterward, looking back, piecing things together, would he understand.

FOTIUS THE SANDALMAKER HAD actually been eyeing the heavyset, smooth-shaven man in the perfectly pressed blue tunic for some time.

Standing in an unusually mixed cluster of faction partisans and citizens of no evident affiliation, Fotius mopped at his forehead with a damp sleeve and tried to ignore the sweat trickling down his ribs and back. His own tunic was stained and splotched. So was Pappio's green one, beside him. The glassblower's balding head was covered with a cap that might once have been handsome but was now a wilted object of general mirth. It was brutally hot already. The breeze had died with the sunrise.

The big, too-stylish man bothered him. He was standing confidently in a group of Blue partisans, including a number of the leaders, the ones who led the unison cries when the Processions began and after victories. But Fotius had never seen him before, either in the Blue stands or at any of the banquets or ceremonies.

He nudged Pappio, on impulse. "You know him?" He gestured at the man he meant. Pappio, dabbing at his upper lip, squinted in the light. He nodded suddenly. "One of us. Or he was, last year."

Fotius felt triumphant. He was about to stride over to the group of Blues when the man he'd been watching brought his hands up to his mouth and cried the name of Flavius Daleinus aloud, acclaiming that extremely well-known aristocrat for Emperor, in the name of the Blues.

Nothing unique in that, though he wasn't a Blue. But when, a heartbeat later, the same cry echoed from various sections of the Hippodrome—in the name of the Greens, the Blues again, even the lesser colors of Red and White, and then on behalf of one craft guild, and another, and another, Fotius the sandalmaker actually laughed aloud.

"In Jad's holy name!" he heard Pappio exclaim bitterly. "Does he think we are all fools?"

The factions were no strangers to the technique of "spontaneous acclamations." Indeed, the Accredited Musician of each color was, among other things, responsible for selecting and training men to pick up and carry the cries at critical moments in a race day. It was part of the pleasure of belonging to a faction, hearing *"All glory to the glorious Blues!"* or *"Victory forever to conquering Astorgus!"* resound through the Hippodrome, perfectly timed, the mighty cry sweeping from the northern stands, around the curved end, and along the other side as the triumphant charioteer did his victory lap past the silent, beaten Green supporters.

"Probably does," a man beside Fotius said sourly. "What would the Daleinoi know of any of us?"

"They are an honorable family!" someone else interjected.

Fotius left them to debate. He crossed the ground toward the cluster of Blues. He felt angry and hot. He struck the impostor on one shoulder. This close, he could smell a scent on the man. Perfume? In the Hippodrome?

"By Jad's Light, who are you?" he demanded. "You aren't a Blue, how dare you speak in our name?"

The man turned. He was bulky, but not fat. He had odd, pale green eyes, which now regarded Fotius as if he were some form of insect that had crawled out of a wine flask. Fotius actually wondered, amid his own turbulent thoughts, how anyone's tunic could remain so crisp and clean here this morning.

The others had overheard. They looked at Fotius and the man who said, contemptuously, in a clipped, precise voice, "And you are the Accredited Record Keeper of the Blues in Sarantium, dare I suppose? Hah. You probably can't even read."

"Maybe he can't," said Pappio, striding up boldly, "but you wore a Green tunic last fall to our end-of-season banquet. I remember you there. You even made a toast. You were drunk!"

The man seemed, clearly, to classify Pappio as close kin to whatever crawling thing Fotius was. He wrinkled his nose. "And men are forbidden by some new ordinance to change their allegiance now? I am not allowed to enjoy and celebrate the triumphs of the mighty Asportus?"

"Who?" Fotius said.

"Astorgus," the man said quickly. "Astorgus of the Blues."

"Get out of here," said Daccilio, who had been one of the Blue faction leaders for as long as Fotius could remember, and who had carried the banner at this year's Hippodrome opening ceremonies. "Get out, now!"

"Take off that blue tunic first!" someone else rasped angrily. Voices were raised. Heads turned in their direction. From all over the Hippodrome the too-synchronized frauds were still crying the name of Flavius Daleinus. With a roiling, hot anger that was actually a kind of joy, Fotius grabbed a fistful of the impostor's crisp blue tunic in his sweaty hands.

Asportus, indeed.

He jerked hard and felt the tunic tear at the shoulder. The jeweled brooch holding it fell onto the sand. He laughed—and then let out a scream as something smashed him across the back of the knees. He staggered, collapsed in the dust. *Just as the charioteers fall*, he thought.

He looked up, tears in his eyes, pain taking his breath away. Excubitors. Of course. Three of them had come. Armed, impersonal, merciless. They could kill him as easily as crack him across the knees, and with as much impunity. This was Sarantium. Commoners died to make an example every day. A spear point was leveled at his breast.

"Next man who strikes another here gets a spear point, not a shaft," the man holding the weapon said, his voice hollow within his helmet. He was utterly calm. The Imperial Guard were the best-trained men in the City.

"You'll be busy, then," said Daccilio bluntly, unintimidated. "It seems the spontaneous demonstration arranged by the illustrious Daleinoi is not achieving what might have been desired."

The three Excubitors looked up into the stands and the one with the leveled spear swore, rather less calmly. There were fistfights breaking out now, centered around the men who had been shouting that patently contrived acclamation. Fotius lay motionless, not even daring to rub his legs, until the spear point wavered and moved away. The green-eyed impostor in the torn blue tunic was no longer among them. Fotius had no idea where he'd gone.

Pappio knelt beside him. "My friend, are you all right?"

Fotius managed to nod. He wiped at the tears and sweat on his face. His tunic and legs were coated with dust now, from the sacred ground where charioteers raced. He felt a sudden wave of fellow-feeling for the balding glassblower. Pappio was a Green, to be sure, but he was a decent fellow for all that. And he had helped unmask a deception.

Asportus of the Blues! *Asportus?* Fotius almost gagged. Trust the Daleinoi, those arrogant patricians, to have so little respect for the citizens as to imagine this shabby pantomime could get Flavius's rump onto the Golden Throne!

The Excubitors beside them suddenly pulled themselves into a line, bristling with military precision. Fotius glanced quickly past them. A man on a horse had entered the Hippodrome, riding slowly along the spina toward the midpoint.

Others saw the rider. Someone cried his name, and then more voices did. This time it *was* spontaneous. A guard of Excubitors moved into place around him as he reined the horse to a stop. It was the formal array of their ranks, and the silence of them, that drew all eyes and compelled a gradual stillness of twenty thousand people.

"Citizens of Sarantium, I have tidings," cried Valerius, Count of the Excubitors, in the rough, unvarnished soldier's tones.

They couldn't all hear him, of course, but the words were repeated by others—as was always the case here—and ran through that vast space, far up into the stands, across the spina with its obelisks and statues, through the empty kathisma where the Emperor would sit for the racing, and under the arches where some charioteers and Hippodrome staff were watching, shielded from the blazing sun.

Fotius saw the brooch on the sand beside him. He palmed it quickly. No one else seemed to notice. He would sell it, not long after, for enough money to change his life. Just now, though, he scrambled to his feet. He was dusty, grimy, sticky with sweat, but thought he should be standing when his Emperor was named.

He was wrong about what was coming, but why should he have understood the dance being danced that day?

MUCH LATER, THE INVESTIGATION by the Master of Offices, through the Quaestor of Imperial Intelligence, proved unexpectedly and embarrassingly incapable of determining the murderers of the most prominent Sarantine aristocrat of his day.

It was established readily enough that Flavius Daleinus—only recently returned to the City—had left his home on the morning of the death of the Emperor Apius, accompanied by his two older sons, a nephew, and a small retinue. Family members confirmed that he was on his way to the Senate Chamber to offer a formal expression of support to the Senators in their time of trial and decision. There was some suggestion—not confirmed from the Imperial Precinct—that he had arranged to meet the Chancellor there and be escorted afterward by Gesius to the Attenine Palace to pay his last respects.

The condition of Daleinus's body and what remained of his clothing when the dead man was carried on a bier to his home, and then later to his final resting place in the family mausoleum, was such that a widely reported rumor about his attire that morning was also not amenable to official confirmation.

The clothing had all burned—with or without the much-discussed strip of purple—and most of the elegant aristocrat's skin had been charred black or scorched entirely away. What remained of his face was horrifying, the features beneath the once-distinguished silver hair a melted ruin.

His oldest son and the nephew had also died, and four of his entourage. The surviving son, it was reported, was now blind and unfit to be seen. He was expected to take clerical vows and withdraw from the City.

Sarantine Fire did that to men.

It was one of the secrets of the Empire, shielded with ferocity, for it was the weapon that had guarded the City—thus far—from incursions over the water. Terror ran before that molten, liquid fire that set ships and men alight, burning upon the sea.

It had never, in living memory or in any of the military chronicles, been used within the walls, or indeed in any land engagement of the armies.

This, of course, directed informed suspicion upon the Strategos of the Navy and, indeed, any other military commanders who might have been able to suborn the naval engineers entrusted with the technique of training the liquid fire through a hose, or launching it through space upon the seafaring enemies of Sarantium.

In due course a number of appropriate persons were subjected to expert questioning. Their deaths did not, however, serve the ultimate goal of determining who it was who had arranged the hideous assassination of a distinguished patrician. The Strategos of the Navy, a man of the old school, elected to end his life, but left behind a letter declaring his innocence of any crimes and his mortal shame that such a weapon, entrusted to his care, had been used in this way. His death was, accordingly, not a useful one either.

It was reliably reported that three men had wielded the siphon apparatus. Or five. That they were wearing the colors and had the Bassanid-style clothing and the barbarian mustaches and long hair of the most extreme Green partisans. Or of the Blues. Further, that they wore the light brown tunics with black trim of the Urban Prefect's men. It was recounted that they had fled east down an alley. Also west. Or through the back of a house on the exclusive, shaded street where the Daleinoi's City mansion could be found. It was declared, with conviction, that the assassins had been Kindath in their silver robes and blue caps. No evident motive commended itself for this, but those worshippers of the two moons might well do evil for its own sake. Some ensuing, sporadic attacks in the Kindath Quarter were judged excusable by the Urban Prefect, as a way of discharging tensions in the City.

All the licensed foreign merchants in Sarantium were advised to keep to their allotted quarters of the City until further notice. Some of those who recklessly did not—curious, perhaps, to observe the unfolding events of those days—suffered predictable, unfortunate consequences.

The assassins of Flavius Daleinus were never found.

In the meticulous tally of the dead in that difficult time, ordered and executed by the Urban Prefect at the command of the Master of Offices, there was a report of three bodies found washed ashore four days later by soldiers patrolling the coast to the east of the triple walls. They were naked, skin bleached gray-white by the sea, and sea creatures had been at their faces and extremities.

No connection was ever made between this finding and the events of the terrible night the Emperor Apius went to the god, to be followed in the morning by the noble Flavius Daleinus. What connection could have been made? Bodies were found by fishermen in the water and along the stony beaches east all the time.

IN THE PRIVATE, PERHAPS petty way of an intelligent man without any real power, Plautus Bonosus rather enjoyed the expression on the Imperial Chancellor's face when the Master of Offices appeared in the Senate Chamber that morning, shortly after Gesius had arrived.

The tall, thin eunuch pressed his fingers together and inclined his head gravely, as if Adrastus's arrival was a source of support and consolation to him. But Bonosus had been watching his face when the ornate doors—rather the worse for their earlier battering—were pried open by the guards.

Gesius had been expecting someone else.

Bonosus had a pretty good idea who that might have been. It was going to be interesting, he thought, when all the players in this morning's pantomime were assembled. Adrastus, clearly, had arrived on his own behalf. With the two most powerful—and dangerous—strategoi and their forces each more than two weeks' hard marching from Sarantium, the Master of Offices had a legitimate pathway to the Golden Throne—if he moved decisively. His lineage among the "Names" was impeccable, his experience and rank unsurpassed, and he had the usual assortment of friends. And enemies.

Gesius, of course, could not even imagine Imperial status for himself, but the Chancellor could engineer a succession—or try to do so—that would ensure his own continuance at the heart of power in the Empire. It would be far from the first time one of the Imperial eunuchs had orchestrated affairs of succession.

Bonosus, listening to the bland shuffle of speeches from his colleagues—variations on a theme of grievous loss and momentous decisions to come—signaled a slave for a cup of chilled wine and wondered who would take a wager with him.

A charming blond boy—from Karch in the far north, by his coloring—brought his wine. Bonosus smiled at him, and idly watched the boy walk back to the near wall. He reviewed, again, the state of his own relations with the Daleinoi. No conflicts that he knew. Two shared—and profitable—backings of a spice ship to Ispahani some years ago, before his appointment. His wife reported that she greeted the lady wife of Flavius Daleinus when they met at the baths they both preferred, and that she was always responded to politely and by name. This was good.

Bonosus expected that Gesius would win this morning. That his patrician candidate would emerge as the Emperor Designate, with the eunuch retaining his position as Imperial Chancellor. The conjoined power of the Chancellor and the wealthiest family in the City were more than a match for Adrastus's ambition, however silken might be the manner and the intricate webs of intelligence spun by the Master of Offices. Bonosus was prepared to risk a sizable sum on the affair, if he could find a taker.

Later, he, too, would have cause to be privately grateful—amid chaos—that a wager had not taken place that day.

Watching as he sipped his wine, Bonosus saw Gesius, with the smallest, elegant gesture of his long fingers, petition Oradius to be allowed to speak. He saw the Master of the Senate bob his head up and down like a street puppet in immediate acknowledgment. *He's been bought*, he decided. Adrastus would have his supporters here too. Would doubtless make his own speech soon. It *was* going to be interesting. Who could squeeze the hapless Senate harder? No one had tried to bribe Bonosus. He wondered if he ought to be flattered or offended.

As another rote eulogy of the dead, thrice-exalted, luminous, never-to-be-equaled Emperor came to a platitudinous close, Oradius gestured with deference toward the Chancellor. Gesius bowed graciously and moved to the white marble speaker's circle in the center of the mosaics on the floor.

Before the Chancellor began, however, there came another rapping at the door. Bonosus turned, expectantly. This was remarkably well-timed, he noted with admiration. Flawlessly, in fact. He wondered how Gesius had done it.

But it was not Flavius Daleinus who entered the room.

Instead, an extremely agitated officer of the Urban Prefecture told the assembled Senate about Sarantine Fire loosed in the City and the death of an aristocrat.

A short time after that, with a gray-faced, visibly aged Chancellor being offered assistance on a bench by Senators and slaves, and the Master of Offices displaying either stupefied disbelief or brilliant acting skills, the august Senate of the Empire heard a mob outside its much-abused doors for the second time that day.

This time there was a difference. This time there was only one name being cried, and the voices were ferociously, defiantly assertive. The doors banged open hard, and the street life of the City spilled in. Bonosus saw the faction colors again, too many guilds to count, shopkeepers, street vendors, tavern-masters, bathhouse workers, animal-keepers, beggars, whores, artisans, slaves. And soldiers. There were soldiers this time.

And the same name on all their lips. The people of Sarantium, making known their will. Bonosus turned, on some instinct, in time to see the Chancellor suddenly drain his cup of wine. Gesius took a deep, steadying breath. He stood up, unaided, and moved toward the marble speaker's circle again. His color had come back.

Holy Jad, thought Bonosus, his mind spinning like the wheel of a toppled chariot, *can he be this swift*?

"Most noble members of the Imperial Senate," the Chancellor said, lifting his thin, exquisitely modulated voice. "See! Sarantium has come to us! Shall we hear the voice of our people?"

The people heard him, and their voice—responding—became a roar that shook the chamber. One name, again and again. Echoing among marble and mosaic and precious stones and gold, spiraling upward to the dome where doomed Heladikos drove his chariot, carrying fire. One name. An absurd choice in a way, but in another, Plautus Bonosus thought, it might not be so absurd. He surprised himself. It was not a thought he'd ever had before.

Behind the Chancellor, Adrastus, the suave, polished Master of Offices—the most powerful man in the City, in the Empire—still looked stunned, bewildered by the speed of things. He had not moved or reacted. Gesius had. In the end, that hesitation, missing the moment when everything changed, was to cost Adrastus his office. And his eyes.

The Golden Throne had been lost to him already. Perhaps that dawning awareness was what froze him there on a marble bench while the crowd roared and thundered as if they were in the Hippodrome or a theater, not the Senate Chamber. His dreams shattered—subtle, intricate designs slashed apart—as a beefy, toothless smith howled the City's chosen name right in his well-bred face.

Perhaps what Adrastus was hearing then, unmoving, was another sound entirely: the jeweled birds of the Emperor, singing for a different dancer now.

"VALERIUS TO THE GOLDEN THRONE!"

The cry had run through the Hippodrome, exactly as he'd been told it would. He'd refused them, had shaken his head decisively, turned his horse to leave, seen a company of the Urban Prefect's guardsmen running toward him—not his own men—and watched as they knelt before his mount, blocking his way with their bodies.

Then they, too, raised his name in a loud shout, begging that he accept the throne. Again he refused, shaking his head, making a sweeping gesture of denial. But the crowd was already wild. The cry that had begun when he brought them word of Daleinus's death reverberated through the huge space where the chariots ran and people cheered. There were thirty, perhaps forty thousand people there by then, even with no racing this day.

A different contest was proceeding toward its orchestrated end.

Petrus had told him what would happen and what he had to do at every step. That his reporting of the second death would bring shock and fear, but no grief, and even some vindication following hard upon the too-contrived acclamations of Daleinus. He hadn't asked his nephew how he'd known those acclamations would come. Some things he didn't need to know. He had enough to remember, more than enough to keep clearly in sequence this day.

But it had developed precisely as Petrus had said it would, exact as a heavy cavalry charge on open ground, and here he was astride his horse, the Urban Prefect's men blocking his way and the Hippodrome crowd screaming his name to the god's bright sun. His name and his alone. He had refused twice, as instructed. They were pleading with him now. He saw men weeping as they roared his name. The noise was deafening, a wall, punishingly loud, as the Excubitors—his own men this time—moved closer, and then completely surrounded him, making it impossible for a humble, loyal, unambitious man to ride from this place, to escape the people's declared will in their time of great danger and need.

He stepped down from his horse.

His men were around him, pressing close, screening him from the crowd where Blues and Greens stood mingled together, joined in a fierce, shared desire they had not known they even had, where all those gathered in this white, blazing light were calling upon him to be theirs. To save them now.

And so, in the Hippodrome of Sarantium, under the brilliant summer sun, Valerius, Count of the Excubitors, yielded to his fate and suffered his loyal guards to clothe him in the purple-lined mantle Leontes happened to have brought with him.

"Will they not wonder at that?" he had asked Petrus.

"It won't matter by then," his nephew had replied. *"Trust me in this."*

And the Excubitors made way, the outer ring of them parting slowly, like a curtain, so that the innermost ones could be seen holding an enormous round shield. And standing upon that shield as they raised it to their shoulders—in the ancient way soldiers proclaimed an Emperor—Valerius the Trakesian lifted his hands toward his people. He turned to all corners of the thundering Hippodrome—for *here* was the true thunder that day—and accepted, humbly and graciously, the spontaneous will of the Sarantine people that he be their Imperial Lord, Regent of Holy Jad upon earth.

Valerius! Valerius! Valerius!

All glory to the Emperor Valerius!

Valerius the Golden, to the Golden Throne!

His hair *had* been golden once, long ago, when he had left the grainlands of Trakesia with two other boys, poor as stony earth, but strong for a lad, willing to work, to fight, walking barefoot through a cold, wet autumn, the north wind behind them bringing winter, all the way to the Sarantine military camp, to offer their services as soldiers to a distant Emperor in the unimaginable City, long, long ago.

"PETRUS, STAY AND DINE with me?"

Night. A western sea breeze cooling the room through the open windows over the courtyard below. The sound of falling water drifted up from the fountains, and from farther away came the susurration of wind in the leaves of the trees in the Imperial gardens.

Two men stood in a room in the Traversite Palace. One was an Emperor, the other had made him so. In the larger, more formal Attenine Palace, a little way across the gardens, Apius lay in state in the Porphyry Room, coins on his eyes, a golden sun disk clasped between folded hands: payment and passport for his journey.

"I cannot, Uncle. I have promises to be kept."

"Tonight? Where?"

"Among the factions. The Blues were very useful today."

"Ah. The Blues. And their most favored actress? Was she very useful?" The old soldier's voice was sly now. "Or is she to be useful later this evening?"

Petrus looked unabashed. "Aliana? A fine dancer, and I always laugh during her comic turns upon the stage." He grinned, the round, smooth face free of guile.

The Emperor's gaze was shrewd, undeceived. After a moment he said, quietly, "Love is dangerous, nephew."

The younger man's expression changed. He was silent a moment, by one of the doorways. Eventually he nodded his head. "It can be. I know that. Do you . . . disapprove?"

It was a well-timed question. How could his uncle's disapproval attach to anything he did tonight? After the events of the day?

Valerius shook his head. "Not really. You will move into the Imperial Precinct? One of the palaces?" There were six of them scattered on these grounds. They were all his now. He would have to learn to know them.

Petrus nodded. "Of course, if you honor me so. But not until after the Mourning Rites and the Investiture, and the Hippodrome ceremony in your honor."

"You will bring her here with you?"

Petrus's expression, directly confronted, was equally direct. "Only if you approve."

The Emperor said, "Are there not laws? Someone said something, I recall. An actress . . . ?"

"*You* are the source and fount of all laws in Sarantium now, Uncle. Laws may be changed."

Valerius sighed. "We need to talk further on this. And about the holders of office. Gesius. Adrastus. Hilarinus—I don't trust him. I never did."

"He is gone, then. And Adrastus must also be, I fear. Gesius . . . is more complex. You know he spoke for you in the Senate?"

"You said. Did it matter?"

"Probably not, but if he had spoken for Adrastus—unlikely as that may sound—it might have made things . . . uglier."

"You trust him?"

The Emperor watched his nephew's deceptively bland, round face as the younger man thought. Petrus wasn't a soldier. He didn't look like a courtier. He carried himself, more than anything else, Valerius decided, like an academician of the old pagan Schools. There was ambition there, however. Enormous ambition. There was, in fact, an Empire's worth of it. He had cause to know, being where he was.

Petrus gestured, his soft hands spreading a little apart. "Truthfully? I'm not certain. I said it was complex. We will, indeed, have to talk further. But tonight you are allowed an evening of leisure, and I may permit myself the same, with your leave. I took the liberty of commanding ale for you, Uncle. It is on the sideboard beside the wine. Have I your gracious leave to depart?"

Valerius didn't really want him to go, but what was he to do? Ask the other man to sit with him for a night and hold his hand and tell him being Emperor would be all right? Was he a child?

"Of course. Do you want Excubitors?"

Petrus began shaking his head, then caught himself. "Probably a wise idea, actually. Thank you."

"Stop by the barracks. Tell Leontes. In fact, a rotating guard of six of them for you, from now on. Someone used Sarantine Fire here today."

Petrus's too-quick gaze showed he didn't quite know how to read that comment. Good. It wouldn't do to be *utterly* transparent to his nephew.

"Jad guard and defend you all your days, my Emperor."

"His eternal Light upon you." And for the first time ever, Valerius the Trakesian made the Imperial sign of blessing over another man.

His nephew knelt, touched forehead to floor three times, palms flat beside his head, then rose and walked out, calm as ever, unchanged though all had changed.

Valerius, Emperor of Sarantium, successor to Saranios the Great who had built the City, and to a line of Emperors after him, and before him in Rhodias, stretching back almost six hundred years, stood alone in an elegant chamber where oil lanterns hung from the ceiling and were set in brackets on the walls and where half a hundred candles burned extravagantly. His bedroom for tonight was somewhere nearby. He wasn't sure where. He wasn't familiar with this palace. The Count of the Excubitors had never had reason to enter here. He looked around the room. There was a tree near the courtyard window, made of beaten gold, with mechanical birds in the branches. They glittered in the flickering light with jewels and semiprecious stones. He supposed they sang, if one knew the trick. The tree was gold. It was entirely of gold. He drew a breath.

He went to the sideboard and poured himself a flask of ale. He sipped, then smiled. Honest Trakesian brew. Trust Petrus. It occurred to him that he should have clapped hands for a slave or Imperial officer, but such things slowed matters down and he had a thirst. He'd a right to one. It had been a day of days, as the soldiers said. Petrus had spoken true—he was entitled to an evening without further planning or tasks. Jad knew, there would be enough to deal with in the days to come. For one thing, certain people would have to be killed—if they weren't dead already. He didn't know the names of the men who'd wielded that liquid fire in the City—he didn't *want* to know—but they couldn't live.

He walked from the sideboard and sank down into a deep-cushioned, high-backed chair. The fabric was silk. He'd had little experience of silk in his life. He traced the material with a callused finger. It was soft, smooth. It was . . . *silken*. Valerius grinned to himself. He liked it. So many years a soldier, nights on stony ground, in bitter winter or the southern desert storms. He stretched out his booted feet, drank deeply again, wiped his lip with the back of a scarred, heavy hand. He closed his eyes, drank again. He decided he wanted his boots removed. Carefully, he placed the ale flask on an absurdly delicate three-legged ivory table. He sat up very straight, took a deep breath and then clapped his hands three times, the way Apius—Jad guard his soul!—used to do.

Three doors burst open on the instant.

A score of people *sprang* into the room and flung themselves prostrate on the floor in obeisance. He saw Gesius and Adrastus, then the Quaestor of the Sacred Palace, the Urban Prefect, the Count of the Imperial Bedchamber—Hilarinus, whom he didn't trust—the Quaestor of Imperial Revenue. All the highest officers of the Empire. Flattened before him on a green and blue mosaic floor of sea creatures and sea flowers.

In the ensuing stillness, one of the mechanical birds began to sing. Valerius the Emperor laughed aloud.

VERY LATE THAT SAME night, the sea wind having long since died to a breath, most of the City asleep, but some not so. Among these, the Holy

Order of the Sleepless Ones in their austere chapels, who believed—with fierce and final devotion—that all but a handful of them had to be constantly awake and at prayer through the whole of the night while Jad in his solar chariot negotiated his perilous journey through blackness and bitter ice beneath the world.

The bakers, too, were awake and at work, preparing the bread that was the gift of the Empire to all who dwelt in glorious Sarantium. In winter the glowing ovens would draw people from the darkness seeking warmth—beggars, cripples, streetwalkers, those evicted from their homes and those too new to the Holy City to have found shelter yet. They would move on to the glassmakers and the metalsmiths when the gray, cold day came.

In broiling summer now, the nearly naked bakers worked and swore at their ovens, slick with sweat, quaffing watery beer all night, no attendants at their doors save the rats, scurrying from cast light into shadow.

Torches burning on the better streets proclaimed the houses of the wealthy, and the tread and cry of the Urban Prefect's men warned the illicit to take a certain care elsewhere in the night city. The roaming bands of wilder partisans—Green and Blue each had their violent cadres—tended to ignore the patrols, or, more properly, a lone patrol was inclined to be prudently discreet when the flamboyantly garbed and barbered partisans careened into sight from one tavern or another.

Women, save for the ones who sold themselves or patricians in litters with armed escorts, were not abroad after dark.

This night, however, all the taverns—even the filthiest cauponae where sailors and slaves drank—were closed in response to an Imperial death and an Emperor acclaimed. The shocking events of the day seemed to have subdued even the partisans. No shouting, drunken youths in the loose, eastern clothing of Bassania and the hairstyling of western barbarians could be seen—or heard—slewing through empty streets.

A horse neighed in one of the faction stables by the Hippodrome, and a woman's voice could be heard through an open window over a colonnade nearby, singing the refrain of a song that was not at all devout. A man laughed, and then the woman did, and then there was silence there, too. The high screech of a cat in a laneway. A child cried. Children always cried in the darkness, somewhere. The world was what it was.

The god's sun passed in its chariot through ice and past howling daemons under the world. The two moons worshipped—perversely—as goddesses by the Kindath had both set, over west into the wide sea. Only the stars, which no one claimed as holy, shone like strewn diamonds over the city Saranios had founded to be the New Rhodias, and to be more than Rhodias had ever been.

"Oh City, City, ornament of the earth, eye of the world, glory of Jad's creation, will I die before I see you again?"

So, Lysurgos Matanias, posted as ambassador to the Bassanid court two hundred years past, longing in his heart for Sarantium even amid the luxurious eastern splendors of Kabadh. *Oh City, City.*

In all the lands ruled by that City, with its domes and its bronze and golden doors, its palaces and gardens and statues, forums and theaters and colonnades, bathhouses and shops and guildhalls, taverns and whorehouses and sanctuaries and the great Hippodrome, its triple landward walls that had never yet been breached, and its deep, sheltered harbor and the guarded and guarding seas, there was a timeworn phrase that had the same meaning in every tongue and every dialect.

To say of a man that he was sailing to Sarantium was to say that his life was on the cusp of change: poised for emergent greatness, brilliance, fortune—or else at the very precipice of a final and absolute fall as he met something too vast for his capacity.

Valerius the Trakesian had become an Emperor.

Heladikos, whom some worshipped as the son of Jad and placed in mosaic upon holy domes, had died in his chariot bringing fire back from the sun.

Part One

Miracle, bird or golden handiwork,

More miracle than bird or handiwork . . .

CHAPTER I

The Imperial Post, along with most of the civil positions in the Sarantine Empire after Valerius I died and his nephew, having renamed himself appropriately, took the Golden Throne, was under the hegemony of the Master of Offices.

The immensely complex running of the mails—from the recently conquered Majriti deserts and Esperana in the far west to the long, always-shifting Bassanid border in the east, and from the northern wildernesses of Karch and Moskav to the deserts of Soriyya and beyond—required a substantial investment of manpower and resources, and no little requisitioning of labor and horses from those rural communities dubiously honored by having an Imperial Posting Inn located in or near them.

The position of Imperial Courier, charged with the actual carrying of the public mails and court documents, paid only modestly well and involved an almost endless regimen of hard traveling, sometimes through uncertain territory, depending on barbarian or Bassanid activity in a given season. The fact that such positions were avidly solicited, with all the associated bribes, was a reflection of where the position might lead after a few years more than anything else.

The couriers of the Imperial Post were expected to be part-time spies for the Quaestor of Imperial Intelligence, and diligent labor in this unspoken part of the job—coupled with rather more of the associated bribes—might see a man appointed to the intelligence service directly, with more risks, less far-ranging travel, and significantly higher recompense. Along with a chance to be on the receiving end, at last, of some of the bribes changing hands.

As one's declining years approached, an appointment from Intelligence back to, say, running a substantial Posting Inn could actually lead to a respectable retirement—especially if one was clever, and the Inn far enough from the City to permit rather more watering of wine and an enhancing of revenues by accepting travelers without the required Permits.

The position of courier was, in short, a legitimate career path for a man with sufficient means to make a start but not enough to be launched by his family in anything more promising.

This, as it happened, was a fair description of the competence and background of Pronobius Tilliticus. Born with an unfortunately amusing name (a frequently cursed legacy of his mother's grandfather and his mother's unfamiliarity with current army vernacular), with limited skill at law or numbers, and only a modest paternal niche in Sarantine hierarchies, Tilliticus had been told over and again how fortunate he was to have had his mother's cousin's aid in securing a courier's position. His obese cousin, soft rump securely spread on a bench among the clerks in the Imperial Revenue office, had been foremost of those to make this observation at family gatherings.

Tilliticus had been obliged to smile and agree. Many times. He had a gathering-prone family.

In such an oppressive context—his mother was now constantly demanding he choose a useful wife—it was sometimes a relief to leave Sarantium. And now he was on the roads again with a packet of letters, bound for the barbarian Antae's capital city of Varena in Batiara and points en route. He also carried one particular Imperial Packet that came—unusually—directly from the Chancellor himself, with the elaborate Seal of that office, and instructions from the eunuchs to make this delivery with some ceremony.

An important artisan of some kind, he was given to understand. The Emperor was rebuilding the Sanctuary of Jad's Holy Wisdom. Artisans were being summoned to the City from all over the Empire and beyond. It irked Tilliticus: barbarians and rustic provincials were receiving formal invitations and remuneration on a level three or four times his own to participate in this latest Imperial folly.

In early autumn on the good roads north and then west through Trakesia it was hard to preserve an angry mien, however. Even Tilliticus found the weather lifting his spirits. The sun shone mildly overhead. The northern grain had been harvested, and on the slopes as he turned west the vineyards were purple with ripening grapes. Just looking at them gave him a thirst. The Posting Inns on this road were well-known to him and they seldom cheated couriers. He lingered a few days at one of them *(Let the damned paint-dauber wait for his summons a little!)* and feasted on spit-roasted fox, stuffed fat with grapes. A girl he remembered seemed also to enthusiastically remember him. The innkeeper did charge double the price for her exclusive services, but Tilliticus knew he was doing it and saw that as one of the perquisites of a position he dreamed of for himself.

On the last night, however, the girl asked him to take her away, which was simply ridiculous.

Tilliticus refused indignantly and—abetted by a quantity of scarcely watered wine—offered her a lecture about his mother's family's lineage. He exaggerated only slightly; with a country prostitute it was hardly required. She didn't seem to take the chiding with particular good grace and in the morning, riding away, Tilliticus considered whether his affections had been misplaced.

A few days later he was certain they had been. Urgent medical circumstances dictated a short detour north and a further delay of several days at a well-known Hospice of Galinus, where he was treated for the genital infection she had given him.

They bled him, purged him with something that emptied his bowels and stomach violently, made him ingest various unpleasant liquids, shaved his groin, and daubed on a burning, foul-smelling black ointment twice a day. He was instructed to eat only bland foods and to refrain from sexual congress and wine for an unnatural length of time.

Hospices were expensive, and this one, being celebrated, was particularly so. Tilliticus was forced to bribe the chief administrator to record his stay as being for injuries incurred in the course of duties—or else he'd have had to pay for the visit out of his own pocket.

Well, a crab-infested chit in a Posting Inn *was* an injury incurred in the Emperor's service, wasn't it? This way, the administrator could bill the Imperial Post directly—and he would no doubt add to the tally half a dozen treatments Tilliticus hadn't received and designate those sums for his own purse.

Tilliticus left a stiff letter addressed to the innkeeper four days' ride back, to be delivered by the next eastbound courier. Let the bitch hump for slaves and farmhands in an alley back of a caupona if she wasn't going to keep herself clean. The Posting Inns on the roads of the Empire were the finest in the world, and Pronobius Tilliticus regarded it as a positive *duty* to make sure she was gone when next he rode through.

He was in the service of the Sarantine Emperor. These things reflected directly upon the majesty and prestige of Valerius II and his glorious Empress Alixana. The fact that the Empress had been bought and used in her youth in exactly the same way as the chit in the inn was not a matter for open discussion at this stage in the world's progression. A man was allowed his thoughts, however. They couldn't kill you for thinking things.

He lasted a part of the prescribed period of abstinence, but a tavern he knew too well in Megarium, the port city and administrative center of western Sauradia, proved predictably tempting. He didn't remember any of the girls this time around but they were all lively enough, and the wine was good. Megarium had a reputation for decent wine, however barbaric the rest of Sauradia might be.

An unfortunate incident involving jests about his name—made one night by a loutish apprentice and a trader in Heladikian icons—left him with a gashed chin and a twisted shoulder that called for further medical treatment and a longer stay than anticipated in the tavern. The stay became less than pleasant after the first few days because it appeared that two of the once-willing girls had contracted an affliction unfortunately similar to the one he was to have been cured of by now, and they made no secret about blaming Tilliticus.

They didn't throw him out, of course—he *was* an Imperial Courier, and the girls were bodies-for-sale, one of them a slave—but his food tended to arrive cold or overcooked after that, and no one rushed to help a man with an awkward shoulder manage his plates and flasks. Tilliticus was feeling seriously hard done by when he finally decided he was well enough to resume his journey. The tavern-keeper, a Rhodian by birth, gave him mail for relatives in Varena. Tilliticus tossed it in a midden-heap by the harbor.

It was much later in the autumn than it should have been by then and the rains had come. He caught one of the last of the small ships tacking west across the bay to the Batiaran port of Mylasia and docked in a cold, driving rain, having emptied his guts over the ship's railing several times. Tilliticus had little love for the sea.

The city of Varena—where the barbaric, still half-pagan Antae who had sacked Rhodias a hundred years ago and conquered all Batiara held their wretched little court—was three days' ride farther west, two if he hurried. He had not the least interest in hurrying. Tilliticus waited out the rain, drinking morosely by the harbor. His injuries allowed him to do that, he decided. This had been a *very* difficult run. His shoulder still hurt.

And he had *liked* that girl in Trakesia.

IN THE GOOD WEATHER Pardos was outside at the oven making quicklime for the setting bed. The heat of the fire was pleasant when the wind picked up, and he liked being in the sanctuary yard. The presence of the dead under their headstones didn't frighten him, or not in daylight at any rate. Jad had ordained that man would die. War and plague were part of the world the god had made. Pardos didn't understand why, but he had no expectation of understanding. The clerics, even when they disagreed about doctrine or burned each other over Heladikos, all taught submission and faith, not a vainglorious attempt to comprehend. Pardos knew he wasn't wise enough to be vain *or* to comprehend.

Beyond the graven, sculpted headstones of the named dead, a dark earth mound rose—no grass there yet—at the northern end of the yard. Beneath it lay bodies claimed by the plague. It had come two years ago and then again last summer, killing in numbers too great for anything but mass burial by slaves taken in war. There was lime ash in there, too, and some other elements mixed in. They were said to help contain the bitter spirits of the dead and what had killed them. It was certainly keeping the grass from coming back. The queen had ordered three court cheiromancers and an old alchemist who lived outside the walls to cast binding spells as well. One did all the things one could think to do in the aftermath of plague, whatever the clerics or the High Patriarch might say about pagan magics.

Pardos fumbled for his sun disk and gave thanks for being alive. He watched the black smoke of the lime kiln rise up toward the white, swift clouds, and noted the autumn reds and golds of the forest to the east. Birds were singing in the blue sky and the grass was green, though shading to brown near the sanctuary building itself where the afternoon light failed in the shadow of the new walls.

Colors, all around him in the world. Crispin had told him, over and over, to make himself *see* the colors. To think about them, how they played against each other and with each other; to consider what happened when a cloud crossed the sun—as now—and the grass darkened beneath him. What would he name that hue in his mind? How would he use it? In a marinescape? A hunting scene? A mosaic of Heladikos rising above an autumn forest toward the sun? *Look* at the grass—now!—before the light returned. Picture that color in glass and stone tesserae. Embed it in memory, so you could embed it in lime and make a mosaic world on a wall or a dome.

Assuming, of course, there ever emerged a glassworks again in conquered Batiara where they made reds and blues and greens worthy of a name, instead of the muddied, bubbled, streaked excrescences they'd received in the morning shipment from Rhodias.

Martinian, a calm man and perhaps prepared for this, had only sighed when the urgently awaited sheets of new glass were unwrapped. Crispin had foamed into one of his notorious, blasphemous rages and smashed the topmost dirty brown sheet of what was supposed to be red, cutting one hand. "*This* is red! Not that dungheap color!" he had shouted, letting drops of his blood fall on the brownish sheet.

He could be entertaining in his fury, actually, unless you happened to be the one who had given him cause to lose his temper. When they had their beer and crusts of bread at lunch, or walking back toward Varena's walls at sunset after work, the laborers and apprentices would trade stories of things Crispin had said and done when angry. Martinian had told the apprentices that Crispin was brilliant and a great man; Pardos wondered if a temper came with that.

He'd had some shockingly inventive ideas this morning for how to deal with the glassworks steward. Pardos himself would never have been able to even conceive of broken shards being inserted and applied in the ways Crispin had proposed, swearing violently even though they were on consecrated ground.

Martinian, ignoring his younger partner, had set about accepting and discarding sheets, eyeing them with care, sighing now and again. They simply couldn't reject them all. For one thing, there was little chance of better quality in replacements. For another, they were working against time, with a formal re-burial and a ceremony for King Hildric planned by his daughter the queen for the first day after the Dykania Festival. It would take place here in the newly expanded sanctuary they were decorating now. It was already mid-autumn, the grapes harvested. The roads south were muddy after last week's rains. The chances of getting new glass sent up from Rhodias in time were too slim even to be considered.

Martinian was, as usual, visibly resigned to the situation. They would have to make do. Pardos knew that Crispin was as aware of this as his partner. He just had his temper. And getting things *right* mattered to him. Perhaps too much so, in the imperfect world Jad had made as his mortal children's dwelling place. Pardos the apprentice made a quick sign of the sun disk again and stoked the kiln, keeping it as hot as he could.

He stirred the mixture inside with a long shovel. This would not be a good day to become distracted and let the setting lime emerge faulty.

Crispin had imaginative uses for broken glass on his mind.

So attentive was he to the lime mixture cooking in the oven that Pardos actually jumped when a voice—speaking awkwardly accented Rhodian—addressed him. He turned quickly, and saw a lean, red-faced man in the gray and white colors of the Imperial Post. The courier's horse grazed behind him near the gate. Belatedly, Pardos became aware that the other apprentices and laborers working outside the sanctuary had stopped and were looking over this way. Imperial Couriers from Sarantium did not appear in their midst with any frequency at all.

"Are you hard of hearing?" the man said waspishly. He had a recent wound on his chin. The eastern accent was pronounced. "I said my name is Tilliticus. Sarantine Imperial Post. I'm looking for a man named Martinian. An artisan. They said he'd be here."

Pardos, intimidated, could only gesture toward the sanctuary. Martinian, as it happened, was asleep on his stool in the doorway, his much-abused hat pulled over his eyes to block the afternoon sunlight.

"Deaf *and* mute. I see," said the courier. He clumped off through the grass toward the building.

"I'm not," said Pardos, but so softly he wasn't heard. Behind the courier's back, he flapped urgently at two of the other apprentices, trying to signal them to wake Martinian before this unpleasant man appeared in front of him.

HE HAD NOT BEEN ASLEEP. From his favorite position—on a pleasant day, at any rate—in the sanctuary entrance, Martinian of Varena had noticed the courier riding up from a distance. Gray and white showed clearly against green and blue in sunlight.

He and Crispin had used that concept, in fact, for a row of Blessed Victims on the long walls of a private chapel in Baiana years ago. It had been only a partial success—at night, by candlelight, the effect was not what Crispin had hoped it would be—but they'd learned a fair bit, and learning from errors was what mosaic work was about, as Martinian was fond of telling the apprentices. If the patrons had had enough money to light the chapel properly at night, it might have been different, but they'd known the resources when they made their design. It was their own fault. One always had to work within the constraints of time and money. That, too, was a lesson to be learned—and taught.

He watched the courier stop by Pardos at the lime kiln and he tipped his hat forward over his eyes, feigning sleep. He felt a peculiar apprehension. No idea why. And he was never able to give an adequate explanation afterward, even to himself, as to why he did what he did next that autumn afternoon, altering so many lives forever. Sometimes the god entered a man, the clerics taught. And sometimes daemons or spirits did. There were powers in the half-world, beyond the grasp of mortal men.

He was to tell his learned friend Zoticus, over a mint infusion some days later, that it had had to do with feeling old that day. A week of steady rain had caused his finger joints to swell painfully. That wasn't really it, however. He was hardly so weak as to let such a thing lead him into so much folly. But he truly *didn't* know why he'd chosen—with no premeditation whatsoever—to deny being himself.

Did a man always understand his own actions? He would ask Zoticus that as they sat together in the alchemist's farmhouse. His friend would give him a predictable reply and refill his cup with the infusion, mixed with something to ease the ache in his hands. The unpleasant courier would be long gone by then, to wherever his postings had taken him. And Crispin, too, would be gone.

Martinian of Varena feigned sleep as the easterner with the nose and cheekbones of a drinker approached him and rasped, "You! Wake! I'm looking for a man named Martinian. An Imperial Summons to Sarantium!"

He was loud, arrogant as all Sarantines seemed to be when they came to Batiara, his words thick with the accent. Everyone heard him. He meant for them to hear him. Work stopped inside the sanctuary being expanded to properly house the bones of King Hildric of the Antae, dead of the plague a little more than a year ago.

Martinian pretended to rouse himself from an afternoon doze in the autumn light. He blinked owlishly up at the Imperial Courier, and then pointed a stiff finger into the sanctuary—and up toward his longtime friend and colleague Caius Crispus. Crispin was just then attempting the task of making muddy brown tesserae appear like the brilliant glowing of Heladikos's sacred fire, high up on a scaffold under the dome.

Even as he pointed, Martinian wondered at himself. A summons? To the *City*? And he was playing the games of a boy? No one here would give him away to an arrogant Sarantine, but even so . . .

In the stillness that ensued, a voice they all knew was suddenly heard overhead with unfortunate clarity. The resonance of sound happened to be very good in this sanctuary.

"By Heladikos's cock, I will carve slices from his rump with his *useless* glass and force-feed him his own buttocks in segments, I swear by holy Jad!"

The courier looked affronted.

"That's Martinian," said Martinian helpfully. "Up there. He's in a temper."

IN FACT, HE REALLY wasn't anymore. The blasphemous vulgarity was almost reflexive. Sometimes he said things, and wasn't even aware he was speaking aloud, when a technical challenge engaged him entirely. At the moment, he was obsessed, in spite of himself, with the problem of how to make the torch of Heladikos gleam red when he had nothing that was red with which to work. If he'd had some gold he could have sandwiched the glass against a gold backing and warmed the hue that way, but gold for mosaic was a fatuous dream here in Batiara after the wars and the plague.

He'd had an idea, however. Up on the high scaffold, Caius Crispus of Varena was setting reddish-veined marble from Pezzelana flat into the soft, sticky lime coat on the dome, interspersed with the best of the tesserae they'd managed to salvage from the miserable sheets of glass. The glass pieces he laid at angles in the setting bed, to catch and reflect the light.

If he was right, the effect would be a shimmer and dance along the tall shape of the flame, the flat stones mingled with the tilted, glinting tesserae. Seen from below, it ought to have that result in sunlight through the windows around the base of the dome, or by the light of the wall candles and the suspended iron lanterns running the length of the sanctuary. The young queen had assured Martinian that her bequest to the clerics here would ensure evening and winter lighting. Crispin had no reason to disbelieve her—it was her father's tomb, and the Antae had had a cult of ancestor-worship, only thinly masked by their conversion to the Jaddite faith.

He had a cloth knotted around the cut in his left hand, and that made him awkward. He dropped a good stone, watched it fall a long way and swore again, reaching for another one. The setting bed was beginning to harden beneath the flame and torch he was filling in. He would have to work faster. The torch was silver. They were using whitish marble and some river-smooth stones for that—it ought to work. He'd heard that in the east they had a way of frosting glass to make an almost pure white tessera like snow, and that mother-of-pearl was available, for crowns and jewelry. He didn't even like *thinking* about such things. It only frustrated him, here in the west amid ruins.

As it happened, these were his thoughts in the precise moment when the irritated, carrying eastern voice from below penetrated his concentration and his life. A coincidence, or the heard accents of Sarantium carrying his mind sailing that way toward the celebrated channel and the inner sea and the gold and silver and silk of the Emperor?

He looked down.

Someone, short as a snail from this height, was addressing him as Martinian. This would have been merely vexing had Martinian himself—by the doorway, as was usual at this hour—not also been gazing up at Crispin as the easterner barked the wrong name, disturbing all the work in the sanctuary.

Crispin bit back two obscene retorts and then a third response, which was to direct the imbecile in the right direction. Something was afoot. It might only be a jibe directed at the courier—though that would be unlike his partner—or it might be something else.

He'd deal with it later.

"I'll be down when I'm done," he called, *much* more politely than the circumstances warranted. "Go pray for someone's immortal soul in the meantime. Do it quietly."

The red-faced man shouted, “Imperial Couriers are *not* kept waiting, you vulgar provincial! There is a letter for you!”

Interesting as this undoubtedly was, Crispin found it easy to ignore him. He wished he had some red vivid as the courier’s cheeks, mind you. Even from this height they showed crimson. It occurred to him that he’d never tried to achieve that effect on a face in mosaic. He slotted the idea among all the others and returned to creating the holy flame given as a gift to mankind, working with what he had.

HAD HIS INSTRUCTIONS NOT been unfortunately specific, Tilliticus would simply have dropped the packet on the dusty, debris-strewn floor of the shabby little sanctuary, reeking with the worst Heladikian heresy, and stormed out.

Men did *not* come—even here in Batiara—in their own slow time to receive an invitation from the Imperial Precinct in Sarantium. They raced over, ecstatic. They knelt. They embraced the knees of the courier. Once, someone had kissed his muddy, dung-smeared boots, weeping for joy.

And they most certainly offered the courier largess for being the bearer of such exalted, dazzling tidings.

Watching the ginger-haired man named Martinian finally descend from his scaffolding and walk deliberately across the floor toward him, Pronobius Tilliticus understood that his boots were not about to be kissed. Nor was any sum of money likely to be proffered him in gratitude.

It only confirmed his opinion of Batiara under the Antae. They might be Jad-worshippers, if barely, and they might be formal tributary allies of the Empire in a relationship brokered by the High Patriarch in Rhodias, and they might have conquered this peninsula a century ago and rebuilt some of the walls they had leveled then, but they were *still* barbarians.

And they had infected with their uncouth manners and heresies even those native-born descendants of the Rhodian Empire who had a claim to honor.

The man Martinian’s hair was actually an offensively bright red, Tilliticus saw. Only the dust and lime in it and in his untidy beard softened the hue. His eyes, unsoftened, were a hard, extremely unpleasant blue. He wore a nondescript, stained tunic over wrinkled brown leggings. He was a big man, and he carried himself in a coiled, angry way that was quite unappealing. His hands were large, and there was a bloodstained bandage wrapped around one of them.

He's in a temper, the fool by the doorway had said. The fool was still on his stool, watching the two of them from beneath something misshapen that might once have been a hat. The deaf and mute apprentice had wandered in by now, along with all the others from outside. It *ought* to have been a splendid, resonant moment for Tilliticus to make his proclamation, to graciously accept the artisan's stammering gratitude on behalf of the Chancellor and the Imperial Post, and then head for the best inn Varena could offer with some coins to spend on mulled wine and a woman.

"And so? I'm here. What is it you want?"

The mosaicist's voice was as hard as his eyes. His glance, when it left Tilliticus's face and sought that of the older man in the doorway, did not grow any less inimical. An unpleasant character, entirely.

Tilliticus was genuinely shocked by the rudeness. "In truth? I want nothing whatever with you." He reached into his bag, found the fat Imperial Packet and threw it scornfully at the artisan. The man, moving quickly, caught it in one hand.

Tilliticus said, almost spitting the words, "You are Martinian of Varena, obviously. Unworthy as you are, I am charged with declaring that the Thrice Exalted Beloved of Jad, the Emperor Valerius II, requests you to attend upon him in Sarantium with all possible speed. The packet you hold contains a sum of money to aid you in your travels, a sealed Permit signed by the Chancellor himself that allows you to use Imperial Posting Inns for lodging and services, and a letter that I am sure you will be able to find someone to read to you. It indicates that your services are requested to aid in the decoration of the new Sanctuary of Jad's Holy Wisdom that the Emperor, in his own great wisdom, is even now constructing."

There was a mollifying buzz of sound in the sanctuary as the apprentices and lesser artisans, at least, appeared to grasp the significance of what Tilliticus had just said. It occurred to him that he might consider, at future times, relaying the formal words in this blunt tone. It had an effectiveness of its own.

"What happened to the old one?" The red-haired artisan seemed unmoved. Was he mentally deficient? Tilliticus wondered.

"What old one, you primitive barbarian?"

"Sheathe the insults or you'll crawl from here. The old sanctuary."

Tilliticus blinked. The man *was* deranged. "You threaten an Imperial Courier? Your nose will be slit for you if you so much as lift a hand to me. The old sanctuary burned two years ago, in the riot. Are you ignorant of events in the world?"

"We had plague here," the man said, his voice flat. "Twice. And then a civil war. Fires halfway across the world are unimportant at such times. Thank you for delivering this. I will read it and decide what to do."

"Decide?" Tilliticus squeaked. He hated the way his voice rose when he was caught by surprise. The same thing had happened when that accursed girl in Trakesia had asked him to take her away. It had made it difficult to impart the proper tone to the needed dissertation upon his mother's family.

"Why, yes," the mosaicist said. "Dare I assume this is an offer and an invitation, not a command, as to a slave?"

Tilliticus was too stupefied to speak for a moment.

He drew himself up. Pleased to note that his voice was under control, he snapped, "Only a slave would fail to grasp what this means. It seems you are craven and without aspiration in the world. In which case, like a slave, you may burrow back down into your little hovel here and do what you will in the dirt, and Sarantium suffers no loss at all. I have no time for further talk. You have your letter. In the Emperor's thrice-glorious name, I bid you good day."

"Good day," said the man, dismissively. He turned away. "Pardos," he said, "the setting lime was well-done today. And properly laid on, Radulf, Couvry. I'm pleased."

Tilliticus stomped out.

The Empire, civilization, the glories of the Holy City . . . all *wasted* on some people, he thought. In the doorway he stopped in front of the older man, who sat regarding him with a mild gaze.

"Your hat," Tilliticus said, glaring at him, "is the most ridiculous head covering I have ever seen."

"I know," said the man, cheerfully. "They all tell me that."

Pronobius Tilliticus, aggrieved, unassuaged, reclaimed his horse and galloped off, dust rising behind him on the road to Varena's walls.

"WE HAD BETTER TALK," Crispin said, looking down at the man who had taught him most of what he knew.

Martinian's expression was rueful. He stood up, adjusted the eccentric hat on his head—only Crispin among those there knew that it had saved his life, once—and led the way outside. The Imperial Courier, dudgeon lending him speed, was racing toward town. The sanctuary lay in its own enclosure just east of the city walls.

They watched him for a moment, then Martinian began walking south toward a copse of beech trees outside the yard at the opposite end from the burial mound. The sun was low now and the wind had picked up. Crispin squinted a little, emerging from the muted light of the sanctuary. A cow looked up from grazing and regarded them as they went. Crispin carried the Imperial Packet. The name "Martinian of Varena" was writ large upon it in cursive script, quite elegantly. The seal was crimson and elaborate.

Martinian stopped short of the trees, just past the gate that led out from the yard to the road. He sat down on a stump there. They were quite alone. A blackbird swooped from their left, curved into the woods and was lost in leaves. It was cold now at the end of day with the sun going down. The blue moon was already up, above the forest. Crispin, glancing over as he leaned back against the wooden gate, realized that it was full.

Ilandra had died at sunset on a day when the blue moon was full, and the girls—sores ruptured, bodies fouled, their features hideously distorted—had followed her to the god that night. Crispin had walked outside and seen that moon, a wound in the sky.

He handed the heavy packet to Martinian, who accepted it without speaking. The older mosaicist looked down at his name for a moment, then tore open the Chancellor of Sarantium's seal. In silence he began taking out what was within. The weight turned out to be silver and copper coins in a filigreed purse, as promised. A letter explained, as the courier had said, that the Great Sanctuary was being rebuilt and mosaic work was much a part of that. Some compliments upon the reputation of Martinian of Varena. There was a formal-looking document on superb paper which turned out to be the Permit for the Posting Inns. Martinian whistled softly and showed the parchment to Crispin: it was signed by the Chancellor himself, no lesser figure. They were both sufficiently familiar with high circles—if only here in Batiara among the Antae—to know that this was an honor.

Another document proved, when unfolded three times, to be a map showing the location of the Posting Inns and lesser stopping places on the Imperial road through Sauradia and Trakesia to the City. Yet another folded sheet named certain ships calling at Mylasia on the coast as reliable for sea transport if they happened to be in harbor.

"Too late in the year by now for commercial ships," Martinian said thoughtfully, looking at this last. He took out the letter again, opened it. Pointed to a date at the top. "This was issued at the very beginning of autumn. Our red-cheeked friend took his time getting here. I think you were meant to sail."

"*I* was meant to sail?"

"Well, you, pretending to be me."

"Martinian. What in Jad's—?"

"I don't want to go. I'm old. My hands hurt. I want to drink mulled wine this winter with friends and hope there are no wars for a while. I have no desire to sail to Sarantium. This is *your* summons, Crispin."

"Not my name."

"It ought to be. You've done most of the work for years now." Martinian grinned. "About time, too."

Crispin did not return the smile. "Think about this. This Emperor is said to be a patron. A builder. What more could you ask for in life than a chance to see the City and work there in honor? Make something that will last, and be known?"

"Warm wine and a seat by the fire in Galdera's tavern." *And my wife beside me in the night until I die*, he thought, but did not say.

The other man made a disbelieving sound.

Martinian shook his head. "Crispin, this *is* your summons. Don't let their mistake confuse things. They want a master mosaicist. We are known for our work in the tradition of Rhodian mosaic. It makes *sense* for them to have someone from Batiara be a part of this, east-west tensions notwithstanding, and you know which of the two of us ought to make the journey."

"I know that I have not been asked. You have. By name. Even if I *wanted* to go, which I don't."

Martinian, uncharacteristically, said something obscene involving Crispin's anatomy, the thunder god of the Bassanids, and a lightning bolt.

Crispin blinked. "You will now practice speaking like me?" he asked, not smiling. "That will have things even further reversed, won't it?"

The older man was flushed. "Do not even pretend that you don't want to go. Why did you pretend not to know about their sanctuary? *Everyone* knows about the Victory Riot and the burning in Sarantium."

"Why did you pretend not to be yourself?" There was a little silence. The other man looked away, toward the distant woods. Crispin said, "Martinian, I *don't* want to go. It isn't pretending. I don't want to do anything. You know that."

His friend turned back to him. "Then that's why you must go. Caius, you are too young to stop living."

"They were younger and they weren't. They stopped."

He said it quickly, harshly. He hadn't been ready for Martinian's words. He *needed* to be ready when such things came up.

It was quiet here. The god's sun going down red in the west, preparing to journey through the long dark. In sanctuaries throughout Batiara the sunset rites would soon begin. The blue moon was above the eastern trees. No stars yet. Ilandra had died vomiting blood, black sores covering her, bursting. Like wounds. The girls. His girls had died in the dark.

Martinian took off his shapeless hat. His hair was gray, and he had lost most of it in the center. He said, quite gently, "And you honor the three of them by doing the same? Shall I blaspheme some more? Don't make me. I don't like it. This packet from Sarantium is a gift."

"Then accept it. We're nearly done here. Most of what's left is border work and polishing, and then the masons can finish."

Martinian shook his head. "Are you afraid?"

Crispin's eyebrows met when he frowned. "We have been friends a long time. Please do not talk to me that way."

"We have been friends a long time. No one else will," said Martinian implacably. "One in four people died here last summer, following the same numbers the summer before. More than that, they say, elsewhere. The Antae used to worship their own dead, with candles and invocations. I suppose they still do, in Jad's sanctuaries instead of oak groves or crossroads, but not . . . Caius, *not* by following them into a living death."

Martinian looked down as he finished at the twisted hat in his hands.

One in four. Two summers in succession. Crispin knew it. The burial mound behind them was only one among many. Houses, whole quarters of Varena and other cities of Batiara still lay deserted. Rhodias itself, which had never really recovered from the Antae sack, was a hollow place, forums and colonnades echoing with emptiness. The High Patriarch in his palace there was said to walk the corridors alone of a night, speaking to spirits unseen by men. Madness came with the plague. And a brief, savage war had come among the Antae, as well, when King Hildric died, leaving only a daughter after him. Farms and fields everywhere had been abandoned, too large to be worked by those left alive. There had been tales of children sold into slavery by their parents for want of food or firewood as winter came.

One in four. And not only here in Batiara. North among the barbarians in Ferrieres, west in Esperana, east in Sauradia and Trakesia, indeed all through the Sarantine Empire and into Bassania and probably beyond, though tales didn't run that far. Sarantium itself hard hit, by report. The whole world dredged deep by Death's hunger.

But Crispin had had three souls in Jad's creation to live with and love, and all three were gone. Was the knowledge of other losses to assuage his own? Sometimes, half asleep at night in the house, a wine flask empty by his bed, he would lie in the dark and think he heard breathing, a voice, one of the girls crying aloud in her dreams in the next room. He would want to rise to comfort her. Sometimes he *would* rise, and only come fully awake as he stood up, naked, and became aware of the appalling depth of stillness around him in the world.

His mother had suggested he come live with her. Martinian and his wife had invited him to do the same. They said it was unhealthy for him to stay alone with only the servants in a house full of memories. There were rooms he could take above taverns or inns where he would hear the sounds of life from below or along hallways. He had been urged, actively solicited, to marry again after most of the year had passed. Jad knew, enough widows had been left with too-wide beds, and enough young girls needed a decent, successful man. Friends told him this. He still seemed to have friends, despite his best efforts. They told him he was gifted, celebrated, had a life in front of him yet. How could people not understand the irrelevance of such things? He told them that, tried to tell them.

"Good night," Martinian said.

Not to him. Crispin looked over. The others were leaving, following the road the courier had taken back to the city. End of day. Sun going down. It was quite cold now.

"Good night," he echoed, lifting a hand absently to the men who worked for them and to the others engaged in finishing the building itself. Cheerful replies followed. Why should they not be cheerful? A day's work done, the rains had passed for a time, the harvest was in with winter not yet here, and there was splendid new gossip now to trade in the taverns and around hearth fires tonight. An Imperial Summons for Martinian to the City, an amusing game played with a pompous eastern courier.

The stuff of life, bright coinage of talk and shared conjecture, laughter, argument. Something to drink on, to regale a spouse, a sibling, a longtime servant. A friend, a parent, an innkeeper. A child.

Two children.

Who knows love?
Who says he knows love?
What is love, tell me.

"I know love,"
says the littlest one . . .

A Kindath song, that one. Ilandra had had a nurse from among the moon-worshippers, growing up in the wine country south of Rhodias where many of the Kindath had settled. A tradition in her family, to be nursed by them, and to choose among the Kindath for their physicians. A better family than his own, though his mother had connections and dignity. He'd married well, people had said, understanding nothing. People didn't know. How could they know? Ilandra used to sing the tune to the girls at night. If he closed his eyes he could have her voice with him now.

If he died he might join her in the god's Light. All three of them.

"You *are* afraid," Martinian said again, a human voice in the world's twilight, intruding. Crispin heard anger this time. Rare, in a kindly man. "You are afraid to accept that you have been allowed to live, and must *do* something with that grace."

"It is no grace," he said. And immediately regretted the sour, self-pitying tone in the words. Lifted a quick hand to forestall a rebuke. "What must I do to make everyone happy, Martinian? Sell the house for a pittance to one of the land speculators? Move in with you? *And* with my mother? Marry a fifteen-year-old ready to whelp children? Or a widow with land and sons already? Both? Take Jad's vows and join the clerics? Turn pagan? Become a Holy Fool?"

"Go to Sarantium," said his friend.

"No."

They looked at each other. Crispin realized that he was breathing hard. The older man said, his voice soft now in the lengthening shadows, "That is too final for something so large. Say it again in the morning and I'll never speak of this again. On my oath."

Crispin, after a silence, only nodded. He needed a drink, he realized.

An unseen bird called, clear and far from toward the woods. Martinian rose, clapped his hat on his head against the sundown wind. They walked together back into Varena before the night curfew sounded and the gates were locked against whatever lay outside in the wild forests, the night fields and lawless roads, in the moonlit, starlit air where daemons and spirits assuredly were.

Men lived behind walls, when they could.

IN THE LAST OF the light, Crispin went to his favorite baths, nearly deserted at this hour. Most men visited the baths in the afternoon, but mosaicists needed light for their work and Crispin preferred the quiet at the end of day now. A few men were taking exercise with the heavy ball, ponderously lobbing it back and forth, naked and sweating with exertion. He nodded to them in passing, without stopping. He took some steam first, and then the hot and cold waters, and had himself oiled and rubbed down—his autumn regimen, against the chill. He spoke to no one beyond civil greetings in the public rooms at the end, where he had a beaker of wine brought to him at his usual couch. After, he reclaimed the Imperial Packet from the attendant with whom he had checked it and, declining an escort, walked home to drop the packet and change for dinner. He intended not to discuss the matter tonight, at all.

"YOU ARE GOING TO go, then. To Sarantium?"

Certain intentions, in the presence of his mother, remained largely meaningless. That much was unchanged. Avita Crispina signaled, and the servant ladled out more of the fish soup for her son. In the light of the candles, he watched the girl withdraw gracefully to the kitchen. She had the classic Karchite coloring. Their women were prized as house slaves by both the Antae and the native Rhodians.

"Who told you?" They were alone at dinner, reclining on facing couches. His mother had always preferred the formal old fashions.

"Does it matter?"

Crispin shrugged. "I suppose not." A sanctuary full of men had heard that courier. "Why am I going to go, Mother? Do tell me."

"Because you don't want to. You do the opposite of what you think you should. A perversity of behavior. I have no idea where you derived it."

She had the audacity to smile, saying that. Her color was good tonight, or else the candles were being kind. He had no tesserae so white as her hair, none even close. In Sarantium the Imperial Glassworks had, rumor told, a method of making . . .

He halted that line of thought.

"I don't do any such thing. I refuse to be so obvious. I may—sometimes—be a little imprudent when provoked. The courier today was a complete and utter fool."

"And you told him so, of course."

Against his will, Crispin smiled. "He told me *I* was, actually."

"That means he isn't, to be so perceptive."

"You mean it isn't obvious?"

Her turn to smile. "My mistake."

He poured himself another cup of the pale wine and mixed it half-and-half with water. In his mother's house he always did.

"I'm not going," he said. "Why would I want to go so far, with winter coming?"

"Because," said Avita Crispina, "you aren't entirely a fool, my child. We're talking about *Sarantium*, Caius, dear."

"I know what we are talking about. You sound like Martinian."

"He sounds like me." An old jest. Crispin didn't smile this time. He ate some more of the fish soup, which was very good.

"I'm not going," he repeated later, at the doorway, bending to salute her on the cheek. "Your cook is too skillful for me to bear the thought of leaving." She smelled, as always, of lavender. His first memory was of that scent. It ought to have been a color, he thought. Scents, tastes, sounds often attained hues in his mind, but this one didn't. The flower might be violet, almost porphyry, in fact—the royal color—but the *scent* wasn't. It was his mother's scent, simply that.

Two servants, holding cudgels, were waiting to walk him home in the dark.

"There are better cooks than mine in the east. I shall miss you, child," she replied calmly. "I expect regular letters."

Crispin was used to this. It still made him snort with exasperation as he walked away. He glanced back once and saw her in the spill of light, clad in a dark green robe. She lifted a hand to him and went within. He turned the corner, one of her men on either side of him, and walked the short distance to his home. He dismissed his mother's servants and stood a moment outside, cloaked against the chill, looking up.

Blue moon westering now in the autumn sky. Full as his heart once had been. The white moon, rising from the eastern end of his street, framed on both sides and below by the last houses and the city walls, was a pale, waning crescent. The cheiromancers attached meaning to such things. They attached meaning to everything overhead.

Crispin wondered if he could find a meaning to attach to himself. To whatever he seemed to have become in the year since a second plague summer had left him alive to bury a wife and two daughters himself. In the family plot, beside his father and grandfather. Not in a lime-strewn mound. Some things were not to be endured.

He thought about the torch of Heladikos he had contrived today on the small dome. There still remained, like a muted shadow of color, this pride in his craft, this love for it. Love. Was that still the word?

He did want to see this latest artifice by candlelight: an extravagant blazing of candles and oil lanterns all through the sanctuary, lifting fire to light the fire he'd shaped in stone and glass. He had a sense—honed by experience—that what he'd contrived might achieve something of the effect he wanted.

That, Martinian had always said, was the best any man in this fallible world could expect.

He *would* see it, Crispin knew, at the dedication of the sanctuary at autumn's end, when the young queen and her clerics and pompous emissaries from the High Patriarch in Rhodias—if not the Patriarch himself—laid King Hildric's bones formally to rest. They would not stint on candles or oil then. He'd be able to judge his work that day, harshly or otherwise.

He never did, as events unfolded. He never did see his mosaic torch on that sanctuary dome outside the walls of Varena.

As he turned to enter his own house, key to hand—the servants having been told, as usual, not to wait up—a rustling gave him warning, but not enough.

Crispin managed to lash out with a fist and catch a man in the chest, hard. He heard a thick grunt, drew breath to cry out, then felt a sack dropped over his head and tightened expertly at his throat, blinding and choking him at once. He coughed, smelled flour, tasted it. He kicked out violently, felt his foot meet a knee or shin and heard another muffled cry of pain. Lashing and twisting, Crispin clawed at the choking hold on his throat. He couldn't bite, from inside the bag. His assailants were silent, invisible. Three of them? Four? They had almost certainly come for the money that accursed courier had declared to the whole world was in the packet. He wondered if they'd kill him when they found he didn't have it. Decided it was probable. Pondered, with a far part of his mind, why he was struggling so hard.

He remembered his knife, reached for it with one hand, while raking for the arm at his throat with the other. He scratched, like a cat or a woman, drew blood with his fingernails. Found the knife hilt as he twisted and writhed. Jerked his blade free.

HE CAME TO, SLOWLY, and gradually became aware of painful, flickering light and the scent of perfume. Not lavender. His head hurt, not altogether unexpectedly. The flour sack had been removed—obviously: he could see blurred candles, shapes behind them and around, vague as yet. His hands appeared to be free. He reached up and very gingerly felt around the egg-shaped lump at the back of his skull.

At the edge of his vision, which was not, under the circumstances, especially acute, someone moved then, rising from a couch or a chair. He had an impression of gold, of a lapis hue.

The awareness of scent—more than one, in fact, he now realized—intensified. He turned his head. The movement made him gasp. He closed his eyes. He felt extremely ill.

Someone—a woman—said, "They were instructed to be solicitous. It appears you resisted."

"Very . . . sorry," Crispin managed. "Tedious of me."

He heard her laughter. Opened his eyes again. He had no idea where he was.

"Welcome to the palace, Caius Crispus," she said. "We are alone, as it happens. Ought I to fear you and summon guards?"

Fighting a particularly determined wave of nausea, Crispin propelled himself to a sitting position. An instant later he staggered upright, his heart pounding. He tried, much too quickly, to bow. He had to clutch urgently at a tabletop to keep himself from toppling. His vision swirled and his stomach did the same.

"You are excused the more extreme rituals of ceremony," said the only living child of the late King Hildric.

Gisel, queen of the Antae and of Batiara and his own most holy ruler under Jad, who paid a symbolic allegiance to the Sarantine Emperor and offered spiritual devotion to the High Patriarch and to no one else alive, looked gravely at him with wide-set eyes.

"Very . . . extremely . . . kind of you. Your Majesty," Crispin mumbled. He was trying, with limited success, to make his eyes stop blurring and become useful in the candlelight. There seemed to be random objects swimming in the air. He was also having some difficulty breathing. He was alone in a room with the queen. He had never even *seen* her, except at a distance. Artisans, however successful or celebrated, did *not* hold nocturnal, private converse with their sovereign. Not in the world as Crispin knew it.

His head felt as if a small but insistent hammer inside it were trying to pound its way out. His confusion was extreme, disorienting. Had she captured him or rescued him? And *why*, in either case? He didn't dare ask. Amid the perfumes he smelled flour again suddenly. That would be himself. From the sack. He looked down at his dinner tunic and made a sour face. The blue was streaked and smeared a grayish white. Which meant that his hair and beard . . .

"You were attended to, somewhat, while you slept," said the queen, graciously enough. "I had my own physician summoned. He said bleeding was not immediately necessary. Would a glass of wine be of help?"

Crispin made a sound that he trusted to convey restrained, well-bred assent. She did not laugh again, or smile. It occurred to him that this was a woman not unused to observing the effects of violence upon men. A number of well-known incidents, unbidden, came into his head. Some were quite recent. The thought of them did nothing to ease him at all.

The queen made no movement, and a moment later Crispin realized that she had meant what she said quite literally. They *were* alone in this room. No servants, not even slaves. Which was simply astonishing. And he could hardly expect her to serve him wine. He looked around and, more by luck than any effective process of observation, encountered a flask and cups on the table by his elbow. He poured, carefully, and watered two cups, unsure whether that was a presumption. He was *not* conversant with the Antae court. Martinian had taken all their commissions from King Hildric and then his daughter, and had delivered the reports.

Crispin looked up. His eyesight seemed to be improving as the hammer subsided a little and the room elected to stabilize. He saw her shake her head at the cup he had poured for her. He set it down. Waited. Looked at her again.

The queen of Batiara was tall for a woman and unsettlingly young. Seen this closely, she had the straight Antae nose and her father's strong cheekbones. The wide-set eyes were a much-celebrated blue, he knew, though he couldn't see that clearly in the candlelight. Her hair was golden, bound up, of course, held by a golden circlet studded with rubies.

The Antae had worn bear grease in their hair when they'd first come to settle in the peninsula. This woman was not, manifestly, an exponent of such traditions. He imagined those rubies—he couldn't help himself—set in his mosaic torch on the sanctuary dome. He imagined them gleaming by candlelight there.

The queen wore a golden sun disk about her throat, an image of Heladikos upon it. Her robe was blue silk, threaded with fine gold wire, and there was a purple band running down the left side, from high collar to ankle. Only royalty wore purple, in keeping with a tradition going back to the Rhodian Empire at its own beginnings six hundred years ago.

He was alone in a palace room at night with the headache of his life and a queen—his queen—regarding him with a mild, steady appraisal.

It was common opinion, all through the Batiaran peninsula, that the queen was unlikely to live through the winter. Crispin had heard wagers offered and taken, at odds.

The Antae might have moved beyond bear grease and pagan rituals in a hundred years but they were most emphatically not accustomed to being ruled by a woman, and any choice of a mate—and king—for Gisel was fraught with an almost inconceivable complexity of tribal hierarchies and feuds. In a way, it was only due to these that she was still alive and reigning a year and more after her father's death and the savage, inconclusive civil war that had followed. Martinian had put it that way one night over dinner. The factions of the Antae were locked in balance around her; if she died, that balance spiraled away and war came. Again.

Crispin had shrugged. Whoever reigned would commission sanctuaries to their own glory in the god's name. Mosaicists would work. He and Martinian were extremely well-known, with a reputation among the upper classes and reliable employees and apprentices. Did it matter so much, he'd asked the older man, what happened in the palace in Varena? Did any such things signify greatly after the plague?

The queen was still gazing at him beneath level brows, waiting. Crispin, belatedly realizing what was expected, saluted her with his cup and drank. It was magnificent wine. The very best Sarnican. He'd never tasted anything so complex. Under any normal circumstances, he would . . .

He put it down, quickly. After the blow to his head, this drink could undo him completely.

"A careful man, I see," she murmured.

Crispin shook his head. "Not really, Majesty." He had no idea what was expected of him here, or what to expect. It occurred to him that he ought to feel outraged . . . He'd been assaulted and abducted outside his own home. Instead, he felt curious, intrigued, and he was sufficiently self-aware to recognize that these feelings had been absent from his life for some time.

"May I assume," he said, "that the footpads who clapped a flour sack on my head and dented my braincase were from the palace? Or did your loyal guards rescue me from common thieves?"

She smiled at that. She couldn't be older than her early twenties, Crispin thought, remembering a royal betrothal and a husband-to-be dying of some mischance a few years ago.

"They were my guards. I told you, their orders were to be courteous, while ensuring you came with them. Apparently you did some injuries to them."

"I am delighted to hear it. They did some to me."

"In loyalty to their queen and in her cause. Do you have the same loyalties?"

Direct, very direct.

Crispin watched as she moved to an ivory and rosewood bench and sat down, her back very straight. He saw that there were three doors to the room and imagined guards poised on the other side of each of them. He pushed his hands through his hair—a characteristic motion, leaving it randomly scattered—and said quietly, "I am engaged, to the best of my skill, and using deficient materials, in decorating a sanctuary to honor your father. Is that answer enough, Majesty?"

"Not at all, Rhodian. That is self-interest. You are extremely well paid, and the materials are the best we can offer right now. We've had a plague and a war, Caius Crispus."

"Oh, really," he said. Couldn't help himself.

She raised her eyebrows. "Insolence?"

Her voice and expression made him abruptly aware that whatever the proper court manners might be, he was not displaying them, and the Antae had never been known for patience.

He shook his head. "I lived through both," he murmured. "I need no reminders."

She regarded him in silence another long moment. Crispin felt an unexplained prickling along his back up to the hairs of his neck. The silence stretched. Then the queen drew a breath and said without preamble: "I need an extremely private message carried to the Emperor in Sarantium. No man—or woman—may know the contents of this, or that it is even being carried. That is why you are here alone, and were brought by night."

Crispin's mouth went dry. He felt his heart begin to hammer again. "I am an artisan, Majesty. No more than that. I have no place in the intrigues of courts." He wished he hadn't put down the wineglass. "And," he added, too tardily, "I am not going to Sarantium."

"Of course you are," she said dismissively. "What man would not accept that invitation." She knew about it. Of course she did. His *mother* knew about it.

"It is not my invitation," he said pointedly. "And Martinian, my partner, has indicated he will not go."

"He is an old man. You aren't. And you have nothing to keep you in Varena at all."

He had nothing to keep him. At all.

"He isn't old," he said.

She ignored that. "I have made inquiries into your family, your circumstances, your disposition. I am told you are choleric and of dark humor, and not inclined to be properly respectful. Also that you are skilled at your craft and have attained a measure of renown and some wealth thereby. None of this concerns me. But no one has reported you to be cowardly or without ambition. Of course you will go to Sarantium. Will you carry my message for me?"

Crispin said, before he had really thought about the implications at all, "What message?"

Which meant—he realized much later, thinking about it, reliving this dialogue again and again on the long road east—that the moment she told him, he had no real choice, unless he *did* decide to die and seek Ilandra and the girls with Jad behind the sun.

The young queen of the Antae and of Batiara, surrounded by mortal danger and fighting it with whatever tools came to hand, however unexpectedly, said softly, "You will tell the Emperor Valerius II and no one else that should he wish to regain this country and Rhodias within it, and not merely have a meaningless claim to them, there is an unmarried queen here who has heard of his prowess and his glory and honors them."

Crispin's jaw dropped. The queen did not flush, nor did her gaze flicker at all. His reaction was being closely watched, he realized. He said, stammering, "The Emperor is married. Has been for years. He changed the *laws* to wed the Empress Alixana."

Calm and very still on her ivory seat, she said, "Alas, husbands or wives may be put aside. Or die, Caius Crispus."

He knew this.

"Empires," she murmured, "live after us. So does a name. For good or ill. Valerius II, who was once Petrus of Trakesia, has wanted to regain Rhodias and this peninsula since he brought his uncle to the Golden Throne twelve summers ago. He purchased his truce with the King of Kings in Bassania for that reason alone. King Shirvan is bribed so Valerius may assemble an army for the west when the time ripens. There are no mysteries here. But if he tries to take this land in war, he will not hold it. This peninsula is too far away from him, and we Antae know how to make war. And his enemies east and north—the Bassanids and the northern barbarians—will never sit quiet and watch, no matter how much he pays them. There will be men around Valerius who know this, and they may even tell him as much. There is another way to achieve his . . . desire. I am offering it to him." She paused. "You may tell him, too, that you have seen the queen of Batiara very near, in blue and gold and porphyry, and may . . . give him an honest description, should he ask for one."

This time, though she continued to hold his gaze and even lifted her chin a little, she did flush. Crispin became aware that his hands were perspiring at his sides. He pressed them against his tunic. He felt the stirrings, astonishingly, of a long-dormant desire. A kind of madness, that, though desire often was. The queen of Batiara was not, in any possible sense, someone who could be thought of in this way. She was offering her face and exquisitely garbed body to his recording gaze, only that he might tell an Emperor about her, halfway around the world. He had never dreamed of moving—never wanted to move—in this world of royal shadows and intrigue, but his puzzle-solving mind was racing now, with his pulse, and he could begin to see the pieces of this picture.

No man—or woman—may know.

No woman. Clear as it could be. He was being asked to carry an overture of marriage to the Emperor, who was very much married, and to the most powerful and dangerous woman in the known world.

"The Emperor and his lowborn actress-wife have no children, alas," said Gisel softly. Crispin realized his thoughts must have been in his face. He was *not* good at this. "A sad legacy, one might imagine, of her . . . profession. And she is no longer young."

I am, was the message beneath the message he was to bring. *Save my life, my throne, and I offer you the homeland of the Rhodian Empire that you yearn for. I give you back the west to your east, and the sons to your need. I am fair, and young . . . Ask the man who carries my words to you. He will say as much. Only ask.*

"You believe . . ." he began. Stopped. Composed himself with an effort. "You believe this can be kept secret? Majesty, if I am even known to have been brought to you . . ."

"Trust me in this. You can do me no service if you are killed on the way or when you arrive."

"You reassure me greatly," he murmured.

Surprisingly, she laughed again. He wondered what those on the other side of the doors would think, hearing that. He wondered what else they might have heard.

"You could send no formal envoy with this?"

He knew the answer before she gave it. "No such messenger from me would have a chance to bespeak the Emperor in . . . privacy."

"And I will?"

"You might. You have pure Rhodian blood on both sides. They acknowledge that, still, in Sarantium, though they complain about you. Valerius is said to be interested in ivory, frescoes . . . such things as you do with stones and glass. He is known to hold conversation with his artisans."

"How commendable of him. And when he finds that I am not Martinian of Varena? What sort of conversation will then ensue?"

The queen smiled. "That will depend on your wits, will it not?"

Crispin drew another breath. Before he could speak, she added, "You have not asked what return a grateful, newly crowned Empress might make to the man who conveyed this message for her and had success follow upon it. You can read?" He nodded. She reached into a sleeve of her robe and withdrew a parchment scroll. She extended it a little toward him. He walked nearer, inhaled her scent, saw that her eyelashes were accented and extended subtly. He took the parchment from her hand.

She nodded permission. He broke the seal. Uncurled the scroll. Read.

He felt the color leave his face as he did so. And hard upon astonishment came bitterness, the core of pain that walked with him in the world.

He said, "It is wasted on me, Majesty. I have no children to inherit any of this."

"You are a young man," the queen said mildly.

Anger flared. "Indeed? So why no offer here of a comely Antae woman of your court, or an aristocrat of Rhodian blood for my prize? The brood mare to fill these promised houses and spend this wealth?"

She had been a princess and was a queen and had spent her life in palaces where judging people was a tool of survival. She said, "I would not insult you with such a proposal. I am told yours was a love-match. A rare thing. I count you lucky in it, though the allotted time was brief. You are a well-formed man, and would have resources to commend you, as the parchment shows. I imagine you could buy your own brood mare of high lineage, if other methods of choosing a second wife did not present themselves."

MUCH LATER, IN HIS own bed, awake, with the moons long set and the dawn not far off, Crispin was to conclude that it was this answer, the gravity of it with the bite of irony at the end, that had decided him. Had she offered him a mate on paper or in word, he told himself, he would have refused outright and let her kill him if she wanted.

She would have, he was almost certain of it.

And that thought had come in the last of the darkness, even before he learned from the apprentices as they met at the sanctuary for the sunrise prayers that six of the Palace Guard in Varena had been found dead in the night, their throats slit.

Crispin would walk away from the babble of noise and speculation to stand in the sanctuary alone under his charioteer and torch on the dome. The light was just entering through the dome's ring of windows, striking the angled glass. The mosaic torch seemed to flicker as he watched, a soft but unmistakable rippling, as of a muted flame. In his mind's eye he could see it above burning lanterns and candles . . . given enough of them it would work.

He understood something. The queen of the Antae, battling for her life, had made something else as clear as it could be: she would not let the secrecy of his message be endangered in any way, even by her own most trusted guards. Six men dead. Nothing muted there at all.

He didn't know how he felt. Or no, he realized that he did know: he felt like a too small ship setting out from harbor far too late in the year, undermanned, with winter winds swirling all around it.

But he was going to Sarantium. After all.

EARLIER, IN THE DEPTHS of the night, in that room in the palace, feeling a stillness descend upon him, Crispin had said to the woman in the carved ivory seat, "I am honored by your trust, Majesty. I would not want another war here, either among the Antae or a Sarantine invasion. We have endured our share of dying. I will carry your message and try to give it to the Emperor, if I survive my own deception. It is folly, what I am about to do, but everything we do is folly, is it not?"

"No," she said, unexpectedly. "But I do not expect to be the one who persuades you of that." She gestured to one of the doors. "There is a man on the other side who will escort you home. You will not see me again, for reasons you understand. You may kiss my foot, if you feel sufficiently well."

He knelt before her. Touched the slender foot in its golden sandal. Kissed the top of it. As he did, he felt long fingers brush through his hair to the place on his skull where the blow had fallen. He shivered. "You have my gratitude," he heard. "Whatever befalls."

The hand was withdrawn. He stood, bowed again, went out through the indicated portal, and was escorted home by a tongueless, smooth-shaven giant of a man through the windy night streets of his city. He was aware of desire lingering as he walked in blackness away from the palace, from the chamber. He was astonished by it.

In that exquisite, small receiving room, a young woman sat alone for a time after he left. It was rare for her to be entirely solitary, and the sensation was not disagreeable. Events had moved swiftly since one of her sources of privy knowledge had mentioned the spoken-aloud details of a summons conveyed by the Imperial Post to an artisan working at her father's resting place. She'd had little time to ponder nuances, only to realize that this was an unexpected, slender chance—and seize it.

Now there were deaths to attend to, regrettably. This game was lost before it began if it were known to Agila or Eudric or any of the others hovering around her throne that the artisan had had private converse with her in the night before journeying east. The man escorting the mosaic worker now was the only one she fully trusted. For one thing, he could not speak. For another, he had been hers since she was five years old. She would give him further orders for tonight when he returned. It would not be the first time he had killed for her.

The queen of the Antae offered, at length, a small, quiet prayer, asking forgiveness, among other things. She prayed to holy Jad, to his son the Charioteer who had died bringing fire to mortal men, and then—to be as sure as one could ever be sure—to the gods and goddesses her people had worshipped when they were a wild cluster of tribes in the hard lands north and east, first in the mountains, and then by the oak forests of Sauradia, before coming down into fertile Batiara and accepting Jad of the Sun, conquering heirs to an Empire's homeland.

She nursed few illusions. The man, Caius Crispus, had surprised her a little, but he was an artisan only, and of an angry, despairing humor. Arrogant, as the Rhodians still were so much of the time. Not a truly reliable vessel for so desperate an enterprise. This was almost certainly doomed to failure, but there was little she could do but try. She had let him come near to her, kiss her foot. Had brushed his flour-smeared red hair with fingers deliberately slow . . . perhaps longing was the gateway to this man's loyalty? She didn't think so, but she didn't know, and she could only use what few tools, or weapons, she had or was given.

Gisel of the Antae did not expect to see the wildflowers return in spring, or watch the midsummer bonfires burn upon the hills. She was nineteen years old, but queens were not, in truth, allowed to be so young.

CHAPTER II

When Crispin was a boy and free for a day in the way that only boys in summer can be free he had walked outside the city walls one morning and, after throwing stones in a stream for a time, had passed by a walled orchard universally reported among the young Varenans to belong to a spirit-haunted country house where unholy things happened after dark.

The sun was shining. In an effusion of youthful bravado, Crispin had climbed the rough stone wall, leaped across into a tree, sat down on a stout branch among the leaves and begun eating apples. He was heart-poundingly proud of himself and wondering how he'd prove he'd done this to his sure-to-be-skeptical friends. He decided to carve his initials—a newly learned skill—on the tree trunk, and dare the others to come see them.

He received, a moment later, the deepest fright of his young life.

It used to wake him at night sometimes, the memory having turned into a dream he'd have even as an adult, a husband, a father. In fact, he had managed to persuade himself that it mostly *had* been a dream, spun out of overly vivid childhood anxieties, the blazing midday heat, almost-ripe apples eaten too quickly. It had to have been a child's fantasy, breeding ground of nightmare.

Birds did *not* talk.

More particularly, they did not discuss with each other from tree to tree, in the identically bored tones and timbre of an overbred Rhodian aristocrat, which eye of a trespassing boy should be pecked out and consumed first, or how the emptied eye sockets might then offer easy access to slithery morsels of brain matter within.

Caius Crispus, eight years old and blessed or cursed with an intensely visual imagination, had not lingered to further investigate this remarkable phenomenon of nature. There seemed to be several birds in animated colloquy about him, half hidden in the leaves and branches. He dropped three apples, spat out the half-chewed pulp of another, and leaped wildly back to the wall, scraping an elbow raw, bruising a shin, and then doing himself further damage when he landed badly on the baked summer grass by the path.

As he sprinted back, not quite screaming, toward Varena, he heard sardonic crowing laughter behind him.

Or he did in his dreams, after, at any rate.

TWENTY-FIVE YEARS LATER, WALKING the same road south of the city, Crispin was thinking about the power of memories, the way they had of coming back so fiercely and unexpectedly. A scent could do it, the sound of rushing water, the sight of a stone wall beside a path.

He was remembering that day in the tree, and the recollection of terror took him a little further back, to the image of his mother's face when the reserves of the urban militia returned from that same year's spring campaign against the Inicii and his father was not with them.

Horius Crispus the mason had been a vivid, well-liked man, respected and successful in his craft and business. His only surviving son struggled, however, to shape a clear mental picture, after all these years, of the man who had gone marching north to the border and beyond into Ferrieres, red-bearded, smiling, easy-striding. He'd been too young when the militia's deputy commander had come to their door with his father's nondescript shield and sword.

He could remember a beard that scratched when he kissed his father's cheek, blue eyes—his own eyes, people said—and the big, capable hands, scarred and always scratched. A big voice, too, that went soft within the house, near Crispin or his small, scented mother. He had these . . . fragments, these elements, but when he tried to pull them together in his mind to create a whole it somehow slipped away, the way the man had slipped away too soon.

He had stories to go by: from his mother, her brothers, sometimes his own patrons, many of whom remembered Horius Crispus well. And he could study his father's steady, incisive work in houses and chapels, graveyards and public buildings all over Varena. But he couldn't cling to any memory of a face that did not blur into an absence. For a man who lived for image and color—who flourished in the realm of sight—this was hard.

Or it had been hard. Time passing did complex things, to deepen a wound or to heal it. Even, sometimes, to overlay it with another that had felt as if it would kill.

It was a beautiful morning. The wind was behind him, the coming winter in it, but crisp rather than cold while the sun shone, sweeping the mist from the eastern forests and hills to the west and farther south. He was alone on the road. Not always a safe thing, but he felt no danger now, and he could see a long way in the open country south of the city—almost to the rim of the world, it seemed.

Behind him, when he glanced back, Varena gleamed, bronze domes, red roof-tiles, the city walls nearly white in the morning light. A hawk circled above its own warning shadow on the stubble of the fields east of the road. The harvested vines on the slopes ahead looked derelict and bare, but the grapes were inside the city, being made into wine even now. Queen Gisel, efficient in this as in many things, had ordered that city laborers and slaves join in the grain and grape harvests, to cover—as much as possible—the loss of so many people to the plague. The first festivals would be beginning soon, in Varena and in smaller villages everywhere, leading up to the wildness of Dykania's three nights. It would be difficult, though, to shape a truly festive mood this autumn, Crispin thought. Or perhaps he was wrong about that. Perhaps festivals were *more* important after what had happened. Perhaps they were more uninhibited in the presence of death.

As he walked, he could see abandoned farmhouses and outbuildings on both sides of the country path. The rich farmland and vineyards around Varena were all very well, but they needed men to sow and reap and tend, and too many laborers were buried in the mass graves. The coming winter would be hard.

Even with these thoughts, it was difficult to remain grim this morning. Light nurtured him, as did clean, sharp colors, and the day was offering both. He wondered if he'd ever be able to create a forest with the browns and reds and golds and the late, deep green of the one he could see now beyond the bare fields. With tesserae worthy of the name, and perhaps a sanctuary dome designed with windows enough and by the god's grace—good, clear glass for those windows, he might. He might.

In Sarantium these things were to be found, men said. In Sarantium, everything on earth was to be found, from death to heart's desire, men said.

He was going, it seemed. *Sailing to Sarantium.* Walking, actually, for it was too late in the year for a ship, but the old saying spoke of change, not a means of travel. His life was branching, taking him toward whatever might come on the road or at journey's end.

His life. He had a life. The hardest thing was to accept that, it sometimes seemed. To move out from the rooms where a woman and two children had died in ugly pain, stripped of all inherent dignity or grace; to allow brightness to touch him again, like this gift of the morning sun.

In that moment, he felt like a child again himself, seeing a remembered stone wall come into view as the path curved and approached it. Half amused, half genuinely unsettled, Crispin added a few more inward curses to his emergent litany against Martinian, who had insisted that he make this visit.

It seemed that Zoticus, the alchemist, much consulted by farmers, the childless and the lovelorn, and even royalty on occasion, dwelled in the selfsame substantial farmhouse with an attached apple orchard where an eight-year-old boy had heard birds discussing with well-bred anticipation the consumption of his eyeballs and brain matter.

"I will send to tell him to expect you," Martinian had said with firmness. "He knows more useful things than any man I know, and you are a fool if you undertake a journey like this without first speaking with Zoticus. Besides, he makes wonderful herbal infusions."

"I don't like herbal infusions."

"Crispin," Martinian had said warningly. And had given directions.

And so here he was, cloaked against the wind, pacing alongside the rough stones of the wall, booted feet tracing the vanished, long-ago bare footsteps of a child who had gone out from the city alone one summer's day to escape the sorrow in his house.

He was alone now, too. Birds flitted from branch to bough on both sides of the road. He watched them. The hawk was gone. A brown hare, too exposed, made swift, deliberately jerky progress across the field on his left. A cloud swept across the sun and its elongated shadow raced over the same field. The hare froze when the shadow reached it and then hurtled erratically forward again as light returned.

On the other side of the road the wall marched beside him, well built, well maintained, of heavy gray stones. Ahead, he could see the gateway to the farmyard, a marker stone opposite it. Unused though it now was, this had been a road laid down in the great days of the Rhodian Empire. In no great distance—a morning's steady walking—it met the high road that ran all the way to Rhodias itself and beyond, to the southern sea at the end of the peninsula. As a child, Crispin used to enjoy the sensation of being on the same road as someone gazing into those distant ocean waters.

He stopped for a moment, looking at the wall. He had climbed it easily that morning long ago. There were still apples in the trees beyond. Crispin pursed his lips, weighing a thought. This was *not* a time to be dueling with childhood memories, he told himself sternly, repressively. He was a grown man, a respected, well-known artisan, a widower. Sailing to Sarantium.

With a small, resolute shrug of his shoulders, Crispin dropped the package he was carrying—a gift from Martinian's wife for the alchemist—onto the brown grass beside the path. Then he stepped across the small ditch, pushed a hand through his hair, and proceeded to climb the wall again.

Not all skills were lost to the years, and it seemed he wasn't so old after all. Pleased with his own agility, he swung one knee up, then the other, stood on the wide, uneven top of the wall, balanced, and then stepped—only boys leaped—across to a good branch. He found a comfortable spot, sat down and, pausing to be judicious, reached up and picked an apple.

He was surprised to find his heart was racing.

He knew that if they saw this, his mother and Martinian and half a dozen others would be performing a collective rueful headshake like the chorus in one of those seldom-performed tragedies of the ancient Trakesian poets. Everyone said Crispin did things merely because he knew that he *shouldn't* do them. A perversity of behavior, his mother called it.

Perhaps. He didn't think so, himself. The apple was ripe. Tasty, he decided.

He dropped it onto the grass among fallen ones for the small animals and stood up to cross back to the wall. No need to be greedy or childish. He'd proven his point, felt curiously pleased with himself. Settled a score with his youth, in a way.

"Some people never learn, do they?"

One foot on a branch, one on top of the wall, Crispin looked down very quickly. Not a bird, not an animal, not a spirit of the half-world of air and shadow. A man with a full beard and unfashionably long gray hair stood in the orchard below, gazing up at him, leaning on a staff, foreshortened by the angle.

Flushing, acutely embarrassed, Crispin mumbled, "They used to say this orchard was haunted. I . . . wanted to test myself."

"And did you pass your test?" the old man—Zoticus, beyond doubt—queried gently.

"I suppose." Crispin stepped across to the wall. "The apple was good."

"As good as they were all those years ago?"

"Hard to remember. I really don't—"

Crispin stopped. A prickling of fear.

"How do . . . how did you know I was here? Back then?"

"You *are* Caius Crispus, I presume? Martinian's friend."

Crispin decided to sit down on the wall. His legs felt oddly weak. "I am. I have a gift for you. From his wife."

"Carissa. Splendid woman! A neckwarmer, I do hope. I find I need them now, as winter comes. Old age. A terrible thing, let me tell you. How did I know you were here before? Silly question. Come down. Do you like mint leaves in an infusion?"

It didn't seem in the least silly to Crispin. For the moment he deferred a reply. "I'll get the gift," he said, and climbed down—jumping would lack all dignity—on the outside of the wall. He reclaimed the parcel from the grass, brushed some ants from it, and walked up the road toward the farmyard gate, breathing deeply to calm himself.

Zoticus was waiting, leaning on his staff, two large dogs beside him. He opened the gate and Crispin walked in. The dogs sniffed at him but heeled to a command. Zoticus led the way toward the house through a neat, small yard. The door was open, Crispin saw.

"Why don't we just eat him now?"

Crispin stopped. Childhood terror. The very worst kind, that made nightmares for life. He looked up. The voice was lazy, aristocratic, remembered. It belonged to a bird perched on the branch of an ash tree, not far from the doorway.

"Manners, manners, Linon. This is a guest." Zoticus's tone was reproving.

"A guest? Climbing the wall? Stealing apples?"

"Well, eating him would hardly be a proportionate response, and the philosophers teach that proportion is the essence of the virtuous life, do they not?"

Crispin, stupefied, fighting fear, heard the bird give an elaborate sniff of disapproval. Looking more closely, he abruptly realized, with a further shock, that it was not a real bird. It was an artifice. Crafted.

And it was talking. Or else . . .

"You are speaking for it!" he said quickly. "Casting your voice? The way the actors do onstage sometimes?"

"*Mice and blood!* Now he insults us!"

"He is bringing a neckwarmer from Carissa. Behave, Linon."

"Take the neck thing, then let us eat him."

Crispin, his own choler rising suddenly, said bluntly, "You are a construct of leather and metal. You can't eat anything. Don't bluster."

Zoticus glanced quickly over at him, surprised, and then laughed aloud, the sound unexpectedly robust, filling the space before his doorway.

"And that," he said, "will teach you, Linon! If anything can."

"It will teach me that we have an ill-bred guest this morning."

"You did propose eating him. Remember?"

"I am only a bird. Remember? Indeed, I am less than that, it seems. I am a construct of leather and metal."

Crispin had the distinct sense that if the small gray and brown thing with the glass eyes could have moved, it would have turned its back on him, or flown away in disgust and wounded pride.

Zoticus walked over to the tree, turned a screw on each of the tiny legs of the bird, loosening their grip on the branch, and picked it up. "Come," he said. "The water is boiled and the mint was picked this morning."

The mechanical bird said nothing, nestled in his free hand. It looked like a child's toy. Crispin followed into the house. The dogs lay down in the yard.

THE INFUSION WAS GOOD, actually. Crispin, more calm than he'd expected to be, wondered if the old alchemist might have added something besides mint to it, but he didn't ask. Zoticus was standing at a table examining the courier's map Crispin had produced from the inner pocket of his cloak.

Crispin looked around. The front room was comfortably furnished, much as any prosperous farmhouse might be. No dissected bats or pots with green or black liquids boiling in them, no pentagrams chalked on the wooden floor. There were books and scrolls, to mark a learned and an unexpectedly well-off man, but little else to suggest magics or cheiromancy. Still, he saw half a dozen of the crafted birds, made of various materials, perched on shelves or the backs of chairs, and they gave him pause. None of these had spoken yet, and the small one called Linon lay silently on its side on a table by the fire. Crispin had little doubt, however, that any and all of them could address him if they chose.

It amazed him how calmly he accepted this. On the other hand, he'd had twenty-five years to live with the knowledge.

"The Imperial Posting Inns, whenever you can," Zoticus was murmuring, head lowered still to the map, a curved, polished glass in one hand to magnify it. "Comforts and food are unreliable elsewhere."

Crispin nodded, still distracted. "Dog meat instead of horse or swine, I know."

Zoticus glanced up, his expression wry. "Dog is *good*," he said. "The risk is getting human flesh in a sausage."

Crispin kept a composed face with some effort. "I see," he said. "Well spiced, I'm sure."

"Sometimes," said Zoticus, turning back to the map. "Be especially careful through Sauradia, which can be unstable in autumn."

Crispin watched him. Zoticus had taken a quill now and was making notations on the map. "Tribal rites?"

The alchemist glanced up briefly, eyebrows arched. His features were strong, the blue eyes deep-set, and he wasn't as old as the gray hair and the staff might have suggested. "Yes, that. And knowing they will be mostly on their own again until spring, even with the big army camp near Trakesia and soldiers at Megarium. Notorious winter brigands, the Sauradi tribes. Lively women, as I recall, mind you." He smiled a little, to himself, and returned to his annotations.

Crispin shrugged. Sipped his tea. Resolutely tried to put his mind away from sausages.

Some might have seen this long autumn journey as an adventure in itself. Caius Crispus did not. He liked his own city walls, and good roofs against rain, and cooks he knew, and his bathhouse. For him, broaching a new cask of wine from Megarium or the vineyards south of Rhodias had always been a preferred form of excitement. Designing and executing a mosaic was an adventure . . . or had been once. Walking the wet, windswept roads of Sauradia or Trakesia with an eye out for predators—human or otherwise—in a struggle to avoid becoming someone else's sausage was *not* an adventure, and a graybeard's cackling about lively women did not make it one.

He said, "I'd still like an answer, by the way, silly question or not. How did you know I was here all those years ago?"

Zoticus put down the quill and sat in a heavy chair. One of the mechanical birds—a falcon with a silver and bronze body and yellow jeweled eyes, quite unlike the drab, sparrowlike Linon—was fixed to the high back of the chair, screws adjusted so its claws held fast. It gazed inimically at Crispin with a pale glitter.

"You *do* know I am an alchemist."

"Martinian said as much. I also know that most who use that name are frauds, hooking coins and goods from innocents."

Crispin heard a sound from the direction of the fire. It might have been a log shifting, or not.

"Entirely true," said Zoticus, unperturbed. "Most are. Some are not. I am one of those who are not."

"Ah. Meaning you know the future, can induce passionate love, cure the plague, and find water?" He sounded truculent, Crispin knew. He couldn't help it.

Zoticus gazed at him levelly. "Only the last, actually, and not invariably. No. Meaning I can sometimes see and do things most men cannot, with frustratingly erratic success. And meaning I can see things *in* men and women that others cannot. You asked how I knew you? Men have an aura, a presence to them. It changes little, from childhood to death. Very few people dare my orchard, which is useful—as you might guess—for a man living alone in the countryside. You were there once. I knew your presence again this morning. The anger in you was not present in the child, though there was a loss then, too. The rest is little enough altered. It is not," he said kindly, "so complicated an explanation, is it?"

Crispin looked at him, cupping his drink in both hands. His glance shifted to the jeweled falcon gripping the back of the alchemist's heavy chair. "And these?" he asked, ignoring the observations about himself.

"Oh. Well. That's the whole *point* of alchemy, isn't it? To transmute one substance into another, proving certain things about the nature of the world. Metals to gold. The dead to life. I have learned to make inanimate substance think and speak, and retain a soul." He said it much as he might have described learning how to make the mint tea they were drinking.

Crispin looked around the room at the birds. "Why . . . birds?" he asked, the first of fully a dozen questions that occurred. *The dead to life.*

Zoticus looked down, that private smile on his face again. After a moment, he said, "I wanted to go to Sarantium myself once. I had ambitions in the world, and wished to see the Emperor and be honored by him with wealth and women and world's glory. Apius, some time after he took the Golden Throne, initiated a fashion for mechanical animals. Roaring lions in the throne room. Bears that rose on their hind legs. And birds. He wanted birds everywhere. Singing birds in all his palaces. The mechanical artisans of the world were sending him their best contrivances: wind them up and they warbled an off-key paean to Jad or a rustic folk ditty, over and over again until you were minded to throw them against a wall and watch the little wheels spill out. You've heard them? Beautiful to look at, sometimes. And the sound can be appealing—at first."

Crispin nodded. He and Martinian had done a Senator's house in Rhodias.

"I decided," said Zoticus, "I might do better. Far better. Create birds that had their own power of speech. And thought. And that these, the fruits of long study and labor and . . . some danger, would be my conduits to fame in the world."

"What happened?"

"You don't remember? No, you wouldn't. Apius, under the influence of his Eastern Patriarch, began blinding alchemists and cheiromancers, even simple astrologers for a while. The clerics of the sun god have always feared any other avenues to power or understanding in the world. It became evident that arriving in the City with birds that had souls and spoke their own minds was a swift path to blinding if not death." The tone was wry.

"So you stayed here?"

"I stayed. After . . . some extended travels. Mostly in autumn, as it happened. This season makes me restless even now. I did learn on those journeys how to do what I wanted. As you can see. I never did get to Sarantium. A mild regret. I'm too old now."

Crispin, hearing the alchemist's words in his mind again, realized something. *The clerics of the sun god.* "You aren't a Jaddite, are you?"

Zoticus smiled, and shook his head.

"Odd," said Crispin dryly, "you don't *look* Kindath."

Zoticus laughed. There came that sound again, from toward the fire. A log, almost certainly. "I have been told I do," he said. "But no, why would I exchange one fallacy for another?"

Crispin nodded. This was not a surprise, all things considered. "Pagan?"

"I honor the old gods, yes. And their philosophers. And believe with them that it is a mistake to attempt to circumscribe the infinite range of divinity into one—or even two or three—images, however potent they might be on a dome or a disk."

Crispin sat down on the stool opposite the other man. He sipped from his cup again. Pagans were not all that rare in Batiara among the Antae—which might well explain why Zoticus had lingered safely in this countryside—but this was still an extraordinarily frank conversation to be having. "I'd imagine," he said, "that the Jaddite teachers—or the Kindath, from what little I know—would simply say that all modes of divinity may be encompassed in one if the one is powerful enough."

"They would," Zoticus agreed equably. "Or two for the pure Heladikians, three with the Kindath moons and sun. They would all be wrong, to my mind, but that is what they'd say. Are we about to debate the nature of the divine, Caius Crispus? We'll need more than a mint infusion in that case."

Crispin almost laughed. "And more time. I leave in two days and have a great deal to attend to."

"Of course you do. And an old man's philosophizing can hardly appeal just now, if ever. I have marked your map with the hostelries I understand to be acceptable, and those to be particularly avoided. My last travels were twenty years and more ago, but I do have my sources. Let me also give you two names in the City. Both may be trusted, I suspect, though not with *everything* you know or do."

His expression was direct. Crispin thought of a young queen in a candlelit room, and wondered. He said nothing. Zoticus crossed to the table, took a sheet of parchment and wrote upon it. He folded the parchment twice and handed it to Crispin.

"Be careful around the last of this month and the first day of the next. It would be wise not to travel those days, if you can arrange to be staying at an Imperial Inn. Sauradia will be a . . . changed place."

Crispin looked his inquiry.

"The Day of the Dead. Not a prudent time for strangers to be abroad in that province. Once you are in Trakesia you'll be safer. Until you get to the City itself and have to explain why you aren't Martinian. That ought to be amusing."

"Oh, very," said Crispin. He had been avoiding thinking about that. Time enough. It was a long journey by land. He unfolded the paper, read the names.

"The first is a doctor," said Zoticus. "Always useful. The second is my daughter."

"Your what?" Crispin blinked.

"Daughter. Seed of my loins. Girl child." Zoticus laughed. "One of them. I told you: I did travel a fair bit in my youth."

They heard a barking from the yard. From farther within the house a long-faced, slope-shouldered servant appeared and made his unhurried way to the door and out. He silenced the dogs. They heard voices outside. A moment later he reappeared, carrying two jars.

"Silavin came, master. He says his swine is recovered. He brought honey. Promises a ham."

"Splendid!" said Zoticus. "Store the honey in the cellar."

"We have thirty jars there, master," said the servant lugubriously.

"Thirty? So many? Oh dear. Well . . . our friend here will take two back for Carissa and Martinian."

"That still leaves twenty-six," said the glum-faced servant.

"At least," agreed Zoticus. "We shall have a sweet winter. The fire is all right, Clovis, you may go."

Clovis withdrew through the inner doorway—Crispin caught a glimpse of a hallway and a kitchen at the end before the door closed again.

"Your daughter lives in Sarantium?" he asked.

"One of them. Yes. She's a prostitute."

Crispin blinked again.

Zoticus looked wry. "Well. Not quite. A dancer. Much the same, if I understand the theater there. I don't really know. I've never seen her. She writes me, at times. Knows her letters."

Crispin looked at the name on the paper again. *Shirin.* There was a street name, as well. He glanced up. "Trakesian?"

"Her mother was. I was traveling, as I say. Some of my children write to me."

"Some?"

"Many are indifferent to their poor father, struggling in his aged loneliness among the barbarians."

The eyes were amused, the tone a long way from what the words implied. Crispin, out of habit, resisted an impulse to laugh, then stopped fighting it.

"You had an adventurous past."

"Middling so. In truth, I find more excitement now in my studies. Women were a great distraction. I am mostly freed of that now, thank the high gods. I actually believe I have a proper understanding of some of the philosophers now, and *that* is an adventure of the spirit. You will take one of the birds? As my gift to you?"

Crispin put his drink down abruptly, spilling some on the table. He snatched at the map to keep it dry. "What? Why would you—?"

"Martinian is a dear friend. You are his colleague, his almost-son. You are going a long way to a dangerous place. If you are careful to keep it private, one of the birds will be of assistance. They can see, and hear. And offer companionship, if nothing else." The alchemist hesitated. "It . . . pleases me to think one of my creations will go with you to Sarantium, after all."

"Oh, splendid. I am to walk the arcades of the City conversing with a companionable jeweled falcon? You want me blinded in your stead?"

Zoticus smiled faintly. "Not a choice gift, were that so. No. Discretion will be called for, but there are other ways of speaking with them. With whichever of them you can *hear* inwardly. You have no training. It is not certain, Caius Crispus. Nothing is in my art, I fear. But if you can hear one of the birds, it may become yours. In the act of hearing, a transference can be achieved. We will know soon enough." His voice changed. "All of you, shape a thought for our guest."

"Don't be absurd!" snapped an owl screwed onto a perch by the front door.

"A fatuous notion!" said the yellow-eyed falcon on the high back of Zoticus's chair. Crispin could imagine it glaring at him.

"Quite so," said a hawk Crispin hadn't noticed, from the far side of the room. "The very idea is indecent." He remembered this jaded voice. From twenty-five years ago. They sounded utterly identical, all of them. He shivered, unable to help himself. The hawk added, "This is a petty thief. Unworthy of being addressed. I refuse to dignify him so."

"That is enough! It is commanded," said Zoticus. His voice remained soft but there was iron in it. "Speak to him, within. Do it now."

For the first time Crispin had a sense that this was a man to be feared. There was a change in the alchemist's hard-worn, craggy features when he spoke this way, a look, a manner that suggested—inescapably—that he had seen and done dark things in his day. And he had *made* these birds. These crafted things that could see and hear. And speak to him. It came to Crispin, in a rush, exactly what was being proposed. He discovered that his hands were clenched together.

It was silent in the room. Unsure of what to do, Crispin eyed the alchemist and waited.

He heard something. Or thought he did.

Zoticus calmly sipped his drink. "And so? Anything?" His voice was mild again.

There had been no actual sound.

Crispin said, wonderingly, fighting a chill fear, "I thought . . . well, I believe I did hear . . . something."

"Which was?"

"I think . . . it sounded as if someone said, *Mice and blood.*"

There came a shriek of purest outrage from the table by the fire.

"*No! No, no, no!* By the chewed bones of a water rat, I am *not* going with him! Throw me in the fire! I'd rather *die*!"

Linon, of course. The small brown and dark gray sparrow, not the hawk or owl or the imperious yellow-eyed falcon, or even one of the oracular-looking ravens on the untidy bookshelf.

"You aren't even properly alive, Linon; don't be dramatic. A little travel again will be good for you. Teach you manners, perhaps."

"Manners? He sloughs me off to a stranger after all these years and speaks of manners?"

Crispin swallowed and, genuinely afraid of what underlay this exercise, he sent a thought, without speaking: *"I did not ask for this. Shall I refuse the gift?"*

"Pah! Imbecile."

Which did, at least, confirm something.

He looked at the alchemist. "Do you . . . did you hear what it said to me?"

Zoticus shook his head. His expression was odd. "It feels strangely, I confess. I've only done this once before and it was different then."

"I'm . . . honored, I think. I mean, of course I am. But I'm still confused. This was not asked for."

"Go ahead. Humiliate me!"

"I daresay," said Zoticus. He didn't smile now. Nor did he seem to have heard the bird. He toyed with his earthenware cup. From the chairback, the falcon's harsh eyes seemed fixed on Crispin, malevolent and glittering. "You could hardly ask for what you do not comprehend. Nor steal it, like another apple."

"Unkind," Crispin said, controlling his own quick anger.

Zoticus drew a breath. "It was. Forgive me."

"We can undo this, can we not? I have no desire to become enmeshed in the half-world. Do the cheiromancers of Sarantium all have creatures like this? I am a mosaicist. That is *all* I want to be. It is all I want to do, when I get there. If they let me live."

It was almost all. He had a message to convey if he could. He had undertaken as much.

"I know this. Forgive me. And no, the charlatans at the Imperial Court, or those casting maledictions on chariot racers for the Hippodrome mob, cannot do this. I am more or less certain of it."

"None of them? Not a single one? You, alone, of Jad's mortal children on earth can . . . make creatures such as these birds? If you can do it—"

"—why can no one else? Of course. The obvious question."

"And the obvious answer is?" Sarcasm, an old friend, never far away of late.

"That it is *possible* someone has learned this, but unlikely, and I do not believe it has happened this way. I have discovered . . . what I believe to be the only access to a certain kind of power. Found in my travels, in a . . . profoundly guarded place and at some risk."

Crispin crossed his arms. "I see. A scroll of chants and pentagrams? Boiled blood of a hanged thief and running around a tree seven times by double moonlight? And if you do the least thing wrong you turn into a frog?"

Zoticus ignored this. He simply looked at Crispin from beneath thick, level brows, saying nothing. After a moment, Crispin began to feel ashamed. He might be unsettled here, this staggering imposition of magic might be unlooked-for and frightening, but it *was* an offered gift, generous beyond words, and the implications of what the alchemist had actually achieved here . . .

"If you can do this . . . if these birds are thinking and speaking with their own . . . will . . . you ought to be the most celebrated man of our age!"

"Fame? A lasting name to echo gloriously down the ages? That would be pleasant, I suppose, a comfort in old age, but no, it couldn't happen . . . think about it."

"I am. Why not?"

"Power tends to be co-opted by greater power. This magic isn't particularly . . . intimidating. No half-world-spawned fireballs or death spells. No walking through walls or flying over them, invisible. Merely fabricated birds with . . . souls and voices. A small thing, but how could I defend myself, or them, if it was known they were here?"

"But why should—?"

"How would the Patriarch in Rhodias, or even the clerics in the sanctuary you are rebuilding outside Varena, take to the idea of pagan magic vesting a soul in crafted birds? Would they burn me or stone me, do you think? A difficult doctrinal decision, that. Or the queen? Would Gisel, rising above piety, not see merit in the idea of hidden birds listening to her enemies? Or the Emperor in Sarantium; Valerius II has the most sophisticated network of spies in the history of the Empire, east *or* west, they say. What would be my chances of dwelling here in peace, or even surviving, if word of these birds went out?" Zoticus shook his head. "No, I have had years to ponder this. Some kinds of achievement or knowledge seem destined to emerge and then disappear, unknown."

Thoughtful now, Crispin looked at the other man. "Is it difficult?"

"What? Creating the birds? Yes, it was."

"I'm certain of that. No, I meant being aware that the world cannot know what you have done."

Zoticus sipped his tea. "Of course it is difficult," he said at length. Then he shrugged, his expression ironic. "But alchemy always was a secret art, I knew that when I began to study it. I am . . . reconciled to this. I shall exult in my own soul, secretly."

Crispin could think of nothing to say. Men were born and died, wanted something, somehow, to live after them—beyond the mass burial mound or even the chiseled, too-soon-fading inscription on the headstone of a grave. An honorable name, candles lit in memory, children to light those candles. The mighty pursued fame. An artisan could dream of achieving a work that would endure, and be known to have been one's own. Of what did an alchemist dream?

Zoticus was watching him. "Linon is . . . a good consequence, now I think on it. Not conspicuous at all, drab, in fact. No jewels to attract attention, small enough to pass for a keepsake, a family talisman. You will arouse no comment. Can easily make up a story."

"Drab? *Drab?* By the *gods*! It is enough! I formally request," said Linon, speaking aloud, "to be thrown into the fire. I have no desire to hear more of this. Or of anything. My heart is broken."

Several of the other birds were, in fact, making sounds of aristocratic amusement.

Hesitantly, testing himself, Crispin sent a thought: *"I don't think he meant any insult. I believe he is . . . unhappy that this happened."*

"You shut up," the bird that could speak in his mind replied bluntly.

Zoticus did indeed look unsettled, notwithstanding his practical words: visibly trying to come to terms with which of the birds his guest seemed to have inwardly heard in the room's deep silence.

Crispin—here only because Martinian had first denied being himself to an Imperial Courier, and then *demanded* Crispin come to learn about the roads to Sarantium—who had asked for no gift at all, now found himself conversing in his mind with a hostile, ludicrously sensitive bird made of leather and—what?—tin, or iron. He was unsure whether what he most felt was anger or anxiety.

"More of the mint?" the alchemist asked, after a silence.

"I think not, thank you," said Crispin.

"I had best explain a few matters to you. To clarify."

"To clarify. Yes. Please," Crispin said.

"My heart," Linon repeated, in his mind this time, *"is broken."*

"You shut up," Crispin replied swiftly, with undeniable satisfaction.

Linon did not address him again. Crispin was aware of the bird, though, could almost *feel* an affronted presence at the edge of his thoughts like a night animal beyond a spill of torchlight. He waited while Zoticus poured himself a fresh cup. Then he listened to the alchemist in careful silence while the sun reached its zenith on an autumn day in Batiara and began its descent toward the cold dark. *Metals to gold, the dead to life . . .*

The old pagan who could breathe into crafted birds patrician voice, sight without eyes, hearing without ears, and the presence of a soul, told him a number of things deemed needful, in the wake of the gift he'd given.

Certain other understandings Crispin obtained only afterward.

"SHE WANTS YOU, THE *shameless whore! Are you going to? Are you?"*

Keeping his expression bland, Crispin walked beside the carried litter of the Lady Massina Baladia of Rhodias, sleekly well-bred wife of a Senator, and decided it had been a mistake to wear Linon on a thong around his neck like an ornament. The bird was going into one of his traveling bags tomorrow, on the back of the mule plodding along behind them.

"You must be *so* fatigued," the Senator's wife was saying, her voice honeyed with commiseration. Crispin had explained that he enjoyed walking in the open country and didn't like horses. The first was entirely untrue, the second was not. "If only I had thought to bring a litter large enough to carry both of us. And one of my girls, of course . . . we couldn't *possibly* ride just alone!" The Senator's wife tittered. Amazingly.

Her white linen chiton, wildly inappropriate for traveling, had—quite unnoticed by the lady, of course—slipped upward sufficiently to reveal a well-turned ankle. She wore a gold anklet, Crispin saw. Her feet, resting on lambswool throws within the litter, were bare this mild afternoon. The toenails were painted a deep red, almost purple. They hadn't been yesterday, in their sandals. She'd been busy last night at the inn, or her servant had been.

"Mice and blood, I'll wager she reeks of scent! Does she? Crispin, does she?"

Linon had no sense of smell. Crispin elected not to reply. The lady did, as it happened, have a heady aroma of spice about her today. Her litter was sumptuous, and even the slaves carrying it and accompanying her were appreciably better garbed—in pale blue tunics and dark blue dyed sandals—than was Crispin. The rest of their party—Massina's young female attendants, three wine merchants and their servants journeying the short distance to Mylasia and then down the coast road, a cleric continuing toward Sauradia, and two other travelers heading for the same healing medicinal waters as the lady—walked or rode mules a little ahead or behind them on the wide, well-paved road. Massina Baladia's armed and mounted escort, also clad in that delicately pale blue—which looked significantly less appropriate on them—rode at the front and back of the column.

None of the party was from Varena itself. None had any reason to know who Crispin was. They were three days out from Varena's walls, still in Batiara and on a busy stretch of road. They had already been forced to step onto the gravel side-path several times as companies of archers and infantry passed them on maneuvers. There was some need for caution on this road, but not the most extreme soft. The leader of the lady's escort gave every indication of regarding a red-bearded mosaicist as the most dangerous figure in the vicinity.

Crispin and the lady had dined together the night before, in the Imperial Posting Inn.

As a part of their careful dance with the Empire, the Antae had permitted the placement of three such inns along their own road from Sauradia's border to the capital city of Varena, and there were others running down the coast and on the main road to Rhodias. In return, the Empire paid a certain sum of money into the Antae coffers and undertook the smooth carriage of the mails all the way to the Bassanid border in the east. The inns represented a small, subtle presence of Sarantium in the peninsula. Commerce necessitated accommodations, always.

The others in their company, lacking the necessary Imperial Permits, had made do with a rancid hostel a short distance farther back. The Lady Massina's distant attitude to the artisan who had been trudging along in their party, lacking even a mount, had undergone a wondrous change when the Senator's wife understood that Martinian of Varena was entitled to use the Imperial Inns, and by virtue of a Permit signed by Chancellor Gesius in Sarantium itself—where, it seemed, he was presently journeying in response to an Imperial request.

He had been invited to dine with her.

When it had also become clear to the lady, over spit-roasted capons and an acceptable local wine, that this artisan was not unfamiliar with a number of the better people in Rhodias and in the elegant coastal resort of Baiana, having done some pretty work for them, she grew positively warm in manner, going so far as to confide that her journey to the medical sanctuary was for childbearing reasons.

It was quite common, of course, she had added with a toss of her head. Indeed, some silly young things regarded it as fashionable to attend at warm springs or hospices if they were wed a season and not yet expecting. Did Martinian know that the Empress Alixana herself had made several journeys to healing shrines near Sarantium? It was hardly a secret. It had started the fashion. Of course, given the Empress's earlier life—did he know she had changed her name, among . . . other things?—it was easy enough to speculate what bloody doings in some alley long ago had led her to be unable to give the Emperor an heir. Was it true that she dyed her hair now? Did Martinian actually *know* the luminaries in the Imperial Precinct? How exciting that must be.

He did not. Her disappointment was palpable, but short-lived. She seemed to have some degree of difficulty finding a place for her sandaled foot that did not encounter his ankle under the table. The capons were followed by an overly sauced fish plate with olives and a pale wine. Over the sweet cheese, figs and grapes, the lady, grown even further confiding, informed her dinner companion that it was her privy belief that the unexpected difficulties she and her august spouse were experiencing had little to do with her.

It was, she added, eyeing him in the firelight of the common room, difficult to *test* this, of course. She had been willing, however, to make the trip north out of too-boring Rhodias amid the colors of autumn to the well-known hospice and healing waters near Mylasia. One sometimes met—only *sometimes*, of course—the most interesting people when one traveled.

Did not Martinian find this to be so?

"CHECK FOR BEDBUGS."

"I know that, you officious lump of metal." He had dined a second time tonight with the lady; they had had a third flask of wine this time. Crispin was aware of the effect of it on himself.

"And talk to me in your head, unless you want people to assume you are mad."

Crispin had been having difficulty with this. It was good advice. So, as it happened, was the first suggestion. Crispin held a candle over the sheets, with the blanket pulled back, and managed to squash a dozen of the evil little creatures with his other hand.

"And they call this an Imperial Posting Inn. Hah!"

Linon, Crispin had learned quite early in their journeying together, was not short of opinions or shy with regard to their expression. He could still bring himself up short in a quiet moment with the realization that he was holding extended conversations in his mind with a temperamental sparrowlike bird made of faded brown leather and tin, with eyes fashioned from blue glass, and an incongruously patrician Rhodian voice both in his head and when speaking aloud.

He had entered a different world.

He had never really stopped to consider his attitude to what men called the half-world: that space where cheiromancers and alchemists and wise-women and astrologers claimed to be able to walk. He knew—everyone knew—that Jad's mortal children lived in a world that they shared, dangerously, with spirits and daemons that might be indifferent to them, or malevolent, or sometimes even benign, but he had never been one of those who let his every waking moment be suffused with that awareness. He spoke his prayers at dawn, and at sunset when he remembered, though he seldom bothered to attend at a sanctuary. He lit candles on the holy days when he was near a chapel. He paid all due respect to clerics—when the respect was deserved. He believed, some of the time, that when he died his soul would be judged by Jad of the Sun and his fate in the afterlife would be determined by that judgment.

The rest of the time, of late, very privately, he remembered the unholy ugliness of the two plague summers and was deeply, even angrily unsure of such spiritual things. He would have said, if asked a few days ago, that all alchemists were frauds and that a bird such as Linon was a deception to gull rustic fools.

That, in turn, meant denying his own memories of the apple orchard, but it had been easy enough to explain away childhood terrors as trickery, an actor's voice projection. Hadn't they all spoken with the same voice?

They had, but it wasn't a deception after all.

He had Zoticus's crafted bird with him as a companion and—in principle, at least—a guardian for his journey. It sometimes seemed to him that this irascible, ludicrously touchy creature—or creation—had been with him forever.

"I certainly didn't end up with a mild spirit, did I?" he remembered saying to Zoticus as he took his leave from the farmhouse that day.

"None of them are," the alchemist had murmured, a little ruefully. "A constant regret, I assure you. Just remember the command for silence and use it when you must." He'd paused, then added wryly, "You aren't particularly mild yourself. It may be a match."

Crispin had said nothing to that.

He had already used the command several times. In a way it was hardly worth it . . . Linon was almost intolerably waspish after being released from darkness and silence.

"Another wager," the bird said now, inwardly, *"leave the door unlocked and you won't sleep alone tonight."*

"Don't be ridiculous!" Crispin snapped aloud. Then, recollecting himself, added silently, *"This is a crowded Imperial Inn, she's a Rhodian aristocrat. And,"* he added peevishly, *"you have nothing to wager in any case, you lump of stuff."*

"A figure of speech, imbecile. Just leave the door unbolted. You'll see. I'll watch for thieves."

This, of course, was one of the benefits of having the bird, Crispin had already learned. Sleep was meaningless to Zoticus's creation, and as long as he hadn't silenced Linon he could be alerted to anything untoward approaching while he slept. He was irked, though, and the more so because a fabricated bird had roused his temper.

"Why would you possibly assume you have the least understanding of a woman like that? Listen to me: she plays little games during the day or over dinner out of sheer boredom. Only a fool would regard them as more." He wasn't sure why he was so irritated about this, but he was.

"You really don't know anything, do you?" Linon replied. Crispin

couldn't sort out the tone this time. *"You think boredom stops with the meal? A stable boy understands women better than you. Just keep playing with your little glass chips, imbecile, and leave these judgments to me!"*

Crispin spoke the silencing command with some satisfaction, blew out his candle and went to bed, resigned to being night food for the predatory insects he'd missed. It would be much worse, he knew, at the common hostel the others in the party had been forced to continue on toward for the night. An extremely small consolation. He didn't like traveling.

He tossed, turned, scratched where he imagined things biting him, then felt something doing so and swore. After a few moments, surprised at his own irresolution, he got up again, walked quickly across the cold floor, and slid home the bolt on the door. Then he crawled back into the bed.

He had not made love to a woman since Ilandra died.

He was still awake some time later, watching the shape of the waning blue moon slide across the window, when he heard the handle tried, then a very soft tapping at the door.

He didn't move, or speak. The tapping came again, twice more—light, teasing. Then it stopped, and there was silence again in the autumn night. Remembering many things, Crispin watched the moon leave the window, trailing stars, and finally fell asleep.

HE WOKE TO MORNING noises in the yard below. In the moment he opened his eyes, surfacing from some lost dream, he had a swift, sure realization about Zoticus's bird, and some wonder that it had taken him so long.

He was not greatly surprised to discover, when he went downstairs for watered ale and a morning meal, that the Lady Massina Baladia of Rhodias, the Senator's wife, and her mounted escorts and her servants had already left, at first daybreak.

There was a mild, unexpected regret here, but it had been almost intolerable to envisage his reentry into this sphere of mortal life as a coupling with a jaded Rhodian aristocrat playing bed games on a country night—not even knowing his true name. In another way, it might have been easier that way, but he wasn't . . . detached enough for that.

On the road again in the chill early-morning breeze, he soon caught up with the merchants and the cleric who had waited for him at the inn up the road. Settling into the long day's striding, he remembered his realization upon first awakening. He drew a breath, released Linon from silence in the bag on the mule's back, and asked a question.

"How dazzlingly brilliant of you," the bird snapped icily. *"She did come last night, didn't she? I was right, wasn't I?"*

White clouds were overhead, swift before the north wind. The sky was a light, far blue. The sun, safe returned from its dark journey under the icy-cold rim of the world, was rising directly in front of them, bright as a promise. Black crows dotted the stubble of the fields. A pale frost glinted on the brown grass beside the road. Crispin looked at it all in the early light, wondering how he'd achieve that rainbow brilliance of color and gleaming with glass and stone. Had anyone ever done frost-tipped autumn grass on a dome?

He sighed, hesitated, then replied honestly, *"She did. You were right. I locked the door."*

"Pah! Imbecile. Zoticus would have kept her busy all night long and sent her back to her own room exhausted."

"I'm not Zoticus."

A feeble answer and he knew it. The bird only laughed sardonically. But he wasn't really up to sparring this morning. Memories were too much with him.

It was colder today, especially when the clouds passed in front of the rising sun. His feet were cold in their sandals; boots tomorrow, he thought. The fields and the vineyards on the north side of the road were bare now, of course, and did nothing to stay the wind. He could see the first dark smudge of forests in the far distance now, northeast: the wild, legendary woods that led to the border and then Sauradia. The road would fork today, south toward Mylasia, where he could have caught a ship earlier in the year for a swift sailing to Sarantium. His slow course overland would angle north, toward that untamed forest, and then east again, the long Imperial road marching along its southernmost edgings.

He slowed a little, opened one of his bags as the mule paced stolidly along over the flawlessly fitted stone slabs of the road, and took out his brown woolen cloak. After a moment, he reached into the bag again and withdrew the bird on its leather thong, dropping it around his neck again. An apology, of sorts.

He'd expected Linon's brittle, waspish tone after the inflicted silence and blindness. He was already growing used to that. What he needed to do now, Crispin thought, closing and retying the bag and then wrapping himself in the cloak, was come to terms with a few other aspects of this journey east under an assumed name, bearing a message from the queen of the Antae for the Emperor in his head, and a creature of the half-world around his neck. And among the things now to be dealt with was the newly apprehended fact that the crafted bird he was carrying with him was undeniably and emphatically female.

TOWARD MIDDAY, THEY CAME to a tiny roadside chapel. *In Memory of Clodius Paresis,* an inscription over the arched doorway said. *With Jad now, in Light.*

The merchants and the cleric wanted to pray. Crispin, surprising himself, went in with them while the servants watched the mules and goods outside. No mosaics here. Mosaic was expensive, a luxury. He made the sign of the sun disk before the peeling, nondescript fresco of fair-haired, smooth-cheeked Jad on the wall behind the altar stone, and knelt behind the cleric on the stone floor, joining the others in the sunrise rites.

It was rather late in the day, perhaps, but there were those who believed the god was tolerant.

CHAPTER III

Kasia took the pitcher of beer, only slightly watered because the four merchants at the large table were regular patrons, and headed back from the kitchen toward the common room.

"Kitten, when you've done with that, you can attend to our old friend in the room above. Deana will finish your tables tonight." Morax gestured straight overhead, smiling meaningfully. She hated when he smiled, when he was so obviously being *pleasant*. It usually meant trouble.

This time it almost certainly meant something worse.

The room overhead, directly above the warmth of the kitchen, was reserved for the most reliable—or generous—patrons of the inn. Tonight it held an Imperial Courier from Sarnica named Zagnes, many years on the road, decent in his manner and known to be easy on the girls, sometimes just wanting a warm body in his bed of an autumn or winter night.

Kasia, newest and youngest of the serving girls at the inn, endlessly slated for the abusive patrons, had *never* been sent to him before. Deana, Syrene, Khafa—they all took turns when he was staying here, even fought for the chance of a calm night with Zagnes of Sarnica.

Kasia got the rough ones. Fair skinned, as were most of the Inicii, she bruised easily, and Morax was routinely able to extract additional payment from her men for damage done to her. This *was* an Imperial Posting Inn; their travelers had money, or positions to protect. No one really worried about injuries to a bought serving girl, but most patrons—other than the genuine aristocrats, who didn't care in the least—were unwilling to appear crude or untutored in the eyes of their fellows. Morax was skilled at threatening outraged indignation on behalf of the entire Imperial Posting Service.

If she was being allowed a night with Zagnes in the best room it was because Morax was feeling a disquiet about something concerning her. Or—a new thought—because they didn't want her bruised just now.

For some days, she had seen small gatherings break up and whispering stop suddenly as she entered a room, had been aware of eyes following her as she did her work. Even Deana had stopped tormenting her. It had been ten days, at least, since pig swill had been dumped on the straw of her pallet. And Morax himself had been far too kind—ever since a visit late one night from some of the villagers, walking up the road to the inn under carried torches and the cold stars.

Kasia wiped sweat from her forehead, pushed her yellow hair back from her eyes, and carried the beer out to the merchants. Two of them grabbed at her, front and rear, pushing her tunic up as she poured for them, but she was used to that and made them laugh by pretending to stamp on the nearest one's boot. These were regulars, who paid Morax a tidy private sum for the privilege of staying here without a Permit, and they wouldn't be trouble unless they had much more beer than this.

She finished pouring, slapped away the hand still squeezing her breast—making sure she never stopped smiling—and turned to go. The evening was young, there were dishes and flasks to be served and cleared and cleaned, fires to be kept up. She was being set free of the drudgery, sent up to an easy man in a warm bedroom. Uncertainly, Kasia walked out from the common room into the darker, colder hallway.

A sudden, nauseating fear gripped her as she began climbing the stairs in the guttering candlelight. She had to stop, leaning sideways against the rail to control it. It was quiet here, the noise from the common room muted. Sweat felt cold on her forehead and neck. A trickle ran down her side. She swallowed. A stale, sour taste in her mouth and throat. Her heart was very fast, her breathing shallow; the blurred shadows of trees beyond the unshuttered, smudged window held terrors without name or shape.

She felt like crying for her mother—a childlike panic, unthinking and primitive—but her mother was in a village three weeks' journey north around the vastness of the Aldwood, and it was her mother who had sold her last autumn.

She couldn't pray. Certainly not to Jad, though she'd been brusquely converted with the others in a roadside chapel at the orders of the Karchite slaver who'd bought them and taken them south. And prayers to Ludan of the Wood were hopelessly beside the point, given what was to happen soon.

It was supposed to be a virgin, and it had been once, but the world had changed. Sauradia was nominally Jaddite now, a tax-paying province of the Sarantine Empire supporting two army camps and the troops based in Megarium, and though certain of the ancient tribal rites were still quietly observed, and ignored by the Jaddite clerics if they weren't *forced* to notice them, no one thought it necessary to offer their maiden daughters anymore.

Not when a whore from the Posting Inn would do.

It was certain, Kasia thought, gripping the railing, looking out the small window at the night from halfway up the stairs. She felt helpless, and enraged by that. She had a knife, hidden by the smith's forge, but what possible good was a knife? She couldn't even try to run. They were watching her now, and where could a female slave go in any case? Into the woods? Along the road to be hunted with the dogs?

She couldn't see the forest through the streaky glass, but she was aware of it, a presence in the blackness, very near. No deceiving herself. The whispers, the watching, those inexplicable kindnesses, a never-before-seen softness in the eyes of that bitch Deana, the moist hunger in the face of Morax's fat wife, the mistress, looking too quickly away whenever Kasia met her gaze in the kitchen.

They were going to kill her two mornings from now, on the Day of the Dead.

CRISPIN HAD USED HIS Permit to take a servant at the first Posting Inn in Sauradia just past the marker stones at the border with Batiara. He was in the Sarantine Empire now, for the first time in his life. He considered taking a second mule for himself, but he really didn't like riding, and his feet were bearing up surprisingly well in the good boots he'd bought. He could lease a small two-wheeled birota and a horse or mule to pull it, but that would mean an outlay, over and above what the Permit allowed him, and they were notoriously uncomfortable, in any case.

Vargos, the hired servant, was a big, silent man, black-haired—unusual for an Inici—with a vivid crosshatched scar high on one cheek and a staff even heavier than the one Crispin carried. The scar looked like a pagan symbol of some kind; Crispin had no desire to know more about it.

Crispin had refused to bring any of the apprentices with him, despite Martinian's urging. If he was doing this crazed journey under a name not his own to try to remake his life or some such thing, he was *not* going to do so in the company of a boy from home. He'd quite enough to deal with without bearing the burden of a young life on a dangerous road, to an even more uncertain destination.

On the other hand, he was not going to be an idiot—or an imbecile, as Linon was altogether too fond of saying—about traveling alone. He didn't *like* being outside the city walls, and this road through western Sauradia, skirting the brooding forest with the wind-scoured mountains to the south, was not even remotely the same as it had been in densely settled, heavily trafficked Batiara. He'd ascertained that Vargos knew the road to the Trakesian border, sized up the man's obvious strength and experience, and claimed him with the Permit. The Chancellor's office would be debited by the Imperial Post. It was all very efficient. He just didn't like how *black* the forest was, north of the road.

The merchants and their wine had forked south well before the border, following the path of Massina Baladia, half a day ahead of them. The cleric—a decent, good-natured man—had only been going as far as a holy retreat just inside Sauradia. They had prayed together and parted company early of a morning before the cleric turned off the road. Crispin might join up with other travelers heading east—there should be some coming up from Megarium—and would certainly try to do so, but in the meantime, a large, capable person walking with him represented minimal good sense. It was one of the virtues of the Post system: he could claim a man like Vargos and release him at any Posting Inn on the road for travelers going on, or coming back the other way. The Sarantine Empire today might not *really* be akin to Rhodias as it had been at the apex of its glory, but it wasn't so very far from it, either.

And if Gisel, the young queen of the Antae, was correct, Valerius II wanted to restore the western Empire, one way or another.

As far as the Rhodian mosaicist Caius Crispus of Varena was concerned, unhappy and cold in autumn rain, any and all measures that increased the degree of *civilized* order in places like this were to be vigorously encouraged.

He really didn't like the forest, at all.

It was interesting, the degree of uneasiness he'd felt as the days passed and they walked the road within constant sight of it. He was forced to acknowledge, with some chagrin, that he was even more a man of the city than he'd known himself to be. Cities, for all their dangers, had walls. Wild things—whether animals or men without laws—could generally be assumed to be outside those walls. And so long as one took care not to be abroad alone after dark or enter the wrong alleyway, a purse-snatcher in the market or an overly impassioned holy man strewing spittle and imprecations was the greatest danger one was likely to encounter.

And in cities were buildings, public and private. Palaces, bathhouses, theaters, merchants' homes, apartments, chapels and sanctuaries—with walls and floors and sometimes even domes whereon people with sufficient means sometimes desired mosaics to be designed and set.

A living, for a man of experience and certain skills.

There was extremely little call for Crispin's particular gifts in this forest, or the wild lands south of it here. The feuding Sauradian tribes had been a byword for barbaric ferocity since the early days of the Rhodian Empire. Indeed, the worst single defeat a Rhodian army had *ever* suffered before the slow decline and final overthrow had been not far north of here, when a full legion sent to quell one tribal rising had been trapped between swampland and wood and cut to pieces.

The legions of reprisal had waged war for seven years, according to the histories. They had succeeded. Eventually. Sauradia was not an easy place to fight in phalanx and column. And enemies that melted like spirits into the trees and then dismembered and ate their captives in blood-soaked ceremonies in the drumming, shrouded forests could inspire a certain apprehension in even the most disciplined soldiery.

But the Rhodians had not taken most of the known world under their aegis by being reluctant to employ harsh measures themselves, and they had the resources of an Empire. The trees of the Sauradian woods had ultimately borne the dead bodies of tribal warriors—and their women and small children—with limbs and privates hacked off, hanging from sacred branches by their greased yellow hair.

It was not a history, thought Crispin one morning, calculated to elicit tranquil reflection, however long ago it had taken place. Even Linon had fallen silent today. The dark woods marched beside the road, very near at this point, seemingly endless ahead to the east and when he looked back west. Oak, ash, rowan, beech, other trees he didn't know, leaves fallen or falling. Smudged black smoke rose at intervals: charcoal-burners, working the edgings of the forest. To the south the land swept upward in a series of ascents toward the barrier of mountains that hid the coastline and the sea. He saw sheep and goats, dogs, smoke from a shepherd's hut. No other sign of human life. It was a gray day, a fine, cold rain falling, the mountain peaks lost under clouds.

Beneath the hood of his traveling cloak, Crispin tried—with only marginal success—to remember why he was doing this.

He attempted to conjure forth bright, multihued images of Sarantium—the fabled glories of the Imperial City, center of Jad's creation, eye and ornament of the world, as the well-known phrase had it. He couldn't. It was too far away. Too unknown to him. The black forest and the mist and the cold rain were too oppressively, demandingly present. And the lack of walls, warmth, people, shops, markets, taverns, baths, *any* man-made images of comfort, let alone beauty.

He was a town person, it was simply the truth. This journey was forcing him to accept, however ruefully, all the associations that carried . . . of decadence, softness, corruption, overbred luxury. Those last sardonic caricatures of Rhodias before it fell: effete, posturing aristocrats who hired barbarians to fight for them and were helpless when their own mercenaries turned. He and the lady Massina Baladia with her cushioned litter, her exquisite travel garb, her scent, and her painted toenails were more akin than unlike, after all, whatever he might wish to say. Town walls defined the boundaries of Crispin's world as much as hers. What he most wanted right now—if he was honest with himself—was a bath, oiling, a professional massage, then a glass of hot, spiced wine on a couch in a warm room with civilized talk washing over him. He felt anxious and disoriented, *exposed* out here in this wilderness. And he had a long way to go.

Not so far to the next bed, however. A steady pace through the steady rain, with only a brief halt for a midday piece of cheese and bread and a flask of sour wine at a smoky, midden-smelling tavern in a hamlet, brought them by late afternoon near to the next Imperial Inn. The rain had even stopped by then, the clouds breaking up to the south and west, though not over the woods. He saw the tops of some of the mountains. The sea would be beyond. He might have sailed, had the courier come in time. A wasted thought.

He might still have a family, had the plague bypassed their house.

Behind them, as he and Vargos and the mule went through another cluster of houses, the sun appeared for the first time that day, pale and low, lighting the mountain slopes, underlighting the heavy clouds above the peaks, glinting coldly in pools of rainwater in the ditch by the road. They passed a smithy and bakehouse and two evil-looking hostelries in the village, ignoring the scrutiny of the handful of people gathered and a coarse invitation from a gaunt whore in the laneway by the second inn.

Not for the first time Crispin offered thanks for the Permit folded in the leather purse at his belt.

The Posting Inn was east of the village, exactly as indicated on his map. Crispin liked his map. He took great comfort in the fact that as he walked places appeared each day when and where the map said they should. It was reassuring.

The inn was large, had the usual stable, smithy, inner courtyard, and no piles of rotting refuse in the doorway. He glimpsed a well-tended vegetable and herb garden beyond a gate toward the back, sheep in the meadow beyond and a sturdy shepherd's hut. Long live the Sarantine Empire, Crispin thought wryly, and the glorious Imperial Post. Smoke rising from broad chimneys offered the promise of warmth within.

"We'll stay two nights," Linon said.

The bird was on the thong around his neck again. She hadn't spoken since morning. The blunt, sudden words startled Crispin.

"Indeed? Why? Your little feet are tired?"

"Mice and blood! You are too stupid to be allowed out of doors without a nursemaid. Remember the calendar and what Zoticus told you. You're in Sauradia, imbecile. And tomorrow is the Day of the Dead."

Crispin had, in fact, forgotten, and cursed himself for it. It irritated him, however unreasonably, when the bird was right.

"So what happens?" he demanded sourly. *"They boil me into soup if I'm found abroad? Bury my bones at a crossroad?"*

Linon didn't bother to reply.

Feeling obscurely at a disadvantage, Crispin left Vargos to see to the mule and his goods while he strode past two barking dogs and a scatter of chickens in the sodden courtyard. He walked through the doorway into the front room of the inn to show his Permit and see if a hot bath could be had immediately for coinage of the Empire.

The entranceway was encouragingly clean, large, high-ceilinged. Beyond it, through a door to the left, the common room had two fires going. A cheerful buzz of speech in many accents drifted out to him. After the wet, cold road all day it was undeniably alluring. He wondered if someone in this kitchen knew how to cook. There had to be deer and boar, perhaps even the elusive Sauradian bison in these woods; a well-seasoned platter of game and a halfway adequate flask or two of wine would go some way to easing him.

It occurred to Crispin, looking around, noting the swept, dry tiling on the floor, that this inn might indeed be a perfectly decent place to rest his feet for two days and nights. Zoticus had been unambiguous in advising him to stay in one place and indoors on the Day of the Dead. For all his sardonic attitude to such things, it wouldn't do to be foolish merely to win a battle with an artificial bird. If nothing else, he thought suddenly, Linon was proof that the half-world was real.

Not an entirely comforting reflection.

He waited for the innkeeper, blessed Permit in hand, letting himself relax already into the sensation of being dry with the near prospect of warmth and wine. He heard a sound from the back of the inn, behind the stairs, and turned, a civil expression ready. He was aware that he was hardly distinguished-looking at the moment, nor did traveling on foot with one temporarily hired servant commend him as affluent, but a Permit with his name elegantly written upon it—or Martinian's name—and the privy Seal and signature of no less a figure than the Imperial Chancellor could make him instantly formidable, he'd discovered.

It wasn't the innkeeper who came from backstairs. Only a thin serving girl in a stained, knee-length brown tunic, barefoot, yellow-haired, carrying a stoppered jug of wine too heavy for her. She stopped dead when she saw him, staring openly, wide-eyed.

Crispin smiled briefly, ignoring the presumption of her gaze. "What do they call you, girl?"

She swallowed, looked down, mumbled, "Kitten."

He felt himself grinning crookedly. "Why that?"

She swallowed again, seemed to be having trouble speaking. "Don't know," she managed finally. "Someone thought I looked like one."

Her eyes never left the floor, after that first naked stare. He realized he hadn't spoken to anyone, other than some instructions to Vargos, all day. It was odd, he didn't know how he felt about that. He did know he wanted a bath, not to be making talk with a serving girl.

"You don't. What's your proper name, then?"

She looked up at that, and then down again. "Kasia."

"Well, Kasia, run find the keeper for me. I'm wet outside and dry within. And never dream of telling me there are no rooms to be had."

She didn't move. Continued to stare at the floor, clutching at the heavy wine jug with both hands beneath it. She was quite young, very thin, wide-set blue eyes. From a northern tribe, obviously. Inicii, or one of the others. He wondered if she'd understood him, his jest; they'd been speaking Rhodian. He was about to repeat his request in Sarantine, without the witticism, when he saw her draw a breath.

"They are going to kill me tomorrow," was what she said, quite clearly this time. She looked up at him. Her eyes were enormous, deep as a forest. "Will you take me away?"

ZAGNES OF SARNICA HAD not been willing, at all.

"Are you simple?" the man had cried the night before. In his agitation he had pushed Kasia right out of the bed to land sprawling on the floor. It was cold, even with the kitchen fires directly below. "What in Jad's holy name would I do with a bought girl from Sauradia?"

"I would do anything you like," she'd said, kneeling beside the bed, fighting back tears.

"Of course you would. What *else* would you do? That is *not* the point." Zagnes was quite exercised.

It wasn't the request to buy her and take her away. Imperial Couriers were used to such pleas. It must have been her reason. The very immediate, particular reason. But she'd *had* to tell him . . . otherwise there was no cause at all for him to even consider it, among all the usual requests. He was said to be a kindly man . . .

Not enough so, it seemed. Or not foolish enough. The courier was white-faced; she had given him a genuine fright. A balding, paunchy man, no longer young. Not cruel at all, merely refusing prudently to involve himself in the under-the-surface life of a Sauradian village, even if it involved the forbidden sacrifice of a girl to a pagan god. Perhaps especially so. What would happen if he reported this story to the clerics, or at the army camp east of them? An investigation, questions asked, probably painful questions—even fatal ones—for these were matters of holy faith. Stringent measures to follow against resurgent paganism?

Fulminating clerics, soldiers quartered in the village, punitive taxes imposed? Morax and others might be punished; the innkeeper could be relieved of his position, his nose slit, hands cut off.

And no more of the best treatment, the warmest rooms at this inn or any of the others in Sauradia for Zagnes of Sarnica. Word traveled swiftly along the main roads, and no one, anywhere, liked an informer. He was an Imperial Officer, but he spent most of his days—and nights—far from Sarantium.

And all this for a serving girl? How could she possibly have expected him to help?

She hadn't. But she didn't want to die, and her options were narrowing by the moment.

"Get back in bed," Zagnes had said brusquely. "You'll freeze on the floor and then you're no good to me at all. I'm *always* cold, these days," he'd added, with a contrived laugh. "Too many years on the road. Rain and wind get right inside my bones. Time to retire. I would, if my wife wasn't at home." Another false, unconvincing laugh. "Girl, I'm sure you are frightened by nothing. I've known Morax for years. You girls are *always* afraid of shadows when this silly . . . when this day comes round."

Kasia climbed silently back into the bed and slipped under the sheet, naked, next to him. He withdrew from her a little. No surprise, she thought bitterly. Would any wise man bed a girl marked for Ludan of the Wood? Her sacred death might pass straight into him.

That wasn't it, though. It seemed Zagnes was a more prosaic sort. "Your feet are *cold*, girl. Rub them together or something. And your hands," he said. "I'm always cold."

Kasia heard herself make an odd sound; half a laugh, half a renewed struggle with panic. She rubbed her feet obediently against each other, trying to warm them so she could warm the man beside her. She heard the wind outside, a branch tapping against the wall. The clouds had come, with rain. No moons.

SHE'D SPENT THE NIGHT with him. He hadn't put a hand on her. Stayed close, curled up like a child. She'd lain awake listening to the wind and the branch and the fall of rain. Morning would come, and then night, and the next day she would die. It was amazing to her that she could shape this sequence, this thought. She wondered if it would be possible to kill Deana before they bound her or bludgeoned her unconscious. She wished she could pray, but she hadn't been raised believing in Jad of the Sun, and none of his invocations came easily to her. On the other hand, how did the sacrifice pray to the god to whom she was being offered? What could she ask of Ludan? That she be dead before they cut her in pieces? Or whatever they did here in the south. She didn't even know.

She was up well before the sleeping courier in the black, damp chill before dawn. She pulled on her underclothes and tunic, shivering, and went down to the kitchen. It was still raining. Kasia heard sounds from the yard: the stableboys readying the changes of mounts for the Imperial Couriers and the horses and mules of those who had brought their own or claimed them. She gathered an armful of firewood from the back room, returned for two more, and then knelt to build up the kitchen fire. Deana came down, yawning, and went to do the same for the front-room fires. She had a new bruise on one cheek, Kasia saw.

"Sleep well, bitch?" Deana said as she walked by. "You'll never get that one again, trust me."

"He told me you were as sloppy below as you are above," Kasia murmured, not bothering to turn. She wondered if Deana would hit her. She had firewood to hand.

But they didn't want her bruised, or marred in any way. It might almost have been amusing . . . she could say whatever she wanted today, without fear of a blow.

Deana stood still for a moment, then went past without touching her.

THEY WERE WATCHING HER closely. Kasia had been made aware of it when she snatched a moment from emptying the chamber pots to stand on the porch in back of the inn to breathe the cold, wet air. The mountains were wrapped in mist. It was still raining. Very little wind now. The chimney smoke went straight up and disappeared in the grayness. She could barely see the orchard and the sheep on the slopes. Sounds were muffled.

But Pharus the stablemaster was casually leaning against a pillar at the far end of the porch, whittling at a wet stick with his knife, and Rugash, the old shepherd, had left his flock to the boys and was standing in the open doorway of the hut beyond the orchard. When he saw her glance at him he turned away and spat through the gap in his teeth into the mud.

They actually thought she might run. Where could a slave girl run? Barefoot up the mountain slopes? Into the Aldwood? Would a death by exposure or animals be better? Or would daemons or the dead find her first and claim her soul forever? Kasia shivered. A wasted fear: she would never even make it to the forest or the hills, and they'd track her if she did. They had the dogs.

Khafa appeared in the open doorway behind her. Without turning, Kasia knew her step.

"I tell mistress, you get whipping of idleness," she said. She'd been ordered to speak nothing but Rhodian, to learn it adequately.

"Fuck yourself," Kasia said without force. But she turned and went in, walking straight past Khafa, who was probably the most decent of them all.

She put all the chamber pots in their rooms, going up and down and up and down the stairs, and then went back into the kitchen to finish with the dishes of the morning. The fire was too low; you were beaten or locked in the wine cellar among the rats if your fire was too low—or too high, wasting wood. She built it up. The smoke stung tears into her eyes. She wiped her cheeks with the backs of her hands.

She had that blade hidden in the smith's shed by the stables. She decided she would go out for it later in the day. She could use it on herself tonight, if nothing else. Deny them what they wanted. A kind of triumph, that.

She never got the chance. Another group of merchants came in, stopping early because of the rain. They had no Permits, of course, but paid Morax, after the usual quiet exchange, for the right to stay illegally. They sat by one of the fires in the common room and drank a considerable amount of wine very quickly. Then three of them wanted girls to pass a wet afternoon. Kasia went up with one of them, a Karchite; Deana and Syrene took the others. The Karchite smelled of wine, wet fur, fish.

He put her face down on the bed as soon as they entered the room and pushed up her tunic, not bothering to take it off or his own clothing. When he finished he fell immediately asleep, sprawled across her. Kasia squirmed out from beneath him. She looked out the window. The rain was easing; it would stop soon.

She went downstairs. The Karchite was snoring loudly enough to be heard in the hallway; she'd no excuse for lingering. Morax, crossing through the front room, looked closely at her as she came down—checking for bruises, no doubt—and gestured to the kitchen wordlessly. It was time to begin readying dinner. Another cluster of men were already in the common room, drinking. The inn would be crowded tonight. Tomorrow had people nervous, excited, wanting a drink and company. Through the archway Kasia saw three of the villagers with a fourth glass at their table. Morax had been with them.

Deana came down a little later, walking carefully, as if something hurt her inside. They stood opposite each other, slicing potatoes and onions, laying out olives in small bowls. The mistress was watching them; neither spoke. Morax's wife beat the girls for talking while they worked. She said something to the cook. Kasia didn't hear what it was. She was aware that the mistress kept looking at her. Keeping her head down, she carried out the bowls of olives and baskets of small bread from the bakehouse and set them on the tables beside the jars of oil. This was a Posting Inn; amenities were offered—for a price paid. The three villagers became engaged in animated talk as soon as she walked in. None of them looked up as she gave them their olives and bread. The two fires were low, but that was Deana's job.

In the kitchen the cook was cutting up chickens now and dropping pieces in the pot with the potatoes and onions for a stew. Already there wasn't enough wine to hand. A wet, cold day. Men drank. At a nod from the mistress, Kasia went toward the back again to the wine storage, taking the key. She unlocked and pulled up the heavy, hinged door set in the floor and hoisted a jug from the cold, shallow cellar. She remembered that when Morax had bought her from the trader a year ago she hadn't been able to lift them out. They had beaten her for that. The large, stoppered jug was still heavy for her and she was awkward with it.

She locked the cellar and came back through the hallway and saw a man standing alone in the front room by the door.

IT WAS THE WILD look of him, she decided later. The full red beard, disordered hair when he pushed back the hood of his muddy cloak. He had large, capable-looking hands with red hairs visible on the backs of them, and his soaked brown outer garment was bunched up at his waist, hoisted above his knees and belted for hard striding. Expensive boots. A heavy staff. On this road of merchant parties and civil servants, uniformed army officers and Imperial Couriers, this solitary traveler reminded her of one of the hard men of her own distant, northern world.

There was an extreme irony to this, of course, but she had no way of knowing that.

He was standing alone, no companion or servant in sight, and there was no one nearby, amazingly, for this one moment. He spoke to her in Rhodian. She barely heard him or the replies she managed to mumble. About her name. She stared at the floor. There was an odd sensation of roaring in her ears, like a wind in the room. She was afraid she would fall down, or drop the wine jug, shattering it. It occurred to her, suddenly, that it didn't matter if she did. What could they do to her?

"They are going to kill me tomorrow," she said.

She looked up at him. Her heart was pounding like a northern drum. "Will you take me away?"

He didn't recoil like Zagnes, or stare in shock or disbelief. He looked at her very closely. His eyes narrowed; they were blue and cold.

"Why?" he said, almost harshly.

Kasia felt tears coming. She fought them. "The . . . the Day of the Dead," she managed. Her mouth felt full of ashes. "The . . . because of the oak god . . . they . . ."

She heard footsteps. Of course. Time had run. Never enough time. She might have died of the plague at home, as her father and brother had. Or of starvation in the winter that followed, had her mother not sold her for food. She *had* been sold, though. She was here. A slave. Time had run. She stopped abruptly, stared straight down at the floor, gripping the heavy wine. Morax walked through the arched door from the common room.

"About time, keeper," said the red-bearded man calmly. "Do you normally keep patrons waiting alone in your front room?"

"Kitten!" roared Morax. "You little bitch, how *dare* you not tell me we had a distinguished guest?" Her own eyes down, Kasia imagined his practiced gaze assessing the unkempt man in his front room. Morax switched to his formal voice. "Good sir, this *is* an Imperial Inn. You do know that Permits are required."

"I rely upon it to ensure fellow guests of some respectability," said the man coolly. Kasia watched them, from the corners of her eyes. He was not a northerner, of course. Not with that accent. She was such a fool, sometimes. He had spoken Rhodian, was regarding Morax bleakly. He glanced through the archway at the crowded common room. "It appears that a surprising number of Permit holders are abroad on a wet day, so late in the year. I congratulate you, keeper. Your welcome must be exceptionally gracious."

Morax flushed. "You have a Permit, then? I am delighted to welcome you, if that is so."

"It is. And I wish to see your delight made extremely tangible. I want the warmest room you have for two nights, a clean pallet for my man wherever you put the servants, and hot water, oil, towels, and a bathtub carried to my room immediately. I will bathe before I dine. I will consult with you as to the food and wine while the bath is being prepared. And I want a girl to oil and wash me. This one will do."

Morax looked stricken. He was good at that. "Oh dear, oh dear! We are just now preparing the evening meal, good sir. As you see, the inn is crowded today and we have far too little staff. I am grieved to say that we cannot accommodate bathing until later. This is merely a humble country inn, good sir. Kitten, get that wine into the kitchen. Now!"

The red-bearded man lifted a hand. He held a paper there. And a coin, Kasia saw. She lifted her head. "You have not yet asked for my Permit, keeper. An oversight. Do read it. You will no doubt recognize the signature and the Seal of the Chancellor himself, in Sarantium. Of course, a great many of your patrons probably have Permits personally signed by Gesius."

Morax went from red-faced to bone white in a moment.

It was almost amusing, but Kasia was afraid she was about to drop the wine. Permits were signed by Imperial functionaries in various cities or by junior officers at army camps, *not* by the Imperial Chancellor. She felt herself gaping. Who *was* this man? She shifted her grip beneath the wine jug. Her arms were trembling with the weight. Morax reached out and took the paper —and the coin. He unfolded the Permit and read, his mouth moving with the words. He looked up, unable to resist staring. His color was slowly coming back. The coin had helped.

"You . . . your servants you said are outside, good my lord?"

"Just the one, taken at the border to get me to Trakesia. There are reasons why it is useful to Gesius and the Emperor for me to travel without display. You run an Imperial Inn. You will understand." The red-bearded man smiled briefly, and then held a finger to his lips.

Gesius. The Chancellor. This man had named him by name, and had a Permit with his privy Seal and signature.

Kasia did begin to pray then, silently. To no god by name, but with all her heart. Her arms were still trembling. Morax had ordered her to the kitchen. She turned to go.

She saw him give the Permit back. The coin was gone. Kasia had never yet learned to follow the motion with which Morax palmed such offerings. He reached out, stopped her with a hand on the shoulder.

"Deana!" he barked, as he saw her walking through the common room. Deana quickly set down her armful of firewood and hurried over. "Take this jug to the kitchen, and tell Breden to carry the largest bathtub to the room above it. Kitten, you will take hot water from the kettle up with Breden. Immediately. The two of you will fill the bath. You will *run* as you do so, to keep it hot. Then you will attend upon his lordship, here. If he complains in the least regard you will be locked in the wine cellar for the night. Am I understood?"

"Do not," said the red-bearded man quietly, "call me your lordship, if you will. I travel this way for a reason, recall?"

"Of course," said Morax, cringing. "Of course! Forgive me! But what shall . . . ?"

"Martinian will do," said the man. "Martinian of Varena."

"MICE AND BLOOD! *What are you doing?"*

"I'm not sure," Crispin replied honestly. *"But I need your help. Does her story sound true to you?"*

Linon, after that first ferocity, grew instantly subdued. After an unexpected silence, she said, *"It does, in fact. What is more true is that we must keep entirely out of this. Crispin, the Day of the Dead is not a thing to meddle with."* She never used his name. *Imbecile* was her preferred form of address.

"I know. Bear with me. Help, if you can."

He looked at the pudgy, slope-shouldered innkeeper and said aloud, "Martinian will do. Martinian of Varena." He paused and added confidingly, "And I will thank you for your discretion."

"Of course!" cried the innkeeper. "My name is Morax, and I am *entirely* at your service, my . . . Martinian." He actually winked. A greedy, petty man.

"The best room is over the kitchen," Linon said silently. *"He is doing what you asked."*

"You know this inn?"

"I know most of them on this road, imbecile. You are taking us into perilous waters."

"I'm sailing to Sarantium. Of course I am," Crispin replied wryly, in silence. Linon gave an inward snort and was still. Another girl, with a purpling bruise on one cheek, had taken the wine jug from the yellow-haired one. Both of them hurried away.

"May I suggest our very best Candarian red wine with your dinner?" the innkeeper said, gripping his own hands in the way all innkeepers seemed to have. "There is a modest surcharge, of course, but . . ."

"You have Candarian? That will be fine. Bring it unmixed, with a jug of water. What is dinner, friend Morax?"

"Aren't we the lordly one!"

"We have some choice country sausages of our own making. Or a stew of chicken, even now being prepared."

Crispin opted for the stew.

On the way up to the room over the kitchen he tried to understand why he'd done what he'd just done. No clear answer came. In fact, he hadn't *done* anything. Yet. But it occurred to him, with something near to actual pain, that he'd last seen that huge-eyed look of terror in his older daughter's face, when her mother lay vomiting blood before she died. He'd been unable to do anything. Enraged, nearly insane with grief. Helpless.

"THEY PERFORM THIS ABOMINATION all over Sauradia?"

He was naked in the metal tub in his room, knees drawn up to his chest. The largest tub wasn't particularly large. The yellow-haired girl had oiled him, not very competently, and was now scrubbing his back with a rough cloth, for want of any strigil. Linon lay on the window-sill.

"No. No, my lord. Only here at the southing of the Old Wood . . . Aldwood, we say . . . and at the northern edge. There are two oak groves sacred to Ludan. The . . . forest god." Her voice was low, close to a whisper. Sound carried through these walls. She spoke Rhodian acceptably, though not easily. He switched to Sarantine again.

"You are Jaddite, girl?"

She hesitated. "I was brought to the Light last year."

By the slave trader, no doubt. "And Sauradia is Jaddite, is it not?"

Another hesitation. "Yes, my lord. Of course, my lord."

"But these pagans still take young girls and . . . do whatever they do to them? In a province of the Empire?"

"Crispin. You are better not knowing this."

"Not in the north, my lord," said the girl. She scrubbed the cloth across his ribs. "In the north a thief or a woman taken in adultery . . . someone who has already forfeited their life is hanged on the god's tree. Only hanged. Nothing . . . worse."

"Ah. A *milder* barbarism. I see. And why is it different here? No thieves or adulterous women to be had?"

"I don't know." She did not react to his sarcasm. He was being unfair, he knew. "I'm sure it isn't that, my lord. But . . . it may be that Morax uses this to keep peace with the village. He . . . allows travelers without Permits to stay, especially in autumn and winter. He's wealthy because of it. The village inns suffer. Perhaps this is his way of making it up to them? He gives one of his slaves. For Ludan?"

"Enough. It is blindingly obvious no one has ever taught you how to give a rubdown. Jad's blood! An Imperial Inn without a strigil? Disgraceful. Get me a dry towel, girl." Crispin was aware of a familiar, hard anger within him and struggled to keep his voice down. "A fine reason to kill a slave, of course. Relations with the neighbors."

She rose and hurriedly fetched a towel from the bed—the excuse for a towel they had sent up. This was *not* his bathhouse in Varena. The room itself was nondescript but of decent size, and some warmth did seem to be rising from the kitchen below. He had already noted that the door had one of the newer iron locks, opened with a copper key. The merchants would like that. Morax knew his business, it seemed, both the licit and the illicit sides of it. He *was* probably wealthy, or on the way to it.

Crispin controlled his anger, thinking hard. "I was correct down below? There are people here tonight without Permits?"

He stood up and stepped, dripping, out of the small tub. She was flushed from his rebuke, anxious, visibly afraid. It only made him more angry. He took the towel, rubbed his hair and beard, then wrapped himself against the cold. Then he swore, bitten by some crawling creature in the towel.

She stood by, hands awkwardly at her sides, eyes downcast. "Well?" he demanded again. "Answer. Was I correct?"

"Yes, my lord." Speaking Sarantine, which she clearly understood more readily, she sounded intelligent for her station, and there was life in the blue eyes when the terror was at bay. "Most of them are illegal. Autumn is a quiet time. If the taxing officers or soldiers come he bribes them, and the Imperial Couriers are back and forth too often to complain . . . so long as they are not put out by the other patrons. Morax takes good care of the couriers."

"I'm sure he does. I know that kind of man. All for a price."

Absently, Crispin nodded his agreement with the bird and then collected himself. He began to dress. Dry clothes from the satchel they had brought up for him. His wet outer garments had been left to dry by a downstairs fire.

"Quiet, Linon. I'm thinking!"

"May all the powers gather to protect us!"

It had grown gradually easier to ignore this sort of thing over the past little while. Something in Linon was peculiar today, however. Crispin put that away for later, along with the rather deeper question of why he was involving himself in this. Slaves died all over the Empire every day, were abused, whipped, sold—made into sausages. Crispin shook his head: was he really so simple that the ridiculous association of a terrified girl with his daughter was drawing him into a world that had no safe place for him at all? Another hard question. For later.

Back in the days when he still enjoyed things, Crispin had always had a puzzle-solving mind. In work, in play. Designing a wall mosaic, gambling at his bathhouse. Now, as he dressed quickly in the twilight chill, he found himself engaged in slotting pieces of information like tesserae within his mind to make a picture. He turned it, tilted it like glass to catch angles of light.

"What will they do to her?" He asked it impulsively.

Linon was still for so long this time he thought the bird was ignoring him. He put on his sandals, waiting. The voice in his mind when it came was cold, uninflected, unlike anything he had heard before from her.

"She will have the juice of poppies in the morning, with whatever she drinks. She will be given to whoever comes for her. From the village, probably. They will take her away. Sometimes they mate them with an animal, for the sake of the fields and the hunters; sometimes the men do it themselves, one after another. They wear masks then, of animals. After, a priest of Ludan cuts out her heart. He may be a smith, a baker in the village. The innkeeper downstairs. We would not know. It is considered a good omen if she lives until the heart is removed. It is buried in the fields. They peel her skin from her and burn it, as the dross of life. Then she is hanged by her hair from the holy oak at the moment the sun sets, for Ludan to take as his own."

"Holy Jad! You can't be—"

"Be silent! Imbecile! I told you you were better off not knowing!"

The girl had looked up, startled. Crispin glared at her and her glance instantly dropped away, a different sort of fear in her now.

Sickened, unbelieving, Crispin began worrying the puzzle again with a part of his mind, struggling for calm. Turning pieces of glass to find the light. Even a dim, precarious light, like candles in a breeze or a slant of winter sun through an arrow slit.

"I can't let them do this to her," he said inwardly to Linon.

"Ah! Let sound the soldiers' drums! Caius Crispus of Varena, bold hero of a later age! You can't? I don't see why not. They will only find someone else. And kill you for trying to interfere. Who are you, artisan, to step between a god and his sacrifice?"

Crispin had finished dressing. He sat down on the bed again. It creaked.

"I don't know how to answer that."

"Of course you don't," said Linon.

The girl whispered, "My lord. I will do anything you like, always."

"What else does a slave do?" he snapped, distracted. She flinched, as if struck. He drew a breath.

"I need your help," he said again to the bird. The puzzle had taken a shape, poor though it might be. He rocked back and forth a little, creaking the bed. *"Here's what I want to happen . . ."*

A few moments later he explained to the girl what steps she, in her turn, had to take if she wanted to live through the day to come. He made it sound as if he knew what he was doing. What became almost intolerable was the look that entered her eyes as he spoke and she understood that he was going to try to save her. She wanted to survive, so much. It burned in her, this desire to live.

He had told Martinian, back home, that he felt no real desire for anything, not even life. Perhaps, Crispin thought, that made him the perfect man for the folly of this.

He sent the girl downstairs. She knelt in front of him first, looked as if she wanted to say something, but he quelled that with a glance and gestured to the door. After she left he sat for another moment, then stood up and began attending to what needed to be prepared in the room.

"Are you angry?" he asked Linon suddenly, surprising himself.

"Yes," said the bird, after a moment.

"Will you tell me why?"

"No."

"Will you help me?"

"I am a lump of leather and metal, as someone once said. You can render me blind, deaf, and silent with a thought. What else can I do?"

Going down the stairs toward the noise and warmth of the common room, Crispin glanced outside. It was full dark outside, the forest lost to sight in the black. Clouds again, no moons or stars to be seen. He ought to have been going down with no more on his mind than the anticipation of a good red wine from Candaria and some modest hopes for the stew. Instead, every shadow, every movement in the shadows beyond the streaked windows, carried an aura of dread. *It is considered a good omen if she lives until the heart is removed.*

He was committed, just about. He carried the copper key at his belt, but he had left the door to his room ajar, like an ineffectual Rhodian fool unused to the harsh realities of travel, the real dangers of the road.

IT HAD BECOME CLEAR that the red-bearded Rhodian drinking and even sharing a steadily replenished quantity of expensive wine was traveling all the way to Sarantium with a Permit signed by the Imperial Chancellor himself. The entire common room knew it by now. The man kept dropping the name of Gesius into every third sentence. It would have been irritating, had he not been so genial . . . and generous. It appeared he was an artisan of some sort, a soft, city fellow summoned to help with one of the Emperor's projects.

Thelon of Megarium considered himself adept at sizing up such men, and the opportunity they represented.

For one thing, the artisan—Martinian, he'd named himself—was quite evidently not carrying his purse. Which meant that the Permit, and whatever moneys he had been advanced or had carried with him from Batiara—obviously a sufficient sum to allow the real indulgence of Candarian wine—were not on his person, unless he'd stuffed them in his underclothes. Thelon grinned behind his hands at the thought of a crumpled, shit-smeared paper being presented at the next Posting Inn.

No, the Imperial Permit was not in Martinian's clothing, he'd wager a good deal.

Or if he'd had a good deal to wager, he would have. Thelon was without resources and attached to his uncle's mercantile party only out of the goodness of his uncle's heart—as his uncle was prone to remind him. They were on their way home to Megarium, having made some useful transactions at the military camp toward Trakesia where the Fourth and the First Sauradian legions were based. Useful for Uncle Erytus, that was. Thelon had no direct interest in any profits. He wasn't even being paid. He was here merely to learn the route, his uncle had said, and the people to be dealt with, and to show he could conduct himself properly among a class of folk better than waterfront rabble.

If he proved a decently quick study, Uncle Erytus had allowed, he *might* be permitted to come into the business at a fair salary and lead some minor trading expeditions himself. Eventually, perhaps, after time had run and maturity had demonstrated itself, he might become a partner with his uncle and cousins.

Thelon's mother and father had showered Uncle Erytus with abject, embarrassing gratitude. Thelon's creditors, including several shit-faced dice players in a certain caupona by the harbor, had declined to express similar enthusiasm.

All things considered, Thelon had to admit that this had been a usefully timed journey away from home, though the weather was ghastly and his pious uncle and bloodless cousins took the sunrise invocations too seriously by more than half and frowned at the very mention of whores. Thelon had been actively pondering how to arrange a quick tension-relieving encounter with their pretty blond serving girl tonight, when the artisan's voluble indiscretions at the next table had steered his thoughts in another direction entirely.

Certain hard facts were unfortunately inescapable. He was going to be home in a few too-short days. There had been an intimation from some parties that if he wished to continue enjoying the use and comfort of his legs he had best be prepared to make a significant payment toward eliminating his dicing debt. Thelon's uncle, as mulishly stupid about a little gambling as he was about girls, was not about to advance him any sums. That much had become obvious, despite Uncle Erytus's almost reluctant good humor after his successful transactions in boots and cloaks and whatever for the soldiers, and the purchase of crudely carved religious artifacts in a town east of the army camp. Trakesian wooden sun disks, he'd informed Thelon, were *much* in demand in Megarium, and even more so across the bay in Batiara. There was a good profit to be made, as much as fifteen percent, after all expenses. Thelon had heroically refrained from yawning.

He had also decided, long before this, not to point out that his uncle's piety and scruples appeared not to make him averse to bribing innkeepers—all of whom appeared to know Erytus well—to allow them to stay illicitly at a sequence of Imperial Inns along the road. Not that he was complaining, mind you, but there was a *principle* here, somewhere.

"Would it be a very great presumption," Uncle Erytus was now saying, leaning toward the red-bearded man, "to ask to be honored with a glimpse of the illustrious Permit you are honored with?" Thelon cringed at the fawning, unctuous language. His uncle, licking someone's boots, was an ugly sight.

The artisan's face darkened. "You don't think I *have* it?" he growled, affronted.

Thelon lifted a hand quickly, to hide another smirk. His uncle, drinking a polite cup of the other man's Candarian, flushed red as the wine. "No, *no*, not at all! I am *sure* you . . . of course you . . . it is just that I've never actually *seen* the Seal or the signature of the august Chancellor Gesius. So *celebrated* a man. Three Emperors served! You would be honoring me, good sir! A glimpse . . . the handwriting of so glorious a figure . . . an example for my sons."

His uncle, Thelon reflected sourly, had all the social-climbing traits one might expect in a modestly successful provincial merchant. He would endlessly regale his family with the unspeakably trivial story of this Permit if he saw it, and would probably find a religious moral to impose upon them, too. Virtue, the rewards thereof. Thelon diverted himself by imagining just what sort of example a eunuch was for his cousins.

"S'all right," the Batiaran artisan was saying with a lordly gesture that nearly toppled his latest flask of wine. "Show you tomorrow. Permit's up'n the room. The *best* room. Over the kitchen. Thash *mush* too far away t'night!" He laughed, finding himself extremely amusing, it seemed. Uncle Erytus, visibly relieved, also laughed loudly. He had a terrible, unconvincing laugh, Thelon decided. The red-bearded man stood up, swayed toward their table, poured again for Erytus. He lifted the flask in unsteady inquiry; Thelon's cousins hastily covered their glasses and so he, of necessity, had to do the same.

It was, quite abruptly, too much to endure. Candarian on offer and he was forced to decline? And here he was, in the midst of some utterly unholy nowhere, without any funds at all and only a few days from an encounter that placed his legs—and Jad knew what else—at more than some risk. Thelon made his decision. He'd just had a confirmation of his earlier guess in any case. The man was *such* a fool.

"My excuses, Uncle," Thelon said, standing, a hand at his belly. "Too much of the sausage. Must purge myself, I fear."

"Moderation," said his uncle predictably, a finger lifted in admonition, "is a virtue at table, as elsewhere."

"I *agree*!" said the fatuous artisan, sloshing his wine.

This, Thelon decided, heading toward the archway to the shadowed front room, was actually going to be a pleasure. He didn't go to the latrine across the hall. He went up the stairway, quietly. He was quite good with locks, as it happened.

As it happened, he didn't even need to be.

"BE READY," CRISPIN SAID inwardly, *"I believe we have landed our fish."*

"How very nautical of you," Linon replied sardonically. *"Do we eat him in salt or sauce?"*

"No wit, please. I need you."

"Witless?"

Crispin ignored this. *"I'm sending the girl up now."*

"Kitten!" he called out, his voice slurred, too loud. "Kitten!"

The girl who had called herself Kasia came over quickly, blue eyes anxious, wiping her hands on the sides of her tunic. Crispin gave her a brief, very direct look, then tilted sideways, spilling some more of his wine, as he pulled the room key from his belt.

He'd had, truly, no idea who might fall for the baits he was offering . . . the unlocked door, the garrulous drunkenness, crude hints dropped over dinner and wine. Indeed, it had been entirely possible no one would succumb. He had no fallback plan. No brilliant constellations of tesserae. A door left foolishly open, careless words about a purse upstairs . . . all he'd been able to devise.

But it seemed someone *had* risen to his lure. Crispin refused to let himself ponder the ethics of what he was doing when the sullen nephew he'd been watching gave him a too-naked glance and excused himself.

He squinted owlishly up at the girl and pointed an unsteady finger at Erytus of Megarium. "Thish *very* good friend of mine wants to see my Permit. Gesius's Seal. S'in the leather purse. On the bed. You know the room, 'bove the kitchen. Go get it. And Kitten . . ." He paused, waggled a finger at her. "I know *'xactly* how much money's in the purse, Kitten."

The Megarian merchant was protesting faintly, but Crispin winked at him and squeezed the girl's rump as she took the key. "Room's not too far for *young* legs," he laughed. "Might let her wrap 'em round me, later, too." One of the merchant's sons let out an alarming giggle before blushing ferociously under his father's swift gaze.

A Karchite at a table across the room laughed loudly, waving his beer at them. Crispin had thought, when he'd first entered the common room, that one of that group might slip away and up. He'd spoken loudly enough for them to hear . . . but they'd been drinking steadily since mid-afternoon, it seemed, and two of them were fast asleep, heads on the table among the food. The others weren't moving anywhere quickly.

Erytus's bored, angry nephew with the thin mouth and long, fidgety hands had said he was going to the latrine. He wasn't. Crispin was sure of it. He was the fish, and hooked.

If he goes into a room intending to steal, he told himself, he deserves whatever happens. Crispin was utterly sober, however—having spilled, or shared, almost all of his wine—and he didn't really convince himself.

It occurred to him, suddenly, before he could push the thought away, that it was possible that a mother, somewhere, loved that young man.

"He's here," Linon said, from the room upstairs.

SHE WENT UP THE stairs again, moving quickly this time past the wall torches, her passage making them waver, leaving a casting of uneven brightness behind and below her. She carried a key. Her heart was pounding, but in a different way this time. This time there was hope, however faint. Where there has been uttermost blackness a candle changes the world. There was nothing to be seen through the windows. She could hear the wind.

She reached the top, went straight on back to the last room over the kitchen. The door was ajar. He had said it might be. He hadn't explained why. Only that if she saw anyone in there when he sent her up, anyone at all, she was to do exactly as he told her.

She entered the room. Stood in the doorway. Saw the outline of a startled, turning figure in the blackness. Heard him swear. Couldn't tell who it was, at all.

Screamed, as she had been told.

THE GIRL'S FIERCE CRY ripped through the inn. They heard it clearly, even in the noisy common room. In the sudden rigid silence that ensued, her next frantic shout rang clearly: "There is a thief! *Help* me! *Help!*"

"Jad rot his eyes!" roared the red-bearded fellow, first to react, leaping to his feet. Morax rushed out of the kitchen in the next moment, hurrying for the stairs. But the artisan, ahead of him to the archway, went the other way, inexplicably. Seizing a stout stick from by the front door, he stormed out into the black night.

"MICE AND BLOOD!" LINON had gasped. *"We're jumping!"* The inner words came right on the heels of the girl's cry.

"Where?" Crispin demanded as he scrambled to his feet downstairs and snarled a curse for the benefit of the others in the room.

"Where do you think, imbecile? Courtyard out the window. Hurry!"

THE WRETCHED GIRL'S SCREAM had frightened him almost out of his head; that was the trouble. It was too loud, too . . . piercingly terrified. There was something raw in it that went far beyond spotting a thief in an upstairs room. But Thelon had no time at all to sort out why; only to know, almost immediately after he did the wrong thing, that what he *ought* to have done was turn calmly to her and, laughing, order her to bring a light so he could more easily fetch the Imperial Permit for the Rhodian to show his uncle, as promised. He'd have so easily been able to talk his way through an explanation of how, on an impulse, a desire to be of assistance, he had come up to the room. He was a respectable man, traveling with a distinguished mercantile party. What *else* did anyone imagine he was doing?

He ought to have done that.

Instead, panicked, stomach churning, knowing she couldn't see him clearly in the dark and seizing that saving thought, he'd grabbed the leather satchel lying on the bed, with papers, money, and what felt like an ornament sticking out halfway, and darted for the window. He'd banged the wooden shutter open hard, swung his feet out and jumped.

It took courage in the darkness of night. He'd no idea what lay below in the courtyard. He might have broken his leg on a barrel or his neck when he landed. He didn't, though the blind fall drove him staggering to his knees in the muck. He kept hold of the satchel, was up quickly, stumbling across the muddy yard toward the barn. His mind was racing. If he dropped the satchel in the straw there, he could double back to the front of the inn and lead the chase out onto the road in pursuit of a thief he'd glimpsed on his way back from the latrine after the girl screamed. Then he could reclaim the satchel—or the worthwhile parts of it—before they left.

It was a *good* strategy, born of swift thinking and urgent cunning.

Had he not been felled by a blow that knocked him senseless and nearly killed him as he angled across toward the shadow of the barn under scudding clouds and a few faint, emergent stars, it might even have worked.

"IMBECILE! YOU COULD HAVE *hit me!*"

"Learn to duck," Crispin snapped. He was breathing hard. *"I'm sorry. Couldn't see clearly enough."* There was only a faint spill of light from the shuttered windows of the common room.

He shouted, "Over here! I've got him! A light, rot you all! Light, in Jad's name!"

Men calling, a confusion of voices, accents, languages, someone rasping something in an unknown dialect. A torch appeared overhead, at the open shutter of his own room. He heard footsteps approaching, the loud voices nearing as men from the common room and the servants from the other side streamed out the front door and rushed over. Some excitement on a wet autumn night.

Crispin said no more, looking down in the light of the single overhead torch, and then in the gradually brightening orange glow as a ring of men surrounded him, some with light in their hands.

The merchant's nephew lay at his feet, a black flow that would be blood seeping from his temple into the mud. The strap of Crispin's satchel was still looped through one of his hands.

"Holy Jad preserve us!" Morax the innkeeper said, wheezing with exertion. He'd raced upstairs and then back down. Robbery in an inn would hardly be unknown, but this was a little different. This was no servant or slave. Crispin, dealing with complex emotions, and aware that they were only at the beginning of what had to be done here, turned and saw the innkeeper's frightened gaze shift quickly from his own face to that of the merchant, Erytus, who was now standing over the body of his nephew, expressionless.

"Is he dead?" Erytus asked finally. He didn't kneel to check for himself, Crispin noted.

"What is happening? I can't see! He shoved me inside!"

"Listen, then. Little to see. But be quiet. I need to be careful, now."

"Now, you need to be careful? After I'm almost broken in pieces?"

"Please, my dear."

It occurred to Crispin that he'd never said anything like that to the bird before. It might have occurred to Linon, too. She fell silent.

One of the cousins did kneel, head bent to the prone man. "He's alive," he said, looking up at his father. Crispin closed his eyes briefly; he had swung hard, but not as hard as he could. He was still holding the staff.

It was cold in the courtyard. A north wind blowing. None of them had had time for cloaks or mantles. Crispin felt mud oozing beneath his sandaled feet. It wasn't raining now, though there was a feel of rain in the wind. Neither moon was visible, and only a changing handful of stars where the racing clouds parted to the south toward the unseen mountains.

Crispin drew a breath. It was time to move this forward and he needed an audience. He looked directly at the innkeeper and said, in his most frigid voice—the one that terrified the apprentices at home—"I wish to know, keeper, if this thief, indeed his entire party, are in possession of Permits that allow them to stay at an Imperial Posting Inn. I wish to know it now."

There was an abrupt, shuffling silence in the courtyard. Morax actually staggered. This was *not* what he had expected. He opened his mouth. No words came out.

New voices now. Others approaching, out of the dark toward the circle of torches. Crispin glanced over and saw the girl, Kasia, being hustled over, two of the inn's servants on either side of her, hands gripping her elbows. They weren't being gentle. She stumbled and they dragged her forward.

"What is happening? I can't see!"

"The girl's here."

"Make her the hero."

"Of course. Why do you think I sent her up?"

"Ah! You were thinking, this afternoon."

"Alarming, I know."

"Let her go, rot you!" he said aloud to the men jostling her. "I owe this girl my Permit and my purse." They released her quickly. Crispin saw that she was barefoot. Most of the servants were.

He turned deliberately back to Morax. "I haven't had an answer to my question, keeper." Morax gestured helplessly, then clasped his hands together pleadingly. Crispin saw the man's wife behind him. Her eyes were burning: a rage without immediate direction, but deep.

"I will answer that. We have no Permit, Martinian." It was Erytus, the uncle. His narrow face was pale in the ring of torches. "It is autumn. Morax has been kind enough to allow us his hearth and rooms on occasions when the inn is less busy."

"The inn is full, merchant. And I assume Morax's kindness has a price and the price is of no benefit to the Imperial Post. Was I to pay a surcharge to your nephew?"

"Oh, well-done! A bowshot at both of them!"

"Linon! Hush!"

The satchel strap remained in the nephew's hand. No one had dared touch it. Lying on his back in the mud, Thelon of Megarium had not moved since Crispin felled him. He was breathing evenly, though. Crispin saw it with relief. Killing the man had not been part of his plans, though he was unavoidably aware that someone else might. *In the north, a thief is hanged on the god's tree.* He was moving quickly here, little time to assess, and less to sort out why he was doing it.

Erytus swallowed, said nothing. Morax cleared his throat, glanced at the merchant, then back at Crispin. His wife was right behind him and he knew it. His shoulders were hunched forward. He looked like a hunted man.

Crispin, no longer a fisherman with a lure but a hunter with a bow, said icily, "It becomes clear that this contemptible thief was staying here illicitly with the sanction of the authorized keeper of an Imperial Posting Inn. How much are they paying you, Morax? Gesius might want to know. Or Faustinus, the Master of Offices."

"My lord! You will *tell* them?" Morax's voice actually squeaked and then broke. It might have been comical, in another setting.

"You wretched man!" It wasn't hard for Crispin to summon a tone of fury. "My Permit and purse are stolen by someone who is here *only* because of your greed—and you ask if I will complain? You haven't even said a word about punishment yet, and all I've seen so far is a manhandling of the girl who stopped this! He would have got away if not for her! What do they do to caught thieves here in Sauradia, Morax? I know what they do in the City to Imperial keepers who breach their trust for private gain. You imbecile!"

"Hah! But be careful. He could kill you. His livelihood is at risk in this."

"I know. But there is a crowd."

Crispin was painfully aware that no one in this courtyard could be considered an ally, though. Most of them were staying illegally and would want to continue to be able to do so. He was a threat to more than Morax right now.

"All of the . . . My lord, in autumn, or winter, almost all the Imperial Inns allow honest travelers to stay. A courtesy."

"Honest travelers. Indeed. I see. I will be prompt to offer this in your defense, should the Chancellor ask. I have put you another question, though: what do you do with thieves here? And how do you recompense aggrieved patrons who are here legitimately?"

Crispin saw Morax glance quickly again at Erytus. The innkeeper was almost cringing.

It was the merchant who spoke. "What compensation would assuage you, Martinian? I will accept responsibility for my nephew."

Crispin, who had spoken of recompense in the fervent hope of hearing exactly this, turned to Erytus and let the anger seem to drift from his voice. "An honorable thing to say, but he is of age, is he not? He answers for himself, surely."

"He should. But his . . . failings are manifest here. A grief to his parents. And to myself, I assure you. What will serve to make this right?"

"We hang thieves back home," one of the Karchites growled. Crispin glanced over. It was the one who'd raised his beer mug to him, earlier. He had a bright, inebriated glint in his eye. The prospect of violence, to cheer a dull night.

"We hang 'em here, too!" said someone else, unseen, at the back of the crowd. There was a sharp murmur. An edge of excitement now. Torches danced, pressed nearer in the cold.

"Or cut off their hands," said Crispin, feigning indifference. He pushed away a torch that came too close to his face. "I care not what the course of law dictates here. Do with him what you will. Erytus, you are an honest man, I can see it. You cannot redress the risk to my Permit, but match the sum in the purse—the sum I would have lost—and I will accept that."

"Done," said the merchant, without a pause. He was a dried-out, humorless man, but impressive in his way.

Crispin said, trying to keep the same casual tone, "And then buy me the girl who saved my purse. I will let you fix your price with the keeper. Don't let him cheat you."

"What?" said Morax.

"The *girl*!" said the wife from behind him, urgently. "But . . ."

"Done," said Erytus, again, quite calmly. He looked faintly disapproving and relieved, at the same time.

"I will need household servants when I reach the City, and I owe her for this." They would think he was a greedy Rhodian pig; that was all right, that was fine. Crispin bent down and hooked the satchel strap from the fingers of the prone man. He straightened, and looked at Morax.

"I am aware that you are not the only keeper to do this. Nor am I, by nature, a teller of tales. I would suggest you be *extremely* fair with Erytus of Megarium in naming your price, and I am prepared to report that because of the intervention of one of your honest and well-trained serving girls no lasting harm has been done."

"No hanging?" the Karchite complained. Erytus looked over at him stonily.

Crispin smiled thinly. "I have no idea what they will do to him. I don't care. I won't be here to see it. The Emperor has summoned me and I will not linger, even for justice and a hanging. I do understand that the good-hearted Morax, *deeply* contrite at our having been driven outside into the cold, now offers Candarian wine to all those who feel the need of warmth. Am I correct, keeper?"

There was a burst of raucous laughter and agreement from the men crowded around them. Crispin let his smile deepen as he met a few glances.

"Nicely done, again. Mice and blood! Will I be forced to respect you?"

"How would we ever deal with that?"

"Husband! Husband!" the wife was saying urgently, for the third or fourth time. Her face was a blotchy red in the torchlight. She was staring at Kasia, Crispin saw. The girl looked stunned, uncomprehending. Either she was, or she was an extremely good actress.

Morax didn't turn to his wife. He drew a shaky breath and took Crispin by the elbow, walking him a little way into the dark.

"The Chancellor? The Master of Offices . . . ?" he whispered.

". . . have more pressing concerns. I will not trouble them with this. Erytus makes good my risk of loss, and you sell the girl with all her countersigned papers as compensation. Make the price fair, Morax."

"My lord, you want . . . *that* girl, of all of them?"

"I can hardly use all of them, keeper. That is the one who saved my purse." He let himself smile again. "She's a favorite of yours?"

The innkeeper hesitated. "Yes, my lord."

"Good," said Crispin briskly. "You *ought* to lose something in this, if only a yellow-haired bed-partner. Pick another of your girls to mount in the dark while your wife sleeps." He paused, his smile disappearing. "I am being generous, keeper."

He was, and Morax knew it. "I don't . . . that is, she isn't . . . my wife . . ." The innkeeper fell silent. He drew a shaky breath. "Yes, my lord," he said. Tried to smile. "I do have other girls here."

Crispin knew what that meant, as it happened.

"I told you," Linon said.

"No help for it," he replied, silently. There were questions embedded in this that he could not answer. Aloud, he said, "I mean it, Morax . . . a *very* fair price for Erytus. And serve out the wine."

Morax swallowed, and nodded unhappily. Crispin was uncontrite. The expensive wine would be the innkeeper's only real loss, and Crispin needed the other patrons to feel kindly toward him now, and for Morax to know that they did.

It began to rain. Crispin looked up. Dark clouds blotted all the sky. The forest was north, very near, a presence. Someone approached them from beyond the torches: a hefty, reassuring figure, with Crispin's cloak in his hands. Crispin smiled briefly at him. "It's all right, Vargos. We're going inside." Vargos nodded, his expression watchful.

They had picked up Thelon of Megarium and were carrying him in. His uncle and cousins walked beside him; servants carried torches. The girl, Kasia, lingered uncertainly, and so did the innkeeper's wife, her gaze poisonous.

"What is happening?"

"You heard. We are going in."

"Go upstairs, Kitten," Crispin said mildly, walking back toward the light. "You are being sold to me. You have no more tasks in this inn, do you understand?" She didn't move for a moment, her eyes enormous, then she nodded once, jerkily, like a rabbit. She was shivering, he saw. "Wait for me in the room. I've some good wine promised me, before I come up. Warm the bed. Don't fall asleep." It was important to be casual about this. She was a slave, bought on impulse; he knew nothing more than that.

"About the wine, my lord?" Morax's voice at his elbow was low, complicitous. "The Candarian? It is wasted on almost all of them, my lord." That happened to be true.

"I don't care," Crispin replied icily.

That happened to be untrue. He found it almost painful. Candarian island wine was celebrated, it was *far* too good to waste. Under ordinary circumstances.

"Mice and blood, artisan. You are still an imbecile. You do know what this means for tomorrow?"

"Of course I do. No help for it. We won't be able to stay. I count on you to protect us all." He meant it ironically but it didn't quite come out that way. The bird made no reply.

There was a god's tree somewhere in that forest beyond the road and tomorrow was the Day of the Dead. And despite what Zoticus had advised him, they were going to have to be away from here and traveling at sunrise or before.

He went inside with the innkeeper. Sent the girl upstairs with the key. Sat again at his table in the common room to drink a flask or two of the wine, prudently watered, and earn what goodwill he could from those who shared in the liquid bounty. He kept his purse on him this time, with his money, his Permit, and the bird.

After a time, Erytus of Megarium reappeared, having concluded an encounter with Morax. He presented Crispin with certain papers that indicated that the Inici slave girl Kasia was now the legal property of the artisan Martinian of Varena. Erytus also insisted on finalizing the financial compensation upon which they had agreed. Crispin allowed him to count the contents of his purse; Erytus produced his own, and matched it. The Karchite merchants watched them but were too far away to see anything clearly.

Erytus accepted only a very small cup of wine, in earnest of goodwill. He looked weary and unhappy. He extended renewed apologies for his nephew's disgraceful conduct and rose to leave a few moments later. Crispin stood and exchanged a bow with him. The man had behaved impeccably. Crispin had, in fact, relied upon that.

Looking at the papers and the quite heavy purse on the table beside him, Crispin sipped the good wine. He expected the Megarium party to be gone even before he was in the morning—if the nephew was allowed to leave. He suspected that some further outlays on Erytus's part would achieve that end, if they hadn't done so already. He found himself hoping so. The young man was a rogue, but he'd been seduced into this crime, had his skull dented for it, and would doubtless suffer extremely at his family's hands. Crispin did not particularly want to be the agency of his being hanged from a pagan oak in Sauradia.

He looked around. The revived Karchites and several of the other guests—including a cheerful, gray-clad courier—were quaffing Candarian red wine unwatered, downing it like beer. He managed not to wince at the sight, raising his own glass in a genial salute. He felt very far from his own world. Ordinary circumstances had been left a long way off, at home, behind city walls. Where he ought to have stayed, shaping images of beauty with such materials as came to hand. There was no beauty here.

It occurred to him that he ought not to leave his new slave alone for too long, even with a lock on the door. There wasn't much he could do if she went missing now and never turned up. He went upstairs.

"Are you going to stick it in her?" Linon cackled suddenly. The crudeness and the patrician voice and Crispin's mood were all janglingly at odds with each other. He made no reply.

The girl had the key. He knocked softly and called to her. She unbolted to his voice and opened the door. He stepped inside and closed and bolted it again. It was very dark in the room. She had lit no candles, had closed the shutters again and latched them. He could hear the rain outside. She stood very near to him, not speaking. He was embarrassed, surprisingly aware of her, still wondering why he had done what he had done tonight. She knelt with a rustle, a blurred female shape, and then bent her head to kiss his foot before he could withdraw. He stepped quickly back, clearing his throat, uncertain what to say.

He gave her the topmost blanket from the bed and bade her sleep on the servant's pallet by the far wall. She never spoke. Aside from that instruction, neither did he. He lay in the bed listening to the rain for a long time. He thought of the queen of the Antae, whose foot he himself had kissed, before this journey had begun. He remembered a Senator's wife, tapping at his door. Another inn. Another country. He finally fell asleep. He dreamt of Sarantium, of making a mosaic there, with brilliant tesserae and all the shining jewels he needed: images on a towering dome of an oak tree in a grove, lightning bolts in a livid sky.

They would burn him in the City for such an impiety, but this was only a dream. No one died for his dreams.

He woke in the darkness before dawn. After a moment of disorientation, he swung out of bed and crossed the cold floor to the window. He opened the shutters. The rain had stopped again, though water was still dripping off the roof. A heavy fog had drifted in; he could scarcely see the courtyard below. There were men stirring down there—Vargos would be among them, readying the mule—but sounds were muted and distant. The girl was awake, standing beside her pallet, a pale, thin figure, ghostlike, silently watching him.

"Let's go," he said, after a moment.

Not long afterward they were on the road, three of them walking east in a mist-shrouded half-world as dawn came without a sunrise on the Day of the Dead.

CHAPTER IV

Vargos of the Inicii was not a slave.

Many of the Posting Inns' servants-for-hire along the main Imperial roads were, of course, but Vargos had chosen this job of his own will, as he was quick to point out to those who erred in addressing him. He'd signed his second five-year indenture with the Imperial Post three years ago, carried his copy of the paper on his person, though he couldn't read it, and collected a payment twice a year, in addition to his guaranteed room and board. It wasn't much, but over the years he'd bought new boots twice, a woolen cloak, several tunics, an Esperanan knife, and he could offer a copper follis or two to a whore. The Imperial Post preferred slaves, naturally, but there weren't enough of them, since the Emperor Apius had elected to pacify the northern barbarians rather than subdue them, and stout men were badly needed for parties on the roads. Some of those stout men, including Vargos, were northern barbarians.

At home, Vargos's father had often expressed—generally with spilled ale and a table-thumping fist—his views on working or soldiering for Sarantium's fat-rumped catamites, but Vargos had been of the habit of disagreeing with his parent on occasion. Indeed, it had been after the last such discussion that he had left their village one night and begun his journey south.

He couldn't remember the details of the argument anymore—something to do with a superstition about plowing beneath a blue full moon—but it had ended with the old man, blood dripping from his scalp, deliberately branding his youngest son on the cheek with a hunting knife while Vargos's brothers and uncles enthusiastically held him down. Vargos, for all his violent, injurious struggling at the time, had had to concede to himself afterward that the scarring had probably been deserved. It was not really acceptable among the Inicii for a son to hammer his father half to death with a stick of firewood in the course of an agrarian dispute.

He'd chosen not to linger for further debate or familial chastisement, however. There was a world beyond their village, and precious little within it for a youngest son. He had walked out of the house that same spring night, the two nearly full moons high above the newly planted fields and the dense, well-known forests, and had set his marred face to the far south, never looking back.

He'd expected, of course, to join the Imperial army, but someone in a roadside caupona had mentioned positions on offer at the Posting Inns, and Vargos had thought he might try that for a season or two.

That had been eight summers ago. Amazing, when you thought about it: how quickly-made decisions became the life you lived. He'd his share of newer scars since then, for the roads *were* dangerous and hungry men turned outlaw easily enough in Sauradia, but the work suited Vargos. He liked open spaces, had no single master to knuckle his forehead to, and didn't share his father's bone-deep hatred of the Empires—either Sarantine or the old one in Batiara.

Even though he was known as a keep-to-himself man, he had acquaintances at every Posting Inn and roadside tavern from the Batiaran border to Trakesia by now. That meant decently clean sleeping straw or pallets, a fireside sometimes in winter, food and beer, and some of the girls could be soft enough on the occasions when they weren't commanded elsewhere. It helped that he was one of the freemen, and had a coin or two to spend. He had never been out of Sauradia. Most of the Imperial Post servants stayed in their province, and Vargos had never had the least desire to wander farther than he already had eight years ago, cheek dripping blood, from the north.

Until this morning, on the Day of the Dead, when the red-haired Rhodian who'd hired him at Lauzen's inn by the border set out in fog from Morax's with a slave girl marked for the oak god.

Vargos had converted to the Jaddite faith years ago, but that didn't mean a man from the northern reaches of the Aldwood couldn't recognize one who'd been named to the tree. She was of the Inicii herself, sold off to a slave trader, perhaps even from a village or farm near his own. In her eyes, and in the looks given her by some of the men and women at Morax's, Vargos had read the signs the night before. No one had said a word, but no one had to. He knew what day was coming.

Vargos's conversion to the sun god's faith—along with a contentious belief in the holiness of Heladikos, the god's mortal son—had been a real one, as it happened. He prayed each dawn and at sunset, lit candles at chapels for the Blessed Victims, fasted on the days that called for fasts. And he disapproved now, deeply, of the old ways he'd left behind: the oak god, the corn maiden, the seemingly endless thirst for blood and human hearts eaten raw. But he'd never have dreamt of interfering, and certainly hadn't done so, the two other times he'd been here at Morax's, close to the southern godtree on this day.

None of his business, he'd have said, if the thought had even occurred to him or been raised by anyone else. A servant didn't summon the Imperial army or clergy to halt a pagan sacrifice. Not if he wanted to go on living and working on this road. And what was one girl a year, among all of them? There had been plagues two summers in a row. Death was everywhere in the midst of them.

The red-headed Batiaran hadn't raised anything at all with Vargos. He'd simply bought the girl—or had her bought for him—and was taking her away to save her life. His choice of her could have been an accident, chance, but it wasn't, and Vargos knew it.

They'd been planning to stay here two nights, in order not to be traveling on this day.

That intention had been in line with what every halfway prudent man on the roads of Sauradia was doing on the Day of the Dead. But late last night, before going up the stairs to his room after the extremely strange capture of the thief, Martinian of Varena had summoned Vargos out to the hallway from his pallet in the servants' room and told him they'd be leaving tomorrow after all, before sunrise, with the girl.

Vargos, taciturn as he was, had been unable not to repeat, "Tomorrow?"

The Rhodian, unexpectedly sober despite all the wine they'd been noisily drinking in the other room, had looked at Vargos for a long moment in the dimly lit corridor. It was difficult to make out his expression behind the full beard, in the shadows. "I don't think it is safe to stay here," was all he'd said, speaking Rhodian. "After what has happened."

It wasn't in the *least* safe outside, Vargos thought but did not say. He'd considered that the other man might be testing him, or trying to say something without putting it into words. But he hadn't been prepared for what came next.

"It is the Day of the Dead tomorrow," said Martinian, speaking carefully. "I will not make you go with us. You do not owe me that. If you prefer to stay, I will release you freely and hire another man when I can."

That wouldn't be tomorrow, Vargos knew. There would be expressions of regret but no one would be free to travel with the artisan tomorrow. Not for a fistful of silver solidi.

No one would have to.

Vargos had made a swift decision or two in his day. He shook his head. "You asked for a man to come to the Trakesian border, I recollect. I'll be ready with the mule before the sun-up prayers. Jad's Light will see us through the day."

The Batiaran was not a fellow with an easy smile, but he'd smiled briefly then and placed a hand on Vargos's shoulder before heading up the stairs. He said, "Thank you, friend," before he went.

In eight years, no one had ever offered to release him from duty in that way before, or offered a thank-you to a short-term hired servant for simply performing—or continuing—his contracted service.

This meant two things, Vargos had finally decided, back on his narrow pallet, elbowing away a too-close, snoring Trakesian. One was that Martinian had known exactly what he was doing—somehow—when he'd had the merchant buy him that girl. And the other was that Vargos was his man now.

Courage spoke to him. The courage of Jad in his chariot battling cold and darkness each long night under the world, of Heladikos driving his horses far too high to bring back fire from his father, and of a single traveler risking his own death for a girl who had been named to a savage ending on the morrow.

Vargos had seen some celebrated men in his time on this road. Merchant princes, aristocrats from the far-off City itself, clad in gold and white, soldiers in bronze armor and regimental colors, austere, immensely powerful figures in the clergy of the god. Some years ago, memorably, Leontes himself, Supreme Strategos of all the Empire's armies, had passed with a company of his own picked guard on their way back east from Megarium. They'd been riding to the military camp near Trakesia, then heading north and east against the restive Moskav tribes. Vargos, in a dense press of men and women, had caught only a flashing glimpse of golden hair, helmetless, as people screamed in ecstasy beside the road. That had been in the year after the great victory against the Bassanids beyond Eubulus, and after the Triumph the Emperor had granted Leontes in the Hippodrome. Even in Sauradia they had heard about that. Not since Rhodias had an Emperor granted a strategos such a processional.

It was this artisan from Varena, though, a descendant of the legions, the Rhodians, the blood Vargos had been raised to hate, who had done the bravest thing he knew, last night and now. And Vargos was going to follow him.

They were unlikely to get far, he thought grimly. *Jad's Light will see us through,* he'd said in the hallway the night before. There was no light to speak of as they led the mule out of the courtyard in a black, blanketing thickness of predawn fog. The pale autumn sun would be rising ahead of them soon—and they would have no way of even knowing.

The three of them walked from the yard in an unnatural, muffled stillness. Men—or the blurred outlines of men—stood and watched them pass. No one offered to help, though Vargos knew every man there. They had tasted no food or drink, on Martinian's instructions. Vargos knew why. He still wasn't sure how Martinian knew.

The girl was barefoot, wrapped in the artisan's second cloak, the hood hiding her face. No other travelers were moving, though the Megarian merchants had left earlier, in full darkness, carrying the wounded man in a litter. Vargos, awake and loading the mule by torchlight, had seen them go. They wouldn't travel far today, but they had little choice but to move on. Where Vargos came from, the apprehended thief would have been an obvious candidate to be hanged from Ludan's Tree.

Here, he wasn't sure. The girl had been named. They might choose another, or they might not relinquish her, fearing a year's bad luck if they did. Things were different in the south. Different tribes had settled here, different histories had set their stamp. Would they kill him and the Batiaran to take her back? Almost certainly, if they wanted her and the two men resisted. This sacrifice was the holiest rite of the year in the old religion; men interfered at absolute peril of their lives.

Vargos was quite certain Martinian would resist.

He was somewhat surprised to feel an equal certainty in himself, a cold anger overriding fear. As they passed out from the courtyard he walked past the stablemaster, Pharus, a burly figure in the mist. Pharus was staring at them in a certain way, no proper respect in his bearing at all, and though Vargos had known him for years he did not hesitate. He stopped in front of the man just long enough to swing the bottom of his staff upward, hard, hammering Pharus right between the legs without a word spoken. The stablemaster let out a high-pitched screech and crumpled in the mud, hands clutching for his groin as he thrashed on the cold, wet ground.

Vargos bent low in the fog and spoke softly in the ear of the gasping, writhing man. "A warning. Leave her be. Find another, Pharus."

He straightened, carried on, not looking back. He never looked back. Not since he'd left home. He saw Martinian and the girl gazing at him, cloaked shadows on the almost invisible surface of the road. He shrugged, and spat. "Private quarrel," he said. He knew they would know it was a lie, but some things were best not spoken aloud, Vargos had always felt. He did not, for example, tell them he expected to die before midday.

HER MOTHER USED TO call her *erimitsu*, "clever one" in their own dialect. Her sister was *calamitsu*, which was "beautiful one," and her brother was, of course, *sangari*, which was "beloved." Her brother and father had died last summer, black sores bursting all over their bodies, blood running from their mouths when they tried to scream at the end. They buried them in the pit with all the others. In the autumn, faced with winter coming, imminent starvation, and two daughters, her mother had sold one to the slavers: the one who had the intelligence to perhaps survive in the harsh world far away.

Kasia had had a reputation already that made her almost unmarriageable at home. Too clever by half, and too thin by more than that in a tribe where women were valued for full hips and soft figures—promise of comfort in the long cold and children easily birthed. Her mother had made a bitter, brutal choice but not a unique one that year as the first snows fell on the mountains above them. The Karchite slave traders knew what they were doing that season, traveling the northern villages of Trakesia and then Sauradia in a slow circuit of acquisition.

The world was a place of grief, Kasia had understood, beyond tears, after the first two nights journeying south with shackles on her wrists. Man was born to sorrow, and women knew more of it. She'd lain on the cold ground, head averted, watching the last sparks of the dying fire as she lost her maidenhead to two of the slavers in the dark.

A year in Morax's inn had done nothing to change her thinking, though she had not starved and had learned what to do to avoid being beaten too often. She was alive. Her mother and sister might be dead by now. She didn't know. Had no way of knowing. The men hurt her sometimes, upstairs, but not always and not most of them. You learned, if you were clever, to shield that cleverness and gather a blank, stolid endurance about you like a cloak. And you passed days and nights and days and nights that way. The first winter in this alien south, spring, summer, then the coming of autumn again with turning leaves and memories you wanted to avoid.

You tried never to think of home. Of being free to walk out of doors when work was done, following the stream uphill to places where you could sit entirely alone beneath circling hawks and among the small quick woodland creatures they hunted, listening to the heartbeat of the world, dreaming in daylight with open eyes. You didn't dream, here. You endured, behind the cloak. Who had ever said existence offered more?

Until the day you understood they were going to kill you, and you realized—with genuine astonishment—that you wanted to survive. That somehow life still burned inside like the obdurate embers of a fire more fierce than desire or grief.

On the almost-invisible road, walking east with two men in gray, sound-swallowing fog on the Day of the Dead, Kasia watched them dealing with fear and the rawness of their danger and was unable to deny her joy. She struggled to hide it, as she had hidden every emotion for a year. She was afraid if she smiled they would think her simple, or mad, so she kept close to the mule, a hand on its rope, and tried not to meet the eyes of either man when the mist swirled and showed their faces.

They might be followed. They might die here on the road. This was a day of sacrifice and the risen dead. There might be demons abroad, in search of mortal souls. Her mother had believed that. But Kasia had claimed her knife in the mist before dawn, darting through fog to the smithy and taking it from its hiding place. She could kill someone, or herself, before they took her for Ludan.

She had seen the shape of Pharus the stablemaster in the courtyard as they walked past. He had been leaning forward intently, still watching her as he had for the past two days. And though his eyes had been almost hidden in the enveloping grayness she could feel the fury in him. She had wondered suddenly if he was the oak priest here, the one who offered the heart of the sacrifice.

Then Vargos—who had simply been one of many servants on the road, a man who'd slept here so many nights without exchanging a single word with her—had stopped in front of Pharus and clubbed him upward between the legs with his staff.

It was when Pharus collapsed with an appalling inhalation of breath that Kasia had begun struggling not to show the fierceness of her joy. With every step they took down the road after that blow—wrapped in fog as in a blanket, a womb, unable to see ten paces ahead or behind—she felt herself being reborn, remade.

It was wrong, she *knew* it was. There was death out here today, and no sane person ought to be abroad. But death had been summoned and waiting for her at the inn already, a certainty, and it might or might not find her out in the mist. Any way you looked at it, a chance was better than none at all. And she had her little knife.

Vargos was leading them, the Rhodian behind. They walked in silence, save for the muffled snorting of the mule and the creaking of the weight on its back. They listened. Ahead and behind. The world had shrunk nearly to nothingness. They moved, unseeing, in an endless gray on a straight road the Rhodians had built five hundred years ago in their Empire's bright glory.

Kasia thought about the artisan behind her. She should be ready to die for him, given what he'd done. She might be, in fact. But she was the *erimitsu*, and thought too much for her own good. So her mother used to say, and her father, brother, aunts—just about everyone.

She wasn't sure why he hadn't touched her last night. He might prefer boys, or find her thin, or simply have been tired. Or he might have been being kind. Kindness was not a thing she knew much about.

He had cried a name in the middle of the night. She'd been dozing herself, on the pallet, fully clothed, and had startled awake to the sound of his voice. She couldn't remember the name and he'd never quite awakened, though she'd waited, listening.

The other thing she didn't understand was how he'd known to run to the courtyard instead of up the stairs with everyone else when she screamed. The thief might have escaped, otherwise. It had been black in the room; she couldn't have identified anyone. Pacing along by the mule, Kasia worried that puzzle like a dog with a scrap of meat on a bone and eventually gave it up. She wrapped herself more tightly in Martinian's cloak. The cold was damp, penetrating. She had no shoes, but she was used to that. She looked over to left and right, couldn't see a thing beyond the road, could barely see the road itself beneath her feet. It would be easy enough, actually, to fall into the ditches. She knew where the forest was, to their left, knew it would draw nearer as they continued east.

Around mid-morning—at a guess—they came to one of the small roadside chapels. Kasia hadn't even seen it until Vargos spoke softly and they stopped. She peered through the grayness and made out the dark outline of the tiny chapel. They'd have gone right past had Vargos not been looking for it. Martinian called a halt. Standing where they were, listening all the time for sounds in all directions, they quickly ate chunks of dark bread with some beer, and shared out a wheel of cheese Vargos had taken from the servants' table. When they finished, Vargos looked an inquiry at Martinian. The red-bearded man hesitated, then Kasia saw him nod. He led them into the empty chapel for the invocation to Jad. Somewhere the sun had risen by now, was shining. Kasia listened to the two men hurry through the litany, and joined them for the responses she had been taught: *Let there be Light for our lives, lord, and Light eternal when we come to you.*

They went back out into the fog, untied the mule, began walking again. There was nothing to be seen at all. In front of her the world ended beyond Vargos. It was like walking in a dream, no passage of time, no sense of movement, the slabs of the road cold underfoot, walking away and away.

Kasia's hearing was extremely good. She heard the voices before either of the men did.

She reached back, touched Martinian on the arm, pointed back down the road. In the same moment Vargos said, very softly, "They are coming. Left, just up here. Cross over."

There was a short, flat cart bridge spanning the ditch, leading into the fields. She wouldn't have seen that, either. They took the mule across, went a short way through the muddy stubble in the dense, impenetrable grayness, and stopped. Listening. Kasia's heart was racing now. They had come for her, after all. It was not over. They ought not to have stopped to pray, she thought.

Let there be Light. There was no light. At all.

Martinian stood on the other side of the mule, his red beard and hair dulled by the grayness. Kasia saw him hesitate, then slip an old, heavy sword silently free of the ropes that strapped it to the mule's side. Vargos watched him. They heard the noises clearly now, voices approaching from the west, men talking too loudly, to encourage themselves. Footsteps now on the road—eight men? ten?—muffled but very near, just across the ditch. Kasia strained to see, prayed she would not be able to. If the fog lifted for even a moment now, they were lost.

Then she heard growling, and a sharp, urgent bark. They had brought the dogs. Of course. And they all knew her scent. They *were* lost.

Kasia laid one hand across the mule's shoulders, felt its nervousness, willed it to silence. She fumbled for her knife. She had the power to die before they took her, if no other power at all. Her brief, mad joy had gone, was lost, swift as a bird into grayness all around.

She thought of her mother a year ago, alone on a leaf-strewn path with a small bag of coins in her hands, watching the slave train take her daughter away. It had been a brilliantly clear day, snow gleaming on the mountain peaks, birdsong, the leaves red and gold, and falling.

CRISPIN CONSIDERED HIMSELF AN articulate man and knew he was a reasonably educated one. He'd had a tutor for many years after his father died, at his mother's insistence and his uncle's. Had struggled through the classical authors on rhetoric and ethics, and the tragic dramas of Arethae, greatest of the city-states in Trakesia: those thousand-year-old confrontations between men and gods written in an almost lost form of the language men now called Sarantine. Writings from a different world, before stern Rhodias had shaped its empire and Trakesia's cities had dwindled into islets of pagan philosophy and then, latterly, not even that, as the Schools were closed. It was merely another province of Sarantium now, barbarians in the north of it and beyond its northern borders, and Arethae was a village huddled under the grandeur of its ruins.

Even more than his education, Crispin thought, fifteen years of working for and then alongside Martinian of Varena would have honed the thinking of any man. Gentle as his older partner might be in manner, Martinian was unrelenting and even joyful in chasing a dialectic down to its conclusions. Crispin had learned, of necessity, to give as good as he got and to derive a certain pleasure in marshalling words to guide premises to resolutions. Color and light and form had always been his chief delight in the world, the realm of his own gift, but he took no little pride in being able to order and formulate his thoughts.

It was therefore with real distress that he had come to understand earlier this morning that he wasn't even *close* to having words to express how uncomfortable he was out here in the fog. He couldn't *begin* to say how passionately he wanted to be anywhere else but here in Sauradia on an almost-invisible road. It went beyond fear and awareness of danger: his was the distress of a soul that felt itself to be in entirely the wrong sort of world.

And that was before they'd heard the men and dogs.

They stood now in the wet earth of a bare field, in silence. He was aware of the girl beside him, her steadying hand on the mule, keeping it quiet. Vargos was a shrouded shape a little ahead of them, with his staff. Crispin, on a thought, turned and carefully worked his sword free of the ropes on the mule's back. He felt awkward holding it, a fool, and at the same time genuinely afraid. If anything at all turned on the swordplay of Caius Crispus of Varena . . . He expected Linon, on her thong about his neck, to say something caustic, but the bird had been silent from the moment they awoke this morning.

He had brought the sword at the last moment, an impulse, an afterthought, and only because it had been his father's and he was leaving home and going far away. His mother had said nothing, but her arched eyebrows had been—as ever—infinitely expressive. She'd sent a servant for the heavy footsoldier's blade Horius had carried when summoned to militia duty.

In the house where he'd grown up, Crispin had drawn it from its scabbard and noted with surprise that blade and sheath were oiled and cared for, even after a quarter of a century. He'd made no comment on that, merely raised his own eyebrows and then offered a few dramatic, self-mocking passes with the sword in his mother's receiving room. He'd struck a martial pose, weapon leveled at a bowl of apples on the table.

Avita Crispina had winced to see it. She'd murmured dryly, "Try not to hurt yourself, dear." Crispin had laughed, and sheathed the blade, claiming his wine with relief.

"You are supposed to tell me to come home with it or upon it," he'd murmured indignantly.

"That's a shield, dear," his mother had said gently.

He had no shield, no real idea how to use the sword, and there were dogs here with the hunters. Would the fog impede them, or the water in the ditch by the road? Or would the hunting hounds simply follow the girl's known scent right across the small bridge and lead the men right to them? The barking grew strident in that moment. Someone shouted, almost directly in front of them:

"They've crossed to the field! Come on!"

One question answered, at any rate. Crispin took a breath and lifted his father's blade. He did not pray. He thought of Ilandra, as he always did, but he did not pray. Vargos spread his feet wide and held his staff before him in both hands.

"He's here!" said Linon suddenly, in a tone Crispin had never heard from the bird. *"Oh, lord of worlds, I knew it! Crispin, do not move! Don't let the others move."*

"Hold still!" Crispin said sharply, instinctively, to Vargos and the girl.

In that moment several things seemed to happen at once. The accursed mule brayed stridently, legs gone rigid as tree trunks. The dogs' triumphant barking went suddenly high with shrill, yelping panic. And the shouting man screamed in terror, the sound ripping through the fog.

The mist swirled about the road, parted for a moment.

And in that instant Crispin saw something impossible. A shape from tormented dream, from nightmare. His mind slammed down, desperately denying what his eyes had just told him. He heard Vargos croak something that must have been a prayer. Then the fog closed in again like a curtain. Sight was gone. There was still screaming, high-pitched, appalling, from the vanished road. The mule trembled in every stiffened limb. He heard the streaming sound of it urinating beside him. The dogs were whining like whipped puppies. They heard them fleeing, back to the west.

There came a rumbling sound, as of the earth itself, shaking beneath them. Crispin stopped breathing. Ahead of them, among the hunters, the first man's scream went sharply, wildly higher, and then was cut off. The rumbling stopped. Crispin heard running footsteps, men screaming and the dogs' yelping sounds receding swiftly back the way they had come. Vargos had now dropped to his knees in the cold, sodden field, the staff fallen from his fingers. The girl was clutching at the trembling mule, struggling to steady it. Crispin saw that his hand holding the sword was shaking helplessly.

"What is it? Linon! What is this?"

But before the bird on his neck could make any reply, the mist parted again ahead of them, more than a swirling this time, a withdrawal, revealing the road across the narrow ditch for the first time that morning, and Crispin saw clearly what had, indeed, come on this day. His understanding of the world and the half-world changed forever in that moment as he, too, sank to his knees in the mud, his father's sword dropping from his fingers. The girl remained standing by the mule, transfixed. He would remember that.

VERY FAR TO THE west in that moment the autumn sun had long since risen above the woods near Varena. The sky was blue and the sunlight caught the red of the oak leaves and of the last apples on the trees in an orchard beside a road that joined the great highway to Rhodias a little farther south.

In the courtyard of the farmhouse adjoining that orchard an old man sat on a stone bench by his door, wrapped in a woolen cloak against the crispness of the breeze, enjoying the morning light and the colors. He held an earthenware bowl of herbal tea in both hands, warming them. A servant, grumbling out of ancient habit, fed the chickens. Two dogs slept by the open gate in the sunlight. In a distant field sheep could be seen but no shepherd. It was clear enough to make out the towers of Varena to the north and west. A bird trilled from the rooftop of the farmhouse.

Zoticus stood up, very abruptly. He set down his tea on the bench, spilling some of it. A watcher might have seen his hands tremble. The servant was not watching. The alchemist took a step or two toward his front gate and then turned to face the east, a grave, intent expression on his weathered face.

"What is it? Linon!" he said sharply and aloud. "What is this?"

He was, of necessity, unaware that he was echoing another man's question. He received no reply, either. Of course. One of the dogs stood up, though, head tilted a little to one side, questioningly.

Zoticus remained that way for a long time, motionless, as if listening for something. He had closed his eyes. The servant ignored him, used to this. The chickens were fed, and then the goat, and he milked the one cow. The eggs were collected. Six of them this morning. The servant carried them inside. All this time the alchemist did not move. The dog hesitated, and then padded over to lie down beside him. The other dog remained by the gate, in the light.

Zoticus waited. But the world, or the half-world, gave nothing more back to him. Not after that one sharp vibration in the soul, in the blood, a gift—or a punishment—offered someone who had walked and watched in shadows most men never knew.

"Linon," he said again, at length, but softly this time, a breath. He opened his eyes, looking out at the distant trees of the forest through the gate before his home. Both dogs sat up this time, watching him. He reached down without looking and patted the one at his knee. After a while he went back into the house, leaving his forgotten tea to grow cold on the stone bench outside. The sun rose higher through the morning, in the clear and cloudless blue of the autumn sky.

TWICE IN HIS LIFE Vargos thought (he was never entirely certain) he had seen one of the *zubir*. A glimpse in half-light, no more than that, of the Sauradian bison, lord of the Aldwood and all the great forests, emblem of a god.

Once, at summer sunset, working alone in his father's field, he had looked up squinting to see a bulky, shaggy shape at the edge of the wood. The light had been fading, the distance great, but something too large had moved against the dark curtain of the trees and then disappeared. It might have been a stag but it had been enormous, and he hadn't seen the high, branched horns.

His father had beaten him with an ax handle for suggesting that evening that he might actually have seen one of the sacred beasts of the wood. To see a *zubir* was an awesome thing, reserved for priests and sacred warriors consecrated to Ludan. Fourteen-year-old boys with a disrespectful turn of mind were not granted such felicities in the scheme of the world as the Inicii—and Vargos's father—saw it.

The second time had been eight years ago on his solitary springtime journey south with a branded cheek and a hard, sustaining anger. He had fallen asleep to the howling of wolves and awakened in moonlight to the sound of something roaring in the woods. He had heard an answering roar from nearer yet. Peering into a night made strange by the noises and the blue moon, Vargos had again seen something massive move at the forest's edge and withdraw. He had lain awake, listening, but the roaring had not come again, and nothing else appeared at the limits of his sight as the blue moon swung west after the white one and then set, leaving a sky strewn with stars, and the distant wolves, and the murmuring of a dark stream beside him.

Twice, then, and uncertainty both times.

This time there was no doubt. The fear that went into Vargos lodged like a knife between two ribs. In fog and a damp cold on the Day of the Dead he stood in a stubbled field between the ancient Rhodian high road to Trakesia and the southernmost edgings of the infinitely more ancient forest and fell to his knees at what he saw on the road when the mist parted.

There was a dead man there. The others had already fled, and the dogs. Vargos saw that it was Pharus, the stablemaster from Morax's. He lay flat on his back, limbs wide outflung like a child's discarded doll. It could be seen—even from there—that his entrails were spilling out. Blood was spreading all around him. His belly and chest had been ripped apart.

But that wasn't what drove Vargos to his knees as if felled by a blow. He had seen men die badly before. It was the other thing in the road.

The creature that had done this to the man. The *zubir* that was—Vargos knew this in that moment as he knew his own name—more than only an emblem, after all, however awesome that might be in itself. His ideas of faith and power crumbled in that cold muddy field.

He had adopted the teachings of the sun god, had worshipped and invoked Jad and Heladikos his son almost from the time he had first come south, forsaking the gods of his tribe and the blood-soaked rituals as he had forsaken his home.

And here now was the presence of Ludan, the Ancient One, the oak god, before him in a swirling away of grayness on the Imperial high road, in one of his known guises. *Zubir.* The bison. Lord of the forest.

And this *was* a god who demanded blood. And this was the day of sacrifice. Vargos's heart was pounding. He saw that his hands were shaking and was not ashamed. Only afraid. A mortal man in a place where he should not have been.

The mist swirled again, fog wrapped the road like a cloak. The obliterating bulk of the bison was lost. And then it was not. It was, somehow, in the field right beside them, enormous and black, an overpowering presence, a rank smell of animal and blood, wet fur and rotting earth, leaving the dead man alone on the empty road, torn apart, his heart exposed to the day this was.

HER HAND ON THE neck of the shuddering mule, Kasia saw the mist part, saw what had come to be in the road, and she went straight through her own fear and beyond in an instant.

In a kind of trance of unfeeling, she watched the fog descend again, and was utterly unsurprised when the *zubir* materialized in the field beside them. Vargos had fallen to his knees.

How, she thought, how should one be surprised at what a god could do? She realized suddenly that the donkey had stopped trembling and was standing very still, unnaturally so, given the smell and presence of the monstrous creature not ten paces away now. But what could be strange, what *could* be strange when one had strayed from a known road this far into the world of the powers? A bison stood before them, so big it would have blotted half the road from her sight if the road had not been lost. Three men could sit between the sharp, short curving of its horns. She saw blood on those horns, and streaky, viscous matter dripping slowly from them. She had seen the stablemaster in the road, ripped into meat.

She had thought this morning, foolishly, that she might escape.

She knew now—oh, she knew!—that Ludan was not to be escaped. Not like this. Not by some clever Rhodian with a scheme. Not by a girl named, however unfairly, however cruelly, to the god. Cruelty had no . . . *place* here in the field. It was a word that had no meaning, no *context*. The god was, and did what he did.

In this suspended state of calm, Kasia looked into the eyes of the *zubir*, eyes so deep a brown they were black, and she saw them clearly even in mist, and seeing, she surrendered her mortal will and the meaning of her soul to the ancient god of her people. What man—what woman, even more than man—had ever been immune to destiny? Where could you run when your name was known to a god? The secret pagan priest here, the whispering villagers, Morax's gross, small-eyed wife . . . none of them mattered. Their own destinies awaited them, or had found them already. Ludan signified, and he was here.

Kasia was serene, unresisting, as one drugged with the juice of poppies, when the bison began moving toward the forest. It looked back at the three of them, slowly turning its massive shaggy head. Kasia thought she understood. She had been named. He knew her. There was no path in the world that would not lead her here. Her tread, barefoot in the mud and crushed grass, was steady as she began to follow. Fear was behind her, in another world. She wondered if she would have time to wish a prayer that mattered, for her mother and her sister far away, if such things were allowed, if they were still alive, if the sacrifice had any power in what she was. She knew without turning back that the two men were coming behind her. Choice was not granted here, to any of them.

They went into the Aldwood on the Day of the Dead following the *zubir*, and the black trees swallowed them even more completely than the fog had done before.

"THE NUMINOUS," THE PHILOSOPHER Archilochus of Arethae had written nine hundred years ago, "is not to be directly apprehended. Indeed, if the gods wish to destroy a man, they need only show themselves to him."

Crispin struggled to barricade his soul behind ancient learning, a desperately conjured image of a marble portico in sunlight, a white-clad, white-bearded teacher serenely illuminating the world for attentive disciples in the most celebrated of the city-states of Trakesia.

He failed. Terror consumed him, asserting mastery, dominance, as he followed the girl and the stupefying creature that was . . . more than he could grasp. A god? The showing forth of one? The numinous? Upwind of them now, it stank. Things crawled and oozed through the thick, matted fur that hung from its chin, neck, shoulders, even the knees and breast. The bison was enormous, impossibly so, taller than Crispin was, wide as a house, the great, horned head vast and appalling. And yet, as they entered the woods, the first black trees like sentinels, wet leaves falling about them and upon them, the creature moved lightly, gracefully, never turning after that first look back—certain they were following.

And they were. Had there been choice, any kind of volition here, Caius Crispus of Varena, son of Horius Crispus the mason, would have died in that wet, cold field and joined his wife and daughters in the afterworld—whatever it turned out to be—rather than enter the Aldwood as a living man. The forest had frightened him even at a distance, in sunlight, seen from the safety of the road in Batiara. This morning, this otherworldly morning in Sauradia, there was no place on the god's earth he would not rather be than here in this dank, inhuman wilderness where even the *smells* could horrify.

The god's earth. What god? What power ruled in the world as he knew it? As he *had* known it: for this unnatural creature appearing in fog on the road had changed all that forever. Crispin spoke in his mind to the bird again, but Linon was silent as the dead, hanging about his throat as if she were, truly, no more than an amulet, a pedestrian little creation of leather and metal, worn for sentimental reasons.

He reached up with one hand on impulse and clasped the alchemist's creation. He flinched. The bird was burning hot to the touch. And this, as much as any other thing—this change where no such change should have been possible—was what made Crispin finally accept that he had left the world he knew and was unlikely ever to walk back into it again. He had made a choice last night, had intervened. Linon had warned him. He regretted Vargos, suddenly: the man did not deserve a fate such as this, randomly hired at a border inn to attend an artisan walking the road to Trakesia.

No man deserved this fate, Crispin thought. His throat was dry; it was difficult to swallow. The fog drifted and swirled, trees disappeared then loomed around them, very close. Wet leaves and wet earth defined a hopelessly twisting path. The bison led them on; the forest swallowed them like the jaws of a living creature. Time blurred, much as the seen world had blurred; Crispin had no idea how far they had come. Unable not to, awed and afraid, he reached up and touched the bird again. He couldn't hold her. The heat had penetrated now through his cloak and tunic. He felt her on his chest like a coal from a fire.

"Linon?" he said again, and heard only the silence of his own mind.

He surprised himself then, and began to pray, wordlessly, to Jad of the Sun—for his own soul, and his mother's and his friends', and the taken souls of Ilandra and the girls, asking Light for them, and for himself.

He had told Martinian little more than a fortnight ago that he wanted nothing in life anymore, had no desires, no journeys sought, no destinations in a hollowed, riven world. He ought not to be trembling so, to be so profoundly apprehensive of the shifting textures of the forest around them and the mist clinging like fingers to his face, and of the creature that was leading them farther and farther on. He ought to be ready to die here if what he'd been saying was true. It was with a force of real discovery that Crispin realized he wasn't, after all. And that truth, a hammer on the beating heart, smashed through the illusions he'd gathered and nourished for a year and more. He had things unfinished in his mortal house, it seemed. He did have something left.

And he knew what it was, too. Walking in a world where sight was nearly lost—tree trunks and twisted branches in the grayness, heavy wet leaves falling, the black bulk of the bison ahead of him—he could see what he wanted now, as if it were illuminated by fire. He was too clever a man, even amid fear, not to perceive the irony. All the ironies here. But he did know now what he wanted, in his heart, to make, and beyond cleverness, was wise enough not to deny it in this wood.

Upon a dome, with glass and stone and semiprecious gems and streaming and flickering light through windows and from a glory of candles below, Crispin knew he wanted to achieve something of surpassing beauty that would last.

A creation that would mean that he—the mosaic-worker Caius Crispus of Varena—had been born, and lived a life, and had come to understand a portion of the nature of the world, of what ran through and beneath the deeds of women and men in their souls and in the beauty and the pain of their short living beneath the sun.

He wanted to make a mosaic that would endure, that those living in after days would know had been made by him, and would honor. And this, he thought, beneath black and dripping trees, walking over sodden, rotting leaves in the forest, would mean that he had set his mark upon the world, and had been.

It was so strange to realize how it was only at this brink of the chasm, threshold of the dark or the god's holy Light, that one could grasp and accept one's own heart's yearning for more of the world. For life.

Crispin realized that his terror had gone now, with this. More strangeness. He looked around at the thick shadows of the forest and they did not frighten him. Whatever lay beyond sight could not be half so overwhelming as the creature that walked before him. Instead of fear, he felt a sadness beyond words now. As if all those born into the world to die were taking this shrouded walk with them, each one longing for something they would never know. He touched the bird again. That heat, as of life, in the damp, gray cold. No glow. Linon was as dark and drab as she had ever been. There was no shining in the Aldwood.

Only the awesome thing that led them, delicate for all its bulk, through the tall, silent trees for a measureless time until they came to a clearing and into it, one by one, and without a word spoken or a sound,

Crispin knew that this was the place of sacrifice. Archilochus of Arethae, he thought, had not been born when men and women were dying for Ludan in this grove.

The bison turned.

They stood facing him in a row, Kasia between the two men. Crispin drew a breath. He looked across the girl at Vargos. Their eyes met. The mist had lifted. It was gray and cold, but one could see clearly here. He saw the fear in the other man's eyes and also saw that Vargos was fighting it. He admired him then, very much.

"I am sorry," he said, words in the wood. It seemed important to say this. Something—an acknowledgment—from the world beyond this glade, these encircling trees where the wet leaves fell silently on the wet, cold grass. Vargos nodded.

The girl sank to her knees. She seemed very small, a child almost, lost inside his second cloak. Pity twisted in Crispin. He looked at the creature before them, into the dark, huge, ancient eyes, and he said, quietly, "You have claimed blood and a life already on the road. Need you take hers as well? Ours?"

He had not known he was going to say that. He heard Vargos suck in his breath. Crispin prepared himself for death. The earth rumbling as before. The ripping of those horns through his flesh. He continued to look into the bison's eyes, an act as courageous as anything he'd ever done in his life.

And what he saw there, unmistakably, was not anger or menace but loss.

And it was in that moment that Linon finally spoke.

"He doesn't want the girl," the bird said very gently, almost tenderly, in his mind. *"He came for me. Lay me on the ground, Crispin."*

"What?" He said it aloud, in bewildered astonishment.

The bison remained motionless, gazing at him. Or not, in fact, at him. At the small bird about his throat on the worn leather thong.

"Do it, my dear. This was written long ago, it seems. You are not the first man from the west to try to take a sacrifice from Ludan."

"What? Zoticus? What did—"

His mind spinning, Crispin remembered something and clutched it like a spar. That long conversation in the alchemist's home, holding a cup of herbal tea, hearing the old man's voice: "I have the only access to certain kinds of power. Found in my travels, in a guarded place . . . and at some risk."

Something began—only just began—to come clear for him. A different kind of mist beginning to rise. He felt the beating of his own heart, his life.

"Of course, Zoticus," Linon said, still gently. *"Think, my dear. How else would I have known the rites? There is no time, Crispin. This is in doubt, still. He is waiting, but it is a place of blood. Take me from your neck. Lay me down. Go. Take the others. You have brought me back. I believe you will be permitted to leave."*

Crispin's mouth was dry again. A taste like ashes. No one had moved since the girl sank to her knees. There was no wind in the clearing, he realized. Mist hung suspended about the branches of the trees. When the leaves fell, it was as if they descended from clouds. He saw puffs of white where the bison breathed in the cold.

"And you?" he asked silently. *"Do I save her and leave you behind?"*

He heard, within, a ripple of laughter. Amazingly. *"Oh, my dear, thank you for that. Crispin, my body ended here when you were still a child in the world. He thought the released soul might be freely taken when the sacrifice was made. In the moment of that power. He was right and wrong, it seems. Do not pity me. But tell Zoticus. And tell him, also, for me . . ."*

An inward silence, to match the one in the gray, still glade. And then: *"There is no need. He will know what I would have said. Tell him goodbye. Put me down now, dear. You must leave, or never leave."*

Crispin looked at the bison. It still had not moved. Even now, his mind could not compass the vastness of it, the presence of so huge and raw a power. The brown eyes had not changed, ancient sorrow in gray light, but there was blood on the horns. He took a shaky breath and slowly reached up with both hands, removing the little bird from his neck. He knelt—it seemed proper to kneel—and laid her gently on the cold ground there. He realized she was no longer burning, but warm, warm as a living thing. A sacrifice. There was a pain in him; he had thought he was past such grief, after Ilandra, after the girls.

And as he laid her down, the bird said then, aloud, in a voice Crispin had never heard from her, the voice of a woman, grave, serene, "I am yours, lord, as I ever was from the time I was brought here."

A stillness, rigid as suspended time. Then the bison's head moved, down, and up again, in acquiescence, and time began once more. The girl, Kasia, made a small, whimpering sound. Vargos, beyond her, put a hand to his mouth, an oddly childlike gesture.

"Go quickly now. Take them and go. Remember me." And in his mind now Linon's voice was that same mild woman's voice. The voice of the girl who had been sacrificed here so long ago, cut open, flayed, her beating heart torn out, while an alchemist watched from hiding nearby and then performed an act or an art Crispin could not begin to comprehend. Evil? Good? What did the words mean here? *One thing to another. The dead to life. The movement of souls.* He thought of Zoticus. Of a courage he could scarcely imagine, and a presumption beyond belief.

He stood up, unsteadily. He hesitated, utterly uncertain of rules and rituals in this half-world he had entered, but then he bowed to the vast, appalling, stinking creature before him that was a forest god or the living symbol of a god. He put a hand on Kasia's arm, tugging her to her feet. She glanced at him, startled. He looked at Vargos, and nodded. The other man stared, confused.

"Lead us," Crispin said to Vargos, clearing his throat. His voice sounded reedy, strange. "To the road." He would be lost, himself, ten paces into the forest.

The bison remained motionless. The small bird lay on the grass. Tendrils of mist drifted in the utterly still air. A leaf fell, and another. *"Goodbye,"* Crispin said, silently. *"I will remember."* He was weeping. The first time in more than a year.

They left the glade, Vargos leading them. The bison slowly turned its massive head and watched them go, the dark eyes unfathomable now, the horns wet and bloody beneath the circling trees. It made no other movement at all. They stumbled away and it was lost.

Vargos found their path, and nothing in the Aldwood stayed them upon it. No predator of the forest, no demon or spirit of the air or dark. The fog came again, and with it that sense of movement without passage of time. They came out where they had gone in, though, left the forest and crossed into the field. They reclaimed the mule, which had not moved. Crispin bent and picked up his sword from where it had fallen; Vargos took his staff. When they came to the road, over the same small bridge across the ditch, they stood above the body of the dead man there, and Crispin saw amid all the blood that his chest had been torn entirely open, both upward from the groin and to each side, and his heart was gone. Kasia turned away and vomited into the ditch. Vargos gave her water from a flask, his own hands shaking. She drank, wiped her face. Nodded her head.

They began walking, alone on the road, in the gray world.

The fog began to lift some time afterward. Then a pale, weak, wintry sun appeared through a thinning of the clouds for the first time that day. They stopped without a word spoken, looking up at it. And from the forest north of them in that moment there came a sound, high, clear, wordless, one sung note of music. A woman's voice.

"Linon?" Crispin cried urgently, in his mind, unable not to. *"Linon?"*

There was no reply. The inner silence was absolute. That long, unearthly note seemed to hang in the air between forest and field, earth and sky, and then it faded away like the mist.

LATER THAT DAY, TOWARD twilight far to the west, a gray-haired, gray-bearded man rode a jostling farmer's cart toward the city walls of Varena.

The farmer, having had more than one animal cured of an ailment by his passenger, was happy to oblige with irregular rides into the city. The passenger, at the moment, could not have been said to appear happy, or pleased, or anything but preoccupied. As they approached the walls and merged with the streaming traffic heading into and out of Varena before sunset closed the gates, the solitary passenger was recognized by a number of people. Some greeted him with deference and awe, others moved quickly to the far side of the road or fell back making a sign of the sun disk as the farmer's cart passed carrying an alchemist. Zoticus was, in fact, long accustomed to both responses and knew how to deal with each. Today he scarcely noticed them.

He'd had a shock this morning that had greatly undermined the wry detachment with which he preferred to view the world and what transpired within it. He was still dealing—not entirely successfully—with that.

"I think you should go into the city," had said the falcon earlier that day. He'd named her Tiresa when he'd claimed her soul. *"I think it would be good for you tonight."*

"Go to Martinian and Carissa," little Mirelle had added, softly. *"You can talk with them."* There'd been a murmur of agreement from the others, a rustling of leaves in his mind.

"I can talk with all of you," he'd said aloud, irritated. It offended him when the birds became solicitous and protective, as if he were growing fragile with age, needed guarding. Soon they'd be reminding him to wear his boots.

"Not the same," Tiresa had said briskly. *"You know it isn't."*

Which was true, but he still didn't like it.

He'd tried to read—Archilochus, as it happened—but his concentration was precarious and he gave it up, venturing out for a walk in the orchard instead. He felt extremely strange, a kind of hollowness. Linon was gone. Somehow. She'd been gone, of course, since he'd given her away, but this was . . . different. He'd never quite stopped regretting the impulse that had led him to offer a bird to the mosaicist traveling east. Or not just east: to Sarantium. The city he'd never seen, never would see now. He'd found a power in his life, claimed a gift, his birds. There were other things he would not be allowed, it seemed.

And the birds weren't really *his*, were they? But if they weren't, then what could they be said to be? And where was Linon, and how had he heard her voice this morning from so far?

And what was he doing shivering in his orchard without a cloak or his stick on a windy, cold autumn day? At least he had his boots on.

He'd gone back inside, sent Clovis off, complaining, with a request to Silavin the farmer down the road, and had taken the birds' collective counsel after all.

He couldn't talk to his friends *about* what was troubling him, but sometimes talking about other things, any other things, the very timbre of human voices, Carissa's smile, Martinian's gentle wit, the shared warmth of a fire, the bed they'd offer him for the night, a morning visit to the bustle of the market . . .

Philosophy could be a consolation, an attempt to explain and understand the place of man in the gods' creation. It couldn't *always* succeed, though. There were times when comfort could only be found in a woman's laughter, a friend's known face and voice, shared rumors about the Antae court, even something so simple as a steaming bowl of pea soup at a table with others.

Sometimes, when the shadows of the half-world pressed too near, one needed the world.

He left Silavin at the city gates, with thanks, and made his way to Martinian's home late in the day. He was welcomed there, as he'd known he would be. His visits were rare; he lived a life outside the walls. He was invited to spend a night, and his friends made it seem as if he was doing them a great honor by accepting. They could see he was disturbed by something but—being friends—they never pressed him to speak, only offered what they could, which was a good deal just then.

In the night he woke in a strange bed, in darkness, and went to the window. There were lights burning in the palace, on the upper floors where the beleaguered young queen would be. Someone else awake, it seemed. Not his grief. His gaze went beyond, to the east. There were stars above Varena in the clear night. They blurred in his sight as he stood there, holding memory to himself like a child.

CHAPTER V

They walked for a long time, moving through a world becoming gradually more familiar as the mist continued to lift. And yet, for all the reemergence of the ordinary, Crispin thought, it had also become a landscape changed beyond his capacity of description. Where the bird had been about his neck there was an absence that felt oddly like a weight. There were crows in the field again, toward the woods, and they heard a songbird in a thicket south of the road. A flash of russet was a fox, though they never saw the hare it pursued.

At what must have been mid-afternoon they stopped. Vargos unwrapped the food again. Bread, cheese, ale for each of them. Crispin drank deeply. He looked away to the south. The mountains were visible again, rifts in the clouds above them showed blue and there was snow on the peaks. Light, shafts of color, coming back into the world.

He became aware that Kasia was looking at him.

"She . . . the bird spoke," she said. Apprehension in her face, though there had not been in the forest, in the gray mist of the field.

He nodded. He had made himself ready for this during the silent walking. He had guessed it would come, that it had to come.

"I heard," he said. "She did."

"How? My lord?"

Vargos watched them, holding his flask.

"I don't know," he lied. "The bird was a talisman given me by a man said to be an alchemist. My friends wanted me to have such a thing for protection. They believe in forces I do not. Did not. I . . . understand next to nothing of what happened today."

And that was not a lie. Already the morning felt to be a recollection of being wrapped in mist, with a creature in the Aldwood larger than the world, than his comprehension of the world. Thinking back, the only vivid color he could remember was the red blood on the bison's horns.

"He took her, instead of . . . me."

"He took Pharus, as well," said Vargos quietly, pushing the stopper back into his flask. "We saw Ludan, or his shadow, today." There was something near to anger in the scarred face. "How do we worship Jad and his son after this?"

Real anguish here, Crispin thought, and was moved. They had lived through something together this morning. Wildly different paths to that glade seemed to matter less than one might have expected.

He drew a breath. "We worship them as the powers that speak to our souls, if it seems they do." He surprised himself. "We do so knowing there is more to the world, and the half-world, and perhaps worlds beyond, than we can grasp. We always knew that. We can't even stop children from dying, how would we presume to understand the truth of things? Behind things? Does the presence of one power deny another?" It was posed as a rhetorical question, a flourish, but the words hung in the brightening air. A blackbird lifted from the stubble of the field and flew away west in a low, sweeping arc, wings beating.

"I do not know," said Vargos, finally. "I have no learning. Twice, when I was younger, I thought I saw the *zubir*, the bison. I was never sure. Was I being marked? For today, in some way?"

"I am not the man to answer that," said Crispin.

"Are we . . . safe now?" the girl asked.

"Until the next thing comes," Crispin said, and then, more kindly, "Safe from those who followed, yes, I believe so. From whatever was in the wood? I . . . also believe so." *He doesn't want the girl. He came for me.*

It took a certain act of will, but he kept his mind from calling out again to the silence. Linon had been with him for so little time—abrasive, unyielding—but no one else, not even Ilandra, had ever been *within* him in that way. *My dear*, she had said, at the end. *Remember me.*

If he understood any of this rightly, Linon had been a woman, named as Kasia had been named to the forest god, but she had *died* in that grove a long time ago. Heart cut out, body hanging from a sacred tree. And soul . . . ? Soul claimed by a mortal man who had been watching, insanely daring, and drawing upon some arcane power Crispin's mind could not compass.

He remembered, unexpectedly, the look on Zoticus's face when it had emerged that of all his birds it was Linon whose inward voice Crispin had heard. *She was his first,* Crispin thought, and knew it was true.

Tell him goodbye, the bird had said silently at the end, in what would once have been her own voice. Crispin shook his head. He had thought once, in his arrogance, that he knew something of the world of men and women.

"There is a chapel we will come to soon," Vargos said. Crispin pulled his thoughts back, and realized they had both been watching him. "Before sunset. A real one, not just a roadside shrine."

"Then we will enter it and pray," said Crispin.

There *would* be comfort in the well-worn rituals, he realized. A returning to the customary, where people lived out their lives. Where they *had* to live their lives. The day, he thought, had done all it could do, the world had revealed all it would just now. They would calm themselves, he would order his thoughts, begin adjusting to the absence about his throat and in his mind, begin thinking of what to say in a difficult letter to Zoticus, perhaps even begin looking forward to wine and a meal at tonight's inn. A returning to the customary, indeed, as if coming home from a very long journey.

Men, when they think in this way—that the crisis, the moment of revealed power, has passed—are as vulnerable as they will ever be. Good leaders of armies at war know this. Any skilled actor or writer for the stage knows it. So do clerics, priests, perhaps cheiromancers. When people have been very deeply shaken in certain ways they are, in fact, wide-open to the next bright falling from the air. It is not the moment of birth—the bursting through a shell into the world—that imprints the newborn gosling, but the next thing, the sighting that comes after and marks the soul.

They went on, two men and a woman, through an opening world. No one else was on the road. It was the Day of the Dead. The autumn light became mild as the sun swung west, palely veiled. A cool breeze moved the clouds. More rifts of blue could be seen overhead. Crows in the fields, jays, and another small bird Crispin didn't know, swift-flying on their right, with a bright tail red as blood. Snow far off, on the distant mountain peaks emerging one by one. The sea beyond. He could have sailed, if the courier . . .

They came to the place of which Vargos had spoken. It was set behind iron gates, some distance back from the road on the south side. It faced the forest. The chapel was much larger than the usual roadside places of prayer. A real one, as Vargos had put it: a gray stone octagon with a dome above, neatly cropped grass around it, a dormitory beside, outbuildings behind, a graveyard. It was very peaceful here. Crispin saw cows and a goat in the meadow beyond the graves.

Had he been more aware of time and place, had his mind not been wrestling with unseen things, he might have realized where they were and been prepared. He did not, and he was not.

They tied the mule by the low wall, went through the unlocked iron gate and up the stone path. There were late-season flowers growing beside it, lovingly tended. Crispin saw an herb garden to the left, back toward the meadow. They opened the heavy wooden door of the chapel and the three of them went in and Crispin looked at the walls, as his eyes slowly adjusted to the muted light, and then, stepping forward, he looked up at the dome.

DIVISIONS OF FAITH IN the worship of Jad had led to burnings and torture and war almost from the beginning. The doctrine and liturgy of the sun god, emerging from the promiscuous gods and goddesses of Trakesia during the early years of the Empire of Rhodias, had not evolved without their share of schisms and heresies and the frequently savage responses to these. The god was in the sun, or he was behind the sun. The world had been born in light, or it had been released from ice and darkness by holy light. At one time the god was thought to die in winter and be reborn in the spring, but the gentle cleric who had expounded this had been ordered torn apart between cavalry horses by a High Patriarch in Rhodias. For a brief time, elsewhere, it had been taught that the two moons were Jad's offspring—a belief more than halfway to the doctrines of the Kindath, who named them sisters of the god and equal to him in disturbing ways. This unfortunate fallacy, too, had required a number of deaths to extirpate.

The varying forms of belief in Heladikos—as mortal son, as half-mortal child, as god—were only the most obdurate and enduring of these conflicts waged in the holy name of Jad. Emperors and Patriarchs, first in Rhodias and then Sarantium, wavered and grew firm and then reversed their positions and tolerance, and Heladikos the Charioteer moved in and out of acceptance and fashion, much as the sun moved in and out of cloud on a windy day.

In the same way, amongst all these bitter wars, fought with words and iron and flame, the rendered image of Jad himself had become a line of demarcation over the years, a battlefield of art and belief, of ways of imagining the god who sent life-bringing light and battled darkness every night beneath his world while men slept their precarious sleep.

And this modest, beautifully made old chapel in a quiet, isolated place on the ancient Imperial road in Sauradia was that dividing line.

HE'D HAD NO WARNING at all. Crispin took some steps forward in the subdued, delicate light of the chapel, noting, absently, the old-fashioned mosaics of intertwined flowers on the walls, and then looked up.

A moment later, he found himself lying on the cold stones of the floor, struggling to breathe, gazing up at his god.

He ought to have known what was waiting for him in this place. Even setting out from Varena it had crossed his mind that the road through Sauradia would take him past this chapel at some point—he wasn't certain exactly where, but he knew it was on the Imperial road—and he'd even been looking forward to seeing what the old craftsmen had done in their primitive fashion, rendering Jad in the eastern way.

But the intensity and the terror of what had happened this morning in the fog and the wood had driven that thought so far from him that he was wide-open, defenseless, utterly exposed to the force of what had been done by mortal men on this dome. After the Aldwood and the bison and Linon, Crispin had no barriers within himself, no refuge, and the power of the image above hammered into him, driving all strength from his body so that he fell down like a pantomime grotesque or a helpless drunk in an alley behind a caupona.

He lay flat on his back staring up at the figure of the god: the bearded face and upper torso of Jad massively rendered across virtually the entirety of the dome. A gaunt image, battle-weary and grim, weighted down—he registered the heavy cloak, the bowed shoulders—by his burdens and the stern evils of his children. A figure as absolute and terrifying as the bison had been: another dark, massive head, against the pale, golden tesserae of the sun behind him. A figure seeming as if it would descend in overwhelming judgment from above. The image encompassed the head and shoulders, both lifted hands. No more, no *room* on the dome for more. Spreading across the softly illuminated space, gazing down with eyes large as some figures Crispin had made in his day, it was so out of scale it should never have worked, and yet Crispin had not in all his life seen anything made that touched the strength of this.

He had *known* this work was here, westernmost of all the renderings of the god done with the full dark eastern beard and those black, haunted eyes: Jad as judge, as worn, beleaguered warrior in deathly combat, not the shining, blue-eyed, golden sun-figure of Crispin's west. But knowing and *seeing* were so far from the same thing it was as if . . . as if one was the world and the other the half-world of hidden powers.

The old craftsmen. Their primitive fashion.

So he had thought, back home. Crispin felt an aching in his heart for the depths of his own folly, the revealed limitations of his understanding and skill. He felt naked before this, grasping that in its own way this work of mortal men in a domed chapel was as much a manifestation of the holy as the bison with its blood-smeared horns in the wood, and as appalling. The fierce, wild power of Ludan, accepting sacrifice in his grove, set against the immensity of craft and comprehension on this dome, rendering in glass and stone a deity as purely humbling. How did one move from one of these poles to the other? How did mankind *live* between such extremes?

For the deepest mystery, the pulsing heart of the enigma, was that as he lay on his back, paralyzed by revelation, Crispin saw that the eyes were the same. The world's sorrow he'd seen in the *zubir* was here in the sun god above him, distilled by nameless artisans whose purity of vision and faith unmanned him. Crispin was actually unsure for a moment if he'd ever be able to get up, to reassert his self-control, his will.

He struggled to disentangle the elements of the work here, to gain some mastery over it and himself. Deep brown and obsidian in the eyes, to make them darker and stronger than the framing brown hair, shoulder length. The long face made longer by that straight hair and the beard; the arched, heavy eyebrows, deeply etched forehead, other lines scoring the cheeks—the skin so pale between beard and hair it showed as nearly gray. Then down to the rich, luxurious blue of the god's robe beneath his cloak which was shot through, Crispin saw, with a dazzling myriad of contrasting colors for a woven texture and the hinted play and power of light in a god whose power *was* light.

And then the hands. The hands were heartbreaking. Contorted, elongated fingers with the ascetic spiritualism suggested by that, but there was more: these were no cleric's fingers, no hands of repose and clasped meditation; they were both scarred. One finger on the left hand had clearly been broken; it was crooked, the knuckle swollen: red and brown tesserae against white and gray. These hands had wielded weapons, had been cut, frozen, known savage war against ice and black emptiness in the endless defense of mortal children whose understanding was . . . that of children, no more.

And the sorrow and judgment in the dark eyes was linked to what had happened to those hands. The colors, Crispin saw—the craftsman in him marveling—brought hands and eyes inescapably together. The vivid, unnaturally raised veins on the wrists of both pale hands used the same brown and obsidian that were in the eyes. He knew, intuitively, that this precise pairing of tesserae would exist nowhere else on the dome. The eyes of sorrow and indictment, the hands of suffering and war. A god who stood between his unworthy children and the dark, offering sunlight each morning in their brief time of life, and then his own pure Light afterward, for the worthy.

Crispin thought of Ilandra, of his girls, of the plague ravaging like a rabid carnivore through all the world, and he lay on cold stone beneath this image of Jad and understood what it was saying to him, to all those here below: that the god's victory was never assured, never to be taken for granted. It was *this*, he realized, that the unknown mosaicists of long ago were reporting on this dome to their brethren with this vast, weary god against the soft gold of his sun.

"Are you all right? *My lord!* Are you all right?"

He became aware that Vargos was addressing him with an urgency and concern that almost seemed amusing, after all they had survived today. It wasn't especially uncomfortable on the stones, though cold. He moved a hand vaguely. It was still somewhat difficult to breathe, actually. It was better when he didn't look up. Kasia, he saw as he turned his head, was standing a little apart, staring at the dome.

Looking over at her, he grasped something else: Vargos knew this place. He'd been along this road, back and forth, for years. The girl would never have seen this incarnation of Jad either, had most likely never even heard of it. She'd only come from the north a year ago, forced into slavery and the faith of the sun god, had only *known* Jad as a young, fair-haired, blue-eyed god, a direct descendant—though this she wouldn't know—of the solar deity in the pantheon of the Trakesians centuries ago.

"What do you see?" he said to her. His voice rasped in his throat.

Vargos turned to follow his gaze to the girl. Kasia looked over at him anxiously, then away. She was very pale.

"I . . . he . . ." She hesitated. They heard footsteps. Crispin struggled to a sitting position and saw a cleric approaching in the white robes of the order of the Sleepless Ones. He understood now why it was so quiet here. These were the holy men who stayed awake all night praying while the god fought daemons beneath the world. *Mankind has duties*, the figure overhead was saying, *this is an unending war*. These men believed that and embodied it in their rituals. The image above and the order of clerics praying in the long nights fit together. The men who made the mosaic, so long ago, would have known that.

"Tell us," he said quietly to Kasia as the white-clad figure, small, round-faced, full-bearded, came over to them.

"He . . . doesn't think he is winning," she said finally. "The battle."

The cleric stopped at that. He eyed the three of them gravely, apparently unsurprised to find a man sitting on the floor.

"He isn't *certain* he is," the cleric said to Kasia, speaking Sarantine, as she had. "There are enemies, and man does evil, abetting them. It is never sure, this battle. Which is why we must be a part of it."

"Do we know who achieved this?" Crispin asked quietly.

The cleric looked surprised. "Their names? The craftsmen?" He shook his head. "No. There must have been many of them, I suppose. They were artisans . . . and a holy spirit possessed them for a time."

"Yes, of course," Crispin said, rising to his feet. He hesitated. "Today is the Day of the Dead here," he murmured, not sure why he was saying that. Vargos steadied him with a hand at his elbow and then stepped back.

"I understand as much," the cleric said mildly. He had an unlined, gentle face. "We are surrounded by pagan heresies. They do evil to the god."

"Is that all they are to you?" Crispin asked. In his mind was a voice—a young woman, a crafted bird, a soul: *I am yours, lord, as I ever was from the time I was brought here.*

"What else should they be to me?" the white-robed man said, raising his eyebrows.

It was a fair question, Crispin supposed. He caught an anxious look from Vargos and let the matter rest. "I am sorry for . . . how you found me," he said. "I was affected by the image."

The cleric smiled. "You aren't the first. Might I guess you are from the west . . . Batiara?"

Crispin nodded. It wasn't a difficult conjecture. His accent would have given that away.

"Where the god is yellow-haired and comely, his eyes blue and untroubled as summer skies?" The white-robed man was smiling complacently.

"I am aware of how Jad is rendered in the west, yes." Crispin had never been much inclined to be lectured by anyone.

"And as a last hazarded guess, may I assume you are an artisan of some sort?"

Kasia looked astonished, Vargos wary. Crispin eyed the cleric coolly. "A clever surmise," he said. "How would you know this?"

The man's hands were clasped at his waist. "As I said, you aren't the first westerner to react this way. And it is often those who make their own attempts at such things who . . . are most affected."

Crispin blinked. He might feel humbled by what was on the dome, but "attempts at such things" was not acceptable.

"I am impressed by your sagacity. It is indeed a fine piece of work. After I attend to certain requests from the Emperor in Sarantium, I might be willing to return and supervise the needed repairs to the erratic groundwork done on the dome."

The cleric's turn to blink, pleasingly. "That work was done by holy men with a holy vision," he said indignantly.

"I have no doubt of it. One shame is that we don't know their names, to honor them, another is that they lacked technique equal to their vision. You do know that tiles have begun to dislodge toward the right side of the dome, as we face the altar. Parts of the god's cloak and left forearm appear to have recklessly chosen to detach themselves from the rest of his august form."

The cleric looked up, almost reluctantly.

"Of course, you may have a parable or a liturgical explanation for this," Crispin added. In the oddest way, fencing with the man was restoring his equilibrium. Not necessarily a *proper* thing, he supposed, but he needed it just now.

"You would propose *changing* the figure of the god?" The man seemed genuinely aghast.

Crispin sighed. "It has *been* changed, good cleric. When your extremely pious artisans did this work centuries ago, Jad had a robe and a left arm." He pointed. "Not the remains of dried-out groundwork."

The cleric shook his head. His features had reddened. "What manner of man looks up at glory and speaks of daring to set his own hands upon it?"

Crispin was quite calm now. "A descendant in the craft of those who did it in the first place. Lacking, perhaps, their piety, but with a better understanding of the technique of mosaic. I should add that the dome also appears near to losing some of its golden sun, to the left. I'd need to be up on a scaffold to be certain, but it seems some tesserae have dislodged there as well. If that goes, then the god's hair will soon begin to fall out, I fear. Are you prepared to have Jad come down upon you, not in a thunderous descent but in a dribble of glass and stone?"

"This is the most profane heresy!" the cleric snapped, making the sign of the disk.

Crispin sighed. "I am sorry you see it that way. I do not mean to provoke you. Or not only that. The setting bed on the dome was done in an old-fashioned way. One layer, and most likely with a mixture of materials we now understand to be less enduring than others. It is—as we all know—not holy Jad above us, but his rendering by mortal men. We worship the god, not the image, I understand." He paused. This was a matter of extreme contention in some quarters. The cleric opened his mouth as if to answer, but then closed it again.

Crispin went on. "Mortals have their limitations, and this, too, we all know. Sometimes new things are discovered. It is no criticism of those who achieved this dome to note such a truth. Lesser men may preserve the work of greater. With competent assistants I could probably ensure the restored image above us would remain for several hundred years to come. It would take a season of work. Perhaps a little less or more. But I can tell you that without such intervention those eyes and hands and hair will begin to litter the stones around us soon. I would be sorry to see it. This is a singular work."

"It is unmatched in the world!"

"I believe that."

The cleric hesitated. Kasia and Vargos, Crispin saw, were eyeing him with astonishment. It occurred to him—with a restorative amusement—that neither of them had had any reason to believe he was *good* for anything to this point. A worker in mosaic had little enough chance to show his gifts or skill walking the emptiness of Sauradia.

In that moment, in an intervention Crispin could have called divine, a tinkling sound was heard across the floor. Crispin repressed a smile and walked over. He knelt, looking carefully, and found a brownish tessera without difficulty. He turned it over. The backing was dry, brittle. It crumbled to powder as he brushed it with a finger. He rose and walked back to the other three, handing the mosaic piece to the cleric.

"A holy message?" he said dryly. "Or just a piece of dark stone from"—he looked up—"most likely the robe again, on the right side?"

The cleric opened his mouth and closed it, exactly as he had before. He was undoubtedly regretting, Crispin thought, that this had been his day to be awake in daylight and deal with visitors to the chapel. Crispin looked up again at the severe majesty overhead and regretted his bantering tone. Attempts at such *things* had rankled, but it hadn't been personal, and he ought to have been above such pettiness. Especially today, and here.

Men, he thought—perhaps especially *this* man, Caius Crispus of Varena—seemed to escape so rarely from the concerns and trivial umbrages that made up their daily lives. He ought to have been moved beyond them today, surely. Or perhaps—a sudden, quite different sort of thought—perhaps it was because he'd been taken so far beyond that he needed to find his way back in this manner?

He looked at the cleric, and then up again at the god. The god's image. It *could* be done, with skillful people. Probably close to half a year, however, realistically. He decided, abruptly, that they would stay the night here. He would speak to the leader of this holy order, make amends for irony and levity. If they could be made to understand what was happening on the dome, perhaps when Crispin reached the City bearing a letter from them, the Chancellor, or someone else—the Imperial Mosaicist?—might be enlisted in an attempt to preserve this splendor. He'd teased and been flippant, Crispin thought. Perhaps he'd make redress by an act of restoration, in memory of this day and perhaps of his own dead.

In the unfolding of events, of a man's life, so many things can intervene. Just as he was not to see his torch of Heladikos in the chapel outside Varena by glittering candlelight, so this, too, was a task Crispin was never to perform, though his intentions in that moment were deeply sincere and nearly pious. Nor did they, in fact, end up spending that night in the dormitory of the ancient sanctuary.

The cleric slipped the brown tessera into his robe. But before anyone could speak again, they heard a distant and then a growing thunder of horses from the road.

The cleric looked to the doors, startled. Crispin exchanged a sharp glance with Vargos. Then they heard, even through the doors and well back from the road, a loudly shouted command to halt. The hoofbeats stopped. There was a jingling, then boots on the path and the voices of men.

The doors burst open admitting a spearshaft of daylight and half a dozen cavalry soldiers. They strode forward, heavy steps on stone. None of them looked up at the dome. Their leader, a burly, black-haired, very tall man, carrying his helmet under one arm, stopped before the four of them. He nodded to the cleric, stared at Crispin.

"Carullus, tribune of the Fourth Sauradian. My respects. Saw the mule. We are looking for someone on this road. Would you be named Martinian of Varena, by any chance?"

Crispin, unable to think of any adequate reason to do otherwise, nodded his head in agreement. He was, in fact, speechless.

Carullus of the Fourth's formal expression gave way on the instant to mingled disdain and triumph—a remarkable conjunction, in fact, a challenge ever to render in tesserae. He leveled a thick, indicting finger at Crispin. "Where the *fuck* have you been, you shit-smeared Rhodian slug? Sticking it into every poxed whore on the road? What are you *doing* on the road instead of at sea? You've been awaited in the fucking City for *weeks* now by his thrice-exalted Majesty, His Imperial Magnificence, the fucking Emperor Valerius II himself. You turd."

"YOU ARE A MENTALLY defective idiot of a Rhodian, you know."

An entirely unexpected memory came to Crispin with the words, forming slowly, retrieved from some lost corner of childhood. It was amazing, really, what the mind could dredge forth. At the most absurd moments. He had been stunned unconscious when he was about nine years old, playing "Siege" with friends around and on top of a woodshed. He'd failed to repel a ferocious Barbarian assault from two older boys and had pitched from the shed roof, landing on his head among logs.

From that morning until the guardsmen of Queen Gisel had clapped a sack of flour over his head and clubbed him into submission the experience had not been repeated.

It had now, Crispin grasped through the miasma of an excruciating headache, been duplicated twice in the same autumn season. His thoughts were extremely muddled. For a moment he'd attributed the obscene words he'd just heard to Linon. But Linon was sardonic not profane, she called him *imbecile* not *idiot*, spoke Rhodian not Sarantian, and she was gone.

Recklessly, he opened his eyes. The world shifted and heaved, appallingly. He closed them again quickly, near to throwing up.

"A genuine fool," the heavy voice went on implacably, "ought never to be allowed out of doors. What in holy thunder do you *expect* to happen when a foreigner—a *Rhodian* at that!—calls a Sarantine cavalry tribune a fart-faced goat-fucker in the presence of his own men?"

It wasn't Linon. It was the soldier.

Carullus. Of the Fourth Sauradian. That was the swine's name.

The swine went on, his tone a gross exaggeration of patience now. "Have you the least idea of the position you put me in? The Imperial army is *entirely* dependent on respect for authority . . . and regular payment, of course . . . and you left me next to no choice at all. I couldn't draw a sword in a chapel. I couldn't strike you with my fist . . . giving you far too much dignity. Flattening you with a helm was just about the only *possible* course. I didn't even swing hard. Be grateful that I'm known for a kindly man, you snot-faced Rhodian prig, and that you've a beard. The bruise won't show as much before it heals. You'll be as ugly as you've always been, not more than that."

Carullus of the Fourth chuckled. He actually chuckled.

He'd been slugged with a helmet. It was coming back to him. On the cheekbone and jaw. Crispin had a memory of a swift, heavy arm coming across, then nothing more. He attempted to move his jaw up and down, and then from side to side. A searing pain made him gasp, but movement was possible, it seemed. He continued to try opening his eyes at intervals, but the world insisted upon moving about in a sick-making fashion whenever he did.

"Nothing's broken," Carullus said easily. "Told you, I'm a good-natured man. Bad for discipline, but there it is. There it is. The god made me what I am. You really must not think you can walk the roads of the Sarantine Empire making insults—however clever—to the face of military officers in the presence of their troops, my western friend. I have fellow tribunes and chiliarchs who would have dragged you straight outside and run you through in the graveyard to save lugging your corpse anywhere. I, on the other hand, do not entirely subscribe to the general loathing and contempt for the sanctimonious, cowardly, shit-smeared Rhodian catamites that most soldiers of the Empire profess. I actually find you people amusing at times and, as I said before, I'm a kindly man. Ask my troops."

Carullus, a tribune of the Sauradian Fourth, liked the cadences of his own voice, it appeared. Crispin wondered how and how soon he could kill this kindly man.

"Where . . . am I?" It hurt to talk.

"In a litter. Traveling east."

This information brought no inconsiderable relief: it seemed the world was indeed moving, and the perception of a weaving landscape and an up-and-down-bobbing military conversationalist beside him was not merely a product of his braincase having being rearranged again.

There was something urgent to be said. He struggled and then remembered what it was. Forced his eyes open again, finally grasping that Carullus was riding beside him, on a dark gray horse. "My man?" Crispin asked, moving his jaw as little as possible. "Vargos."

Carullus shook his head, his own mouth a thin line in a smooth-shaven face. "Slaves who strike a soldier—any soldier, let alone an officer—are torn apart in a public execution. Everyone knows that. He nearly knocked me down."

"He's not a slave, you contemptible shit!"

Carullus said, mildly enough, "Careful. My men might hear you, and I'd have to respond. I know he isn't a slave. We looked at his papers. He'll be whipped and castrated when we get to camp, but not killed between the horses."

Crispin felt his heart thump then, hard. "He's a free man, an Imperial citizen and my hired servant. You touch him at absolute peril. I mean it. Where's the girl? What's happened to her?"

"She *is* a slave, from one of the inns. And young enough. We can use her at camp. She spat in my face, you know."

Crispin forced himself to be calm; anger would make him nauseated again, and useless. "She was sold from the inn. She belongs to me. You will know this, having gone through those papers, too, you pustulent excrescence. If she is touched or harmed, or if the man is harmed in any way, my first request of the Emperor will be your testicles sliced off and bronzed into gaming dice. Be clear about this."

Carullus sounded amused. "You really are an idiot, aren't you? Though *pustulent excrescence* is good, I must say. How do you tell anything to the Emperor at all if it is reported that you and your companions were found by our company to have been robbed, sexually penetrated in various ways, and foully murdered by outlaws on the road today? I repeat, the man and the girl will be dealt with in the usual manner."

Crispin said, still struggling to keep his composure, "There is an idiot here, but he's on the horse not in the litter. The Emperor will receive a precise report of our encounter from the Sleepless Ones, along with their earnest petition that I return to supervise the restoration of the image of Jad on the dome, as we were discussing when you burst in. We were neither robbed nor killed. We were accosted in a holy place by slovenly horsemen under an incompetent dung-faced tribune, and a man personally summoned by Valerius II to Sarantium was struck by a weapon in the face. Do you prefer a reprimand leavened by my conceding I provoked you, or castration and death, Tribune?"

There was a satisfying period of silence. Crispin brought up a hand and tenderly touched his jaw.

He looked over and up at the horseman, squinting into the light. Odd specks and colors danced erratically in his vision. "Of course," he added, "you could turn back west, kill the clerics—all of them will know the story by now—and claim we were *all* robbed and violated and killed by those evil brigands on the road. You could do that, you dried-out rat dropping."

"Stop insulting me," Carullus said, but without force this time. He rode some further distance in silence. "I had forgotten about the fucking cleric," he admitted, at length.

"You forgot about who signed my Permit, too," Crispin said. "And who requested me to come to the City. You've read the papers. Get on with it, Tribune: give me half a reason to be forgiving. You might consider begging."

Instead, Carullus of the Fourth Sauradian began to swear. Impressively, in fact, and for quite some time. Finally he swung down from his horse, gestured at someone Crispin couldn't see, and handed off the reins to the soldier who hurried up. He began walking alongside Crispin's litter. "Rot your eyes, Rhodian. We *can't* have civilians—especially foreigners—insulting army officers! Can't you *see* that? The Empire is six months behind in their pay. Six months, with winter coming! Everything's going for *buildings*." He said the word like another obscenity. "Have you any notion what morale is like?"

"The man. The girl," Crispin said, ignoring this. "Where are they? Are they hurt?"

"They're here, they're here. She's not been touched, we've no time for play. You are *late*, I told you. That's why we were riding to look for you. An undignified, Jad-cursed order if ever there was one."

"Oh, shit yourself! The *courier* was late. I wrapped up affairs and left five days after he came! It was past the season for sailing. You think I *wanted* to be on this road? Find *him* and ask questions. Titaticus, or something. An idiot with a red nose. Kill him with your helmet. How is Vargos?"

Carullus looked back over his shoulder. "He's on a horse."

"What? Riding?"

The tribune sighed. "Tied across the back of one. He was . . . worked over a little. He *struck* me after you fell. He can't *do* that!"

Crispin tried to sit up, and failed, miserably. He closed his eyes and opened them again when this seemed practical. "Listen to me carefully. If that man has been seriously injured, I *will* have your rank and your pension revoked, if not your life. This is an oath. Get him in a litter and have him tended to. Where's the nearest physician who doesn't kill people?"

"At camp. He *struck* me," Carullus repeated, plaintively. But he turned, after a moment, and gestured again, behind him. When another soldier trotted up on his horse, Carullus murmured a rapid volley of instructions, too softly for Crispin to hear. The cavalryman muttered unhappily but turned to obey.

"It is done," Carullus said, turning back to Crispin. "They say he's had nothing broken. Won't walk or piss easy for a while, but nothing that won't pass. Are we friends?"

"Fuck yourself with your sword. How far to your camp?"

"Tomorrow night. He's all right, I'm telling you. I don't lie."

"No, you just shit all over your uniform when you realize you've made the mistake of your life."

"Jad's blood! You swear more than I do! Martinian, there is fault here both ways. I am being reasonable."

"Only because a holy man saw what happened, you bloated fart, you pantomime buffoon."

Carullus laughed suddenly. "True enough. Number it among the great blessings of your life. Give money to the Sleepless Ones until the day you die. *Bloated fart* is also good, by the way. I like it. I'll use it. Do you want a drink?"

The situation was outrageous, and he was only moderately reassured about Vargos's condition, but it did begin to appear that Carullus of the Fourth Sauradian was not entirely a lout, and he did want a drink.

Crispin nodded his head, carefully.

They brought him a flask, and later an aide to the tribune cleaned Crispin's bloodied cheek and jawline with decent care when they halted for a brief rest. He saw Vargos then. They had indeed worked him over, and more than a little, but had evidently chosen to reserve more substantial chastisement until such time as everyone at their camp could watch the fun. Vargos was awake by then. His face was puffy from the blows and there was an ugly gash on his forehead, but he was in a litter now. Kasia was led up, apparently untouched, though with that furtive, doe-like look in her eyes again, as if caught in torchlight by night hunters and frozen in place with apprehension. He remembered his first sight of her. Yesterday at about this time in the front room of Morax's inn. *Yesterday?* That was astonishing. It would give him another headache if he dwelled on it. He was an idiot. An imbecile.

Linon was gone, to her god, into silence in the Aldwood.

"We have an escort to the military camp," Crispin said to both of them, still moving his jaw as little as possible. "I have achieved an understanding with the tribune. We will not be harmed further. In return I will allow him to continue functioning as a man and a soldier. I am sorry if you were hurt, or frightened. It seems I am now to be accompanied to Sarantium the rest of the way. There was more urgency to my summons than was evident in the documents themselves or their delivery. Vargos, they have promised a physician at their camp tomorrow night to tend to you, and I will release you from my service then. The tribune swears you will come to no harm and I believe he is honest. A gross pig, but honest."

Vargos shook his head. He mumbled something Crispin couldn't make out. His lips were badly swollen, the words garbled.

"He wants to come with you," Kasia said softly. The sun was low, now, behind her, almost straight along the road. It was growing colder, twilight coming. "He says he cannot serve on this road anymore, after this morning. They will kill him."

Crispin, after a moment's thought, realized that had to be true. He remembered a blow struck by Vargos in the dark of the innyard before dawn this morning. Vargos, too, had intervened in this sacrifice. His own was not the only life in the midst of change, it seemed. In the last bronze glow of the sun underlighting clouds he looked closely at the man in the other litter. "This is correct? You wish me to retain your services all the way to the City?"

Vargos nodded his head.

Crispin said, "Sarantium is a different world, you know that."

"Know that," Vargos said, and this time Crispin heard it clearly. "Your man."

He felt something unexpected then, like a shaft of light through everything else that day. It took him a moment to recognize it as happiness. Crispin stretched out a hand from his litter and the other man reached across the space between to touch it with his own.

"Rest now," said Crispin, struggling to keep his own eyes open. His head was hurting a great deal. "It will be all right." He wasn't sure he believed that, but after a moment he saw that Vargos had indeed closed his eyes and was asleep. Crispin touched his bruised chin again and struggled not to yawn: it hurt when he opened his mouth so much. He looked at the girl. "We'll talk tonight," he mumbled. "Need to sort out your life, too."

He saw that quick, flaring apprehension in her again. Not a surprise, really. Her life, what had happened to her this year, and this morning. He saw Carullus coming over: long strides, his shadow behind him on the road. Not a bad man, really. An easy laugh, sense of humor. Crispin *had* provoked him. In front of his soldiers. It was true. Not the wisest thing. Might admit that later. Might not. Might be better not.

He was asleep before the tribune reached his litter.

"Don't hurt him!" Kasia said to the officer as he came up, though Crispin never heard it. She stepped quickly between the litter and the soldier.

"I *can't* hurt him, girl," said the tribune of the Fourth Sauradian, shaking his head bemusedly, looking at her. "He has both my balls on a smith's anvil and the hammer in his hand."

"Good!" she said. "Keep remembering that." Her expression was fierce, northern, not at all doelike just then.

The soldier laughed aloud. "Jad rot the moment I saw the three of you in that chapel," he said. "Now Inici slave girls tell me what to do? What were you even doing abroad on the fucking Day of the Dead, anyhow? Don't you know it is dangerous today in Sauradia?"

She went pale, he saw, but made no reply. There was a tale here, his instincts told him. They also told him he wasn't likely to hear it. He could have her beaten for disrespect, but knew he wouldn't. He really was a kindhearted man, Carullus told himself. The Rhodian didn't know how lucky he was.

Carullus also had a sense—a mild one, to be sure—that his own future might *possibly* be at risk as a result of this encounter at the sanctuary. He'd seen, a little too late, the Rhodian's Permit, and who had signed it, and had read the specific terms of the Emperor's request for the presence of a certain Martinian of Varena.

An artisan. Only an artisan, but personally invited to the City to lend his *great expertise and knowledge* to the Emperor's new Sanctuary of Jad's Holy Wisdom. Another building. Another fucking building.

Wisdom, holy or wholly practical, suggested to Carullus that he exercise a measure of caution here. The man talked a *very* confident game, and he had papers to back him up. He did own the girl, too; those documents had been in the satchel as well. Only since last night, mind you. Part of that story he wasn't going to learn, Carullus guessed. The girl was still glaring at him with those blue northern eyes. She had a strong, clever face. Yellow hair.

If the cleric hadn't been watching what had happened, Carullus *could* have had the three of them killed and dropped in a ditch. He probably wouldn't have. He was far too soft, he told himself. Hadn't even broken the Rhodian's jaw with his helmet. Shameful, really. Respect for the army had disappeared in this generation. The Emperor's fault? Possibly, though you could be drummed out of the ranks with a slit nose for saying as much. Money went to monuments these days, to Rhodian artisans, to shameful payments to the butt-fucked Bassanids in the east, instead of to honest soldiers who kept the City and the Empire safe. Word was that even Leontes, the army's beloved, the golden-haired Supreme Strategos, spent all his time now in the City, in the Imperial

Precinct, dancing courtly attendance on the Emperor and Empress, playing games of a morning with balls and mallets on horseback, instead of smashing Bassanid or northern enemies into the puling rabble they were. He had a rich wife now. Another reward. Wives could be a world of trouble to a soldier, Carullus thought, had always thought. Whores, if they were clean, were *much* less bother.

They had halted long enough. He gestured to his second in command. Darkness was coming and the next inn was a ways yet. They could only move as fast as the carried men. The litters were hoisted, the litter-bearers' horses collected and led along. The girl gave him a last fierce glare, then began walking between the two sleeping men, barefoot, looking small and fragile in a brown, too-large cloak in the last of the light. She was pretty enough. Thin for his taste, but spirited, and one couldn't have everything. The artisan would be useless to her tonight. One had to exercise a bit of discretion with the personal slaves of other men, but Carullus wondered absently what his best smile might achieve here. He tried to catch her eye, but failed.

HE WAS IN SOME real pain but his father and brothers had given him worse beatings in his day and Vargos was not by nature inclined to feel sorry for himself or surrender to discomfort. He had struck an army tribune in the chest today, nearly felled him; by rights they could kill him for that. They had intended to, he knew, when they reached the camp. Then Martinian had intervened, somehow. Martinian did . . . unexpected things. In the darkness of the inn's crowded main-floor sleeping room, Vargos shook his head. So much had happened since last night at Morax's.

He thought he had seen the old god this morning.

Ludan, in his guise of the *zubir*, in the Aldwood. In a sacred grove of the Aldwood. He had stood there, knelt in that grove . . . and had walked alive from there out into the misty field again because Martinian of Varena had carried some kind of magicked bird about his neck.

The *zubir*. Against the memory of that, what were bruises or a swollen mouth or a stream of red when he pissed tonight? He had seen what he had seen, and lived. Was he blessed? *Could* such a man as he be blessed? Or was he being warned—a sudden thought—to forsake the other god, the one behind the sun, Jad and his chariot-driving son?

Or was Martinian right about this, too: that the one power need not mean a denial of the other? No cleric Vargos knew would accept that, but Vargos had already decided that the Rhodian was worth listening to. And staying with.

All the way to Sarantium, it seemed. There was apprehension in that thought. Megarium, on the coast in the west of Sauradia, was the largest city Vargos had ever seen, and he hadn't liked it. The confining walls, the crowded, filthy, noisy streets. Carts rumbling by all night long, brawling voices when the taverns spilled their denizens, no calm or quietude even in the dark when the moons rode. And Vargos knew by tale what Sarantium was: as much beyond provincial Megarium as golden-haired Leontes, Strategos of the Empire, was beyond Vargos of the Inicii.

He couldn't stay here, though. It was the simplest of truths. He'd made a decision in the dark of a hallway in Morax's late last night and had sealed it with a blow of his staff in the predawn courtyard amid smoky torches and fog. When you can't go back and you can't stay still, you move forward, nothing to think about, get on with it. The sort of thing his father would have said, draining another flask of home-brewed ale, wiping his mustache with his wet sleeve, gesturing with a thick arm for one of the women to bring more beer. It wasn't a complex decision, seen a certain way, and the grace here was that there was a man worth following and a place to go.

Vargos lay on a perfectly decent cot in the next inn east from Morax's and listened to snoring soldiers and laughter from the common room. They were still drinking there, Martinian and the tribune.

He lay quietly, unable to sleep, and thought of the Aldwood again. Of the *zubir* in the middle of the Imperial road in a swirling away of fog, then appearing—somehow—right beside them in the misty field an instant after. He would think of these things all his days, Vargos knew. And remember how Pharus had looked in the road when they came back out.

The stablemaster had been dead before they went into the wood, but when they stood above his body, after, they saw what else had been done to him. Vargos would swear by his mother's life and his own soul that no man had walked up to where the dead man lay. Whatever had claimed the man's heart had not been mortal.

He'd heard a lifeless bird speak aloud with a woman's voice to the *zubir*. He'd led a man and a woman through the Aldwood and out. He'd even—and here, for the first time, Vargos smiled a little in the close darkness—struck a Sarantine officer, a *tribune*, and they'd only roughed him up a little, and then they had put him in a litter—a litter!—and *carried* him to this inn, because Martinian had made them. That memory, too, would stay with him. He would have enjoyed having his Jad-cursed father watch cavalrymen dismount to carry him along the Imperial road like some senator or merchant prince.

Vargos closed his eyes. An unworthy, vain thought, today of all days. Pride had no place in the soul tonight. He struggled to shape a proper prayer to Jad and to his son, the fire-bearer, asking guidance and forgiveness. In his mind's eye, though, he kept seeing again and again that ripped open chest of a dead man he'd known and the black *zubir* with blood on the short, curved horns. To whom did one pray?

He was going to the City. Sarantium. Where the Imperial Palace was and the Emperor, the Triple Walls and the Hippodrome. A hundred holy sanctuaries, he'd heard, and half a million people. He didn't really *believe* that last. He wasn't a northern lout anymore, to be gulled with gross, exaggerated tales. Men told lies in their pride.

Growing up, he had never imagined himself living anywhere but in their village. Then, after that changed one mild, bloody spring night, he'd expected to spend his days going back and forth along the Imperial road in Sauradia until he grew too old for that and took a position at the stable or the forge in one of the inns.

Life did unexpected things to you, Vargos of the Inicii thought in the darkness. You made a decision, or someone else made one, and there you were. There you were. He heard a familiar rustling sound, then a grunt and a sigh; someone had a woman with him on the far side of the room. He turned over on his side, carefully. He'd been kicked in the lower back. That was why his piss was red, why it hurt to turn.

They had a phrase along the Imperial road. *He's sailing to Sarantium*, they said when some man threw himself at an obvious and extreme hazard, risking all, changing everything one way or another, like a desperate gambler at dice putting his whole stake on the table. That was what he was doing.

Unexpected, really. Not his nature. Exciting, he had to admit. He tried to remember the last time he'd felt *excited*. Perhaps with a girl, but not really; that was different. Nice enough, though. Vargos wished he felt a little better. He knew two of the girls here fairly well and they liked him enough. On the other hand there were soldiers here. The girls would be busy all night. Just as well. He needed his sleep.

They were still laughing—and starting to sing now—in the common room. He felt himself drifting off. Martinian was there with the burly, smooth-faced tribune. Unexpected.

He dreamt that night that he was flying. Out of the inn and across the road under both moons and all the stars. West first, over the chapel of the Sleepless Ones, hearing their slow chanting in the night, seeing the candles burning through the windows of the dome. He flew past that image of holy Jad and turned north over the Aldwood.

League upon league he flew above the forest, north and farther north and farther, seeing the black trees touched by mingled moonlight in the iron cold. League upon league the great forest rolled, and Vargos wondered in his dream how anyone could do other than worship a power that dwelled therein.

Then west again for a time across the grass-covered ridges of soft hills and over the wide, slow river meandering south with the road beside it. Another forest on the other side of the gleaming water, as black, as vast, as Vargos flew over it, north and north in the clear, cold night. He saw where the oaks ended and the pines began, and then at last he saw by the moons a range of mountains he had always known, and he was flying lower over fields he had tilled himself in childhood, seeing a stream he had swum in during summers gone, and the first tiny outlying houses of the village, his own home near the small shrine and the Elder's house with the branch bound above the door, and then he saw the graveyard in his dream, and his father's grave.

IT WAS UNUSUAL FOR a man to travel any distance with a female slave, but it was learned by the soldiers of the Fourth Sauradian that the artisan had taken possession of the girl only the night before—some sort of wager won, the story went—and it was not at all unusual that a man might want a body with him on a windy autumn night. Why pay for a whore when you had your own woman to do the needful? The girl was too skinny to be really warm, but she was young, and yellow-haired, and probably had other talents.

The soldiers were aware by now that the Rhodian was more important than he looked. He had also formed an unlikely bond with their tribune over dinner. This was sufficiently surprising as to elicit its own measure of respect. The girl had been escorted, untouched, to the room assigned the artisan. Orders had been explicit. Carullus, who liked to describe himself to anyone who would listen as a gentle soul, was known to have had men crippled and turned out of his company to beg for botching orders on an assignment. His principal centurion was the only one who knew that this had been done once only, soon after Carullus's promotion to tribune and his command of five hundred. The centurion was under standing orders to make certain all new recruits knew the tale, properly embellished. It was useful for soldiers to be somewhat afraid of their officers.

KASIA, ABOUT TO SLEEP under a different roof from Morax's for the first time in a year, had settled beside the fire in the bedroom, feeding it the occasional log, to wait for the man who owned her now. The room was smaller than the better ones in Morax's inn, but it did have this fire. She sat on her cloak—Martinian's cloak—and gazed into the flames. Her grandmother had been skilled at reading futures in tongues of fire, but Kasia lacked any such gift and only found her mind drifting as she watched the fire dance. She was sleepy but there was no pallet in the room, only the one bed, and she had no idea what to expect when the Rhodian came upstairs. She could hear singing from below: Martinian and the man who had knocked him senseless. Men were very strange. She remembered the night before, in Morax's, when she had been sent up to find a thief in Martinian's room and everything had changed. He had saved her life twice now. At the inn and then, somehow, with a magical bird in the Aldwood.

She had been in the Aldwood today.

Had seen a power of the wood, known only in her grandmother's tales told by another smoky northern fire. She had walked from the sacred glade and the black forest alive, unsacrificed, to see that someone else's heart had been torn from his chest. A man she had known, had been forced to sleep with more than once. She had been violently ill, looking down at what remained of Pharus, unable not to remember him using her body, seeing what had now been done to his. She remembered the mist in the field, her hand on the mule. Voices, and the dogs hunting her. Martinian drawing his sword.

Already, curiously, the interlude in the forest itself was receding, blurring, becoming lost in a kind of fog of its own, too difficult to master or retain. Had she actually seen a *zubir* with those dark eyes, that dwarfing size? Had it really been that large? Kasia had the strangest sense, drowsy and half-entranced by the fire, that she was meant to have been dead by now, that her entire being was . . . unrooted, oddly light, because of that. A spark flew and landed on the cloak; she brushed it quickly away. Could the future of such a person be known? Could her grandmother have seen anything at all in this fire, or was Kasia now a blankness, unwritten from this moment forward, unknowable? A kind of living ghost? Or freed from fate because of that? *We'll talk tonight*, Martinian had said in the litter, before drifting to sleep again. *Need to sort out your life.*

Her life. A north wind was blowing outside; a clear night tonight but very cold, winter behind the wind. She put more wood—a little wastefully—on the fire. Saw that her hands were shaking. She laid one palm against her chest, feeling for the presence, the beating of her heart. After a while she realized her cheeks were wet and she wiped away the tears.

SHE HAD FALLEN INTO a shallow, fitful sleep, but they made a great deal of noise coming up the stairs and one of the merchants in the room across the hall shouted at them, causing a soldier to pound truculently on the shouter's door, eliciting further laughter from his fellows. Kasia was therefore on her feet in the middle of the room when they pushed open the unlocked door and Martinian stumbled in, supported—almost carried, in fact—by two soldiers of the Fourth Sauradian, with two more behind.

Weaving erratically, they led him over and spilled him onto the bed, good-humored and amused, despite—or because of—another furious volley of shouts from the room across. It was very late and they weren't being quiet. Kasia knew all about this: by law, the Imperial Inns had to put up as many as twenty soldiers at a time free of charge, doubling up paying guests to make room for them. They had to do it, but no one needed to *enjoy* the disruption of those nights.

One of the soldiers, a Soriyyan by his coloring, gazed at Kasia in the flicker of the firelight. "He's all yours," he said, gesturing to the man sprawled untidily on the bed. "Not much *good* to you. Want to come down with us? Men who c'n *hold* their wine, then hold a girl?"

"Shut fucking up," another said. "Orders."

The Soriyyan looked for a moment as if he'd object, but just then the man on the bed intoned, quite clearly, though with his eyes closed, "It is considered indisputable that the rhetoric of Kallimarchos was instrumental in the onset of the First Bassanid War. Given this as a proposition, ought later generations then lay the blame for so many cruel deaths at the philosopher's tomb? A vexing question."

There was an extreme, disconcerted silence, then two of the soldiers laughed. "Go to sleep, Rhodian," one of them said. "With luck, your head will be working again in the morning. Better men than you have been knocked senseless or bested in a drinking bout by the tribune."

"Not too many've had *both* happen," the Soriyyan added. "All hail the Rhodian!" More laughter. The Soriyyan grinned, pleased with himself. They left, closing the door with a bang.

Kasia winced, then walked over and slid home the bolt. She heard the four of them pound, in sequence, on the merchant's door across, then their boots sounded on the stairs descending to the ground-floor sleeping room.

She hesitated, then walked back toward the bed, looking uncertainly at the man lying there. The firelight made unstable shadows in the room. A log settled with a snapping sound. Martinian opened his eyes. "I begin to wonder if I was meant for the theater," he said, speaking in Sarantine and in his normal voice. "Two nights in succession I've had to do this. Have I a future in the pantomime, do you think?"

Kasia blinked. "You aren't . . . drunk, my lord?"

"Not especially."

"But . . . ?"

"Useful to let him best me in something. And Carullus can hold his wine. We might have been down there all night, and I need to sleep."

"Best you in *something*?" Kasia heard herself say, in a voice her mother and others in the village would have recognized. "He knocked you senseless and nearly broke your jaw."

"Trivial. Well, for him it was." Martinian rubbed absently at his bearded cheek. "He had a weapon, no great achievement. Kasia, they *carried* me here. And carried a servant who struck an army officer. I made them do that. He lost a lot of prestige, Carullus did. Decent enough man, for an Imperial soldier. And I wanted to sleep." He lifted a booted foot and she wrestled the boot off and then did the same with the other.

"They said my father could drink most men down onto the tavern floor or off their couches at a banquet. Guess I inherited that from him," Martinian murmured vaguely, pulling his tunic over his head. Kasia said nothing. Slaves did not ask questions. "He's dead," Martinian of Varena added. "On campaign against the Inicii. In Ferrieres." He wasn't *entirely* sober, she realized, whatever he might say. The drinking had gone on a long time. He was bare-chested now, had matted curls of dark red hair on his chest. She had seen that when she bathed him yesterday.

"I'm . . . Inici," she said, after a moment.

"I know. So's Vargos. Odd, in a way."

"The tribes in Sauradia are . . . different from those who went west to Ferrieres. The ones who went are . . . wilder."

"Wilder. I know. Why they went."

There was a silence. He pushed himself up on an elbow and looked around the room in the wavering light. "A fire," he said. "Good. Build it up, Kasia." He didn't call her Kitten. She went over quickly and knelt, putting on another log, pushing at it with the stick.

"They didn't bring you a cot," he said from the other side of the room. "They'll assume there's only one reason I bought you. I must tell you I was informed at great length downstairs that Inici girls, especially skinny ones, are evil-tempered and a waste of money. Is this true? Carullus did offer to spare me the duty of bedding you tonight while I was in pain. Nice of him, I thought. They should have put a cot in here."

Kasia stayed where she was, looking at the fire. It was difficult to sort out his tone sometimes. "I have your cloak to sleep on," she said finally. "Over here."

She busied herself sweeping ashes into the hearth. He probably *did* like boys, she decided. The pure-blooded Rhodians were said to be inclined that way, like Bassanids. It would make her nights easier.

"Kasia, where's home? Your home?" he said.

She swallowed abruptly. This was not what she'd expected.

She turned, still kneeling, to look at him. "North, my lord. Most of the way to Karch." He had finished undressing himself, she saw, and was under the blanket now, sitting up, arms around his knees. The firelight moved on the wall behind him.

"How were you captured? Or were you sold?"

She clasped her hands in her lap. "Sold," she said. "Last autumn. The plague took my father and brother. My mother had no choice."

"Not so," he said quickly. "There's always a choice. Sold her daughter off to feed herself? How civilized."

"No," Kasia said, clenching her fists. "She . . . we . . . talked about it. When the slave train came. It was me or my sister, or we'd all have died in the winter. You won't understand. There weren't enough men to do the fields or hunt; nothing had been harvested. They bought six girls from my village, with grain, and coins for the market town. There was a *plague*. That . . . changes things."

"Oh, I know," he said softly. Then, after another silence, "Why you? Not your sister?"

She hadn't expected that, either. No one had asked these things. "My mother thought she was . . . more likely to marry. With nothing to offer but herself."

"And you thought?"

Kasia swallowed again. Behind the beard and in the dim, uneven light it was impossible to discern his expression.

"Why . . . how does this matter?" she dared to ask.

He sighed. "You're right. It doesn't. Do you want to go home?"

"What?"

"Your village. I'm going to free you, you know. I have not the least need for a girl in Sarantium, and after what . . . happened to us today I do not propose to tempt any gods at all by making a profit on you." A Rhodian voice, a firelit room. Night, the edge of winter. The world being remade.

He said, "I don't think that . . . whatever we saw today . . . spared your life to clean house or heat bath water on a fire for me. Not that I have any notion why it spared *my* life. So, do you want to go back to your . . . oh, Jad. Jad's blood. Stop that, woman!"

She tried, biting her lip, wiping with the sooty backs of her hands at her streaming face. But how did one not weep, confronted with this? Last night she had known she would be dead today.

"Kasia, I mean it. I will throw you downstairs and let Carullus's men take turns with you! I *detest* crying women!"

She didn't think he really did. She thought he was pretending to be angry and fierce. She wasn't sure of what else she thought. Sometimes things happened too quickly. How does the riven tree explain the lightning bolt?

THE GIRL HAD FALLEN asleep, close to what remained of the fire's warmth. She was still in her tunic, wrapped in one cloak, pillowed on the other, under one of his blankets. He could have had her come into the bed, but the habit of sleeping alone since Ilandra died was entrenched by now, had become something mystical, talismanic. It was morbid and spirit-ridden, Crispin thought sleepily, but he wasn't about to try to break free of it this night with a slave girl bought for him the night before.

Though *slave girl* was unfair, really. She'd been as free as he was a year ago, a victim of the same plague summer that had smashed his own life. There were, he thought, any number of ways a life could be ruined.

Linon would have declared him an imbecile for having the girl sleep by the fire, he knew. Linon wasn't here. He had laid her down on wet grass by wet leaves in a forest this morning and walked away. *Remember me.*

What happens to an unhoused soul when a body and its heart are sacrificed to a god? Did Zoticus know the answer to that? What happens to the soul when the god comes to claim it, after all? Could an alchemist know? He had a difficult letter to write. *Tell him goodbye.*

A shutter was banging along the wall. Windy tonight; would be cold on the road tomorrow. The girl was coming east with him. It seemed both of these Inicii were. So odd, really, the circles and patterns one's life made. Or seemed to make. Patterns men tried to impose on their lives, for the comforting illusion of order?

He'd overheard men talking in a cookshop one day when he was still a boy. His father's head, he'd learned, had been completely severed from his shoulders. By an ax blow. Had landed some distance away, blood spraying from the toppling, headless body. Like a red fountain, one of the men told the other in an awed voice. It was dramatic enough, unsettling enough even for soldiers, to have become a tale: the death of the stonemason, Horius Crispus.

Crispin had been ten years old when he'd heard that. An Inici ax. The tribes that went west to Ferrieres had been wilder. Everyone said that. The girl had said it tonight. They'd pressed south into Batiara constantly, harrying the northern farms and villages. The Antae sent armies, including the urban militia, into Ferrieres just about every year. Usually they were successful campaigns, bringing back needed slaves. There were casualties, however. Always. The Inicii, even outnumbered, knew how to fight. A red fountain. He ought not to have heard such a thing. Not at ten years of age. He'd had dreams after, for a long time, had been unable to tell them to his mother. He was certain, even then, that the men in that cookshop would have been appalled had they known Horius's boy had been listening to them.

When her tears had stopped, Kasia's explanation tonight had been clear enough: there was no *place* for her at home anymore. Once sold, once a slave, sent up or down a hall to any man's room, she had no hope of a life among her own people. There was no going back, marrying, raising a family, sharing in the traditions of a tribe. Those traditions did not allow space for what she'd been forced to become, whatever she had been in the time before the plague when she had a father and brother for shelter.

A man captured and enslaved might escape and return to his village with honor and status—a living emblem of defiant courage. Not a girl sold to the traders for winter grain. The village of her childhood was barred to her now, on the far side of a doorway to the past, and there was no key. One could feel some sorrow for others' griefs, Crispin thought, awake and listening to the wind.

In the crowded, roiling streets of Sarantium, amid the arcades and workshops and sanctuaries and so many people from so many lands, she could—perhaps—create a life for herself. Not an easy or a sure thing for a woman, but she was young, had intelligence and spirit. No one need learn she had been an inn girl in Sauradia, and if they did . . . well, the Empress Alixana herself had been little better in her day. More expensive, but not different in kind, if any of the rumors were true.

Crispin supposed they slit your nose, or worse, for saying that. It was blowing hard outside. He could hear that shutter banging and the high keening of the wind. The Day of the Dead. *Was* it the wind?

The fire had taken the edge off the chill in the room, and he was under two good blankets. He thought, unexpectedly, of the queen of the Antae, young and afraid, her fingers in his hair as he knelt before her. The last time his head had been cracked like this. He was tired and his jaw hurt. He really shouldn't have been drinking with the soldiers tonight. Extremely stupid. Imbecilic, someone would have said. Decent man, though, Carullus of the Fourth. A surprise. Liked to hear himself talk. That image of the god, on the chapel dome. Mosaicists had made it, artisans, like himself. But not. Something else. He wished he knew their names, wished *someone* did. Would write to Martinian about that; try to order his thoughts. He could see the god's eyes in his mind right now. As vividly as he had ever seen anything. That fog this morning, nothing to see at all, all colors leached from the world. Voices pursuing, the dogs, the dead man. The forest and what took them into it. He had feared those woods at first sight, all the way back at the border, and yet he had walked in the Aldwood, after all, black, dense trees, leaves falling, a sacrifice in the glade. No. Not quite. The completion of a sacrifice.

How did one deal with so much? By drinking wine with soldiers? Perhaps. Oldest refuge, one of the oldest. By pulling blankets up to one's bruised face in bed, and falling asleep, sheltered from the knife of wind and the night? Though not the night that was always there now.

Caius Crispus, too, had a dream in that cold dark, though in his he did not fly. He saw himself walking the echoing corridors of an empty palace and he knew what it was, where he was. Had been there with Martinian years ago: the Patriarchal Palace in Rhodias, most glittering emblem of religious power—and wealth—in the Empire. Once, at any rate. In its day.

Crispin had seen it in dusty, emptied-out decay, long after the Antae sack and conquest: most of the rooms looted and empty, closed up. He and Martinian had been walking through it—a cadaverous, coughing cleric as their guide—to view a celebrated old wall mosaic a patron wanted copied for his summer house in Baiana by the sea. The two of them had been admitted, reluctantly, by virtue of a letter—and probably a sum of money—from their wealthy patron, to walk through echoing emptiness and dust.

The High Patriarch lived, worshipped, schemed, dictated his ceaseless flow of correspondence to all quarters of the known world on the two upper floors, seldom venturing from there save on holy days, when he crossed the covered bridge over the street to the Great Sanctuary and led services in the name of Jad, bright gold in glory on the dome.

The three men had walked endless empty ground-level corridors—their resonating footsteps a kind of reproach—and had finally come to the room with the to-be-copied work. A reception hall, the cleric muttered, fumbling through a ring of keys on his belt. He tried several, coughing, before finding the correct one. The mosaicists walked in, paused, and then set about opening shutters, though from the first glance they had both seen there was little point.

The mosaic—running the length and full height of a wall—was a ruin, though not from the wearing of time or the effects of inadequate technique. Hammers and axes had been taken to this, daggers, sword hilts, maces, staves, boot heels to the lower parts, scrabbling fingers. It had been a marinescape—they knew that much. They knew the studio that had been commissioned, though not the names of those who had actually done the work: mosaicists' names, like those of other decorative artisans, were not deemed worth preserving.

Hues of dark blue and a splendid green were still there as evidence of the original scheme near the wood-paneled ceiling. There would have been precious stones used here: for the eyes of a squid or sea horse, the shining scales of fish, coral, shells, the gleam of eels or undersea vegetation. They had all been looted, the mosaic hacked apart in the process. One would feel ill, Crispin thought, were this not so much the expected thing in Rhodias after the fall. There had been a fire set in the room at some point. The charred walls bore black, silent witness.

They stood gazing a while in silence, noses tickled by stirred dust in streaming sunlight, then methodically closed all the shutters again and walked with the afflicted cleric back down the same branching corridors and out into the vast, nearly empty spaces of the city once the center of the world, of an Empire, once thronged with teeming, vibrant, brutal existence.

In his dream, Crispin was alone in that palace, and it was even darker, emptier than he had known it that one time in a life that seemed frighteningly remote now. Then, he'd been a newly married man, rising in his guild, acquiring some wealth, the beginnings of a reputation, flush with the wondrous, improbable reality that he adored the woman he'd wed the year before and she loved him. In the corridors of dream he walked a palace looking for Ilandra, knowing she was dead.

Door after locked door opened somehow to the one heavy iron key he carried, and room after empty room showed dust and the charred black evidence of fire and nothing more. He seemed to hear a wind outside, saw a blue slant of moonlight once through broken slats in shutters. There were noises. A celebration far away? The sacking of the city? From a sufficient distance, he thought, dreaming, the sounds were much the same.

Room after room, his footprints showing behind him in the long-settled dust where he walked. No one to be seen, all sounds outside, from somewhere else. The palace unspeakably vast, unbearably abandoned. Ghosts and memories and sounds from somewhere else. *This is my life,* he thought as he walked. Rooms, corridors, random movement, no one who could be said to matter, who could put life, light, even the *idea* of laughter into these hollow spaces, so much larger than they had ever needed to be.

He opened another door, no different from any of the others, and walked into yet another room, and in his dream he stopped, seeing the *zubir.*

Behind it, dressed as for a banquet in a straight, ivory-colored gown banded at collar and hem with deep blue, her hair swept back and adorned with gems, her mother's necklace about her throat, was his wife.

Even dreaming, Crispin understood.

It wasn't difficult; it wasn't subtle or obscure the way dream messages could be, requiring a cheiromancer to explain them for a fee. She was barred to him. He was to understand she was gone. As much as his youth was, his father, the glory of this ruined palace, Rhodias itself. Gone away. Somewhere else. The *zubir* of the Aldwood proclaimed as much, an appalling, interposed wildness here, bulking savage and abso lute between the two of them, all black, tangled fur, the massive head and horns, and the eyes of however many thousand thousand years teaching this truth. He could not be passed. You came from him and came back to him, and he claimed you or he let you go for a time you could not measure or foretell.

Then, just as Crispin was thinking so, struggling to make a dream's peace with these apprehended truths, beginning to lift a hand in farewell to the loved woman behind the forest god, the *zubir* was gone, confounding him again.

It disappeared as it had in the road in fog, and did not reappear. Crispin stopped breathing in his dream, felt a hammer pounding within him, and did not know that he cried aloud in a cold room in a Sauradian night.

Ilandra smiled in the palace. They were alone. No barriers. Her smile cut the heart from him. He might have been a body lying on a road then, his chest torn open. He wasn't. In his dream he saw her step lightly forward: nothing between, nothing to bar her now. "There are birds in the trees," his dead wife said, coming into his arms, "and we are young." She rose up on her toes and kissed him on the mouth. He tasted salt, heard himself say something terribly, hugely important, couldn't make out his words. His own words. Couldn't.

Woke to the wild wind outside and a dead fire and the Inici girl—a shadow, a weight—sitting on his bed beside him wrapped in his cloak. Her hands clutched her own elbows.

"What? What *is* it?" he cried, confused, aching, his heart pounding. She had kissed . . .

"You were shouting," the girl whispered.

"Oh, dear Jad. Oh, Jad. Go to sleep . . ." He struggled to remember her name. He felt drugged, heavy, he wanted that palace again. Wanted it like some men want the juice of poppies, endlessly.

She was silent, motionless. "I'm afraid," she said.

"We're all afraid. Go to sleep."

"No. I mean, I would comfort you, but I'm afraid."

"Oh." It became unfairly needful to order his thoughts. To be *here*. His jaw hurt, his heart. "People I loved died. You can't comfort me. Go to sleep."

"Your . . . children?"

Every word spoken was drawing him farther from that palace. "My daughters. Last summer." He took a breath. "I am ashamed to be here. I let them die." He had never said this. But it was true. He had failed them. And had survived.

"*Let* them die? Of the *plague*?" the Inici woman on his bed said, incredulous. "No one can *save* anyone from that."

"I know. Jad. I *know*. It doesn't matter."

After a moment, she said, "And your . . . their mother?"

He shook his head.

The god-cursed shutter was still banging. He wanted to go out into the savage night and rip it from the wall and lie down in the icy wind with Ilandra. "Kasia," he said. That was her name. "Go to sleep. It isn't your duty to comfort here."

"Not a duty," she said.

So much anger in him. "Jad's blood! What do you propose? That your lovemaking skills transport me to joy?"

She went rigid. Drew a breath. "No. No. No, I . . . have no skills. That wasn't . . . what I meant."

He closed his eyes. Why did he have to even *address* these things now? So vivid, so rich a dream: on tiptoe, within his arms, a gown he remembered, the necklace, a scent, softness of parted lips.

She was dead, a ghost, a body in a grave. *I am afraid,* Kasia of the Inicii had said. Crispin let out a ragged breath. That shutter still banging along the wall outside. Over and over and over. So inane. So . . . ordinary. He shifted in the bed.

"Sleep here then," he said. "There is nothing to fear. What happened today is over now." A lie. It didn't end until you died. Life was an ambush, wounds waiting for you.

He turned on his side, facing the door, making room for her. She didn't move at first, then he felt her slide under both blankets. Her foot touched his, moved quickly away, but he realized from the icy touch how cold she must have been with the fire dead. It was the bottom of the night. Spirits in the wind? Souls? He closed his eyes. They could lie together. Share mortal warmth. Men bought tavern girls on winter nights for no more than this sometimes.

The *zubir* had been there in the palace and had disappeared. No obstacle. Nothing between. But there was. Of course there was. *Imbecile,* he could hear a voice saying. *Imbecile.* Crispin lay still for another long moment; then, slowly, he turned.

She was lying on her back, staring up at darkness, still afraid. She had thought for a long time that she would die today, he knew. Die brutally. He tried to comprehend what such an expectation would be like. Moving as if through water, or in dream, he laid a hand to her shoulder, her throat, brushed some of the long golden hair back from her cheek. She was so young. He took another breath, deeply unsure, even now, still half lost in another place, but then he touched one small, firm breast through the thinness of her tunic. She never took her eyes from his.

"Skills are a very small part of it," he said. His own voice sounded odd. Then he kissed her, as gently as he could.

He tasted salt again as he had in the dream. Drew back, looking down at her, at the tears. But she lifted a hand, touched his hair, then hesitated as if unsure what to do next, how to move—how to *be*—when it was by choice. The pain of others, he thought. The night so dark with the sun beneath the world. He lowered his head very slowly and kissed her again, then moved and brushed her nipple with his lips, through the tunic. Her hand stayed in his hair, tightening. Sleep was a refuge, he thought, walls were, wine, food, warmth, and this. And this. Mortal bodies in the dark.

"You are not at Morax's," he said. Her heart was so fast, he could feel it. The year she must have lived through. He intended to be careful, patient, but it had been a long time for him, and his own gathering urgency surprised and then mastered him. She held him close after, her body softer than he would have guessed, hands unexpectedly strong against his back. They slept like that for a while and later—nearer morning when they both awoke—he guided their pace more attentively, and in time he heard her begin to make her own sequence of discoveries, on a taken breath and another—like a climber reaching one ridge and then a higher one—before the god's sun finally rose in testament to battles won again, if at cost, in the night.

THE SENIOR PHYSICIAN AT the army base was a Bassanid, and skillful. The former was strictly against regulations, the latter so rare—and valuable—as to have caused the military governor commanding southern Sauradia to ignore all applicable bureaucratic and ecumenical rules. He wasn't, as it happened, the only senior military official in the Empire to take this view. There were openly pagan physicians, Bassanids worshipping Perun and Anahita, Kindaths with their moon goddesses, all through the army. As between a regulation and a good doctor . . . there was no decision at all.

Unfortunately, from a practical viewpoint, the physician took a careful look at the mildly admonished Inici servant, examined a red sampling of his urine, and declared he was unable to ride a horse for a fortnight. This meant they had to commandeer a cart or a wagon for him. And since the girl was traveling east as well and women couldn't ride horses, the wagon had to be large enough for two.

Then the artisan revealed that he had an acute dislike of riding, and since they were using wheeled transport in any case . . .

The military governor had his secretary sign the papers, wasting no more time than absolutely necessary on this distraction. The Emperor in his supreme wisdom wanted this man for something to do with the newest sanctuary in Sarantium. The newest, insanely expensive sanctuary. He had—through the lofty offices of the Chancellor—ordered good soldiers to spend their time tracking a Rhodian artisan on the road. A four-person military carriage was only one more insult.

In the prevailing circumstances the governor proved amenable to a diffident—if loquacious—suggestion from one of the tribunes of the Fourth Sauradian, the man who had found this party.

Carullus proposed that he accompany the artisan, following in the wake of a rapidly couriered letter from the governor, to add a direct personal appeal to the Master of Offices and to the Supreme Strategos, Leontes, that the arrears of pay be attended to as expeditiously as possible. The god knew, Carullus could talk, the governor thought glumly, dictating his letter for the military messenger. Might as well put his tongue to use.

It also appeared that the Rhodian had not, after all, been lax in responding to his invitation. The postal courier charged with the Imperial papers had taken an unconscionably long time to reach Varena. His name and civil service number were, as usual, on the envelope below the broken seal—the governor's secretary had recorded them. Tilliticus. Pronobius Tilliticus.

The governor spent an irritated moment pondering what sort of foolish mother gave her son a name almost identical to that for female genital organs in current military slang. Then he dictated a postscript, suggesting to the Master of Offices that the courier be reprimanded. He was unable to resist adding an offer that *important* communications west to the Antae kingdom in Batiara might better be entrusted to the military. Despite his recently chronic stomach pains, the governor did smile sourly to himself, dictating that part of the letter. He sent off the messenger.

The artisan's party stayed at the camp for two nights only, though the physician was unhappy about this speed. During the brief stay a notary attended upon the Rhodian to record and archive in his files—and forward copies, as requested, to the civil registry in the City—documents attesting to the freed status of the woman, Kasia of the Inicii.

At the same time, the recruiting centurion of the Fourth Sauradian cavalry dealt with the necessary protocols for the military conscription of the man, Vargos—a procedure that released him from his contract with the Imperial Post and triggered the immediate right to all moneys owing under his civil contract. Paperwork arranging the transfer of the appropriate sums to the military paymaster in the City was also processed. The centurion was entirely happy to do this, in fact . . . relations between the military and the civil service were about as cordial here as they were anywhere else. Which was to say, not at all.

The centurion was markedly less enthused about signing the release of the same fellow from his all-too-transitory military service. Had his instructions not been explicit about this, he might well have demurred. The man was strong and fit, and once he recovered from his accidental injuries would make an excellent soldier. They'd been coping with desertions—with pay more than half a year in arrears, it was not in the least surprising—and all the units were undermanned.

It was not to be. Both Carullus and the governor appeared anxious to get the red-bearded Rhodian and his party on their way. Imperial papers signed by Chancellor Gesius himself *could* have that sort of effect, the centurion supposed. The governor was near enough to his retirement to have an extreme disinclination to ruffle feathers in the City.

Carullus, for his own part, was apparently going with the artisan to Sarantium, leading an escort himself. The centurion had no idea why.

IN FACT, THERE WERE several reasons, the tribune of the Fourth Sauradian cavalry thought, during the days of traveling east and then, in Trakesia, curving gradually down south. A tribune commanded five hundred men, was much more significant than any messenger bearing yet another letter of complaint. He could have a legitimate expectation of at least being received and obtaining a formal answer as to the arrears for the Sauradian troops. The Master of Offices might not give him more than platitudes, but Carullus had hopes of seeing either Leontes himself or one of his personal cadre of officers and getting a clearer picture.

In addition, he hadn't been to Sarantium in years, and the chance to visit the City was too appealing to be passed up. He'd calculated that they could arrive—even moving slowly—before the season-ending races in the Hippodrome during the Dykania Festival. Carullus had a lifelong passion for the chariots and his beloved Greens that found little satisfaction in Sauradia.

Beyond this, he had developed an unanticipated but quite genuine liking for the red-bearded Rhodian he'd clipped with his helmet. Martinian of Varena was not an especially genial man—not that Carullus really needed *other* people to keep a conversation going—but the artisan could hold his wine almost as well as a soldier, knew a number of startlingly obscene western songs, and showed none of the arrogance most Rhodians displayed when confronting an honest Imperial soldier. He also swore with an inventiveness of phrase worth copying.

In addition, Carullus had reluctantly come to acknowledge to himself—looking around to determine the whereabouts of certain others in the party as they rode—that he was being continually assailed by an entirely new emotion.

It was the *most* unexpected thing.

FOR CENTURIES, THE JOURNALS and correspondence of seasoned travelers had made it clear that the most imposing way to first see Sarantium was from the deck of a ship at sunset.

Sailing east, the god's sun behind you lighting the domes and towers, gleaming on the seaward walls and the cliffs that lined the infamous channel—the Serpent's Tooth—into the celebrated harbor, there was no way, all travelers reported, to escape the awe and majesty Saranios's city evoked. *Eye of the world, ornament of Jad.*

The gardens of the Imperial Precinct and the flat *churkar* ground where the Emperors played or watched the imported Bassanid game of horses and mallets, could be seen from far out at sea, amid the gold- and bronze-roofed palaces—the Traversite, Attenine, Baracian, all of them. The mighty Hippodrome could be descried, just beyond: and across the forum from it—in this year of the reign of the great and glorious beloved, of Jad, the thrice-exalted Valerius II, Emperor of Sarantium, heir of Rhodias—could be seen the tremendous golden dome, the latest wonder of the world, stretching across the new Sanctuary of Jad's Holy Wisdom.

From out at sea, sailing to Sarantium, all of this and more would spread itself out for the traveler like a feast for the famished eye, too dazzling, too manifold and vividly manifest to be compassed. Men had been known to cover their faces with their cloaks in awe, to close their eyes, turn away, to kneel in prayer on the ship's deck, to weep. *Oh City, City, my eyes are never dry when I remember you. My heart is a bird, winging home.*

Then the ships would be met by the small harbor boats, officials would board, papers would be cleared, customs documents affirmed, cargoes examined and duly taxed, and finally they would be permitted to sail up the curve of the Serpent's Tooth—the great chains drawn back in this time of peace—passing between the narrow cliffs, looking up at walls and guards on each side, thinking of Sarantine Fire unleashed on hapless foes who thought to take Jad's holy and defended City. Awe would give way to—or be joined by—a proper measure of fear. Sarantium was no harbor or haven for the weak.

To port, as instructed by the Harbor Master with shouts and signal horns and flares, and then, papers examined and cleared yet again, the traveler could at last set foot on land, upon the thronged, noisy docks and quays of Sarantium. One could stride unsteadily away from the water after so long at sea and come into the City that was, and had been for more than two hundred years, both the crowning glory of Jad and the eastern Empire and the most squalid, dangerous, overcrowded, turbulent place on earth.

That was if you came by sea.

If you first approached by land down through Trakesia—as the Emperor himself was known to have done thirty years ago—what you saw before anything else were the Triple Walls.

There were those dissenters, as there always are among travelers—a segment of mankind inclined to have, and voice, strong opinions—who urged that the might and scale of Sarantium were made most evident and overwhelming by these titanic walls, seen gleaming at a sunrise. And this was how Caius Crispus of Varena saw them on a morning exactly six weeks after he had set out from his home to answer an invitation from the Emperor addressed to another man, and seeking to discover a reason to live—if they didn't kill him as an impostor first.

There was a paradox embedded in that, he thought, gazing at the brutal sweep of the walls that guarded the landward access to the City on its promontory. He didn't have the frame of mind just then to deal with paradoxes. He was here. On the threshold. Whatever was to begin could now begin.

Part Two

A starlit or a moonlit dome disdains,

All that man is,

All mere complexities,

The fury and the mire of human veins.

CHAPTER VI

It was with uncharacteristic intensity of thought and feeling for such an early hour that Plautus Bonosus, Master of the Senate, walked with his wife and unmarried daughters toward the small, elite Sanctuary of the Blessed Victims near their home to offer the dawn invocation on the second anniversary of the Victory Riot in Sarantium.

Having arrived home discreetly in chilly darkness, he had washed off the scent of his young lover—the boy insisted on wearing a particularly distinctive herbal concoction—and changed his clothes in time to meet his womenfolk in the foyer at sunrise. It was when he noticed the sprig of evergreen each of the three women was wearing in her hair for Dykania that Bonosus suddenly and vividly recalled doing exactly this same thing (having left a different boy) two years before on the morning of the day the City exploded in blood and fire.

Standing in the exquisitely decorated sanctuary, actively participating, as a man of his position was expected to, in the antiphonal chants of the liturgy, Bonosus allowed his mind to wander back—not to the sulky sleekness of his lover, but to the inferno of two years before.

Whatever anyone said, whatever the historians might one day write—or had already written—Bonosus had been there: in the Attenine Palace, in the throne room with the Emperor, with Gesius the Chancellor, with the Strategos, the Master of Offices, all the others, and he knew which person had spoken the words that turned the two days' tide that had already swamped the Hippodrome and the Great Sanctuary, and had been lapping even then at the Bronze Gates of the Imperial Precinct.

Faustinus, the Master of Offices, had been urgently proposing the Emperor withdraw from the City, take to sea from the hidden wharf below the gardens, across the straits to Deapolis or even farther, to wait out the chaos engulfing the capital.

They had been trapped within the Precinct since the morning before. The Emperor's appearance in the Hippodrome to drop the handkerchief at the outset of the Dykania Festival's racing had led not to cheering but to a steadily growing rumble of rage, and then men boiling out of the stands to stand below the kathisma shouting and gesticulating. They wanted the head of Lysippus the Calysian, the Empire's chief taxation officer, and they were making certain Jad's anointed Emperor knew it.

The Hippodrome Prefects guards, routinely sent down to disperse the crowd, had been swallowed up and killed, savagely. Anything resembling the routine had disappeared with that.

"Victory!" someone shouted, hoisting aloft the severed arm of a guardsman like a banner. Bonosus remembered the moment; he dreamt of it, at times. *"Victory to the glorious Blues and Greens!"*

Both factions had joined together in the cry. Unheard of. And the shout was picked up until it echoed through the Hippodrome. The killings took place directly below the Emperor. It was judged prudent that Valerius II and his Empress withdraw through the back of the kathisma at that point and return down the enclosed, elevated corridor to the Imperial Precinct.

The first deaths are always the hardest for a mob. After that, they are in a different country, they have crossed a threshold, and things become truly dangerous. More blood will follow, and fire. Both had, for a day and a brutal night already, and this was the second day.

Leontes had just returned, sword bloodied, from a reconnoiter through the city with Auxilius of the Excubitors. They reported entire streets and the Great Sanctuary burning. Blues and Greens were marching side by side in the smoke, chanting together as they brought Sarantium to its knees. Several names were being declaimed, the tall Strategos said quietly, as replacements for the Emperor.

"Any of them in the Hippodrome yet?" Valerius was standing beside his throne, listening attentively. His soft, smooth-cheeked features and gray eyes betrayed no immediate distress, only an intensity of concentration as he wrestled with a problem. *His city is on fire,* Bonosus remembered thinking, *and he looks like an academic in one of the ancient Schools, considering a problem of volumes and solids.*

"It appears so, my lord. One of the Senators. Symeonis." Leontes, ever courteous, refrained from looking over at Bonosus. "Some of the faction leaders have draped him in purple and crowned him with a necklace of some sort in the kathisma. I believe it is against his will. He was found outside his doors and seized by the mob."

"He is an old, frightened man," Bonosus said. His first words in that room. "He has no ambitions. They are using him."

"I know that," Valerius said quietly.

Auxilius of the Excubitors said, "They are trying to get Tertius Daleinus to come out to them. They broke into his house, but word is, he's already left the city."

Valerius did smile then, but not with his eyes. "Of course he has. A cautious young man."

"Or a coward, thrice-exalted lord," said Auxilius. Valerius's Count of the Excubitors was a Soriyyan, a sour-faced, often angry man. Not a disadvantage, given his office.

"It might be he's simply loyal," Leontes said mildly, with a glance at the other soldier.

It was possible but unlikely, Bonosus thought privately. The pious Strategos was known for offering benign interpretations of other men's actions, as if everyone might be measured by his own virtues. But the youngest son of the murdered Flavius Daleinus would not have any more loyalty toward this Emperor than he'd had for the first Valerius. He *would* have ambitions, but would be unlikely to reach for the dice cup so early in a game this large. From the Daleinoi's nearest country estate he could gauge the mood of the City and return very swiftly.

Bonosus, in the tight grip of his own fear, was unable not to look over and glare at the man sitting near him: Lysippus the Calysian, Quaestor of Imperial Revenue, who had caused all of this.

The Empire's chief taxation officer had been silent throughout the discussions, his prodigious bulk spilling over the edges of the carved bench on which he sat, threatening to bring it crashing down. His face was blotchy with strain and fear. Perspiration stained his dark robe. His distinctive green eyes shifted uneasily from one speaker to another. He had to know that his public execution—or even throwing him through the Bronze Gates to the enraged mob—was a perfectly viable option at this moment, though no one had yet spoken it aloud. It would not be the first time an Imperial Revenue officer had been sacrificed to the people.

Valerius II had shown no signs of such an intent. His loyalty to the fat, gross man who had so efficiently and incorruptibly funded his building schemes and the expensive co-opting of various barbarian tribes had always been firm. It was said that Lysippus had been a part of the machinations that brought the first Valerius to the throne. Whether that was true or not, an ambitious Emperor needed a ruthless taxation officer as much as he needed an honest one: Valerius had said that once to Bonosus, in the most matter-of-fact way—and the enormous Calysian might be depraved in his personal habits, but no one had ever been known to bribe or suborn him, or quarrel with his results.

Plautus Bonosus, at prayer beside his wife and daughters two years after, could still recall the chaotic intermingling of admiration and terror he'd felt that day. The sound of the mob at the Precinct doors had penetrated even into the room where they were gathered around a golden throne, amid artifacts of sandalwood and ivory and birds crafted of gold and semiprecious stones.

Bonosus knew that he himself would have offered the Quaestor to the factions without a second thought. With taxation levels rising each quarter for the past year and a half, continuing even after the debilitating effects of a plague, Lysippus ought to have known better than to arrest and torture two well-liked clerics for sheltering a tax-evading aristocrat he was seeking. It was one thing to pursue the wealthy (though Bonosus did have his thoughts on that). It was another to go after the clerics who ministered to the people.

Surely any sane official would have made allowance for the unrest of the City, how volatile it was on the eve of the Autumn Festival. The Dykania was *always* a dangerous time for authority. Emperors walked carefully then, placating the City with games and largess, knowing how many of their predecessors had lost sight, limbs, life in those turbulent days at autumn's end when Sarantium celebrated—or went dangerously wild.

Two years later Bonosus lifted his strong voice, intoning, *"Let there be Light for us, and for our dead, and for us when we die, lord. Holy Jad, let us find shelter with you and never be lost in the dark."*

Winter was coming again. The months of long, damp, windy darkness. There had been light that afternoon two years ago . . . the red light of the Great Sanctuary uncontrollably afire. A loss so great it was almost unimaginable.

"The northern army can be here from Trakesia in fourteen days," Faustinus had murmured that day, dry and efficient. "The Supreme Strategos will confirm that. This mob has no leadership, no clear purpose. Any puppet they acclaim in the Hippodrome will be hopelessly weak. Symeonis as Emperor? It is laughable. Leave now and you will reenter the City in triumph before full winter comes."

Valerius, a hand laid across the back of his throne, had looked at Gesius, the aged Chancellor, first, and then at Leontes. Both the Chancellor and the golden-haired Strategos, longtime companion, hesitated.

Bonosus knew why. Faustinus might be right, but he might be perilously wrong: no Emperor who had fled from the people he ruled had ever returned to govern them. Symeonis might be a terrified figurehead, but what would stop others from emerging once Valerius was known to have left Sarantium? What if the Daleinus scion found his courage, or had it handed to him?

On the other hand, in the most obvious way, no Emperor torn apart by a howling throng intoxicated by its own power had ever governed after that either. Bonosus wanted to say as much, but kept silent. He wondered if the mob, should they come this far, would understand that the Master of the Senate was here for purely *formal* reasons, that he had no authority, posed no danger, had done them no harm? That he was even, financially, as much a victim of the evil Quaestor of Imperial Revenue as any of them?

He doubted it.

No man spoke a word in that moment fraught with choice and destiny. They saw leaping flames and black smoke through the open windows—the Great Sanctuary burning. They could hear the dull, heavy roar of the mob at the gates and inside the Hippodrome. Leontes and Auxilius had reported at least eighty thousand people gathered in and around the Hippodrome, spilling into the forum there. As many more seemed to be running wild through the rest of the city, from the triple walls down, and had been for much of the night just past. Taverns and cauponae had been overrun and looted, they'd said. Wine was still being found and passed out from the cellars and then from hand to hand in the reeling, smoky streets.

There was a smell of fear in the throne room.

Plautus Bonosus, chanting gravely in his neighborhood sanctuary two years later, knew he would never forget that moment.

No man spoke. The one woman in the room did.

"I would sooner die clothed in porphyry in this palace," the Empress Alixana said quietly, "than of old age in any place of exile on earth." She had been standing by the eastern window while the men debated, gazing out at the burning city beyond the gardens and the palaces. Now she turned and looked only at Valerius. "All Jad's children are born to die. The vestments of Empire are seemly for a shroud, my lord. Are they not?"

Bonosus remembered watching Faustinus's face go white. Gesius opening his mouth, and then closing it, looking old suddenly, wrinkles deep in pale parchment flesh. And he remembered something else he thought he would never lose in his life: the Emperor, from near his throne, smiling suddenly at the small, exquisite woman by the window.

Among many other things, Plautus Bonosus had realized, with a queer kind of pain, that he had never in all his days looked at another man or woman in that way, or received a gaze remotely like the one that the dancer who had become their Empress bestowed upon Valerius in return.

"IT IS *INTOLERABLE*," SAID Cleander, speaking loudly over the tavern noise, "that a man like that should possess such a woman!" He drank, and wiped at the mustache he was trying to grow.

"He doesn't possess her," Eutychus replied reasonably. "He may not even be bedding her. And he *is* a man of some distinction, little sprout."

Cleander glared at him as the others laughed.

The volume of sound in The Spina was considerable. It was midday and the morning's races were done, with the afternoon chariots slated to begin after the break. The most ambitious of the drinking places near the Hippodrome was bursting with a sweating, raucous, bipartisan crowd.

The more fervent followers of Blue and Green had made their way to less expensive taverns and cauponae dedicated to their own factions, but the shrewd managers of The Spina had offered free drinks to retired and current charioteers of all colors from the day they'd opened their doors, and the lure of hoisting a beer or a cup of wine with the drivers had made The Spina a dramatic success from that first day.

It had to be . . . they'd put a fortune into it. The long axis of the tavern had been designed to simulate the real spina—the central island of the Hippodrome, around which the chariots wheeled in their furious careen. Instead of thundering horses, this spina was ringed by a marble counter, and drinkers stood or leaned on both sides, eyeing scaled reproductions of the statues and monuments that decorated the real thing in the Hippodrome. Against one long wall ran the bar itself, also marbled, with patrons packed close. And for those prudent—and solvent—enough to have made arrangements ahead of time, there were booths along the opposite wall, stretching to the shadows at the back of the tavern.

Eutychus was always prudent, and Cleander and Dorus were notably solvent, or rather, their fathers were. The five young men—all Greens, of course—had a standing arrangement to prominently occupy the highly visible second booth on race days. The first booth was always reserved for charioteers or the occasional patrons from the Imperial Precinct amusing themselves among the crowds of the city.

"No man ever truly possesses a woman, anyhow," said Gidas moodily. "He has her body for a time if he's lucky, but only the most fleeting glimpse into her soul." Gidas was a poet, or wanted to be.

"If they have souls," said Eutychus wryly, drinking his carefully watered wine. "It is, after all, a liturgical issue."

"Not anymore," Pollon protested. "A Patriarchal Council settled that a hundred years ago, or something."

"By a single vote," Eutychus said, smiling. Eutychus knew a lot; he didn't hide the fact. "Had one of the august clerics had an unfortunate experience with a whore the night before, the Council would likely have decided women have no souls."

"That's probably sacrilege," Gidas murmured.

"Heladikos defend me!" Eutychus laughed.

"That *is* sacrilege," Gidas said, with a rare, quick smile.

"They don't," Cleander muttered, ignoring this last exchange. "They *don't* have souls. Or *she* doesn't, to be permitting that gray-faced toad to court her. She sent back my gift, you know."

"We know, Cleander. You've told us. A dozen times." Pollon's tone was kindly. He ruffled Oleander's hair. "Forget her. She's beyond you. Pertennius has a place in the Imperial Precinct *and* in the military. Toad or not, he's the sort of man who sleeps with a woman like that . . . unless someone of even higher rank pushes him out of her bed."

"A place in the military?" Oleander's voice swirled upward in indignation. "Jad's cock, that's a bad joke! Pertennius of Eubulus is a bloodless, ass-licking secretary to a pompous strategos whose courage is long behind him since he married above himself and decided he liked soft beds and gold."

"Lower your voice, idiot!" Pollon gripped Oleander's arm. "Eutychus, water his fucking wine before he gets us into a fight with half the army."

"Too late," Eutychus said sorrowfully. The others followed his glance toward the marble spina running down the middle of the room. A broad-shouldered man in an officer's uniform had turned from contemplating a replica of the Greens' second statue to the charioteer Scortius and was gazing across at them, his expression stony. The men on either side of him—neither one a soldier—had also glanced over, but then returned to their drinks at the counter.

With Pollon's firm hand on his arm, Cleander kept silent, though he gazed truculently back at the soldier until the man at the spina bar turned away. Cleander sniffed. "Told you," he said, though quietly. "An army of useless fakers, boasting of imaginary battlefields."

Eutychus shook his head in amusement. "You *are* a rash little sprout, aren't you?"

"Don't call me that."

"What, rash?"

"No. The other. I'm seventeen now, and I don't like it."

"Being seventeen?"

"No! That name. Stop it, Eutychus. You aren't that much older."

"No, but I don't walk around like a boy with his first erection. Someone's going to cut it off for you one day if you aren't careful."

Dorus winced. "Eutychus."

A figure appeared suddenly at their booth. They looked up at a server. He carried a beaker of wine.

"Compliments of the officer at the spina," he said, licking his lips nervously. "He invites you to salute the glory of the Supreme Strategos Leontes with him."

"I don't take wine on conditions," bristled Cleander. "I can buy my own when I want it."

The soldier hadn't turned around. The server looked more unhappy. "He, ah, instructed me to say that if you do not drink his wine and offer his salute, he will be distressed and express this by hanging the . . . loudest of you by his tunic from the hook by the front door." He paused. "We don't want trouble, you know."

"Fuck him!" Cleander said, loudly.

There was a moment before the soldier turned.

This time, so did the two big men on either side of him. One was red-haired and bearded, of indeterminate origin. The other was a northerner of some sort, probably a barbarian, though his hair was close-cropped. The noise of The Spina continued unabated. The server looked from the booth to the three men at the spina and made an earnest, placating gesture.

"Boys don't fuck me," the soldier said gravely. Someone farther along the spina turned at that. "Boys who wear their hair like barbarians they've never faced, and dress like Bassanids they've never seen, do what a working soldier tells them." He pushed off from the bar and walked slowly across to their booth. His expression remained mild. "You style your hair like the Vrachae. If Leontes's army were not on your northern and western borders today, a Vrachae spearman might have been over the walls and up your backside by now. Do you know what they like to do with boys taken in battle? Shall I tell you?"

Eutychus lifted a hand and smiled thinly. "Not on a festival day, thank you. I'm sure it is unpleasant. Do you really propose to start a quarrel over Pertennius of Eubulus? Do you know him?"

"Not at all, but I will quarrel over insults to my Strategos. I've given you a choice. It is good wine. Drink to Leontes and I'll join you. Then we'll toast some of the old Green charioteers and one of you will explain to me how the fucking Blues got Scortius away from us."

Eutychus grinned. "You are, I dare take it, a follower of the glorious and exalted Greens?"

"All my sorry life." The man returned the grin wryly.

Eutychus laughed aloud and made room for the soldier to sit. He poured the offered wine. They toasted Leontes; none of them really disliked him, anyhow. It was difficult, even for Cleander, to be genuinely dismissive of such a man, though he did offer an aside about being known by the secretary one kept.

They went quickly through the soldier's beaker and then two more, saluting a long sequence of Green drivers. The soldier appeared to have a voluminous recollection of Green charioteers from cities all over the Empire in the reigns of the last three Emperors. The five young men had never heard of most of them. The man's two friends watched them from the spina bar, leaning back against it, occasionally joining in the toasts across the aisle. One of them was smiling a little, the other was expressionless.

Then the manager of The Spina had the horns blown, in imitation of those that marked the chariots' Processional in the Hippodrome, and they all began paying their reckonings and tumbling in a noisy spill of people out into the windy autumn sunshine, joining the disgorged crowds from the other taverns and baths to cross the forum for the afternoon's chariots.

The first running after the midday break was the major race of the day and no one wanted to be late.

"ALL FOUR COLORS IN this one," Carullus explained as they hurried across the open space. "Eight quadrigas, two of each color, a big purse. The only purse as large is the last one of the day when the Reds and Whites stay out of it and four Greens and Blues run with bigas—two horses each. That's a cleaner race, this one's wilder. There'll be blood on the track, most likely." He grinned. "Maybe someone will run over that dark-skinned bastard, Scortius."

"You'd like that?" Crispin asked.

Carullus considered the question for a moment. "I wouldn't," he said finally. "He's too much pleasure to watch. Though I'm sure he spends a fortune each year in wards against curse-tablets and spells. There *are* a good many Greens who'd cheerfully see him dragged and trampled for crossing to the Blues."

"Those five we drank with?"

"One of them, anyhow. The noisy one."

The five young men had pushed ahead of them across the Hippodrome Forum, heading for the patrician gates and their reserved seats.

"Who was the woman he was going on about?"

"A dancer. It's always a dancer. Latest darling of the Greens. Name's Shirin, apparently. A looker, it sounds like. They usually are. The young aristocrats are always elbowing each other to get in bed with the dancer or actress of the day. A long tradition. The Emperor married one, after all."

"Shirin?" Crispin was amused. He had that name in his baggage, on a torn-off piece of parchment.

"Yes, why?"

"Interesting. If this is the same person, I'm supposed to visit her. A message to deliver from her father." Zoticus had said she was a prostitute, at first.

Carullus looked astonished. "Jad's fire, Rhodian, you *are* a series of surprises. Don't tell my new friends. The youngest one might knife you—or hire someone to do it—if he hears you have access to her."

"Or be my friend for life if I offer to let him come visit with me."

Carullus laughed. "Wealthy lad. Useful friend." The two men exchanged an ironic glance.

Vargos, on Crispin's other side, listened carefully, saying nothing. Kasia was back at the inn where they'd booked a room last night. She'd been invited to come with them—women were permitted in the Hippodrome under Valerius and Alixana—but had been showing signs of distress ever since they'd passed into the roiling chaos of the City. Vargos hadn't been happy either, but he'd been within city walls before and had some framework for his expectations.

Sarantium dwarfed expectations, but they'd been warned it would.

The long walk from the landward walls to the inn near the Hippodrome had visibly unsettled Kasia the day before. It was a festival; the noise levels and the numbers of people in the streets were overwhelming. They had passed a half-naked ascetic perched precariously on the top of a squared-off triumphal obelisk, his long white beard streaming sideways in the breeze. He was preaching of the City's iniquities to a gathered cluster of the City's people. He'd been up there three years, someone said. It was best to stay upwind, they added.

A few prostitutes had been working the edges of the same crowd. Carullus had eyed one of them and then laughed as she grinned at him and slowly walked away, hips swinging. He'd pointed: the imprint of her sandals in the dust read, quite clearly, "Follow Me."

Kasia hadn't laughed, Crispin remembered.

And she had elected to remain behind at the inn today rather than deal with the streets again so soon.

"You'd really have started a fight with them?" Vargos asked Carullus. His first words of the afternoon.

The tribune glanced over at him. "Of course I would have. Leontes was maligned in my hearing by an effete little City snob who can't even grow a proper mustache yet."

Crispin said, "You'll do a lot of fighting if that's going to be your attitude here. I suspect the Sarantines are free with their opinions."

Carullus snorted. "You are telling *me* about the City, Rhodian?"

"How many times have you been here?"

Carullus looked chagrined. "Well, just twice in point of fact, but—"

"Then I suspect I know rather more than you about urban ways, soldier. Varena isn't Sarantium, and Rhodias isn't what it was, but I do know that if you bridle at every overheard opinion the way you might in a barracks you command, you'll never survive."

Carullus frowned. "He was attacking the Strategos. My commander. I fought under Leontes against the Bassanids beyond Eubulus. In the god's name, I *know* what he's like. That bedbug with his father's money and his stupid eastern robe had no business even *speaking* his name. I wonder where that little boy was two years ago today, when Leontes smashed the Victory Riot? *That* was courage, by Jad's blood! Yes, I would have fought them. It was . . . a matter of honor."

Crispin arched an eyebrow. "A matter of honor," he repeated. "Indeed. Then you should have had rather less difficulty understanding what I did at the walls yesterday when we came in."

Carullus snorted. "Not at *all* the same thing. You could have had your nose slit for declaring a name other than the one on your Permit. Using those papers was a *crime*. In Jad's name, Martinian—"

"Crispin," said Crispin.

An excited, not-entirely-sober cluster of Blues cut in front of them, rushing toward their gate. Vargos was jostled but kept his balance. Crispin said, "I chose to enter Sarantium as Caius Crispus—the name my father and mother gave me, not a false one." He looked at the tribune. "A matter of honor."

Carullus shook his head emphatically. "The only reason, the *only* reason the guard didn't look properly at your papers and detain you when the names didn't match was because you were with me."

"I know," Crispin said, grinning suddenly. "I relied on that."

Vargos, on his other side, snorted with an amusement he couldn't quite control. Carullus glared. "Are you actually planning to give your own name at the Bronze Gates? In the Attenine Palace? Shall I introduce you to a notary first, to arrange for the final disposition of your worldly goods?"

The fabled gates to the Imperial Precinct were, as it happened, visible at one end of the Hippodrome Forum. Beyond them, the domes and walls of the Imperial palaces could be seen. Not far away, north of the forum, scaffolding and mud and masonry surrounded the building site of Valerius II's immense new Sanctuary of Jad's Holy Wisdom. Crispin—or Martinian—had been summoned to play a part in that.

"I haven't decided," Crispin said.

It was true. He hadn't. The declaration at the customs gate in the wall had been entirely spontaneous. Even as he was speaking his own name aloud for the first time since leaving home, he'd realized that being in the company—virtually the custody—of half a dozen soldiers would probably mean his papers would not be examined by an overworked guard at festival time, and that is what had happened. Carullus's blistering, obscene interrogation of him the moment they were out of earshot of the guardhouse had been a predictable consequence.

Crispin had delayed explaining until they'd taken rooms at an inn Carullus knew near the Hippodrome and the new Great Sanctuary. The soldiers of the Fourth Sauradian were sent to a barracks to report, with one of them dispatched to the Imperial Precinct to announce that the Rhodian mosaicist had arrived in Sarantium as requested.

At the inn, over boiled fish and soft cheese with figs and melon after, Crispin had explained to the two men and the woman how he'd come to be traveling with an Imperial Permit belonging to another man. Or, more properly, he'd explained the obvious aspects of that. The rest, having to do with the dead and a barbarian queen, belonged to himself.

Carullus, stunned into unwonted silence through all of this, had eaten and listened without interrupting. When Crispin was done, he'd said only, "I'm a betting man not afraid of odds, but I'd not wager a copper folles on your surviving a day in the Imperial Precinct as Caius Crispus when someone named Martinian was invited on behalf of the Emperor. They don't like . . . surprises at this court. Think about it."

Crispin had promised to do so. An easy promise. He'd been thinking about it, without any answer emerging, since he'd left Varena.

As they crossed the Hippodrome Forum now, the Sanctuary behind them, the Imperial Precinct to their right, a squat, balding man behind a folding, hastily assembled counter was rattling off a sequence of names and numbers as people passed. Carullus stopped in front of him.

"Positions for the first race?" he demanded.

"Everyone?"

"Of course not. Crescens and Scortius."

The tout grinned, showing black, erratic teeth. "Interesting times today. Sixth and eighth. Scortius is outside."

"He won't win from eighth. What are you giving on Crescens of the Greens?"

"For an honest officer? Three to two."

"Copulate with your grandmother. Two to one."

"At two to one I *am* doing that, in her grave, but all right. At least a silver solidus, though. I won't do those odds for beer money."

"A *solidus*? I'm a soldier not a greedy race tout."

"And I run a bet shop, not a military dispensary. You have silver, wager it. Otherwise, stop blocking my booth."

Carullus bit his lower lip. It was a great deal of money.

He dug into his purse, pulled out what Crispin was fairly certain was the only silver piece he had, and passed it across the makeshift counter to the other man. In return he received a green chit with the name "Crescens" on it above the name of the tout. The man had marked, painstakingly, the race number, the amount of the wager, and the odds given on the back of the chit.

They walked on among a tide of people. Carullus was silent amid the noise as they approached the looming gates of the Hippodrome. As they passed within, he appeared to revive. He clutched his betting chit tightly.

"He's in the eighth position, the last one outside. He won't win from there."

"Is the sixth post so much better?" Crispin asked, perhaps unwisely.

"Hah! One morning at the races and the arrogant Rhodian with a false name thinks he knows the Hippodrome! Be silent, you poxed artisan, and pay attention, like Vargos. You may even learn something! If you behave I'll buy you both Sainican red with my winnings when the day is done."

BONOSUS QUITE ENJOYED WATCHING the chariots.

Attending at the Hippodrome, representing the Senate in the Imperial kathisma, was a part of his office that gave him genuine pleasure. The morning's eight races had been splendidly diverting: honors closely divided between Blues and Greens, two wins each for the new Green hero, Crescens, and the truly magnificent Scortius. An exciting surprise in the fifth race when an enterprising fellow racing for the Whites had nipped inside the Greens' second driver in the last turn to win a race he'd no business winning. The Blue partisans treated their junior color's win as if it had been a dazzling military triumph. Their rhythmic, well-coordinated tauntings of the humbled Greens and Reds caused a number of fistfights before the Hippodrome Prefect's men moved in to keep the factions apart. Bonosus thought the young White driver's flushed, exhilarated face beneath his yellow hair as he took his victory lap was very appealing. The young man's name, he learned, was Witticus, a Karchite. He made a mental note of it, leaning forward to applaud politely with the others in the kathisma.

Occurrences of that sort were exactly what made the Hippodrome dramatic, whether it was a startling victory or a charioteer carried off, his neck broken, another victim of the dark figure they called the Ninth Driver. Men could forget hunger, taxes, age, ungrateful children, scorned love, in the drama of the chariots.

Bonosus knew that the Emperor was of a different mind. Valerius would as soon have avoided the racing entirely, sending a stream of court dignitaries and visiting ambassadors to the kathisma in his stead. The Emperor, normally so unruffled, used to fume that he was far too busy to spend an entire working day watching horses run around. He tended not to go to bed at all after a day spent with the chariots, to catch up.

Valerius's work habits were well-known from the reign of his uncle. Then and now he drove secretaries and civil servants to terrified distraction and a state of somnambulant hysteria. They called him the Night's Emperor, and men told tales of seeing him pacing the halls of one palace or another in the very dead of night, dictating correspondence to a stumbling secretary while a slave or a guard walked alongside with a lantern that cast high, leaping shadows on the walls and ceilings. Some said strange lights or ghostly apparitions could be seen flitting in the shadows at such hours, but Bonosus didn't believe that, really.

He settled back into his cushioned seat in the third row of the kathisma and lifted a hand for a cup of wine, waiting for the afternoon's program to begin. Even as he signaled, he heard a telltale rap behind him and rose, very swiftly. The carefully barred door at the back of the Imperial Box was unlocked and swung open by the Excubitors on guard, and Valerius and Alixana, with the Master of Offices, Leontes and his tall new bride, and a dozen other court attendants appeared in the box. Bonosus sank to his knees beside the other early arrivals and performed the triple obeisance.

Valerius, clearly not in good humor, moved briskly past them and stood beside his elevated throne at the front, in full view of the crowd. He hadn't been present in the morning, but he dared not stay away all day. Not today. Not at the end of the festival, the last running of the year, and not, especially, with the memory only two years old of what had happened in this place. He needed to be seen here.

In a way it was perverse, but the all-powerful, godlike Emperors of Sarantium were enslaved by the Hippodrome tradition and the almost mythic force residing within it. The Emperor was the beloved servant and the mortal regent of Holy Jad. The god drove his fiery chariot through the daytime sky and then down through darkness under the world every night in battle. The charioteers in the Hippodrome did battle in mortal homage to the god's glory and his wars.

The connection between the Emperor of Sarantium and the men racing quadrigas and bigas on the sand below had been made by mosaicists and poets and even clerics for hundreds of years—though the clerics also fulminated against the peoples passion for chariot-drivers and their ensuing failure to attend at the chapels. That, Bonosus thought wryly, had been an issue—one way or another—for much longer than a few hundred years, even before the faith of Jad had emerged in Rhodias.

But this underlying link between the throne and the chariots was embedded deep in the Sarantine soul, and much as Valerius might resent time lost from paperwork and planning, his presence here went beyond the diplomatic and entered the holy. The mosaic on the roof of the kathisma showed Saranios the Founder in a chariot behind four horses, a victor's wreath on his head, not a crown. There was a message in that and Valerius knew it. He might complain, but he was here, among his people, watching the chariots run in the god's name.

The Mandator—the Emperor's herald—lifted his staff of office from the right side of the box. A deafening roar immediately went up from eighty thousand throats. They had been watching the kathisma, waiting for this moment.

"Valerius!" cried the Greens, the Blues, all those gathered there: men, women, aristocrats, artisans, laborers, apprentices, shopkeepers, even slaves granted a day to themselves at Dykania. The notoriously changeable people of Sarantium had decided in the past two years that they loved their Emperor again. The evil Lysippus was gone, golden Leontes had won a war and conquered lands all the way to the deserts of the Majriti far to the south and west, restoring memories of Rhodias in its grandeur. *"All hail the thrice-exalted! All hail our thrice-glorious Emperor! All hail the Empress Alixana."*

And well the people should hail her, Bonosus thought. She was one of them in a way that no one else here in the kathisma was. A living symbol of how high someone might rise, even from a rat-infested hovel of an apartment in the bowels of the Hippodrome.

With a wide gesture of encompassing benevolence, Valerius II of Sarantium greeted his welcoming citizens and signaled for a handkerchief for the Empress to drop that the Processional might commence and the afternoon races begin. A secretary was already crouched down—hidden from the crowd by the railing of the kathisma—preparing to deal with the Emperor's flow of dictation that would proceed even while the horses ran. Valerius might accede to the demands imposed by the day and appear before his people, joined to them here in the Hippodrome, united by the sport and the courage down below—mirrors of Jad in his godly chariot—but he would certainly not *waste* an entire afternoon.

Bonosus saw the Empress accept the brilliant white square of silk. Alixana was magnificent. She always was. No one wore—no one was *allowed* to wear—jewelry about their hair and person in the way Alixana did. Her perfume was unique, unmistakable. No woman would even dream of copying it, and only one other was permitted to use the scent: a well-publicized gift Alixana had made the spring before.

The Empress lifted a slender arm. Bonosus, seeing the swift, theatrical gesture, suddenly remembered seeing that arm lifted in the same way fifteen years ago, as she danced, very nearly naked, on a stage.

"The vestments of Empire are seemly for a shroud, my lord. Are they not?" She had said that in the Attenine Palace two years ago. A leading role on a very different stage.

I am growing old, Plautus Bonosus thought. He rubbed his eyes. The past kept impinging upon the present: all he saw now appeared shot through with images of things seen before. Too many interwoven memories. He would die on some tomorrow that lay waiting even now, and then everything would become yesterday—in the god's mild Light, if Jad were merciful.

The weighted handkerchief dropped, fluttering like a shot bird toward the sands below. The wind gusted; it drifted right. Auguries would flow from that, Bonosus knew: fiercely vying interpretations from the cheiromancers. He saw the gates at the far end swing open, heard horns, the high, piercing sound of flutes, then cymbals and martial drums as the dancers and performers led the chariots into the Hippodrome. One man was adroitly juggling sticks that had been set on fire as he capered and danced across the sand. Bonosus remembered flames.

"HOW MANY OF YOUR own men," Valerius had said two years ago, into the rigid stillness that had followed the Empress's words, "would it take to force a way into the Hippodrome through the kathisma? Can it be done?"

His alert gray eyes had been looking at Leontes. His arm had remained casually draped over the back of the throne. There was an elevated, covered passageway, of course, from the Imperial Precinct across to the Hippodrome, ending at the back of the kathisma.

There had been a collective intake of breath in that moment. Bonosus had seen Lysippus the taxation officer look up at the Emperor for the first time.

Leontes had smiled, a hand drifting to the hilt of his sword. "To take Symeonis?"

"Yes. He's the immediate symbol. Take him there, have him defer to you." The Emperor paused for a moment. "And I suppose there will need to be some killing."

Leontes nodded. "We go down, into the crowd?" He paused, thinking. Then amended: "No, arrows first, they won't be able to avoid them. No armor, no weapons. No way to get up to us. It would create chaos. A panic toward the exits." He nodded again. "It might be done, my lord. Depends on how intelligent they are in the kathisma, if they've barricaded it properly. Auxilius, if I can get in with thirty men and cause some disruption, would you be able to cut your way out of here to two of the Hippodrome gates with the Excubitors and move in as the crowd is rushing for the exits?"

"I would, or die in the attempt," Auxilius said, dark-bearded, hard-eyed, revitalized. "I will salute you from the sands of the Hippodrome. These are slaves and commoners. And rebels against Jad's anointed."

Jad's anointed crossed to stand by his Empress at the window, looking at the flames. Lysippus, breathing heavily, was on his overburdened bench nearby.

"It is so ordered, then," said the Emperor quietly. "You will do this just before sundown. We depend upon you both. We place our life and our throne in your care. In the meantime"—Valerius turned to the Chancellor and the Master of Offices—"have it proclaimed from the Bronze Gates that the Quaestor of Imperial Revenue has been stripped of his position and rank for excess of zeal and has been exiled in disgrace to the provinces. We'll have the Mandator announce it in the Hippodrome, as well, if there's any chance he'll be heard. Take him with you, Leontes.

Faustinus, have your spies spread these tidings in the streets. Gesius, inform the Patriarch: Zakarios and all the clerics are to promulgate this in the sanctuaries now and this evening. People will be fleeing there, if the soldiers do their task. This fails if the clergy are not with us. No killing in the chapels, Leontes."

"Of course not, my lord," the Strategos said. His piety was well-known.

"We are all your servants. It shall be as you say, thrice-glorious lord," said Gesius the Chancellor, bowing with a supple grace for so aged a man.

Bonosus saw others beginning to move, react, take action. He felt paralyzed by the gravity of what had just been decided. Valerius was going to fight for his throne. With a handful of men. He knew that if they had but walked a little west from this palace, across the autumn serenity of the gardens, the Emperor and Empress could have been down a stone staircase in the cliff and onto a trim craft and away to sea before anyone was the wiser. If the reports were correct, better than a hundred and fifty thousand people were in the streets right now. Leontes had requested thirty archers. Auxilius would have his Excubitors. Two thousand men, perhaps. Not more. He gazed at the Empress, straight-backed, immobile as a statue, centered in the window. Not an accident, that positioning, he suspected. She would know how to place herself to best effect. *The vestments of Empire. A shroud.*

He remembered the Emperor looking down at his corpulent, sweating taxation officer. There were stories circulating of what Lysippus had done to the two clerics in one of his underground rooms. Tales of what transpired there had made the rounds for some time now. Ugly stories. Lysippus the Calysian had been a well-made man once, Bonosus remembered: strong features, a distinctive voice, the unusual green eyes. He'd had a great deal of power for a long time, however. He couldn't be corrupted or bribed in his duties, everyone knew that, but everyone also knew that corruption could take . . . other forms.

Bonosus was perfectly aware that his own habits went to the borders of the acceptable, but the rumored depravities of the fat man—with boys, coerced wives, felons, slaves—repulsed him. Besides which, Lysippus's tax reforms and pursuit of the wealthier classes had cost Bonosus substantial sums in the past. He didn't know which aspect of the man outraged him more. He did know, because he'd been quietly approached more than once, that there was more to this riot than the blind rage of the common people. A good many of the patricians of Sarantium and the provinces would not be displeased to see Valerius of Trakesia gone and a more . . . pliant figure on the Golden Throne.

Watching in silence, Bonosus saw the Emperor murmur something to the man on the bench beside him. Lysippus looked up quickly. He straightened his posture with an effort, flushing. Valerius smiled thinly, then moved away. Bonosus never knew what was said. There was a bustle of activity at the time and an endless hammering from over by the gates.

Having been summoned to this gathering purely for the procedural formality of it—the Senate still, officially, advised the Emperor on the people's behalf—Bonosus found himself standing uncertainly, superfluous and afraid, between a delicately wrought silver tree and the open eastern window. The Empress turned her head and saw him. Alixana smiled.

Sitting three rows behind her now in the kathisma, his face burning again with the memory, Plautus Bonosus recalled his Empress saying to him, in an intimate tone of arch, diverted curiosity, as if they were sharing a dining couch at a banquet for some ambassador, "Do tell me, Senator, assuage my womanly curiosity. Is the younger son of Regalius Paresis as beautiful unclothed as he is when fully garbed?"

TARAS, FOURTH RIDER OF the Reds, didn't like his position. He didn't like it at all. In fact, being as honest as a man ought to be with himself and his god, he hated it like scorpions in his boots.

While the handlers held his agitated horses in check behind the iron barrier, Taras distracted himself from the pointed glances of the rider on his left by checking the knot of his reins behind his back. The reins had to be well tied. It was too easy to lose a handgrip on them in the frenzy of a race. Then Taras checked the hang of the knife at his waist. More than one charioteer had been claimed by the Ninth Driver because he couldn't cut himself free of the reins when his chariot toppled and he was dragged like a straw toy behind the horses. You raced between one kind of disaster and another, Taras thought. Always.

It occurred to him that this was particularly so for him in this first race of a festival afternoon. He was in the seventh position—a bad post, but it shouldn't have mattered. He drove for the Reds. He wasn't *expected* to win a major race with the first and second drivers of Blue and Green all present.

He did have—as all the White and Red drivers did—a role in every race. And this function was greatly complicated for Taras just now by the undeniable fact that the men in the sixth and eighth slots had *very* strong expectations of winning, despite starting outside, and each carried the fervent hopes of about half the eighty thousand souls in the stands.

Taras tightened his hold on his whip. Each of the men beside him wore the silver ceremonial helmet that marked them as First of their color. They were taking those off now, Taras saw, glancing to each side furtively, as the last of the Processional music gave way to the final preparations to run. On his left and a little behind him, in the sixth post, Crescens of the Greens shoved his leather racing helmet firmly down on his head as a handler cradled the silver one tenderly in his arms. Crescens glared quickly across at Taras, who was unable to glance away in time.

"He gets down in front of you at the Line, worm, I'll have you shoveling manure at some broken-down hippodrome on the frozen border of Karch. Fair warning."

Taras swallowed and nodded. *Oh, very fair,* he thought bitterly but did not say. He gazed past the barrier and down the track. The Line, chalked in white across the sand, was about two hundred paces away. To that point each chariot had to hold its lane, to allow the staggered start position to have its effect and prevent crashes right at the starting gates. After they reached the white line, the outside drivers could begin cutting down. If there was room.

That was the issue, of course.

Taras actually wished, at this moment, that he was still racing in

Megarium. The little hippodrome at his home in the west might not have been very important, a tenth the size of this one, but he'd been a Green there, not a lowly Red, riding a strong Second, fair hopes after a fine season of claiming the silver helmet, sleeping at home, eating his mother's food. A *good* life, tossed aside like a broken whip the day an agent of the Greens of Sarantium had come west and watched him run and recruited him. He would race for the Reds for a while, Taras had been told, starting the way almost everyone began in the City. If he did honorably . . . well, the lives of *all* the great drivers were there to be observed.

If you thought you were good, and wanted to succeed, the Greens' agent said, you went to Sarantium. It was as simple as that. Taras knew it was true. He was young. It was an opportunity. *Sailing to Sarantium,* men called it, when someone took a chance like this. His father had been proud. His mother had cried, and packed him a new cloak and two sealed amphorae of her own grandmother's sovereign remedy for any and all ailments. The most evil-tasting concoction on earth. Taras had taken a spoonful each day since he'd arrived in the City. She'd sent two more jars in the summer, by Imperial Post.

So here he was, healthy as a young horse, on the very last day of his first season in the capital. No bones broken on the year and barely a handful of new scars, only one bad spill that left him dizzy for a few days and hearing flute music. Not a *bad* season, he thought, given that the horses the Reds and Whites drove—especially their lesser drivers—were hopelessly feeble when matched on the great track with those of the Blues and Greens. Taras had an easygoing disposition, worked hard, learned quickly, and had grown more than adequate—or so his factionarius had told him, encouragingly—at the tasks of the lesser colors. They were the same at every track, after all. Blocks, slow-downs, minor fouls (major ones could cost your lead color the race and get you a suspension and a whip across the back—or face—from a First driver in the dressing rooms), even carefully timed spills to bring down a rival team coming up behind you. The trick was to do that last without breaking a bone, or dying, of course.

He'd even won three times in the minor races involving the lesser Green and Blue riders and the Reds and Whites—amusements for the crowd, those were, with careening chariots, reckless corners, dangerous pileups, hotheaded young riders lashing at each other as they strove for recognition. Three wins was perfectly decent for a youngster riding Fourth for the Reds in Sarantium.

Problem was, *perfectly decent* wouldn't suffice at this particular moment. For a veritable host of reasons, the race coming up was hugely important, and Taras cursed fortune that it was his lot to be slotted outside between ferocious Crescens and the whirlwind that was Scortius. He shouldn't even have *been* in this race, but the Reds' second driver had fallen and wrenched a shoulder earlier in the morning and the factionarius had chosen to leave his Third in the next race, where he might have a chance to win.

As a direct result of this, seventeen-year-old Taras of Megarium was sitting here at the starting line, behind horses he didn't know at all well, sandwiched between the two finest drivers of the day, with one of them making it clear that if he didn't cut off the other, his brief tenure in the City might be over.

It was all a consequence of not having enough money to buy adequate protection against the curse-tablets, Taras knew. But what could one do? What could one possibly do?

The first trumpet sounded, warning of the start to come. The handlers withdrew. Taras leaned forward, talking to his horses. He dug his feet deeply into the metal sheaths on the chariot floor and looked nervously to his right and a bit ahead. Then he glanced quickly down again. Scortius, holding his experienced team easily in place, was *smiling* at him. The lithe, dark-skinned Soriyyan had an easy grin—allegedly lethal among the women of the City—and at the moment he was glancing back with amusement at Taras.

Taras made himself look up. It would not do to appear intimidated.

"Miserable position, isn't it?" the First of the Blues said mildly. "Don't worry too much. Crescens is a sweet-natured fellow under that surface. He knows you can't go fast enough to block me."

"The fuck I am, the fuck I do!" Crescens barked from the other side. "I want this race, Scortius. I want seventy-five for the year and I want it in this one. Baras, or whatever your name is, keep him outside or get used to the smell of horse manure in your hair."

Scortius laughed. "We're *all* used to that, Crescens." He clucked reassuringly at his four horses.

The largest of them, the majestic bay in the leftmost position, was Servator, and Taras longed in his heart to stand in a chariot behind that magnificent animal just once in his life. Everyone knew that Scortius was brilliant, but they also knew that a goodly portion of his success—evinced by two statues in the spina before he was thirty years old—had been shaped by Servator. There had even been a bronze statue to the *horse* in the courtyard outside the Greens' banquet hall, until this year. It had been melted down over the winter. When the Greens lost the driver they lost the horse, because Scortius's last contract with them had stipulated—uniquely—that *he* owned Servator, not the faction.

He'd gone over to the Blues in the winter, for a sum and on terms that no one knew for certain, though the rumors were wild. The muscular, tough-talking Crescens had come north from riding First for the Greens in the notoriously rough-and-tumble hippodrome of Sarnica—second city of the Empire—and had assuaged some of his faction's grief by being hard and brave and ruggedly aggressive and by winning races. Seventy-five would be a splendid first season for the Greens' new standard-bearer.

Seventy-*four* would be, Taras desperately wanted to say, but didn't.

Didn't have time, either. His right-side trace horse was restive and needed attention. He had only handled this team once before, back in the summer. The starter's trumpet was up. A handler hurried back and helped Taras hold his position. He didn't look over at Crescens, but he heard the fierce man from Amoria cry, "A case of red from my home if you keep the Soriyyan bastard outside for a lap, Karas!"

"His name's Taras!" Scortius of the hated Blues called back, still laughing—in the very moment the trumpet sounded and the barriers sprang away, laying the wide track open like an ambush or a dream of glory.

"*WATCH THE START!*"

Carullus gripped Crispin's arm, shouting over the deafening noise as thirty-two horses came up to the barriers below and the first warning trumpet blast sounded. Crispin was watching. He and Vargos had learned a great deal through the morning; Carullus was surprisingly knowledgeable and unsurprisingly talkative. The start was almost half the race, they'd come to realize, especially with the best drivers on the track, unlikely to make mistakes on the seven laps around the spina. If one of the top Blues or Greens took the lead at the first turn, it required luck and a great deal of effort to overtake him on a crowded track.

The real drama came when—as now—the two best drivers were so far outside that it was impossible for them to win except by coming from behind, fighting through the blocks and disruptions of the lesser colors.

Crispin kept his eyes on the outside racers. He thought that Carullus's very large wager was a decent bet: the Blues' Scortius was in a miserable position, flanked by a Red driver whose sole task—he had learned through the morning—would be to keep the Blue champion from cutting down for as long as possible. Running wide for a long time on this track was brutally hard on the horses. Crescens of the Greens had his own Green partner on his left, another piece of good fortune, despite his own outside start. If Crispin understood this sport at all by now, that second Green driver would go flying from the barriers as fast as he could and then begin pressing left toward the inside lanes, opening room for Crescens to angle over as well, as soon as they sped past the white chalked line that marked the beginning of the spina and the point when the chaos of maneuvering began.

Crispin hadn't expected to be this engaged by the races but his heart was pounding now, and he'd found himself shouting many times through the morning. Eighty thousand screaming people could make you do that. He'd never been among so large a crowd in his life. Crowds had their own power, Crispin had begun to realize; they carried you with them.

And now the Emperor was here: a new element to the festival excitement of the Hippodrome. That distant purple-robed figure at the western end of the stands—just where the chariots made their first turning round the spina—represented another dimension of power. The men down below them in their frail chariots, whips in hand and reins lashed around their hard, trained bodies, were a third. Crispin looked up for a moment. The sun was high on a clear, windy day: the god in his own chariot, riding above Sarantium. Power above and below and all around.

Crispin closed his eyes for a moment in the brilliance of the day, and just then—without any warning at all, like a flung spear or a sudden shaft of light—an image came to him. Whole and vast and unforgettable, completely unexpected, a gift.

And also a burden, as such images had always been for him: the terrible distance between the art conceived in the eye of the mind and what one could actually execute in a fallible world with fallible tools and one's own crushing limitations.

But sitting there on the marble benches of the Sarantine Hippodrome, assailed by the tumult and the screaming of the crowd, Caius Crispus of Varena knew with appalling certainty what he would like to do on a sanctuary dome here, given the chance. He might be. They'd asked for a mosaicist. He swallowed, his throat suddenly dry. His fingers were tingling. He opened his eyes and looked down at his scarred, scratched hands.

The second trumpet sounded. Crispin lifted his head just as the barriers below were whipped away and the chariots sprang forward like a thunder of war, pushing the inner image back in his mind but not away, not away.

"Come on, you cursed Red! *Come on!*" Carullus was roaring at the top of his considerable voice, and Crispin knew why. He concentrated on the outside chariots and saw the Red driver burst off the line with exceptional speed—the very first team out of the barriers, it seemed to him. Crescens was almost as fast, and the Green second driver in the fifth lane was lashing his horses hard, preparing to lead his champion down and across as soon as they passed the white line. In the eighth position, it seemed to Crispin that Scortius of the Blues had actually been caught unprepared by the trumpet; he seemed to have been turned backward, saying something.

"On!" roared Carullus. "Go! Lash them! *Good man, you Red!"*

The Red driver had already caught Scortius's Blues, Crispin saw, even against the advantage the outside chariot was given at the staggered start. Carullus had said it this morning: half the races were decided before the first turn. It looked like this one might be. With the Red already right beside him—and now pulling *ahead* with the ferocity of his start—the Blue champion had no way to cut down from his position so far outside. His cohorts in the inside lanes were going to be hard-pressed to keep Crescens outside or blocked, especially with the Greens' second driver there to clear a path.

The first chariots reached the white line. The whip hand of the Red driver in the seventh lane seemed a blur of motion as he lashed his mounts forward, first to the line. It didn't matter where that team finished, Crispin knew. Only that they keep Scortius outside for as long as they could.

"He's *done* it!" Carullus howled, clutching Crispin's left arm in his vise of a grip.

Crispin saw the two Green chariots cross the line and begin an immediate angling downward—they had room. The White chariot in the fourth lane hadn't started fast enough to fend them off. Even if the White driver fouled the Green leading the way and they both went down, that would only open up more space for Crescens. It was wonderfully well-done; even Crispin could see that.

Then he saw something else.

Scortius of the Blues, in the worst position, farthest outside, with a fiercely determined Red driver lashing his horses into a frenzy to get ahead of him, *let that chariot go by*.

Then the Blue driver suddenly leaned over, so far left his upper body was outside the platform of his chariot, and from that position he sent his whip forward—for the first time—and lashed his right trace horse. At the same time the big bay on the left side of the team, the one called Servator, *pulled* sharply left and the Blue chariot almost pivoted on the sands as Scortius hurled his body back to the right to balance it. It seemed impossible it could remain upright, keep rolling, as the four horses passed *behind* the still accelerating Red driver at an unbelievably sharp angle, straight across the open track and *right up to the back of Crescens's chariot.*

"Jad rot the soul of the man!" Carullus screamed, as if in mortal agony. "I don't believe it! I do *not* believe it! It was a trick! That start was deliberate! He *wanted* to do this!" He shook both fists in the air, a man in the grip of a vast passion. "Oh, Scortius, my heart, why did you *leave* us?"

All around them, even in the stands of those not formally aligned with one faction or another, men and women were screaming as Carullus was, so startling and spectacular had that angled, careening move been. Crispin heard Vargos and he heard himself shouting with all of them as if his own spirit were down there in the chariot with the man in the blue tunic and leather straps. The horses thundered into the first turn passing beneath the Imperial Box. Dust swirled, the noise was colossal. Scortius was right behind his rival, his four horses almost trampling on the back of the other man's chariot. None of Crescens's allies could block him without also impeding the Green driver or fouling so flagrantly from the side as to disqualify their color from victory.

The chariots whipped along the far stands as Crispin and the others strained to see across the spina and its monuments. The Blues' second driver had used his inside position to seize and hold the lead and he was first into the second turning, straining to keep his horses from drifting outside. Right behind him, surprisingly, was the young Red driver from the seventh lane. Having failed to block Scortius, he had done the only thing he could and pressed downward himself, taking advantage of his spectacular—and spectacularly unsuccessful—start from the barriers.

The first of the seven bronze sea horses tilted and dived from above, down into the silver tank of water at one end of the spina. An egg-shaped counter flipped over at the opposite end. One lap done. Six to go.

IT WAS PERTENNIUS OF Eubulus who had most comprehensively chronicled the events of the Victory Riot. He was Leontes's military secretary, an obvious sycophant and flatterer, but educated, manifestly shrewd, and carefully observant, and since Bonosus had been present himself for many of the events the Eubulan recorded in his history, he could vouch for their essential accuracy. Pertennius was, in fact, the sort of man who could make himself so colorless, so unobtrusive, that you forgot he was there . . . which meant he heard and saw things others might not. He enjoyed this, a little too obviously, letting slip occasional bits of information, clearly expecting confidences in return. Bonosus didn't like him.

Notwithstanding this, Bonosus was inclined to credit his version of events in the Hippodrome two years ago. There were a good many corroborating sources, in any case.

The subversive work of men strewn through the crowd by Faustinus had managed to set Blues and Greens somewhat at odds toward the end of that day. Tempers frayed with uncertainty, and the allegiance between the factions seemed to be wearing thin in places. Everyone knew the Empress favored the Blues, having been a dancer for them herself. It had not been difficult to make the Greens in the Hippodrome anxious and suspicious that they might be the prime victims of any response to the events of the past two days. Fear could bring men together, and it could drive them apart.

Leontes and his thirty archers of the Imperial Guard made their way silently down the enclosed corridor from the Precinct to the rear of the kathisma. There followed an ambiguous incident with a number of the Hippodrome Prefect's men, guarding the corridor for those in the box, allegedly undecided where their immediate loyalties lay. In Pertennius's account, the Strategos made a quietly impassioned speech in that dark corridor and swayed them back to the Emperor's side.

Bonosus had no obvious reason to doubt the report, though the eloquence of the speech as recorded, and its length, seemed at odds with the urgency of the moment.

The Strategos's men—each one armed with his bow as well as a sword—then burst in through the back door of the kathisma, joined by the Prefect's soldiers. They discovered Symeonis actually sitting on the Emperor's seat. This was confirmed: everyone in the Hippodrome had seen him there. He was to argue plausibly, afterward, that he'd had no choice.

Leontes personally ripped the makeshift crown and the porphyry robe from the terrified Senator. Symeonis then dropped to his knees and embraced the booted feet of the Supreme Strategos. He was permitted to live; his abject, very public, obeisance was a useful symbol, since everything happening could be seen clearly throughout the Hippodrome.

The soldiers made ruthlessly short work of those in the kathisma who had placed Symeonis on the Emperor's chair. Most were popular agitators, though not all. Four or five of those in the box with Symeonis were aristocrats who saw themselves as having cause to dispense with an independent Emperor and be the powers behind the throne of a figurehead.

Their hacked bodies were immediately thrown down to the sands, landing bloodily on the heads and shoulders of the crowd, which was so densely packed that people could scarcely move.

This, of course, became the principal cause of the slaughter that followed.

Leontes had the Mandator proclaim the exile of the hated taxation officer. Pertennius reported this speech at some length as well, but as Bonosus understood events, it was likely that next to no one heard it.

This was so because, even as the Mandator was declaring the Emperor's decision, Leontes directed his archers to begin shooting. Some arrows were fired at those directly below the kathisma; others arched high to fall like deadly rain on unprotected people far off. No one on the sands had any weapons, any armor. The arrows, randomly strewn, steadily and expertly fired, caused an immediate, panic-stricken hysteria. People fell, were trampled to death in the chaos, lashed out at each other in desperate attempts to flee the Hippodrome through one of the exits.

It was at this point, according to Pertennius, that Auxilius and his two thousand Excubitors, divided into two groups, appeared at entrances on opposite sides. One of these—the tale would linger and gain resonance—was the Death Gate, the one through which dead and injured charioteers were carried out.

The Excubitors wore their visored helmets. They had already drawn their swords. What ensued was a slaughter. Those facing them were so packed together they could scarcely lift arms to defend themselves. The massacre continued as the sun went down, autumn darkness adding another dimension to the terror. People died of swords, arrows, underfoot, smothered in the blood-soaked crush.

It was a clear night, Pertennius's chronicle meticulously recorded, the stars and the white moon looking down. A stupefying number of people died in the Hippodrome that evening and night. The Victory Riot ended in a black river of moonlit blood saturating the sands.

Two years later, Bonosus watched chariots hurtle around the spina along that same sand. Another sea horse dived—they had been dolphins until recently—another egg was flipped. Five laps done. He was remembering a white moon suspended in the eastern window of the throne room as Leontes—unscathed, calm as a man at ease in his favorite bath, golden hair lightly tousled as if by steam—returned to the Attenine Palace with a gibbering and palsied Symeonis in tow. The aged Senator hurled himself prone on the mosaic-inlaid floor before Valerius, weeping in his terror.

The Emperor, sitting on the throne now, looked down upon him.

"It is our belief you were coerced in this," he murmured as Symeonis wailed and beat his head against the floor.

Bonosus remembered that.

"Yes! Oh *yes*, oh my dear, thrice-exalted lord! I *was*!"

Bonosus had seen an odd expression in Valerius's round, smooth face. He was not a man—it was known—who enjoyed killing people. He'd had the Judicial Code changed already to eliminate execution as a punishment for many crimes. And Symeonis was an old, pathetic victim of the mob more than anything else. Bonosus was prepared to wager on exile for the elderly Senator.

"My lord?"

Alixana had remained by the window. Valerius turned to her. He hadn't spoken whatever it was he'd been about to say.

"My lord," repeated the Empress quietly, "he was crowned. Garbed in porphyry before the people. Willingly or no. That makes two Emperors in this room. In this city. Two . . . living Emperors."

Even Symeonis fell silent then, Bonosus remembered.

The Chancellor's eunuchs killed the old man that same night. In the morning his naked, dishonored body was displayed for all to see, hanging from the wall beside the Bronze Gates in its flabby, pale white shame.

Also in the morning came the renewed Proclamation, in all the holy places of Sarantium, that Jad's anointed Emperor had heeded the will of his dearly beloved people and the hated Lysippus was already banished outside the walls.

The two arrested clerics, both alive if rather the worse for their tenure with the Quaestor of Imperial Revenue, were released, though not before a careful meeting was held among themselves, the Master of Offices, and Zakarios, the Most Holy Eastern Patriarch of Jad, in which it was made clear that they were to remain silent about the precise details of what had, in fact, been done to them. Neither appeared anxious to elaborate, in any case.

It was, as always, important to have the clerics of the City participate in any attempts to bring order to the people. The cooperation of the clergy tended to be expensive in Sarantium, however. The first formal declaration of the Emperor's *extremely* ambitious plans for the rebuilding of the Great Sanctuary took place in that same meeting.

To this day, Bonosus wasn't at all certain how Pertennius had learned about that. He was, however, in a position to confirm another aspect of the historian's chronicle of the riot. The Sarantine civil service had always been concerned with accurate figures. The agents of the Master of Offices and the Urban Prefect had been industrious in their observations and calculations. Bonosus, as leader of the Senate, had seen the same report Pertennius had.

Thirty-one thousand people had died in the Hippodrome under that white moon two years ago.

AFTER THE WILD BURST of excitement at the start, four laps unrolled with only marginal changes in positioning. The three quadrigas that had started inside had all moved off the line quickly enough to hold their positions, and since they were Red, White, and the Blues' second driver, the pace was not especially fast. Crescens of the Greens was tucked in behind these three next to his own Second, who had led him across the track in their initial move. Scortius's horses were still right behind his rival's chariot. As the racers hurtled past them on the fifth lap, Carullus gripped Crispin's arm again and rasped, "Wait for it! He's giving orders now!" Crispin, straining to see through the swirling dust, realized that Crescens was indeed shouting something to his left and the Greens' number two was relaying it forward.

Right at the beginning of the sixth lap, just as they came out of the turn, the Red team running in second place—the Greens' teammate—suddenly and shockingly went down, taking the Blues' second quadriga with him in an explosion of dust and screams.

A chariot wheel flew off and rolled across the track by itself. It happened directly in front of Crispin, and his clearest single image amid the chaos was of that wheel serenely spinning away, leaving carnage behind. He watched it roll, miraculously untouched by any of the swerving and bouncing chariots, until it wobbled to rest at the outer edge of the sand.

Crescens and the other Green beside him avoided the wreck. So did Scortius, pulling swiftly wide to the right. The trailing White second team wasn't quite quick enough to steer around. Its inside horse clipped the piled, mangled chariots and the driver hacked furiously at the reins tied to his waist as his platform tipped over. He hurtled free, to the inside, rolling and rolling across the track toward the spina. Those behind him, with more time to react, were all heading wide. The driver was in no danger once free of his own reins. One of his inside yoked horses was screaming, though, and down, a leg clearly broken. And beside the initial wreckage, the second driver of the Blues lay very still on the track.

Crispin saw the Hippodrome crew sprinting across the sand to get the men away—and the horses—before the surviving chariots came round again.

"That was deliberate!" Carullus shouted, looking down at the chaos of horses and men and chariots. "Beautifully done! Look at the *lane* he opened for Crescens! *On, Greens!*"

Even as Crispin dragged his eyes away from the downed chariots and the motionless man and focused on the quadrigas flying down the straightaway toward the Emperor's box, he saw the Greens' number two driver, sitting in second place now after the accident, pull his team suddenly wide to the outside as Crescens, just behind him, lashed his own horses hard. The timing was superb, like a dance. The Greens' champion hurtled past his partner and was suddenly right beside the White team that had been leading to this point—and then *past* it, outside but astonishingly close, in an explosion of nerve and speed, before the White driver could react and swing out from the rail to force him wider as they entered the turn.

But even as Crescens of the Greens hurtled brilliantly by, accelerating into a curve, the White charioteer abandoned the attempt to slow him and pulled his own horses up sharply instead, reins gripped hard, holding them *right* on the rail—and Scortius was there.

The Blue champion's magnificent inside bay brushed up against the White's outside horse, so close was the move that his own wheels seemed to blur into those of his teammate, and in that instant Crispin surged again to his feet shouting along with everyone else in the Hippodrome, as if they were one person, melded by the moment.

Crescens was ahead as they swept under the Imperial Box, but his ferocious burst of speed had forced his horses wide on the curve. And Scortius of the Blues, leaning madly over to his left again, his entire upper body *outside* the bouncing, careening chariot, the great bay horse pulling the other three downward, had curled inside him only half a length behind as they exploded out of the curve into the far straight with eighty thousand people on their feet and screaming.

The two champions were alone in front.

Throat raw with his own shouting, straining to see across the spina, past obelisks and monuments, Crispin saw Crescens of the Greens lash his horses, leaning so far forward he was almost over their tails, and he heard a thunderous roar from the Green stands as the animals responded gallantly, opening a little distance from the pursuing Blues.

But a little was enough here. A little could be the race: for with that half length gained back again, Crescens, in his turn, leaned over to the left and, with one quick, gauging glance backward, sacrificed a notch of speed for a sharp downward movement and *claimed the inside lane again.*

"He did it!" Carullus howled, pounding Crispin's back. "*Ho, Crescens!* On, Greens! On!"

"How?" Crispin said aloud, to no one in particular. He watched Scortius belatedly go hard to his own whip, lashing his team now, and saw them respond in turn as the two quadrigas flew down the far straight. The Blue horses came up again, their heads bobbing beside Crescens's hurtling chariot once more—but it was too late, they were on the outside now. The Green driver had seized the rail again with that brilliant move out of the turn, and at this late stage the shorter distance along the inside would surely have to tell.

"Holy Jad!" Vargos suddenly screamed from Carullus's other side, as if the words had been ripped from his throat. "Oh, by Heladikos, *look*! He did it deliberately! Again!"

"*What?*" Carullus cried.

"Look! In front of us! Oh, Jad, how did he *know*?"

Crispin looked to where Vargos was pointing and cried out himself then, incoherent, disbelieving, in a kind of transport of excitement and awe. He clutched at Carullus's arm, heard the other man roaring, a sound suspended between anguish and fierce rapture, and then he simply watched, in the appalled fascination with which one might observe a distant figure hurtling toward a cliff he did not see.

THE TRACK CREWS, ADMINISTERED by the civil office of the Hippodrome Prefect and thus resolutely nonpartisan, were extremely good at their various tasks. These included attending to the state of the racecourse, the condition of the starting barriers, the fairness of the start itself, judging fouls and obstructions during the races, and attempting to police the stables and prevent poisonings of horses or assaults on drivers—at least within the Hippodrome itself. Attacks outside were none of their business.

One of their most demanding activities was clearing the track after a collision. They were trained to remove a chariot, horses, an injured driver with speed and skill, either to the safety of the spina or across to the outside of the track against the stands. They could disentangle a pair of mangled quadrigas, cut free the rearing, frightened horses, push twisted wheels out of the way, and do all of this in time to enable the surviving chariots coming around to proceed apace.

Three downed and wrecked quadrigas, twelve entangled horses, including a broken-legged White yoke horse that had dragged its thrashing, yoked companion awkwardly over on its side when it went down, and an unconscious, badly hurt driver presented something of a problem, however.

They got the injured man on a litter over to the spina. They cut all six trace horses free and unhooked two pairs of the yoke horses. They dragged one chariot as far to the outside as they could. They were working on the other two, struggling to unyoke the terrified healthy horse from the broken-legged one, when a warning shout came that the leaders had come back around—moving *very* fast—and the yellow-garbed track crew had to sprint madly for safety themselves.

The accident had taken place on the inside lanes. There was plenty of room for the thundering quadrigas to pass the wreckage to the outside.

Or, in the alternative, just enough room for one of them, if they happened to be running nearly abreast and the outside driver was disinclined to move over enough to let the inside one pass safely by.

They were, as it happened, running nearly abreast. Scortius of the Blues was outside, a little behind as the two quadrigas came out of the turn and the sea horse dived to signal the last lap. He drifted smoothly outward as they came into the straight—just enough to take his quadriga safely around the wreckage and the two tangled horses on the track.

Crescens of the Greens was thereby faced, in a blur of time and at the apex of fevered excitement, with three obvious but extremely unpalatable choices. He could destroy his team and possibly himself by tearing into the obstruction. He could cut toward Scortius, trying to force his way around the outer edge of the pileup—thereby incurring a certain disqualification and a suspension for the rest of the day. Or he could rein his steaming horses violently back, let Scortius go by, and veer around behind the other driver, effectively conceding defeat with but a single lap to go.

He was a brave man. It had been a stunning, blood-stirring race.

He tried to go through on the inside.

The two fallen horses were farther over. Only a single downed chariot lay near the spina rail. Crescens lashed his own splendid left-side trace horse once, guided it to the innermost rail and *squeezed* his four horses by. The left one scraped hard against the rail. The outside trace horse clipped a leg against a spinning wheel—but they were by. The Green champion's chariot hurtled through as well, *bouncing* into the air so that Crescens appeared to be flying for a moment like an image of Heladikos. But he was through. He came down, brilliantly keeping his balance, whip and reins still in hand, the horses running hard.

It was most terribly unfortunate, given so much courage and skill displayed, that his outside chariot wheel bounced down *behind* him, having been dislodged on the way through the wreckage.

One could not, however brave or skillful, race a one-wheeled chariot. Crescens cut himself free of the reins around his torso. He stood a moment upright in the wildly slewing chariot, lifted his knife in a brief but clearly visible salute to the receding figure of Scortius ahead of him, and jumped free.

He rolled several times, in the way drivers all learned young, and then stood up, alone on the sand. He removed his leather helmet, bowed to the Emperor's box—ignoring the other teams now coming around the curve—then he spread his hands in resignation and bowed equally low to the Green stands.

Then he walked off the track to the spina. He accepted a flask of water from a crewman. He drank deeply, poured the rest in a stream over his head, and stood there blistering the air among the monuments with the profane, passionate fire of his frustration as Scortius turned the last straightaway into a one-chariot Procession, and then ran the formal Victory Lap itself, collecting his wreath, while the Blues permitted themselves to become delirious and the Emperor himself in the kathisma—the indifferent Emperor who favored no faction and didn't even like the racing—lifted a palm in salute to the triumphant charioteer as he went by.

Scortius showed no flamboyance, no exaggerated posture of celebration. He never did. He hadn't for a dozen years and sixteen hundred triumphs. He simply raced, and won, and spent the nights being honored in some aristocratic palace, or bed.

Crescens had had access to the faction ledgers. He knew what the Greens had budgeted for counterspells against the curse-tablets that would have been commissioned against Scortius over the years. He imagined that the Blues had designated half as much again this year.

It would be pleasant, Crescens thought, wiping mud and sweat from his face and forehead among the monuments on the last race day of his first year in Sarantium, to be able to hate the man. He had *no* idea how Scortius had deduced the wreckage would still be there after a simple two-chariot accident. He would never actually ask, but he badly wanted to know. He had been *allowed* to take the inside out of that last turn, and he had done as permitted, like a child who snatches a sweet when he thinks his tutor has turned away.

He noted, with a measure of wryness, that the fellow racing for the Reds in the seventh lane—Baras, or Varas, or whatever—the one who'd been gulled by Scortius at the start, had actually caught a tiring White team coming out of the last turn and taken second place with its considerable prize. It was a wonderful result for a young man riding second for the Reds, and it prevented a sweep for the Blues and Whites.

Crescens decided it would be, under all the circumstances, inappropriate to berate the fellow. Best put this race behind. There were seven more to be run today, he was in four of them, and he still wanted his seventy-five wins.

On his way back to the dressing rooms under the stands to rest before his second appearance of the afternoon, he learned that the Blues' Second, Dauzis, downed in the crash, was dead—his neck broken, either in the fall, or when they moved him.

The Ninth Driver was always running with them. He had shown his face today.

In the Hippodrome they raced to honor the sun god and the Emperor and to bring joy to the people, and some of them ran in homage to gallant Heladikos, and all of them knew—every single time they stood behind their horses—that they could die there on the sands.

CHAPTER VII

Could one forget how to be free?

The question had come to her on the road and it lingered now, unanswered. Could a year of slavery mark your nature forever? Could the *fact* of having been sold? She had been sharp-tongued, quick, astringent at home. *Erimitsu*. Too clever to marry, her mother had worried. Now she felt afraid in the core of her being: anxious, lost, jumping at sounds, averting her eyes. She had spent a year having any man who paid Morax use her in whatever way he wanted. A year being beaten for the slightest failing or for none at all, to keep her mindful of her station.

They had only stopped that at the very end, when they wanted her unmarked, smooth as a sacrifice, for death in the forest.

From her room at the inn Kasia could hear the noise from the Hippodrome. A steady sound like the cascading waters north of home, but rising at intervals—unlike the waters—into a punishing volume of sound, a roar like some many-throated beast when a turn of fortune, terrible or wonderful, happened over there where horses were running.

The *zubir* had made no sound at all in the wood. There had been silence, under and over leaves, shrouded and gathered in fog. The world closing down to the smallest thing, to the one thing. Something terrible or wonderful, and her own existence given back to her, leading her from the Aldwood to Sarantium which had never even been a dream. And to freedom, which had been, every night of that year.

There were eighty thousand people over in the Hippodrome right now. Carullus had said so. It wasn't a number she could even get her mind around. Nearly five hundred thousand in the City, he'd said. Even after the riot two years ago and the plague. How did they all not tremble?

She'd spent the morning in this small room. Had thought to have her meal sent up, reflecting on the change that embodied, wondering what girl, beaten and afraid, would appear with a tray for the lady.

The lady with the soldiers. With the man who was going to the palace. She was that lady. Carullus had made certain they knew it downstairs. Service was a function of status here, as everywhere, and the Bronze Gates opening were the doorway to the world in Sarantium.

Martinian was going there. Or, rather, Caius Crispus was. He'd said they should call him Crispin in private. His name was Crispin. He'd been married to a woman named Ilandra. She was dead and his two daughters were. He had cried her name aloud in the country dark.

He hadn't touched Kasia since that night after the Aldwood. Even then, he'd had her sleep in his cloak on the floor again at the beginning. She'd come to the bed herself, when he cried out. Only then had he turned to her. And only that one time. After, he'd made certain she had her own room as they traveled with the soldiers through the autumn winds and blowing leaves, Sauradia's swift rivers and silver mines becoming Trakesia's harvested grainlands, and then that first appalling sight of the City's triple walls.

Five hundred thousand souls.

Kasia, her world spinning and changing too quickly for even a clever one to deal with, had no idea how to sort through what she was feeling. She was too caught in the movement of things. She could make herself blush—right now—if she remembered some of what she *had* felt, unexpectedly, toward dawn at the end of that one night.

She was in her room, hearing the Hippodrome, mending her cloak—his cloak—with needle and thread. She wasn't skilled with a needle, but it was a thing to do. She'd gone down to the common room for the mid-day meal, after all. She was *erimitsu*, the clever one, and she did know that if she allowed herself to become enclosed within walls and locked doors here she might never get out. Hard as it was, she'd made herself go down. They had served her with casual efficiency, though not with deference. All a woman could ask for, perhaps, especially in the City.

She'd had half a roasted fowl with leeks and good bread and a glass of wine she'd watered more than halfway. It occurred to her, eating at a corner table, that she'd never done this in her life: taken a meal at an inn, as a patron, drinking a glass of wine. Alone.

No one troubled her. The room was almost empty. Everyone was in the Hippodrome, or celebrating the last day of Dykania in the streets, snatching food and too much drink from vendors' stalls, waving noise-makers and banners of guild or racing faction. She could hear them outside, in the sunlight. She forced herself to eat slowly, to drink the wine, even pour a second glass. She was a free citizen of the Sarantine Empire in the reign of Valerius II. It was a public holiday, a festival. She made herself accede when the serving woman asked if she wanted melon.

The woman's hair was the same color as her own. She was older, though. There was a faded scar on her forehead. Kasia smiled at her when she brought the melon but the woman didn't smile back. A little later, however, she brought over a two-handled cup filled with hot spiced wine.

"I didn't order this," Kasia said, worriedly.

"I know. You should have. Cold day. This'll calm you. Your men'll be back soon enough and they'll be excited. They always are, after the chariots. You'll have to get busy again, dear."

She walked away, still without a smile, before Kasia could correct her. It had been a kindness, though. *Dear.* She had meant to be kind. That could still happen, then, in cities.

The spiced wine was good. It smelled of harvests and warmth. Kasia sat quietly and finished it. She watched the open doorway to the street outside. A flow of people, back and forth, unending. From all over the world. She found herself thinking of her mother, and home, and then of where she was, right now. This moment. The place in the god's world where she was. And then she thought about the night she had lain with Martinian—*Crispin*—and that made her flush again and feel extremely strange.

She did as Carullus had instructed and had the serving woman set her meal to the room charges and then she went back upstairs. She had a room of her own. A closed door with a new lock. No one would come in and use her, or order her to do something. A luxury so intense it was frightening. She sat at the small window, needle to hand again, the cloak warm across her knees, but the spiced wine after the other two cups had made her sleepy and she must have drifted off in the slant of sunlight there.

The hard knocking at the door woke her with a start and set her heart to hammering. She stood up hastily, wrapped herself in the cloak—an involuntary, protective gesture—crossed to the locked door. She didn't open it.

"Who is that?" she called. She heard her voice waver.

"Ah. They said he brought a whore." A clipped, eastern voice, educated, sour. "I want to see the westerner, Martinian. Open the door."

She was the *erimitsu*, Kasia reminded herself then. She was. She was free, had rights under law; the innkeeper and his people were below. It was full daylight here. And Martinian might need her to keep her wits just now. She'd heard Morax talk to merchants and patricians often enough. She could do this.

She took a breath. "Who seeks him, may I ask?"

There was a short, dry laugh. "I don't talk to prostitutes through locked doors."

Anger helped, actually. "And I don't open doors to ill-bred strangers. We have a problem, it appears."

A silence. She heard a floorboard creak in the hallway. The man coughed. "Presumptuous bitch. I am Siroes, Mosaicist to the Imperial Court. Open the door."

She opened the door. It might be a mistake, but Marti—*Crispin*—

had been summoned here to do mosaic work for the Emperor, and this man . . .

This man was small, plump and balding. He was dressed in a rich, very dark blue, calf-length linen tunic worked expensively in gold thread, a crimson cloak over that with an intricate design running across it in a band, also in gold. He'd a round, complacent face, dark eyes, long fingers, at odds with the general impression of rotund softness. On his hands she saw the same network of cuts and scars that Crispin bore. He was alone save for a servant, a little distance behind him in the empty hallway.

"Ah," said the man named Siroes. "He likes skinny women. I don't mind them. What do you charge for an afternoon encounter?"

It was important to be calm. She was a free citizen. "Do you insult all the women you meet? Or have I offended you somehow? I was told the Imperial Precinct was known for its courtesies. I appear to have been wrongly informed. Shall I call for the innkeeper to have you thrown out, or shall I simply scream?"

Again the man hesitated, and this time, looking at him, Kasia thought she saw something. It was unexpected, but she was almost sure.

"Thrown out?" He gave that same short rasp of laughter. "You aren't presumptuous, you are ignorant. Where is Martinian?"

Careful, she said to herself. This man was important, and Crispin might depend upon him, work with him, for him. She could *not* give way to panic or anger, either one.

She schooled her voice, cast her eyes downward, thought of Morax, genuflecting to some fat-pursed merchant. "I am sorry, my lord. I may be a barbarian and unused to the City, but I am no one's whore. Martinian of Varena is at the Hippodrome with the tribune of the Fourth Sauradian."

Siroes swore under his breath. She caught it again, then, that hint of something unexpected.

He's afraid, she thought.

"When will he be back?"

"My lord, I would imagine when the racing ends." They heard a roar from across the narrow streets and the expanse of the Hippodrome

Forum. Someone had won a race, someone had lost it. "Will you wait for him? Or shall I leave him a message from you?"

"*Wait?* Hardly. Amusing, I must say, that the Rhodian thinks he is at leisure to go to the games when he's taken the god's time arriving."

"Surely not a failing during Dykania, my lord? The Emperor and the Chancellor were both to be at the Hippodrome, we were told. No court presentations were scheduled."

"Ah. And who is informing you so comprehensively?"

"The tribune of the Fourth Sauradian is very knowledgeable, my lord."

"Hah! The Sauradians? A country soldier."

"Yes, my lord. Of course, he is an officer and does have an appointment with the Supreme Strategos. I suppose that required that he make himself aware of doings in the Imperial Precinct. As best he could. Of course, as you say, he wouldn't *really* know very much."

She looked up in time to catch an uneasy glance from the mosaicist. She cast her eyes quickly downward again. She could *do* this. It was possible, after all.

Siroes swore again. "I cannot wait on an ignorant westerner. There is to be an Imperial Banquet after the chariots tonight. I have an honored couch there." He paused. "Tell him that. Tell him . . . I came as a colleague to extend greetings before he was faced with the . . . strain of a court appearance."

She kept her eyes down.

"He will be honored, I know it. My lord, he will be distressed to have missed your visit."

The mosaicist twitched his cloak up on one shoulder, adjusting the golden brooch that pinned it. "Don't fake proper manners or speech. It hardly suits a bony whore. I do have enough time to fuck you. Will a half solidus get your clothes off?"

She held back the biting retort. She wasn't afraid anymore, astonishingly. *He* was. She met his gaze. "No," she said. "It will not. I shall tell Martinian of Varena you were here and offered, though."

She moved to close the door.

"Wait!" His eyes flickered. "A jest. I made a jest. Country folk *never*

understand court wit. Do you . . . would you . . . by chance have any experience of Martinian's work, or, ah, his views on . . . say, the transfer method of setting tesserae?"

A terrified man. They were dangerous sometimes. "I am neither his whore nor his apprentice, my lord. I shall tell him, when he returns, that this is what you came to learn."

"No! I mean . . . do not trouble yourself. I will discuss the matter with him myself, naturally. I shall have to, ah, ascertain his competence. Of course."

"Of course," Kasia said, and closed the door on the Mosaicist to the Imperial Court.

She locked it, leaned back against the wood, and then, unable not to, began to laugh silently, and then to weep, at the same time.

HAD HE ARRIVED BACK at the inn after the racing, as he had intended, had he spoken with Kasia and learned of her encounter with a visitor—the details of which would have meant rather more to him than they did to her—Crispin would almost certainly have conducted himself differently in certain matters that followed.

This, in turn, might have occasioned a significant change in various affairs, both personal and of much wider import. It could, in fact, have changed his life and a number of other lives, and—arguably—the course of events in the Empire.

This happens, more often than is sometimes suspected. Lovers first meet at a dinner one almost failed to attend. A wine barrel falling from a wagon breaks the leg of someone who chose an impulsive route to his usual bathhouse. An assassin's thrown dagger fails to kill only because the intended victim turns—randomly—and sees it coming. The tides of fortune and the lives of men and women in the god's created world are shaped and altered in such fashion.

Crispin didn't come back to the inn.

Or, rather, as he and Carullus and Vargos approached it at sundown through the roiling, tumultuous festival streets, half a dozen men detached themselves from where they were standing by the front wall of the inn and approached them. They were clad, he noted, in subtly patterned knee-length dark green tunics, with a vertical brown stripe on both sides, brown trousers, dark brown belts. Each wore an identical necklace with a medallion, a badge of office. They were grave, composed, entirely at odds with the chaos around them.

Carullus stopped when he saw them. He looked cautious, but not alarmed. Crispin, taking his cue from this, stood easily as the leader of the six men came up to him. He was admiring the taste and cut of the clothing, in fact. Just before the man spoke, he realized he was a eunuch.

"You are the mosaicist? Martinian of Varena?"

Crispin nodded. "May I know who asks?"

Overhead at her window Kasia was watching. She had been looking out for the three men as soon as the cheering from the Hippodrome had stopped. She looked down and thought of calling out. Did not. Of course.

"We are sent from the Chancellor's Offices. Your presence is requested in the Imperial Precinct."

"So I understand. It is why I have journeyed to Sarantium."

"You do not understand. You are greatly honored. You are to come tonight. Now. The Emperor will be hosting a banquet shortly. After this he will receive you in the Attenine Palace. Do you comprehend? Men of the highest rank wait weeks, months to be seen. Ambassadors sometimes leave the city without an audience at all. You will be presented tonight. The Emperor is greatly engaged by the progress of the new Sanctuary. We are to bring you back with us and prepare you."

Carullus made a small, whistling sound. One of the eunuchs looked at him. Vargos was motionless, listening. Crispin said, "I am honored, indeed. But now? I am to be presented as I am?"

The eunuch smiled briefly. "Hardly as you are." One of the others sniffed audibly, with amusement.

"Then I must bathe and change my clothing. I have been in the Hippodrome all day."

"This is known. It is unlikely that any clothing you have brought will be adequate to a formal court appearance. You are here by virtue of the Chancellor's request. Gesius therefore assumes responsibility for you before the Emperor. We will attend to your appearance. Come."

He went. It was why he was here.

Kasia watched from the window, biting her lip. The impulse to call after him was very strong, though she could not have said why. A premonition. Something from the half-world? Shadows. When Carullus and Vargos came upstairs she told them about the afternoon visitor, about that last, strangely specific question he'd asked. Carullus swore, deepening her fears.

"Nothing for it," he said, after a moment. "No way to tell him now. There's a trap of some kind, but there would have to be, at that court. He has quick wits, Jad knows it. Let us hope he keeps them about him."

"I must go," Vargos said, after a silence. "Sundown."

Carullus looked at him, gave Kasia a shrewd glance, and then led them both briskly out into the crowded, now-darkening streets to a good-sized sanctuary some distance back toward the triple walls. Among a great many people in the space before the altar and the sun disk on the wall behind it they heard the sundown rites chanted by a wiry, dark-bearded cleric. Kasia stood and knelt and stood and knelt between the two men and tried not to think about the zubir, or Caius Crispus, or about all the people packed so closely around her here, and in the City.

Afterward, they dined at a tavern not far away. Crowds again. There were many soldiers. Carullus greeted and was saluted by a number of them when they entered, but then, still being solicitous, chose a booth at the very back, away from the noise. He had her sit with her back to the tumult, so she wouldn't even have to look at anyone but Vargos or himself. He ordered food and wine for the three of them, jesting easily with the server. He had lost a great deal of money on one particular race in the afternoon, Kasia gathered. It didn't seem to have subdued him very much. He was not, she had come to realize, a man easily subdued.

HE FELT OUTRAGED BEYOND words, violated and assaulted, undermined in his very sense of who he was. He had shouted in profane rage, lashed out in wild fury, sending fountains of water splashing from the bath, soaking a number of them.

They had laughed. And given the wide swath already cut from him while he'd lain back at his ease, eyes innocently closed in the wonderfully warm, scented water, Crispin had had no real choice anymore. When he'd finished snarling and swearing and vowing obscenely violent acts that appeared only to amuse them further, he'd had to let them complete what they'd begun—or look like a crazed madman.

They finished shaving off his beard.

It seemed that the fashion at the court of Valerius and Alixana was for smooth-cheeked men. Barbarians, hinterland soldiers, provincials who couldn't know better, wore facial hair, the eunuch wielding the scissors and then the gleaming razor said, making a moue of ineffable distaste. They looked like bears, goats, bison, other beasts, he opined.

"What do you know about bison?" Crispin had rasped bitterly.

"Nothing in the least! Thanks be to holy Jad in his mercy!" the eunuch with the razor had replied fervently, making the sign of the sun disk with the blade, eliciting laughter from his fellows.

Men at court, he explained patiently, manipulating the razor with precision as he spoke, had a duty to the god and the Emperor to appear as civilized as they could. For a redheaded man to wear a beard, he'd added firmly, was as much a provocation, a sign of ill-breeding, as . . . as breaking wind during the sunrise invocation in the Imperial Chapel.

Waiting, some time later, in an antechamber of the Attenine Palace, clad in silk for only the second time in his life, with soft, close-fitting leather shoes and a short, dark green cloak pinned to his shoulder over the long, dove gray tunic bordered in textured black, Crispin couldn't stop touching his own face. His hand kept wandering up of its own accord. They had held up a mirror for him in the bath: a splendid one, ivory-handled, a design of grapes and leaves etched on the silver back, the glass wonderfully true, next to no distortion.

A stranger had gazed back at him, wet and pale and angry-looking. Smooth-cheeked as a child. He'd had the beard since before he met Ilandra. Over a decade now. He hardly knew or remembered the oddly vulnerable, truculent, square-chinned person he encountered in the glass. His eyes showed very blue. His mouth—his entire face—felt unguarded and exposed. He'd essayed a brief, testing smile and stopped quickly. It did not look or feel like his own face. He'd been . . . altered. He wasn't *himself*. Not a secure feeling, as he prepared to be presented at the most intricate, dangerous court in the world, bearing a false name and a secret message.

Waiting, he was still angry, taking a kind of refuge from mounting anxiety in that. He knew the Chancellor's officials had been acting with undeniable goodwill and a good-humored tolerance for his water-spraying fit of temper. The eunuchs *wanted* him to make a good impression. It reflected upon them, he'd been made to understand. Gesius's signature had summoned him and smoothed his way here on the road. He stood now in this sumptuous, candlelit antechamber, hearing the sounds of the court beginning to enter the throne room through doors on the far side, and he was—in some complex way—a representative of the Chancellor, though he'd never even seen the man.

One arrived in the Imperial Precinct, Crispin belatedly realized, already aligned in some fashion, even before the first words or genuflections took place. They had told him about the genuflections. The instructions were precise and he'd been made to rehearse them. Against his will, he'd felt his heart beginning to pound, doing so, and that feeling resumed now as he heard the dignitaries of Valerius II's court on the other side of the magnificent silver doors. There was rising and falling laughter, a lightly murmurous flow of talk. They would be in a good humor after a festival day and a banquet.

He rubbed at his naked chin again. The smoothness was appalling, unsettling. As if a shaven, silk-clad, scented Sarantine courtier were standing in his body, half a world away from home. He felt dislodged from the idea of himself he'd built up over the years.

And that sensation—this imposed change of appearance and identity—probably had much to do with what followed, he later decided.

None of it was planned. He knew that much. He was simply a reckless, contrary man. His mother had always said so, his wife, his friends.

He'd given up trying to deny it long ago. They used to laugh at him when he did, so he'd stopped.

After the protracted wait, watching the blue moon rise across an interior courtyard window, events happened quickly when they did begin. The silver doors swung open. Crispin and the Chancellor's representatives turned quickly. Two guardsmen—enormously tall, in gleaming silver tunics—stepped from within the throne room. Crispin caught a glimpse beyond them of movement and color. There was a drifting fragrance of perfume: frankincense. He heard music, then that—and the shifting movements—stopped. A man appeared behind the guards, clad in crimson and white, carrying a ceremonial staff. One of the eunuchs nodded to this man, and then looked at Crispin. He smiled—a generous thing to do in that moment—and murmured, "You look entirely suitable. You are benevolently awaited. Jad be with you."

Crispin stepped forward hesitantly to stand beside the heraldic figure in the doorway. The man looked over at him indifferently. "Martinian of Varena, is it?" he asked.

It really *wasn't* planned.

The thought was in his mind even as he spoke that he might die for this. He rubbed his too-smooth chin. "No," he said, calmly enough. "My name is Caius Crispus. Of Varena, though, yes."

The herald's startled expression might actually have been comical had the situation been even slightly different. One of the guards shifted slightly beside Crispin, but made no other movement, not even turning his head. "Fuck yourself with a sword!" the herald whispered in the elegant accents of the eastern aristocracy. "You think I'm announcing any name other than the one on the list? You do what you want in there."

And, stepping forward into the room, he thumped once on the floor with his staff. The chattering of the courtiers had already stopped. They'd aligned themselves, waiting, creating a pathway into the room.

"*Martinian of Varena!*" the herald declared, his voice resonant and strong, the name ringing in the domed chamber.

Crispin stepped forward, his head whirling, aware of new scents and a myriad of colors but not really seeing clearly yet. He took the prescribed three steps, knelt, lowered his forehead to the floor. Waited, counting ten to himself. Rose. Three more steps toward the man sitting on the candlelit shimmer of gold that was a throne. Knelt again, lowered his head again to touch the cool stone mosaics of the floor. Counted, trying to slow his racing heart. Rose. Three more steps, and a third time he knelt and abased himself.

This last time he stayed that way, as instructed, about ten paces from the Imperial throne and the second throne beside it where a woman sat in a dazzle of jewelry. He didn't look up. He heard a mildly curious murmuring from the assembled courtiers, come from their feast to see a new Rhodian at court. Rhodians were of interest, still. There was a quip, a quicksilver ripple of feminine laughter, then silence.

Into which a papery thin, very clear voice spoke. "Be welcome to the Imperial Court of Sarantium, artisan. On behalf of the Glorious Emperor and the Empress Alixana I give you leave to rise, Martinian of Varena."

This would be Gesius, Crispin knew. The Chancellor. His patron, if he had one. He closed his eyes, took a deep breath. And remained utterly motionless, his forehead touching the floor.

There was a pause. Someone giggled.

"You have been granted permission to rise," the thin, dry voice repeated.

Crispin thought of the *zubir* in the wood. And then of Linon, the bird—the soul—who had spoken in his mind to him, if only for a little while. He had wanted to die, he remembered, when Ilandra died.

He said, not looking up, but as clearly as he could, "I dare not, my lord."

A rustle, of voices, of clothing, like leaves across the floor. He was aware of the mingled scents, the coolness of the mosaic, no music now. His mouth was dry.

"You propose to remain prostrate forever?" Gesius's voice betrayed a hint of asperity.

"No, good my lord. Only until I am granted the privilege of standing before the Emperor in my own name. Else I am a deceiver and deserve to die."

That stilled them.

The Chancellor appeared to be momentarily taken aback. The voice that next spoke was trained, exquisite, and a woman's. Afterward, Crispin would remember that he shivered, hearing her for the first time. She said, "If all who deceived in this room were to die, there would be none left to advise or amuse us, I fear."

It was remarkable, really, how a silence and a silence could be so different. The woman—and he knew this was Alixana and that this voice would be in his head now, forever—went on, after a gauged pause, "You would rather be named Caius Crispus, I take it? The artisan young enough to travel when your summoned colleague deemed himself too frail to make the journey to us?"

Crispin's breath went from him, as if he'd been hit in the stomach. They knew. They *knew*. How, he had no idea. There were implications to this, a frightening number of them, but he had no chance to work it through. He fought for control, forehead touching the floor.

"The Emperor and Empress know the hearts and souls of men," he managed, finally. "I have indeed come in my partner's stead, to offer what assistance my meager skills might avail the Emperor. I will stand to my own name, as the Empress has honored me by speaking it, or accept what punishment is due my presumption."

"Let us be extremely clear. You are *not* Martinian of Varena?" A new voice, patrician and sharp, from near the two thrones.

Carullus had spent some of the time on the last stages of their journey telling what he knew of this court. Crispin was almost certain this would be Faustinus, the Master of Offices. Gesius's rival, probably the most powerful man here—after the one on the throne.

The one on the throne had said nothing at all yet.

"It seems one of your couriers failed to ensure proper delivery of an Imperial summons, Faustinus," said Gesius in his bone-dry voice.

"It rather seems," said the other man, "that the Chancellor's eunuchs failed to ensure that a man being formally presented at court was who he purported to be. This is dangerous. Why did you have yourself announced as Martinian, artisan? That was a deception."

It was difficult doing this with his head on the floor. "I did not," he said. "It seems that—regrettably—the herald must have . . . misheard my name when I spoke it to him. I did say who I am. My name is Caius Crispus, son of Horius Crispus. I am a mosaicist, and have been all my grown life. Martinian of Varena is my colleague and partner and has been so for twelve years."

"Heralds," said the Empress softly, in that astonishing, silken voice, "are of little use if they err in such a fashion. Would you not agree, Faustinus?"

Which offered its clue, of course, as to who appointed the heralds here, Crispin thought. His mind was racing. It occurred to him he was making enemies with every word he spoke. He still had no idea how the Empress—and so the Emperor, he had to assume—had known his name.

"I shall inquire into this, naturally, thrice-exalted." Faustinus's sharp tone was abruptly muted.

"There does not appear to be," a new voice, blunt and matter-of-fact, inserted itself, "any great difficulty here. An artisan was requested from Rhodias, an artisan has answered. An associate of the named one. If he is adequate to the tasks allotted him, it hardly matters, I would say. It would be a misfortune to mar a festive mood, my lord Emperor, with wrangling over a triviality. Are we not here to amuse ourselves?"

Crispin didn't know who this man—the first to directly address Valerius—would be. He heard two things, though. One, after a heart-beat, was a ripple of agreement and relief, a restoration of ease in the room. Whoever this was had a not-inconsiderable stature.

The other sound he caught, a few moments later, was a slight, almost undetectable creaking noise in front of him.

It would have meant nothing at all to virtually any other person in Crispin's awkward position here, forehead pressed to the floor. But it *did* mean something to a mosaicist. Disbelieving at first, he listened. Heard suppressed laughter from right and left, quick whispers to hush. And the soft, steady creaking sound continuing before him.

The court had been diverting itself tonight, he thought. Good food, wine, amorous, witty talk, no doubt. It was night—a festival night. He pictured female hands laid expectantly on male forearms, scented, silk-clad bodies leaning close as they watched. A Rhodian needing a measure of chastisement might offer wonderful sport.

He didn't feel like offering them sport.

He was here at the Sarantine court in his own family name, son of a father who would have been proud beyond words in this moment, and he wasn't inclined to be the mark for a jest.

He was a contrary man. He'd admitted it already, long ago. It was self-destructive at times. He'd acknowledged that, too. He was also the direct descendant of a people who'd ruled an empire far greater than this one, at a time when this city was no more than a gathering of wind-blown huts on a rocky cliff.

"Very well, then," said the Chancellor Gesius, his voice almost but not quite as dry as it had been. "You have permission to rise, Caius Crispus, Rhodian. Stand now before the all-powerful, Jad's Beloved, the high and exalted Emperor of Sarantium." Someone laughed.

He stood, slowly. Facing the two thrones.

The one throne. Only the Empress sat before him. The Emperor was gone.

High and exalted, Crispin thought. *How terribly witty.*

He was expected to panic, he knew. To look befuddled, disoriented, even terrified, perhaps wheel about in a stumbling bearlike circle looking for an Emperor, reacting in slack-jawed confusion when he did not find him.

Instead, he glanced upward in relaxed appraisal. He smiled at what he saw when he did so. Jad could sometimes be generous, it seemed, even to lesser, undeserving mortals.

"I am humbled beyond all words," he said gravely, addressing the figure on the golden throne overhead, halfway to the height of the exquisite little dome. "Thrice-exalted Emperor, I shall be honored to assist in any mosaic work you or your trusted servants might see fit to assign me. I might also be able to propose measures to improve the effect of your elevation on the glorious Imperial throne."

"Improve the effect?" Faustinus again, the sharp voice aghast. Around the room, a sudden tidal murmuring. The joke was spoiled. The Rhodian, for some reason, hadn't been fooled.

Crispin wondered what the effect of this artifice had been over the years. Barbarian chieftains and kings, trade emissaries, long-robed Bassanid or fur-clad Karchite ambassadors, all would have belatedly looked up to see Jad's Holy Emperor suspended in the air on his throne, invisibly held aloft, elevated as much above them in his person as he was in his might. Or so the message would have been, behind the sophisticated amusement.

He said mildly, still looking upward, not at the Master of Offices, "A mosaicist spends much of his life going up and down on a variety of platforms and hoists. I can suggest some contrivances the Imperial engineers might employ to silence the mechanism, for example."

He was, as he spoke, aware of the Empress regarding him from her throne. It was impossible *not* to be aware of her. Alixana wore a headdress more richly ornamented with jewelry than any single object he'd ever seen in his life.

He kept his gaze fixed overhead. "I should add that it might have been more effective to position the thrice-exalted Emperor directly in the moonlight now entering from the southern and western windows in the dome. Note how the light falls only on the glorious Imperial feet. Imagine the effect should Jad's Beloved be suspended at this moment in the luminous glow of a nearly full blue moon. A turn and a half less, I surmise, on the cables, and that would have been achieved, my lord."

The murmuring took a darker tone. Crispin ignored it. "Any competent mosaicist will have tables of both moons' rising and setting, and engineers can work from those. When we have set tesserae on some sanctuary or palace domes in Batiara it has been our good fortune—Martinian's and mine—to achieve pleasing effects by being aware of when and where the moons will lend their light through the seasons. I should be honored," he concluded, "to assist the Imperial engineers in this matter."

He stopped, still looking up. The murmuring also stopped. There was a silence that partook of a great many things then in the candlelit throne room of the Attenine Palace, among the jeweled birds, the golden and silver trees, the censers of frankincense, the exquisite works of ivory and silk and sandalwood and semiprecious stone.

It was broken, at length, by laughter.

Crispin would always remember this, too. That the first sound he ever heard from Petrus of Trakesia, who had placed his uncle on the Imperial throne and then taken it for himself as Valerius II, was this laughter: rich, uninhibited, full-throated amusement from overhead, a man suspended like a god, laughing like a god above his court, not quite in the fall of the blue moonlight.

The Emperor gestured and they lowered him until the throne settled smoothly to rest beside the Empress again. No one spoke during this descent. Crispin stood motionless, hands at his side, his heart still racing. He looked at the Emperor of Sarantium. Jad's Beloved.

Valerius II was soft-featured, quite unprepossessing, with alert gray eyes and the smooth-shaven cheeks that had led to the attack on Crispin's own beard. His hairline was receding though the hair remained a sandy brown laced with gray. He was past his forty-fifth year now, Crispin knew. Not a young man, but far from his decline. He wore a belted tunic in textured purple silk, bordered at hem and collar with bands of intricately patterned gold. Rich, but without ornament or flamboyance. No jewelry, save one very large seal ring on his left hand.

The woman beside him took a different approach in the matter of her raiment and adornment. Crispin had actually been avoiding looking directly at the Empress. He couldn't have said why. Now he did so, aware of her dark-eyed, amused gaze resting upon him. Other images, auras, awarenesses impinged as he briefly met that gaze and then cast his eyes downward. He felt dizzied. He had seen beautiful women in his day, and much younger ones. There were extraordinary women in this room.

The Empress held him, however, and not merely by virtue of her rank or history. Alixana—who had been merely Aliana of the Blues once, an actress and dancer—was dressed in a dazzle of crimson and gold silk, the porphyry in the robe over her tunic used as an accent, but present, unavoidably present, defining her status. The headdress framing her very dark hair and the necklace about her throat were worth more, Crispin suspected, than all the jewelry in the regalia of the queen of the Antae back home. He felt, in that moment, a shaft of pity for Gisel: young and besieged and struggling for her life.

Her head held high despite the weight of ornament she carried, the Empress of Sarantium glittered in his sight, and the clever, observant amusement in her dark eyes reminded him that there was no one on earth more dangerous than this woman seated beside the Emperor.

He saw her open her mouth to speak, and when someone, astonishingly, forestalled her he saw, because he was looking, the quick pursing of lips, the briefly unveiled displeasure.

"This Rhodian," said an elegant, fair-haired woman behind her, "has all the presumption one might have expected, and none of the manners one dared hope for. At least they chopped off his foliage. A red beard along with an uncouth manner would have been too offensive."

Crispin said nothing. He saw the Empress smile thinly. Without turning, Alixana said, "You knew he was bearded? You have been making inquiries, Styliane? Even newly married? How very characteristic of the Daleinoi."

Someone laughed nervously and was quickly silent. The big, frank-looking, handsome man beside the woman looked briefly uneasy. But from the name that had been spoken, Crispin now knew who these two people were. The pieces slotting into place. He had a puzzle-solving mind. Always had. Needed it now.

He was looking at Carullus's beloved Strategos, the man the tribune had come from Sauradia to see, the greatest soldier of the day. This tall man was Leontes the Golden, and beside him was his bride. Daughter of the wealthiest family in Sarantium. A prize for a triumphant general. She was, Crispin had to concede. She *was* a prize. Styliane Daleina was magnificent, and the single, utterly spectacular pearl that gleamed in the golden necklace at her throat might even be . . .

An idea came to him in that moment, anger-driven. Inwardly he winced at his own subversive thought, and he kept silent. There were limits to recklessness.

Styliane Daleina was entirely unruffled by the Empress's remark. She would be, Crispin realized: she'd revealed her knowledge of him freely with the insult. She would have been ready for a retort. He had an abrupt sense that he was now another very minor piece in a complex game being played between two women.

Or three. He was carrying a message.

"He can beard himself like a Holy Fool if he chooses," said the Emperor of Sarantium mildly, "if he has the skills to assist with the Sanctuary mosaics." Valerius's voice was quiet, but it cut through all other sounds. It would, Crispin thought. Everyone in this room would be tuned to its cadences.

Crispin looked at the Emperor, pushing the women from his mind. "You have spoken persuasively about engineering and moonlight," said Valerius of Sarantium. "Shall we converse a moment about mosaic?"

He sounded like a scholar, an academician. He looked like one. It was said that this man never slept. That he walked one or another of his palaces all night dictating, or sat reading dispatches by lanternlight. That he could engage philosophers and military tacticians in discourse that stretched the limits of their own understanding. That he had met with the aspiring architects of his new Great Sanctuary and had reviewed each drawing they presented. That one of them had killed himself when the Emperor rejected his scheme, explaining in precise detail why he was doing so. This much had reached even Varena: there was an Emperor in Sarantium now with a taste for beauty as well as power.

"I am here for no other reason, thrice-exalted," Crispin said. It was more or less the truth.

"Ah," said Styliane Daleina quickly. "Another Rhodian trait. Here to converse he tells us—no deeds. Thus, the Antae conquered with such ease. It is all *so* familiar."

There was laughter again. In its own way, this second interruption was intensely revealing: she had to feel utterly secure, either in her own person or that of her husband, the Emperor's longtime friend, to break into a colloquy of this sort. What was unclear was *why* the woman was attacking him. Crispin kept his gaze on the Emperor.

"There are a variety of reasons why Rhodias fell," said Valerius II mildly. "We are discussing mosaics, however, for the moment. Caius Crispus, what is your opinion as to the new reverse transfer method of laying tesserae in sheets in the workshop?"

Even with all he'd heard about this man, the technical precision of this question—coming from an Emperor after a banquet, in the midst of his courtiers—caught Crispin completely by surprise. He swallowed. Cleared his throat.

"My lord, it is both suitable and useful for mosaics on very large walls and floors. It enables a more uniform setting of the glass or stone pieces where that is desired, and relieves much of the need for speed in setting tesserae directly before the setting bed dries. I can explain, if the Emperor wishes."

"Not necessary. I understand this. What about using it on a dome?"

Crispin was to wonder, afterward, how the ensuing events would have unfolded had he tried to be diplomatic in that moment. He didn't try. Events unfolded as they did.

"On a *dome*?" he echoed, his voice rising. "Thrice-exalted lord, only a fool would even suggest using that method on a dome! No mosaicist worth the name would consider it."

Behind him someone made what could only be called a spluttering sound.

Styliane Daleina said icily, "You are in the presence of the Emperor of Sarantium. We whip or blind strangers who presume so much."

"And we honor those," said the Empress Alixana, in her exquisite voice, "who honor us with their honesty when directly asked for it. Will you say why you offer this . . . very strong view, Rhodian?"

Crispin hesitated. "The court of the glorious Emperor, on a Dykania night . . . do you really wish such a discussion?"

"The Emperor does," said the Emperor.

Crispin swallowed again. Martinian, he thought, would have done this *much* more tactfully.

He wasn't Martinian. Directly to Valerius of Sarantium he spoke one of the tenets of his soul. "Mosaic," he said, more softly now, "is a dream of light. Of color. It is the play of light *on* color. It is a craft . . . I have sometimes dared call it an art, my lord . . . built around letting the illumination of candle, lantern, sun, both moons dance across the colors of the glass and gemstones and stones we use . . . to make something that partakes, however slightly, of the qualities of movement that Jad gave his mortal children and the world. In a sanctuary, my lord, it is a craft that aspires to evoke the holiness of the god and his creation."

He took a breath. It was incredible to him that he was saying these things aloud, and here. He looked at the Emperor.

"Go on," said Valerius. The gray eyes were on his face, intent, coolly intelligent.

"And on a dome," said Crispin, "on the arch of a dome—whether of sanctuary or palace—the mosaicist has a chance to work with this, to breathe a shadow of life into his vision. A wall is flat, a floor is flat—"

"Well, they *ought* to be," said the Empress lightly. "I've lived in some rooms . . ."

Valerius laughed aloud. Crispin, in mid-flight, paused, and had to smile. "Indeed, thrice-gracious lady. I speak in principle, of course. These are ideals we seldom attain."

"A wall or a floor is flat, in its conception," said the Emperor. "A dome . . . ?"

"The curve and the height of a dome allow us the illusion of movement through changing light, my lord. Opportunities beyond price. It is the mosaicist's natural place. His . . . haven. A painted fresco on a flat wall can do all a mosaic can, and—though many in my guild would call this heresy—it can do more at times. Nothing on Jad's earth can do what a mosaicist can do on a dome *if he sets the tesserae directly on the surface.*"

A voice from behind him, refined and querulous: "I will be allowed to speak to this crass western stupidity, I dare trust, thrice-exalted lord?"

"When it is done, Siroes. If it is stupid. Listen. You will be asked questions. Be prepared to answer them."

Siroes. He didn't know the name. He ought to, probably. He hadn't prepared himself as well as he should have . . . but he had *not* expected to be here at court a day after arriving in the City.

He was also angry now. *Crass?* Too many insults at once. He tried to hold down his temper, but this was the place where his soul resided. He said, "East or west has nothing to do with any of this, my lord. You described the reverse transfer as new. Someone has misled you, I am afraid. Five hundred years ago mosaicists were laying reversed sheets of tesserae on walls and floors in Rhodias, Mylasia, Baiana. Examples still exist, they are there to be seen. There are no such examples on any dome in Batiara. Shall I tell the thrice-exalted Emperor why?"

"Tell me why," said Valerius.

"Because five hundred years ago mosaicists had already learned that laying stone and gems and glass flat on sticky sheets and then transferring that relinquished all the power the curves of the dome gave them. When you set a tessera by hand into a surface, you *position* it. You angle it, turn it. You adjust it in relation to the piece beside it, and the one beside that and beyond it, toward or away from the light entering through windows or rising from below. You can build up the setting bed into a relief, or recede it for effect. You can—if you are a mosaicist, and not merely someone sticking glass in a pasty surface—allow what you know of the proposed location and number of candles in the room below and the placement of the windows around the base of the dome and higher up, the orientation of the room on holy Jad's earth, and the risings of his moons and the god's sun . . . you allow *light* to be your tool, your servant, your . . . gift in rendering what is holy."

"And the other way?" It was Gesius the Chancellor this time, surprisingly. The elderly eunuch's spare, gaunt features were thoughtful, as if chasing a nuance through this exchange. It wouldn't be the subject that engaged him, Crispin suspected, but Valerius's interest in it. This was a man who had survived to serve three Emperors.

"The other way," he said softly, "you turn that gift of a high, curved surface into . . . a wall. A badly made wall that bends. You forgo the play of light that is at the heart of mosaic. The heart of what I do. Or have always tried to do, my lord. My lord Emperor."

It was a cynical, jaded court. He was speaking from the soul, with too much passion. Far too much. He sounded ridiculous. He *felt* ridiculous, and he had no clear idea why he was giving vent in this way to deeply private feelings. He rubbed at his bare chin.

"You treat the rendering of holy images in a sanctuary as . . . play?" It was the tall Strategos, Leontes. And from the blunt, unvarnished soldier's tone, Crispin realized that this was the man who'd intervened earlier. *One western artisan is like another,* he'd suggested then. *Why do we care which one came?*

Crispin took a breath. "I treat the presence of light as something to glory in. A source of joy and gratitude. What else, my lord, is the sunrise invocation? The loss of the sun is a grave loss. Darkness is no friend to any of Jad's children, and this is even more true for a mosaicist."

Leontes looked at him, a slight furrow in the handsome brow. His hair was yellow as wheat. "Darkness is sometimes an ally to a soldier," he said.

"Soldiers kill," Crispin murmured. "It may be a necessary thing, but it is no exaltation of the god. I would imagine you agree, my lord."

Leontes shook his head. "I do not. Of course I do not. If we conquer and reduce barbarians or heretics, those who deride and deny Jad of the Sun, do we not exalt him?" Crispin saw a thin, sallow-faced man lean forward, listening intently.

"Is imposing worship the same as exalting our god, then?" More than a decade of debating with Martinian had honed him for this sort of thing. He could almost forget where he was.

Almost.

"How *extremely* tedious this suddenly becomes," said the Empress, her tone the embodiment of capricious boredom. "It is even worse than talk of which way to lay a piece of glass on some sticky bed. I do *not* think sticky beds are a fit subject here. Styliane's just married, after all."

It was the Strategos who flushed, not the elegant wife beside him, as the Emperor's own thoughtful expression broke into a smile, and laughter with an edge of malice rippled through the room.

Crispin waited for it to die. He said, not sure why he was doing so, "It was the thrice-exalted Empress who asked me to defend my views. My strong views, she called them. It was someone else who described them as a stupidity. In the presence of such greatness as I find myself, I dare choose no subjects, only respond when asked, as best I may. And seek to avoid the chasms of stupidity."

Alixana's expressive mouth quirked a little, but her dark eyes were unreadable. She was a small woman, exquisitely formed. "You have a careful memory, Rhodian. I did ask you, didn't I?"

Crispin inclined his head. "The Empress is generous to recall it.

Lesser mortals cannot but recollect each word she breathes, of course." He was surprising himself with almost every word *he* spoke tonight.

Valerius, leaning back on the throne now, clapped his hands. "Well said, if shameless. The westerner may yet teach our courtiers a few things besides engineering and mosaic technique."

"*My lord Emperor!* Surely you have not *accepted* his prattle about the reverse—"

The relaxed demeanor disappeared. The gray gaze went knifing past Crispin.

"Siroes, when you presented your drawings and your plans to our architects and ourself, you did say this device was new, did you not?"

The tone of the room changed dramatically. The Emperors voice was icy. He was still leaning back in his throne, but the eyes had altered.

Crispin wanted to turn and see who this other mosaicist was but he dared not move. The man behind him stammered, "My lord . . . thrice-exalted lord, it has *never* been used in Sarantium. Never on any other dome. I proposed—"

"And what we have just heard of Rhodias? Five hundred years ago? The reasons why? Did you consider this?"

"My lord, the affairs of the fallen west, I—"

"What?" Valerius II sat upright now. He leaned forward. A finger stabbed the air as he spoke. "This was *Rhodias*, artisan! Speak not to us of the fallen west. This was the Rhodian Empire at its apex! In the god's name! What did Saranios name this city when he drew the line with his sword from channel to ocean for the first walls? Tell me!"

There was fear now in the room, palpably. Crispin saw men and women, elegant and glittering, their eyes fixed on the floor like subdued children.

"He . . . he . . . Sarantium, thrice-exalted."

"And what else? *What else?* Say it, Siroes!"

"The . . . He called it the New Rhodias, thrice-great lord." The patrician voice was a croak now. "Glorious Emperor, we know, we *all* know there has never been a holy sanctuary on earth to match the one you have envisaged and are bringing into being. It will be the glory of Jad's world. The dome, the dome is unmatched in size, in majesty . . ."

"We can only bring it into being if our servants are competent. The dome Artibasos has designed is too big, you are now saying, to use proper mosaic technique upon? Is that it, Siroes?"

"My lord, no!"

"You are being given insufficient resources from the Imperial treasury? Not enough apprentices and craftsmen? Your own recompense is inadequate, Siroes?" The voice was cold and hard as a stone in the depths of winter.

Crispin felt fear and pity. He couldn't even see the man being so ruthlessly annihilated, but behind him he heard the sound of someone sinking to his knees.

"The Emperor's generosity surpasses my worth as much as he surpasses all those in this room in majesty, my thrice-exalted lord."

"We rather believe it does, in fact," said Valerius II icily. "We must reconsider certain aspects of our building plans. You may leave us, Siroes. We are grateful to the lady Styliane Daleina for urging your talents upon us, but it begins to appear that the scope of our Sanctuary might have you overmatched. It happens, it happens. You will be appropriately rewarded for what you have done to this point. Fear not."

Another piece of the puzzle. The aristocratic wife of the Strategos had sponsored this other mosaicist before the Emperor. Crispin's appearance tonight, his swift summons to court, had threatened that man, and so her, by extension.

It was appallingly true, what he'd conjectured earlier: he'd arrived here with allegiances and enemies before he'd even opened his mouth—or lifted his head from the floor. *I could be killed here,* he thought suddenly.

Behind him he heard the silver doors opening. There were footsteps. A pause. The banished artisan would be doing his obeisance.

The doors closed again. Candles flickered in the draft. The light wavered, steadied. It was silent in the throne room, the courtiers chastened and afraid. Siroes, whoever he was, had left. Crispin had just ruined a man by answering a single question honestly without regard for tact or diplomacy. Honesty at a court was a dangerous thing, for others, for oneself. He kept his own eyes on the mosaic of the floor again. A hunting scene in the center. An Emperor of long ago, in the woods with a bow, a stag leaping, the Imperial arrow in flight toward it. A death coming, if the scene continued.

The scene continued.

Alixana said, "If this distressing habit of spoiling a festive evening persists, my beloved, I shall join brave Leontes in regretting your new Sanctuary. I must say, paying the soldiers on time seems to cause so *much* less turmoil."

The Emperor looked unperturbed. "The soldiers will be paid. The Sanctuary is to be one of our legacies. One of the things that will send our names down the ages."

"A lofty ambition to now lay on the shoulders of an untried, ill-mannered westerner," said Styliane Daleina, tartness in her voice.

The Emperor glanced over at her, his expression blank. She had courage, Crispin had to concede, to be challenging him in this mood.

Valerius said, "It would be, were it on his shoulders. The Sanctuary has already risen, however. Our splendid Artibasos, who designed and built it for us, carries the burden of that—and the weight of his heroic dome, like some demigod of the Trakesian pantheon. The Rhodian, should he be capable, will attempt to decorate the Sanctuary for us, in a manner pleasing to Jad and ourselves."

"Then we must hope, thrice-exalted, he finds more pleasing manners in himself," said the fair-haired woman.

Valerius smiled, unexpectedly. "Cleverly put," he said. This Emperor, Crispin was coming to realize, was a man who valued intelligence a great deal. "Caius Crispus, we fear you have earned the displeasure of one of the ornaments of our court. You must endeavor, while you labor among us, to make amends to her."

He didn't feel like making amends, as it happened. She had endorsed an incompetent for her own reasons and was now trying to make Crispin suffer the consequences. "It is a regret to me, already," he murmured. "I have no doubt the Lady Styliane is a jewel among women. Indeed, the pearl she wears about her throat, larger than any single womanly ornament I can see before me, is evidence and reflection of that."

He knew what he was doing this time, as it happened.

It was dangerously rash, and he didn't care. He didn't like this tall, arrogant woman with the perfect features and yellow hair and cold eyes and that stinging tongue.

He heard a collective intake of breath, could not mistake the sudden burning of anger in the woman's eyes, but it was the other woman he was really waiting on, and Crispin, turning to her, found what he was looking for: the briefest flicker of surprised, ironic understanding in the dark gaze of the Empress of Sarantium.

In the awkwardness that followed his making explicit something the lady Styliane Daleina would far rather *not* have had made so clear, the Empress said, with deceptive mildness, "We have many ornaments among us. It occurs to me now that another of them has promised us to lay to rest a wager proposed at the banquet. Scortius, before I retire for the night, if I am to sleep easily, I *must* know the answer to the Emperor's question. No one has come forward to claim the offered gem. Will you tell us, charioteer?"

This time Crispin did turn to look, as the brilliant array of courtiers to his right parted in a shimmer of silk and a small, trim man moved, neat-footed and composed, to stand beside a candelabrum. Crispin moved a little to one side, to let Scortius of the Blues wait alone before the thrones. Unable to help himself, he stared at the man.

The Soriyyan driver he'd seen perform marvels that day had deep-set eyes in a dark face traced lightly—and in one or two cases less lightly—by scars. His easy manner suggested he was no stranger to the palace. He wore a knee-length linen tunic in a natural, off-white color, stripes in a dark blue running down from each shoulder to the knee, gold thread bordering it. A soft blue cap covered his black hair. His belt was gold, simple, extremely expensive. About his throat was a single chain, and from it, on his chest, hung a golden horse with jewels for its eyes.

"We all strive," the charioteer said gravely, "in all we do, to please the Empress." He paused deliberately, then white teeth flashed. "And then the Emperor, of course."

Valerius laughed. "Sheathe that deadly charm, charioteer. Or save it for whomever you are seducing now."

There was feminine laughter. Some of the men, Crispin noted, did not appear amused. Alixana, her own dark eyes flashing now, murmured, "But I *like* when he unsheathes it, my lord Emperor."

Crispin, caught unawares, was unable to control his own sudden burst of laughter. It didn't matter. Valerius and the court around him gave vent to amusement as the charioteer bowed low to the Empress, smiling, unruffled. This was, Crispin understood finally, a court with a nature at least partly defined by its women.

By the woman on the throne, certainly. The Emperor's return to good humor was manifestly unfeigned. Crispin, looking at the two thrones, abruptly thought of Ilandra, with the queer inner twist, as of a blade, that still came whenever he did so. Had his wife made the same sort of openly provocative remark he, too, would have been relaxed enough to find it amusing, so sure had he been of her. Valerius was like that with his Empress. Crispin wondered—not for the first time—what it would have been like to be wed to a woman one could not trust. He glanced at the Strategos, Leontes. The tall man wasn't laughing. Neither was his aristocratic bride. There might be many reasons for that, mind you.

"The jewel," said the Emperor, "is still on offer, until Scortius reveals his secret. A pity our Rhodian didn't see the event; he seems to have so many answers for us."

"The racing today, my lord? I did see it. A magnificent spectacle." It occurred to Crispin, a little too late, that he might be making another mistake.

Valerius made a wry face. "Ah. You are a partisan of the track? We are surrounded by them, of course."

Crispin shook his head. "Hardly a partisan, my lord. Today was the first time I was ever in a hippodrome. My escort, Carullus of the Fourth Sauradian, who is here to meet with the Supreme Strategos, was good enough to be my guide to the running of the chariots." It couldn't hurt Carullus to have his name mentioned here, he thought.

"Ah, well, then. As a first-timer you wouldn't be able to address the question in any case. Go ahead, Scortius. We await enlightenment."

"Oh, no. No, let us ask him, my lord," said Styliane Daleina. There really was malice in her cold beauty. "As our thrice-exalted Emperor says, the artisan seems to know *so* much. Why should the chariots be beyond his grasp?"

"There is much that lies beyond me, my lady," Crispin said, as mildly as he could. "But I shall endeavor to . . . satisfy you." He smiled in turn, briefly. He was paying a price for what he'd done inadvertently to her artisan, and for the deliberate reference to her pearl. He could only hope the price would stop at barbed innuendoes.

Alixana said, from her throne, "The question we debated at dinner, Rhodian, was this: how did Scortius know to surrender the inside track in the first race of the afternoon? He let the Green chariot come inside him, deliberately, and led poor Crescens straight into disaster."

"I recall it, my lady. It led the tribune of the Fourth Sauradian into a financial disaster, as well."

A weak sally. The Empress did not smile. "How regrettable for him. But none of us has been able to offer an explanation that matches the answer our splendid charioteer is holding in reserve. He has promised to tell us. Do you wish to hazard a guess before he does?"

"There is," Valerius added, "no shame attached to not knowing. Especially if this was your first time at the Hippodrome."

It never really occurred to him not to answer. Perhaps it should have. Perhaps a more careful man, judging nuances, would have demurred. Martinian would have been such a man, almost certainly.

Crispin said, "I have a thought, my lord, my lady. I may be very wrong, of course. I probably am."

The charioteer beside him glanced over. His eyebrows were raised a little, but his brown-eyed, observant gaze was intrigued and courteous.

Crispin looked back at him, and smiled. "It is one thing to sit above the track and ponder how a thing was done, it is another to do it at speed on the sands. Whether I am right or not, permit me to salute you. I did not expect to be moved today, and I was."

"You do me too much honor," Scortius murmured.

"What is it, then?" said the Emperor. "Your thought, Rhodian? There is an Ispahani ruby to be claimed."

Crispin looked at him and swallowed. He hadn't known, of course, what was on offer. This was no trivial prize; it was wealth, from the farthest east. He turned back to Scortius, clearing his throat. "Would it have to do with light and dark in the crowd?"

And from the immediate smile on the charioteer's face, he knew that he had it. He did. A puzzle-solving mind. All his life.

In the waiting silence, Crispin said, with growing confidence, "I would say that the very experienced Scortius took his cue from the darkness of the crowd as he reached the turn below the Imperial Box, my lord Emperor. There must have been other things he knew that I cannot even imagine, but I'd hazard that was the most important thing."

"The darkness of the *crowd*," said the Master of Offices. Faustinus glared. "What nonsense is this?"

"I hope it is not nonsense, my lord. I refer to their faces, of course." Crispin said no more. He was looking at the charioteer beside him. Everyone was, by now.

"We seem," the Soriyyan said, at length, "to have a chariot-driver here." He laughed, showing white, even teeth. "I fear the Rhodian is no mosaicist at all. He is a dangerous deceiver, my lord."

"He is *correct*?" said the Emperor sharply.

"He is entirely so, thrice-exalted lord."

"Explain!" It was a command, whiplike.

"I am honored to be asked," said the champion of the Blues, calmly.

"You are not asked. Caius Crispus of Varena, explain what you mean."

Scortius looked abashed, for the first time. Crispin realized that the Emperor was genuinely vexed, and he guessed why: there was, clearly, another puzzle-solving mind in this room.

Crispin said cautiously, "Sometimes a man who sees a thing for the first time may observe that which others, more familiar, cannot truly *see* anymore. I confess that I grew weary of the later races in the long day, and my gaze wandered. It went to the stands across the spina."

"And that taught you how to win a chariot race?" Valerius's brief pique had passed. He was engaged again, Crispin saw. Beside him, Alixana's dark gaze was unreadable.

"It taught me how a better man than I might do so. A mosaicist, as

I told you, my lord, sees the changing colors and light of Jad's world with some . . . precision. He must, or will fail at his own tasks. I spent a part of the afternoon watching what happened when the chariots went past the far stands and people turned to follow their passage."

Valerius was leaning forward now, his brow furrowed in concentration. He held up a hand suddenly. "Wait! I'll hazard this. Wait. Yes . . . the impression is brighter, paler when they look straight ahead—faces toward you—and darker when their heads turn away, when you see hair and head coverings?"

Crispin said nothing. Only bowed. Beside him, Scortius of the Blues wordlessly did the same.

"You have earned your own ruby, my lord," said the charioteer.

"I have not. I still don't . . . You now, Scortius. Explain!"

The Soriyyan said, "When I reached the kathisma turn, my lord Emperor, the stands to my right were many-hued, quite dark as I drove past Crescens to the inside. They ought not to have been, with the Firsts of the Greens and Blues right beneath them. Their faces *ought* to have been turned directly to us as we went by, offering a brightness in the sunlight. There is never time to see actual faces in a race, only an impression—as the Rhodian said—of light or dark. The stands before the turn were dark. Which meant the watchers were turned *away* from us. Why would they turn away from us?"

"A collision behind you," said the Emperor of Sarantium, nodding his head slowly, his fingers steepled together now, arms on the arms of his throne. "Something more compelling, even more dramatic than the two champions in their duel."

"A violent collision, my lord. Only that would divert them, turn their heads away. You will recall that the original accident happened *before* Crescens and I moved up. It appeared a minor one, we both saw it and avoided it. The crowd would have seen it as well. For the Hippodrome to be turned away from the two of us, something violent had to have happened *since* that first collision. And if a third—or a fourth—chariot had smashed into the first pair, then the Hippodrome crews were *not* going to be able to clear the track."

"And the original accident was on the inside," said the Emperor, nodding again. He was smiling with satisfaction now, the gray eyes keen. "Rhodian, you *understood* all of this?"

Crispin shook his head quickly. "Not so, my lord. I guessed only the simplest part of it. I am . . . humbled to have been correct. What Scortius says he deduced, in the midst of a race, while controlling four horses at speed, fighting off a rival, is almost beyond my capacity to comprehend."

"I actually realized it too late," Scortius said, looking rueful. "If I had *truly* been alert, I'd not have been going by Crescens on the inside at all. I'd have stayed outside him around the turn and down the far straight. That would have been the *proper* way to do it. Sometimes," he murmured, "we succeed by good fortune and the god's grace as much as anything else."

No one said anything to this, but Crispin saw the Supreme Strategos, Leontes, make a sign of the sun disk. After a moment, Valerius looked over and nodded to his Chancellor. Gesius, in turn, gestured to another man who walked forward from the single door behind the throne. He was carrying a black silk pillow. There was a ruby on it in a golden band. He came toward Crispin. Even at a distance Crispin saw that this shining prize for an Emperor's idle amusement at a banquet would be worth more money than he'd ever possessed in his life. The attendant stopped before him. Scortius, on Crispin's right, was smiling broadly. Good fortune and the god's grace.

Crispin said, "No man is less worthy of this gift, though I hope to please the Emperor in other ways as I serve him."

"Not a gift, Rhodian. A prize. Any man—or woman—here might have won it. They all had a chance before you, earlier tonight."

Crispin bowed his head. A sudden thought came to him, and before he could resist it, he heard himself speaking again. "Might I . . . might I be permitted to make of this a gift, then, my lord?" He stumbled over the words. He was successful but not wealthy. Neither was his mother, aging, nor Martinian and his wife.

"It is yours," said the Emperor, after a brief, repressive silence. "What one owns one may give."

It was true, of course. But what did one own if life, if love, could be taken away to darkness? Was it *all* not just . . . a loan, a leasehold, transitory as candles?

Not the time, or the place, for that.

Crispin took a deep breath, forcing himself toward clarity, away from shadows. He said, knowing this might be another mistake, "I should be honored if the Lady Styliane would accept this from me, then. I would not have even had the chance to speak to this challenge had she not thought so kindly of my worth. And I fear my own impolitic words earlier might have distressed a fellow artisan she values. May this serve to make my amends?" He was aware of the charioteer beside him, the man's drop-jawed gaze, a flurry of incredulous sound among the courtiers.

"Nobly said!" cried Faustinus from by the two thrones.

It occurred to Crispin that the Master of Offices, powerful in his control of the civil service, might not be an especially subtle man. It also occurred to him in that same moment—noting Gesius's thoughtful expression and the Emperor's suddenly wry, shrewd one—that this might not be accidental.

He nodded at the attendant—vividly clad in silver—and the man carried the pillow over to the golden-haired lady standing near the thrones. Crispin saw that the Strategos, beside her, was smiling but that Styliane Daleina herself had gone pale. This might indeed have been an error; he had no sure instincts here at all.

She reached forward, however, and took the ruby ring, held it in an open palm. She had no real choice. Exquisite as it was, beside the spectacular pearl about her throat it was almost a trifle. She was the daughter of the wealthiest family in the Empire. Even Crispin knew this. She needed this ruby about as much as Crispin needed . . . a cup of wine.

Bad analogy, he thought. He *did* need one, urgently.

The lady looked across the space of the room at him for a long moment, and then said, all icy, composed perfection, "You do me too much honor in your turn, and honor the memory of the Empire in Rhodias with such generosity. I thank you." She did not smile. She closed her long fingers, the ruby nestled in her palm.

Crispin bowed.

"I must say," interjected the Empress of Sarantium, plaintively, "that

I am desolate now beyond all words. Did I, too, not urge you to speak, Rhodian? Did I not stop our beloved Scortius to give you an *opportunity* to show your cleverness? What gift will you make to *me*, dare I ask?"

"Ah, you are cruel, my love," said the Emperor beside her. He looked amused again.

"I am cruelly scorned and overlooked," said his wife.

Crispin swallowed hard. "I am at the service of the Empress in all things I may possibly do for her."

"Good!" said Alixana of Sarantium, her voice crisp, changing on the instant, as if this was exactly what she'd wanted to hear. "*Very* good. Gesius, have the Rhodian conducted to my rooms. I wish to discuss a mosaic there before I retire for the night."

There was another rustle of sound and movement. Lanterns flickered. Crispin saw the sallow-faced man near the Strategos pinch his lips together suddenly. The Emperor, still amused, said only, "I have summoned him for the Sanctuary, beloved. All other diversions must follow our needs there."

"I am not," said the Empress of Sarantium, arching her magnificent eyebrows, "a diversion."

She smiled, though, as she spoke, and laughter followed in the throne room like a hound to her lead.

Valerius stood. "Rhodian, be welcome to Sarantium. You have not entered among us quietly." He lifted a hand. Alixana laid hers upon it, shimmering with rings, and she rose. Together, they waited for their court to perform obeisance. Then they turned and went from the room through the single door Crispin had seen behind the thrones.

Straightening, and then standing up once more, he closed his eyes briefly, unnerved by the speed of events. He felt like a man in a racing chariot, not at all in control of it.

When he opened his eyes again, it was to see the real charioteer, Scortius, gazing at him. "Be very careful," the Soriyyan murmured softly. "With all of them."

"How?" Crispin managed to say just before the gaunt old Chancellor swooped down upon him as upon a prize. Gesius laid thin, proprietary fingers on Crispin's shoulder and smoothly guided him from the room, across the tesserae of the Imperial hunt, past the silver trees and the jeweled birds in the branches and the avidly watchful, silken figures of the Sarantine court.

As he walked through the silver doors into the antechamber again, someone behind him clapped their hands sharply three times and then, amid a resumption of talk and languid, late-night laughter, Crispin heard the mechanical birds of the Emperor begin to sing.

CHAPTER VIII

"Jad boil the bastard in his own fish sauce!" Rasic snarled under his breath as he scrubbed at a stained pot. "We might as well have joined the Sleepless Ones and gotten some holy credit for being up all fucking night!"

Kyros, stirring his soup over the fire with a long wooden spoon, pretended not to be listening. You didn't boil things in the fish sauce, anyhow. Strumosus was known to have exceptionally good hearing, and there was a rumor that once, years ago, the eccentric cook had tossed a dozing kitchen boy into a huge iron pot when the soup in that pot came to a boil unattended.

Kyros was pretty sure that wasn't true, but he *had* seen the rotund master chef bring a chopping knife down a finger's breadth away from the hand of an undercook who was cleaning leeks carelessly. The knife had stuck, quivering, in the table. The undercook had looked at it, at his own precariously adjacent fingers, and fainted. "Toss him in the horse trough," Strumosus had ordered. Kyros's bad foot had excused him from that duty, but four others had done it, carrying the unconscious undercook out the door and down the portico steps. It had been winter then, a bitterly cold, gray afternoon. The surface of the water in the trough across the courtyard was frozen. The undercook revived, spectacularly, when they dropped him in.

Working for a notoriously temperamental cook was not the easiest employment in the City.

Still, Kyros had surprised himself over the course of a year and a half by discovering that he enjoyed the kitchen. There were mysteries to preparing food, and Kyros had found himself thinking about them. It helped that this wasn't just any kitchen, or any chef. The short, hot-tempered, ample-stomached man who supervised the food here was a legend in the City. There were those who held the view that he was far too aware of the fact, but if a cook *could* be an artist, Strumosus was. And his kitchen was the Blues' banqueting hall in Sarantium, where feasts for two hundred people were known to take place some nights.

Tonight, in fact. Strumosus, in a fever of brilliance, controlled chaos, and skin-blistering invective, had coordinated the preparation of eight elaborate courses of culinary celebration, climaxing in a parade of fifty boys—they'd recruited and cleaned up the stablehands—carrying enormous silver platters of shrimp-stuffed whitefish in his celebrated sauce around the wildly cheering banquet room while trumpets sounded and blue banners were madly waved. An overly enthused Clarus—the Blues' principal male dancer—had leaped flamboyantly from his seat at the high table and hastened over to plant a kiss full on the lips of the cook in the doorway to the kitchens. Shouts and ribald laughter ensued as Strumosus pretended to swat the little dancer away and then acknowledged the applause and whistles.

It was the last night of Dykania, end of another racing season, and the Glorious Blues of Great Renown had once more thrashed the hapless whey-faced Greens, both during the long season and today. Scortius's astonishing victory in the first afternoon race already seemed destined to become one of those triumphs that were talked about forever.

The wine had flowed freely all night, and so had the toasts that came with it. The faction's poet, Khardelos, had stood up unsteadily, propped himself with one splayed hand on the table, and improvised a verse, flagon lifted:

Amid the thundering voices of the gathered throng Scortius flies like an eagle across the sand beneath the eagle's nest of the Kathisma!
All glory to the glorious Emperor!
Glory to the swift Soriyyan and his steeds!
All glory to the blues of great Renown!

Kyros had felt prickles of sheer delight running along his spine. *Like an eagle across the sand*. That was wonderful! His eyes misted with emotion. Strumosus, beside him at the kitchen door in the momentary lull of activity, had snorted softly. "A feeble wordsmith," he'd murmured, just loudly enough for Kyros to hear. He often did that. "Old phrases and butchered ones. Must talk to Astorgus. The charioteers are splendid, the kitchen is matchless, as we all know. The dancers are good enough. The poet, however, must go. Must go."

Kyros had looked over and blushed to see Strumosus's sharp, small eyes on him. "Part of your education, boy. Be not seduced by cheap sentiment any more than by a heavy hand with spices. There's a difference between the accolades of the masses and the approval of those who really know." He turned and went back into the heat of the kitchen. Kyros quickly followed.

Later, scarred, craggy-faced Astorgus, once the most celebrated charioteer in the City himself and now the Blues' factionarius, made a speech announcing a new statue to Scortius for the spina in the Hippodrome. There were already two of them, but both had been raised by the pustulent Greens. This one, Astorgus declared, would be made of silver not bronze, to the greater glory of the Blues and the charioteer, both. There was a deafening roar of approval. One of the younger serving boys in the kitchen, startled by the noise, dropped a dish of candied fruit he was carrying out. Strumosus buffeted him about the head and shoulders with a long-handled wooden spoon, breaking the spoon. The spoons broke easily, as it happened. Kyros had noticed that the cook seldom did much actual damage, for all the apparent force of his blows.

When he had a moment, Kyros paused in the doorway again, looking at Astorgus. The factionarius was drinking steadily but to little evident effect. He had an easy, smiling word for everyone who stopped by his seat at the table. A calm, immensely reassuring man. Strumosus said Astorgus was the principal reason for the Blues' current domination of the racing and many other matters. He had wooed Scortius, Strumosus himself, was said to be working on other clever schemes all the time. Kyros wondered, though: how would it feel to be known as a competent administrator when you had once been the object yourself of all the wild cheers, the statues raised, the enraptured speeches and poems comparing you to eagles and lions, or to the great Hippodrome figures of all the ages? Was it hard? It *must* be, he thought, but couldn't really know, not from looking at Astorgus.

The banquet meandered its way to a vague close, as such events tended to. A few quarrels, someone violently ill in a corner of the hall, too sick to make it as far as the room set aside for vomiting. Columella, the horse doctor, slumped in his seat morosely, chanting verses from Trakesia long ago in a monotone. He was always like that late at night. He knew more old poetry than Khardelos did. Those on either side of him were fast asleep with their heads among the platters on the table. One of the younger female dancers was doing a sequence of movements by herself, over and over, face intent, hands fluttering up like paired birds, then falling to rest at her sides as she spun. Kyros seemed to be the only one watching her. She was pretty, he thought. Another pair of dancers took her with them when they left. Then Astorgus left, helping Columella along, and soon no one was left in the hall. That had been a while ago.

As far as Kyros could judge, it had been a very successful banquet. Scortius hadn't been there, of course. He had been summoned to the Imperial Precinct, and so was forgiven his absence. An invitation from the Emperor brought glory to them all.

On the other hand, the brilliant charioteer was also the reason Strumosus—exhausted, dangerously irritable—and a handful of unfortunate boys and undercooks were still awake in the kitchen in the depths of an autumn night after even the most impassioned of the partisans had staggered to their homes and beds. The Blues' staff and administration were asleep by now across the courtyard in the dormitory or their private quarters, if rank had earned them such. The streets and squares beyond the gated compound were quiet at the end of the festival. Slaves under the supervision of the Urban Prefects office would be out already, cleaning the streets. It was cold outside now; a north wind had come slicing down out of Trakesia, winter in it.

Ordinary life would resume with the sun. The parties were over.

But it seemed that Scortius had solemnly promised the master cook of the Blues that he would come to the kitchens after the Emperor's banquet and sample what had been offered tonight, comparing it to the fare in the Imperial Precinct. He was late. It was late. It was *very* late. No approaching footsteps could be heard outside.

They had all been enthused at the prospect of sharing the last of a glorious day and night with the charioteer, but that had been a long time ago. Kyros suppressed a yawn and eyed the low fire, stirring his fish soup, careful not to let it boil. He tasted it, and decided against adding any more sea salt. It was an extreme honor for one of the scullion boys to be entrusted with supervising a dish and there had been indignation when Kyros was given such tasks after barely a year in the kitchen. Kyros himself had been astonished; he hadn't known Strumosus was even aware of his presence.

He hadn't actually wanted to be here at the beginning. As a boy he'd planned to be a charioteer, of course: all of them did. Later, he'd expected to follow his father as an animal trainer for the Blues, but reality had descended upon that idea when Kyros was still very young. A trainer dragging a clubbed foot around with him was unlikely to survive even a season among the big cats and bears. Kyros's father had appealed to the faction administration to find another place for his son when Kyros was of age. The Blues tended to look after their own. Administrative wheels had turned, on a minor scale, and Kyros had been assigned to apprentice in the great kitchen with the newly recruited master cook. You didn't have to run, or dodge dangerous beasts there.

Other than the cook.

Strumosus reappeared in the doorway from the portico outside. Rasic, with his uncanny survival instinct, had already stopped his muttering, without turning around. The chef looked fevered and overwrought, but he often did, so that didn't signify greatly. Kyros's mother would have paled to see Strumosus walking to and from the hot kitchens and the cold courtyard at such an hour as this. If the noxious vapors didn't afflict you in the black depths of night, then the spirits of the half-world would, she firmly believed.

Strumosus of Amoria had been hired by the Blues—at a cost rumored to be outrageous—from the kitchens of the exiled Lysippus, once Quaestor of Imperial Revenue, banished in the wake of the Victory Riot. The two factions competed in the hippodromes with their chariots, in the theaters of the Empire, with their poets' declamations and group chants, and—not at all infrequently—in the streets and alleyways with cudgels and blades. Cunning Astorgus had decided to take the competition into the kitchens of the faction compounds, and recruiting Strumosus—though he was prickly as a Soriyyan desert plant—had been a brilliant stroke. The City had talked about nothing else for months; a number of patricians had discovered a hitherto unknown affiliation to the Blues and had happily fattened themselves in the faction's banquet hall while making contributions that went a long way toward fattening Astorgus's purse for the horse auctions or the wooing of dancers and charioteers. The Blues appeared to have found yet another way to fight—and defeat—the Greens.

Blues and Greens had fought side by side two years ago, in the Victory Riot, but that astonishing, almost unprecedented fact hadn't done anything to stop them from dying when the soldiers had come into the Hippodrome. Kyros remembered the riot, of course. One of his uncles had been killed by a sword in the Hippodrome Forum and his mother had taken to her bed for two weeks after that. The name of Lysippus the Calysian had been one to spit upon in Kyros's household, and in a great many others, of all ranks and classes.

The Emperor's taxation master had been ruthless, but they always were, taxation masters. It was more than that. The stories of what went on after darkfall in his city palace had been ugly and disturbing. Whenever young people of either sex went missing eyes were cast at those blank, windowless stone walls. Wayward children were threatened with the gross Calysian to frighten them into obedience.

Strumosus hadn't added anything to the rumors, being uncharacteristically reticent on the subject of his former employer. He'd arrived in the Blues' kitchens and cellars, spent a day glaring at what he found, thrown out almost all of the implements, much of the wine, dismissed all but two of the undercooks, terrified the boys, and—within days—had begun producing meals that dazzled and amazed.

He was never happy, of course: complaining endlessly, verbally and physically abusing the staff he hired, hectoring Astorgus for a larger budget, offering opinions on everything from poets to the proper diet for the horses, moaning about the impossibility of subtle cooking when one had to feed so many uneducated chewers of food. Still, Kyros had noted, for all the flow of grievances, there never did seem to be an end to the changing dishes they prepared in the great kitchen, and Strumosus didn't seem at all financially constrained in his market purchases of a morning.

That was one of Kyros's favorite tasks: accompanying the cook to market just after the invocation in chapel, watching him appraise vegetables and fish and fruit, squeezing and smelling, sometimes even *listening* to food, devising the day's meals on the spot in the light of what he found.

In fact, it was most likely because of his obvious attention at such times, Kyros later decided, that the cook had elevated him from washing platters and flasks to supervising some of the soups and broths. Strumosus almost never addressed Kyros directly, but the fierce, fat little man seemed always to be talking to himself at the market as he moved swiftly from stall to stall, and Kyros, keeping up as best he could with his bad foot, heard a great deal and tried to remember. He had never imagined, for example, that the difference in taste between the same fish caught across the bay near Deapolis and one netted on this side, near the cliffs east of the City, could be so great.

The day Strumosus found sea bass from Spinadia in the market was the first time Kyros saw a man actually weep at the sight of food. Strumosus's fingers as he caressed the glistening fish reminded Kyros of a Holy Fool's clasp on his sun disk. He and the others in the kitchen were permitted to sample the dish—baked lightly in salt, flavored with herbs—after the dinner party that night was over, and Kyros, tasting, began to comprehend a certain way of living life. He would sometimes date the beginning of his adulthood to that evening.

At other times he would consider that his youth properly ended at the conclusion of Dykania later that same year, waiting for Scortius the charioteer in the depths of a cold night, when they heard a sudden, urgent cry and then running feet in the courtyard.

Kyros wheeled around awkwardly to look at the outside door. Strumosus quickly set down his cup and the wine flask he was holding. Three men bulked in the entranceway, then they burst inside, making the space seem suddenly small. One was Scortius. His clothing was torn, he held a knife in his hand. One of the others gripped a drawn sword: a big man, an apparition, dripping blood, with blood on the sword.

Kyros, his jaw hanging open, heard the Glory of the Blues, their own beloved Scortius, rasp harshly, "We're being pursued! Get help. Quickly!" He said it in a gasp; they had been running.

It occurred to Kyros only later that if Scortius had been a different sort of man he might have shouted for aid himself. Instead, it was Rasic who sprang for the inner doorway and sprinted across the banquet room toward the exit nearest the dormitory, screaming in a blood-chilling voice, *"Blues! Blues! We are attacked! To the kitchen! Up, Blues!"*

Strumosus of Amoria had already seized his favorite chopping knife. There was a mad glint in his eye. Kyros looked around and grabbed for a broom, pointing the shaft toward the empty doorway. There were sounds outside now, in the darkness. Men moving, and the dogs were barking.

Scortius and his two companions came farther into the room. The wounded one with the sword waited calmly, nearest the door, first target of any rush.

Then the sounds of movement in the courtyard ceased. No one could be seen for a moment. There was a frozen interval, eerie after the explosion of action. Kyros saw that the two undercooks and the other boys had each grabbed some sort of weapon. One held an iron poker from the fire. Blood from the wounded man was dripping steadily onto the floor at his feet. The dogs were still barking.

A shadow moved in the darkness of the portico. Another big man. Kyros saw the dark outline of his blade. The shadow spoke, with a northern accent: "We want only Rhodian. No quarrel with Blues or other two men. Lives be spared if you send him out to us."

Strumosus laughed aloud.

"Fool! Do you understand where you are, whoever you are? Ignorant louts! Not even the Emperor sends soldiers into this compound."

"We have no wish to be here. Send Rhodian and we go. I hold my men so you can—"

The man on the portico—whoever he was—never finished that sentence, or any other in his days under Jad's sun or the two moons or the stars.

"Come, Blues!" Kyros heard from outside. A wild, exultant cry from many throats. *"On, Blues! We are attacked!"*

A howling came from the north end of the courtyard. Not the dogs. Men. Kyros saw the big, shadowy figure with the sword break off and half turn to look. Then he staggered suddenly sideways. He fell with a sequence of clattering sounds. Other shadows sprang onto the portico. A heavy staff rose and fell, dark against the darkness, once and then again above the downed man. There was a crunching sound. Kyros turned away, swallowing hard.

"Ignorant men, whoever they are. Or were," said Strumosus in a matter-of-fact voice. He set his knife down on the table, utterly unruffled.

"Soldiers. On leave in the City. Hired for some money. It wouldn't have taken much, if they'd been drinking with borrowed money." It was the bleeding man. Looking at him, Kyros saw that his wounds were in shoulder and thigh, both. He was a soldier himself. His eyes were hard now, angry. Outside, the tumult grew. The other intruders were fighting to get out of the compound. Torches were being brought at a run; they made streams of orange and smoke in the courtyard beyond the open doorway.

"Ignorant, as I say," said Strumosus. "To have followed you in here."

"They killed two of my men, and your fellow at the gates," said the soldier. "He tried to stop them."

Kyros shuffled to a stool and sat down heavily, hearing that. He knew who had been on gate duty. Short straw on a banquet night. He was beginning to feel sick.

Strumosus showed no reaction at all. He looked at the third figure in the kitchen, a smooth-shaven, very well-dressed man with flaming red hair and a grim face.

"You are the Rhodian they wanted?"

The man nodded briefly.

"Of course you are. Do tell me, I pray you," said the master cook of the Blues, while men fought and died in the dark outside his kitchen, "have you ever tasted lamprey from the lake near Baiana?"

There followed a brief silence in the room. Kyros and the others were moderately familiar with this sort of thing; no one else could possibly be.

"I'm . . . ah, very sorry," said the red-haired man, eventually, with a composure that did him credit. "I cannot say I have."

Strumosus shook his head in regret. "A very great pity," he murmured. "Neither have I. A legendary dish, you must understand. Aspalius wrote of it four hundred years ago. He used a white sauce. I don't, myself, actually. Not with lamprey."

This produced a further, similar, silence. A number of torches were in the courtyard now as more and more of the Blues appeared in hastily thrown-on boots and clothing. The latecomers had missed the battle, it seemed. No one was resisting now. Someone had silenced the dogs. Kyros, peering through the doorway, saw Astorgus coming quickly across and then up the three steps to the portico. The factionarius paused there, looking down at the fallen man for a moment, then entered the kitchen.

"There are six dead intruders out there," he said, to no one in particular. His face showed anger but no fatigue.

"All dead?" It was the big soldier. "I'm sorry for that. I had questions."

"They entered our compound," Astorgus said flatly. "With swords. No one does that. Our horses are here." He stared at the wounded man a moment, assessing. Then, looking back over his shoulder, he snapped, "Toss the bodies outside the gate and notify the Urban Prefect's officers.

I'll deal with them when they arrive. Call me when they do. Someone get Columella in here, and send for the doctor." He turned to Scortius.

Kyros couldn't decipher his expression. The two men looked at each other for what seemed a long time. Fifteen years ago Astorgus had been exactly what Scortius was now: the most celebrated chariot-racer in the Empire.

"What happened?" the older man asked, finally. "Jealous husband? Again?"

IN FACT, HE HAD assumed that to be the case, at first.

A measure of his success in the dark after the racing and the feasts had always been due to the fact that he was not a man who actively pursued women. Notwithstanding this, it would have been an inaccuracy to suggest that he didn't desire them acutely, or that his pulse did not quicken when certain invitations were waiting for him at his home when he returned from the Hippodrome or the stables.

That evening—end of the Dykania revels, end of the racing season—when he came home to change for the Imperial banquet, a brief, unsigned, unscented note had been among those waiting for him on the marble table inside the entranceway. He hadn't needed a signature, or scent. The laconic, entirely characteristic phrasing told him that he'd conquered more than Crescens of the Greens in the first race that afternoon.

"If you are equal to avoiding a different set of dangers," the neat, small handwriting read, *"my maidservant will be waiting on the eastern side of the Traversite Palace after the Emperor's feast. You will know her. She is to be trusted. Are you?"*

No more than that.

The remaining letters were set aside. He had wanted this woman for a long time. Wit drew him, of late, and her demeanor of serene, amused detachment, the aura of . . . difficulty about her. He was fairly certain that the withdrawn manner was only a public one. That there was a great deal beneath that formal austerity. That perhaps even her extremely powerful husband had never fathomed that.

He thought he might discover—or begin discovering—if this was so tonight. The prospect had enlivened the whole of the Emperor's banquet with an intense, private anticipation. The privacy of it was central, of course. Scortius was the most discreet of men: another reason the notes came; another reason, perhaps, he hadn't been killed before this.

Not that there hadn't been attempts—or warnings. He'd been beaten once: much younger, lacking the protections of celebrity and his own wealth. He had, in fact, long since reconciled himself to the notion that he was not a man likely to die in his bed, though someone else's bed was a possibility. The Ninth Driver would take him, or a sword in the night as he returned from a chamber where he ought not to have been.

He'd assumed, therefore, that this was the threat tonight, as he slipped out through a small, locked, rarely used gate in the Imperial Precinct wall in the cold autumn dark.

He had a key to that gate, courtesy of an encounter years ago with the black-haired daughter of one of the chiliarchs of the Excubitors. The lady was married now, mother of three children, impressively proper. She'd had an enchanting smile once, and a way of crying out and then biting her lower lip, as if surprised by herself in the dark.

He didn't often use the key, but it was extremely late and there had been more need than usual for caution earlier. He'd spent an unexpectedly intense time in the room the servant had led him to: not the lady's bedroom after all, though there was a divan, and wine, and scented candles burning while he waited. He'd wondered if he'd find passion and intimacy beneath the court mask of cool civility. When she arrived—still dressed as she had been at the banquet and in the throne room after—he'd discovered both, but had then apprehended, through a lingering time together as the images of day were made to recede, rather too deep an awareness of the same things in himself for comfort.

That posed its own particular sort of danger. In his life—the life he had chosen to live—the need for lovemaking, the touch and scent and urgency of a woman in his arms, was central and compelling, but the desire for any sort of ongoing intimacy was a threat.

He was a toy for these ladies of the Imperial Precinct and the patrician houses of the City, and he knew it. They addressed a need of his, and he assuaged desires some of them hadn't known they harbored. A transaction, of a sort. He'd been engaged in it for fifteen years.

In fact, tonight's unexpected vulnerability, his reluctance to leave her and go back out into the cold, offered a first suggestion—like a distant trumpet blowing—that he might be getting old. It was unsettling.

Scortius relocked the small gate quietly behind him and turned to scan the darkness before proceeding. It was an hour he had known before; not a safe one in the streets of Sarantium.

The Blues' compound—his destination, honoring a promise to Strumosus of Amoria—wasn't far away: across the debris-filled, cluttered construction space before the new Sanctuary, along the northern side of the Hippodrome Forum, and then up from the far end, with its pillar and statue of the first Valerius, to the compound gates. Beyond them he expected to find the kitchen fires burning and a fierce, indignant master chef awaiting his declaration that nothing he'd tasted in the Attenine Palace could compare to what he was offered in the prosaic warmth of the Blues' kitchen in an interlude before dawn.

It was likely to be the truth. Strumosus, in his own way, was a genius. The charioteer even had some genuine anticipation of this late meal, for all his fatigue and the disquieting emotions he was dealing with. He could sleep all day tomorrow. He probably would.

If he lived. Following a habit long entrenched, he remained motionless for a time, screened by bushes and the low trees near the wall, and carefully eyed the open spaces he would have to cross, looking from left to right and then slowly back again.

He saw no daemons or spirits or flickers of name on the paving stones, but there were men under the marble roof of the almost-finished portico of the Great Sanctuary.

There ought not to have been. Not at this time of night, and not spread out so precisely, like soldiers. He would not have been surprised to find drunken revelers outstaying the end of Dykania, wending their way in the cold through the construction materials in the square before the Bronze Gates, but this motionless cluster who thought they were concealed by pillar and cloak and darkness sent a different sort of message. From where they waited on the portico, these men—whoever they were—could see the gates clearly, and the first movement he made from his own position would bring him into the open, even if they didn't know this small doorway was here.

He wasn't tired anymore.

Danger and a challenge were the heady, unmixed wine of life to Scortius of Soriyya: another reason he lived for the speed and blood of the track and for these illicit trysts in the Precinct or beyond it. He knew this, in fact, had known it for many years.

He breathed a quick, forbidden invocation to Heladikos and began considering his options. Those shadowed men would be armed, of course. They were here for a purpose. He had only a knife. He could sprint across the open space toward the Hippodrome Forum, catching them by surprise, but they had an angle on him. If any of them could run he'd be cut off. And a footrace lacked . . . any sort of dignity.

He reluctantly decided the only intelligent course, now that he'd spotted them, was to slip back into the Precinct. He could find a bed among the Excubitors in their barracks—they'd be proud to have him and would ask no questions. Or he could go to the Bronze Gates openly from inside, inviting unfortunate speculation at this hour, and request that a message be carried to the Blues' compound. He'd have an escort party in very little time.

Either way, more people would discover how late he'd been here than he really cared to have know. It wasn't as if his nocturnal habits were so very secret, but he did pride himself on doing as little as possible to draw attention to individual episodes. Dignity, again, and a respect for the women who trusted him. He lived much of his life in the eye of the world. He preferred some details to be his own and not the property of every envious or titillated rumor-monger in the bathhouses and barracks and cauponae of Sarantium.

Not much choice here, alas. It was sprint through the street like an apprentice dodging his masters cudgel, or slip back in and put a wry face on things with the Excubitors or at the gates.

He really wasn't about to run.

He'd already taken the key back out of his leather purse when he saw a flare of light on the Sanctuary portico as one of the massive doors swung open. There men stepped out, vividly outlined against the brightness behind them. It was *very* late; this was odd in the extreme. The Great Sanctuary was not yet open to the public; only the workers and architects had been inside. Watching, unseen, Scortius saw the waiting group of men on the portico shift silently and begin to spread out, in immediate response. He was too far away to hear anything, or recognize anyone, but he saw two of the three men before the doors turn and bow to the third, who withdrew inside. And that sent another sort of warning to him.

A blade of light narrowed and disappeared as the heavy door was closed. The two men turned to stand alone and exposed on the porch amid the debris of construction in windy darkness. One of the two turned and said something to the other. They were manifestly unaware of swordsmen spreading out around them.

Men died at night in the City all the time.

People went to the graves of the violently dead with cheiromancers' curse-tablets, ignoring the imprecations of the clergy as they invoked death or dismemberment for the charioteers and their horses, fierce passion from a longed-for woman, sickness to a hated neighbor's child or mule, storm winds for an enemy's merchant vessel. Blood and magic, flames flitting along the night streets. Heladikos's fires. He had seen them.

There were swords across the square, real men carrying them, whatever might be said about the half-world spirits all around. Scortius stood in darkness with the moons set and the stars furtive behind swift clouds. A cold wind blew from the north—where Death was said to dwell in the old tales of Soriyya, the tales told before Jad had come to the people of the south, along with the legend of his son.

What was happening on that portico was none of his business, and he had his own dangers to negotiate through the streets. He was unarmed, save for the trivial knife, could hardly help two defenseless men against sword-wielding attackers.

Some situations required a sense of self-preservation.

He was, alas, deficient in this regard.

"Watch out!" he roared at the top of his voice, bursting out from behind the screening trees.

He drew his little knife as he emerged. Having calmly decided just a moment ago that he was not going to run, he seemed to be running after all, and the wrong way entirely. It did occur to him—a small, belated sign of functioning intelligence—that he was being unwise.

"Assassins!" he cried. *"Get inside!"*

The two men on the portico turned toward him as he sprinted across the square. He saw a low, covered pile of bricks just in time and leaped it, clipping his ankle, almost falling when he landed. He swore like a sailor in a dockside caupona, at himself, at their slowness. Watching as he ran—for enemies, for movement, for more of the accursed bricks—he saw the nearest soldier turn and draw his sword along the western side of the portico. He was close enough to hear the sound as blade slid free of scabbard.

His fervent hope—and inadequate plan—was that the third man had not bolted the door to the Sanctuary, that they could get inside before the assassins closed in. It struck him—rather late—that he *could* have shouted the same warning and not come charging like a schoolboy into the midst of things himself. He was the toast of Sarantium, the Emperor's dinner companion, Glory of the Blues, wealthy beyond all youthful dreams.

Pretty much the same person he'd been fifteen years ago, it seemed. Unfortunately, perhaps.

He bounded up onto the porch, wincing as he landed on the bruised ankle, went straight past the two men and grabbed at the handle of the massive door. Gripped, turned.

Locked. He rattled and jerked the handle uselessly, pounded once on the door, then wheeled around. Saw the two men clearly for the first time. Knew them both. Neither had made any intelligently responsive move. Paralyzed with fear, both of them. Scortius swore again.

The soldiers had encircled them. Predictably. The leader, a big, rangy man, stood directly in front of the portico steps between cloth-covered mounds of something or other and looked up at the three of them. His eyes were dark in the darkness. He held his heavy sword lightly, as if it weighed nothing at all.

"Scortius of the Blues!" he said, his voice odd.

There was a silence. Scortius said nothing, thinking fast.

The soldier went on, still in that bemused tone, "You cost me a fortune this afternoon, you know." A Trakesian voice. He'd guessed this might be it: soldiers on city leave, hired in a caupona to kill and disappear.

"These men are both under the protection of the Emperor," Scortius snapped icily. "You touch either of them, or me, at absolute cost of your lives. *No* one will be able to protect you. Anywhere in the Empire or beyond. Do you understand me?"

The man's sword did not move. His voice did, however, shifting upward in surprise. "What? You thought we were here to *harm* them?"

Scortius swallowed. His knife hand fell to his side. The other two men on the portico were looking at him with curiosity. So were the soldiers below. The wind blew, stirring the coverings on the mounds of bricks and tools. Leaves skittered across the square. Scortius opened his mouth, then closed it, finding nothing to say.

He had made several different, very swift assumptions since emerging from the Imperial Precinct and seeing men waiting in the dark. None of them appeared to have been correct.

"Um, charioteer, may I present to you Carullus, tribune of the Fourth Sauradian cavalry," said the redheaded mosaicist—for it was he who stood on the portico. "My escort on the last part of the journey here, and my guardian in the City. He did lose a lot of money on the first race this afternoon, as it happens."

"I am sorry to hear it," said Scortius, reflexively. He looked at Caius Crispus of Varena, and then at the celebrated architect, Artibasos, standing beside him, rumpled and observant. The builder of this new Sanctuary.

And he was now fairly certain who it was they'd been bowing to while he watched from across the way. He was attaining understanding late here, it seemed. The Bassanids had a philosophic phrase about that, in their own tongue; he'd heard it often from their traders in Soriyya in the seasons when there hadn't been a war. He didn't much feel like being philosophic at the moment.

There was another silence. The north wind whistled through the pillars, flapping the covers over the brick and masonry again. No movement from by the Bronze Gates: they would have heard him shouting but hadn't bothered to do anything about it. Events outside the Imperial Precinct rarely disturbed the guards; their concern was in *keeping* those events outside. He had careened across the open square, roaring like a madman, waving a dagger, banging his ankle . . . to no effect whatsoever. Standing in darkness on the still-unfinished portico of the Great Sanctuary of Jad's Holy Wisdom, Scortius received a swift, unsettling image of the elegant woman he'd lately left. The scent and the touch of her.

He imagined her observing his conduct just now. He winced at the thought of her arched eyebrows, the quirked, amused mouth, and then—failing to see any obvious alternatives—he began to laugh.

EARLIER THAT SAME NIGHT, walking with an escort from the Attenine toward the Traversite Palace, where the Empress of Sarantium had her favored autumn and winter quarters, Crispin had found himself thinking of his wife.

This happened all the time, but the difference—and he was aware of it—was that in his mind the image of Ilandra appeared now as a shield, a defense, though he remained unsure what it was he feared. It was windy and cold crossing the gardens; he wrapped himself in the cloak they'd given him.

Guarded by the dead, hiding behind the memory of love, he was conducted to the smaller of the two main palaces under swiftly moving clouds and the westered, sunken moons and entered, and walked marble corridors with lanterns burning on the walls and paused before soldiers at the doorway of an Empress who had summoned him, so late at night, to her private quarters.

He was expected. The nearest soldier nodded, expressionless, and opened the door. Crispin passed into a space of firelight, candlelight, and gold. The eunuchs and soldiers remained outside. The door was closed behind him. Ilandra's image slowly faded as a lady-in-waiting approached, silk-clad, light on slippered feet, and offered him a silver cup of wine.

He accepted, with real gratitude. She took his cloak and laid it on a bench against the wall by the fire. Then she smiled at him sidelong and withdrew through an inner door. Crispin stood alone and looked around in the light of myriad candles. A room in sumptuous good taste; a little ornate to a western eye, but the Sarantines tended to be. Then he caught his breath.

There was a golden rose on a long table by the wall to his left. Slender as a living flower, seemingly as pliant, four buds on the long stem, thorns among the small, perfect leaves, all of gold, all four buds rendered in stages of unfolding, and a fifth, at the crown, fully opened, achieved, each thin, exquisite petal a marvel of the goldsmith's craft, with a ruby at the center of it, red as a fire in the candlelight.

The beauty caught at his heart, and the terrible fragility. If one were merely to take that long stem between two fingers and twist, it would bend, distort, fall awry. The flower seemed almost to sway in a breeze that wasn't there. So much perfection and so transient, so vulnerable. Crispin ached for the mastery of it—the time and care and craft brought to this accomplishment—and for the simultaneous perception that this artifice, this art, was as precarious as . . . as any joy in mortal life.

As a rose, perhaps, that died in a wind or at summer's end.

He thought suddenly of the young queen of the Antae then, and of the message he carried, and he was aware of pity and fear within himself, a very long way from home.

A silver branching of candles wavered on the table by the rose. There was no sound, but the flicker of movement made him turn.

She had been on the stage in her youth, knew very well—even now—how to move with silence and a dancer's grace. She was small, slender, dark-haired, dark-eyed, exquisite as the rose. She brought thorns to mind, the drawing of blood, the danger at the heart of beauty.

She had changed to a night robe of deep red, had had her women remove the spectacular headdress and the jewels at wrist and throat. Her hair was down now for the night, thick and long and dark, unsettling. There were diamonds still hanging at her ears, her only ornament, catching the light. Her scent was about her, drifting toward him through a space she defined, and surrounding her, also, was an aura: of power, and of amused intelligence, and of something else he could not name but knew he feared and was right to fear.

"How deeply acquainted might you be, Rhodian, with the private chambers of royalty?" Her voice was low, wry, shockingly intimate.

Careful, oh careful, he told himself, setting down his wine cup and bowing low, hiding a surging anxiety with the slowness of the movements. He straightened. Cleared his throat. "Not at all, my lady. I am honored and out of my element."

"A Batiaran far from his peninsula? A fish netted from water? How would you taste, Caius Crispus of Varena?" She did not move. The firelight was caught in her dark eyes and in the diamonds beside them. It flashed from the diamonds, was drowned in her eyes. She smiled.

She was toying with him. He knew this, but his throat was still dry. He coughed again, and said, "I have no idea. I am at your service in all things, thrice-exalted."

"You did say that. They shaved your beard, I understand. Poor man." She laughed, came forward then, straight toward him and then past, as he caught his breath. She stood by the long table, looking at the rose. "You were admiring my flower?" Her voice was honey, or silk.

"Very much, my lady. A work of great beauty and sadness."

"Sadness?" She turned her head, looked at him.

He hesitated. "Roses die. An artifice so delicate reminds us of the . . . impermanence of all things. All beautiful things."

Alixana said nothing for a time. Not a young woman anymore. Her dark, accentuated eyes held his until he looked away and down. Her scent, this near, was intoxicating, eastern, it made him think of colors, many things did: this was near to the red of her robe, but deeper, darker, porphyry, in fact. The purple of royalty. He looked down and wondered: could that be intentional, or was it only him—turning scent, sound, taste into color? There were hidden arts here in Sarantium of which he would know nothing. He was in the City of Cities, ornament of the world, eye of the universe. There were mysteries.

"The impermanence of the beautiful. Well said. That," the Empress murmured, looking at the rose, "is why it is here, of course. Clever man.

Could you, Rhodian, make me something in mosaic that suggests the opposite: a hint of what endures beyond the transitory?"

She had asked him here for a reason, after all. He looked up. "What would suggest that for you, Empress?"

"Dolphins," she said, without any warning at all.

He felt himself go white.

She turned fully around and watched him, leaning against the ivory of the table, hands braced on either side of her, fingers spread. Her expression was thoughtful, evaluating; that disconcerted him more than irony would have done.

"Drink your wine," the Empress said. "It is very good." He did. It was.

It didn't help him. Not with this.

Dolphins were deadly at this point in the story of the world. Much more than simply marine creatures, leaping between water and air, graceful and decorative—the sort any woman might enjoy seeing on the walls of her rooms. Dolphins were entangled in paganism, or trammeled in the nets of Heladikian heresies, or both.

They carried souls from the mortal realm of the living through the echoing chambers of the sea to the realms of the Dead, and judgment. So the Ancients had believed in Trakesia long ago—and in Rhodias before Jad's teachings came. Dolphins had served the many-named god of the Afterworld, conduits of the spirits of the dead, traversing the blurred space between life and what came after.

And some of that old, enduring paganism had crossed—through a different sort of blurred space—into the faith of Jad, and his son Heladikos, who died in his chariot bringing fire to men. When Heladikos's chariot plunged, burning like a torch, into the sea—so the dark tale ran—it was the dolphins who came and bore his ruined beauty upon their backs. Making of themselves a living bier, they carried it to the ends of the uttermost sea of the world to meet his father, sinking low at dusk. And Jad had claimed the body of his child and taken it into his own chariot, and carried it down—as every night—into the dark. A deeper, colder dark that night, for Heladikos had died.

And so the dolphins were said to be the last creatures of the living world to see and touch beloved Heladikos, and for their service to him they were holy in the teachings of those who believed in Jad's mortal son.

One might choose one's deadly sacrilege. The dolphins carried souls to the dark god of Death in the pagans' ancient pantheon, or they bore the body of the one god's only son in a now-forbidden heresy.

Either way, either meaning, an artisan who placed dolphins on a ceiling or wall was inviting mortal consequences from an increasingly vigilant clergy. There had been dolphins once in the Hippodrome, diving to number the laps run. They were gone, melted down. Sea horses counted the running now.

It was this Emperor, Valerius II, who had urged the joint Pronouncement of Athan, the High Patriarch in Rhodias, and Zakarios, the eastern one here in the City. Valerius had worked very hard to achieve that rare agreement. Two hundred years of bitter, deadly dispute in the schismatic faith of Jad had been papered over with that document, but the price for whatever gains an ambitious Emperor and superficially united clergy might enjoy had been the casting of all Heladikians into heresy: at risk of denunciation, ritual cursing in chapels and sanctuaries, fire. It was rare to be executed in Valerius's Empire for breaking the laws of man, but men were burned for heresy.

And it was Valerius's Empress who was asking him now, scented and gleaming in red and threaded gold by late-night candlelight, for dolphins in her rooms.

He felt much too drained by all that had happened tonight to properly sort through this. He temporized, carefully. "They are handsome creatures, indeed, especially when they leap from the waves."

Alixana smiled at him. "Of course they are." Her smile deepened. "They are also the bearers of Heladikos to the place where sea meets sky at twilight."

So much for temporizing. At least he knew which sin he might be burned for committing.

She was making it easier for him, however. He met her eyes, which had not left his face. "Both Patriarchs have banned such teachings, Empress. The Emperor swore an oath in the old Sanctuary of Jad's Wisdom to uphold their will in this."

"You heard of that? Even in Batiara? Under the Antae?"

"Of course we did. The High Patriarch is in Rhodias, my lady."

"And did the king of the Antae . . . or his daughter after . . . swear a similar oath to uphold?"

A stunningly dangerous woman. "You know they did not, my lady. The Antae came to Jad by way of the Heladikian teachings."

"And have not changed their doctrines, alas."

Crispin spun around.

The Empress merely turned her head and smiled at the man who had entered—as silently as she had—and had just spoken from the farthest door of the room.

For the second time, his heart racing, Crispin set down his wine and bowed to conceal a mounting unease. Valerius had changed neither his clothing nor his manner. He crossed to the wall himself and poured his own cup of wine. The three of them were alone, no servants in the room.

The Emperor sipped from his cup and looked at Crispin, waiting. An answer seemed to be expected.

It was very late; an utterly unanticipated mood seized Crispin, though it was one his mother and friends would all have claimed they knew. He murmured, "One of the Antae's most venerated clerics has written that heresies are not like clothing styles or beards, my lord, to go in and out of fashion by the season or the year."

Alixana laughed aloud. Valerius smiled a little, though the gray eyes remained attentive in the round, soft face. "I read that," he said. "Sybard of Varena. *A Reply to a Pronouncement.* An intelligent man. I wrote to him, saying as much, invited him here."

Crispin hadn't known that. Of course he hadn't known that.

What he did know—what *everyone* seemed to know—was that Valerius's manifest ambitions in the Batiaran peninsula derived much of their credibility from the religious schisms and the declared need to rescue the peninsula from "error." It was odd, and at the same time of a piece with what he was already learning about the man, that the Emperor might anchor a possible reconquest of Rhodias and the west in religion, and at the same time praise the Antae cleric whose work challenged, point by point, the document that gave him that anchor.

"He declined the invitation," said Alixana softly, "with some unkind words. Your partner Martinian also declined our invitation. Why, Rhodian, do none of you want to come to us?"

"Unfair, my heart. Caius Crispus has come, on cold autumn roads, braving a barber's razor and our court . . . only to find himself beset by a mischievous Empress with an impious request."

"Better my mischief than Styliane's malice," said Alixana crisply, still leaning back against the table. Her tone changed, slyly. It was interesting: Crispin knew the shadings of this voice, already. He felt as if he always had. "If heresies change by the season," she murmured, "may not the decorations of my walls, my lord Emperor? You have already conquered *here*, in any case."

She smiled sweetly, at both of them. There was a brief silence.

"What poor man," said the Emperor finally, shaking his head, his expression bemused, "may hope to be wise enough to have rejoinders for you?"

His Empress's smile deepened. "Good. I may do it, then? I do want dolphins here. I shall make arrangements for our Rhodian to—"

She stopped. An Imperial hand was uplifted across the room, straight as a judge's, halting her. "After," said Valerius sternly. "*After* the Sanctuary. *If* he chooses to do so. It is a heresy, seasonal or otherwise, and the weight of it, discovered, would fall on the artisan not the Empress. Consider. And decide after."

"After," said Alixana, "is likely to be a long time from now. You have built a very *large* Sanctuary, my lord. My chambers here are lamentably small." She made a moue of displeasure.

Crispin had an emerging sense that this was both a normal byplay for the two of them *and* something contrived to divert him. Why the latter, he wasn't sure, but the thought produced an opposite effect: he remained uneasy and alert.

And there came, just then, a knocking at the outer door.

The Emperor of Sarantium looked over quickly, and then he smiled.

He looked younger when he did, almost boyish. "Ah! Perhaps I *am* wise enough, after all. An encouraging thought. It appears," he murmured, "that I am about to win a wager. My lady, I shall look forward to your promised payment."

Alixana looked put out. "I cannot believe she would do this. It must be something else. Something . . ." She trailed off, biting at her lower lip. The lady-in-waiting had appeared at the inner doorway, eyebrows raised in inquiry. The Emperor set down his drink and silently withdrew past her, out of sight into the interior room. He was smiling as he went, Crispin saw.

Alixana nodded to her woman. The lady-in-waiting hesitated, and gestured toward her mistress and then at her own hair. "My lady . . . ?"

The Empress shrugged, impatience flitting across her face. "People have seen more than my unbound hair, Crysomallo. Leave it be."

Crispin stepped reflexively back toward the table with the rose as the door opened. Alixana stood not far away, imperious, for all the intimacy of her appearance. It did occur to him that whoever this was it could hardly be an intruder, else they'd not have gained entry into this palace, let alone caused the guards to tap on the door so late at night.

The woman stepped back a little and a man entered the room, behind her, though only a pace or two. He cradled a small ivory box in both hands. He handed it to Crysomallo, and then, turning toward the Empress, performed a full court obeisance, head touching the floor three times. Crispin wasn't certain, but he had a sense that such ceremony was excessive here, exaggerated. When the visitor finally straightened and then stood at Alixana's gesture, Crispin recognized him: the lean, narrow-faced man who'd been standing behind the Strategos Leontes in the audience chamber.

"You are a late visitor, secretary. Could this be a personal gift from you, or has Leontes something private he wishes said?" The Empress's tone was difficult to read: perfectly courteous, but no more than that.

"His lady wife does, thrice-exalted. I bring a small gift from Styliane Daleina to her thrice-revered and beloved Empress. She would be honored beyond her worth should you deign to accept it." The man looked quickly around as he finished speaking, and Crispin had the distinct sense that the secretary was memorizing the room. He could not miss the Empress's unbound hair, or the privacy of this situation. Clearly, Alixana did not care in the least. Crispin wondered, again, what game he'd become a small piece in, how he was being deployed now and to what end.

The Empress nodded at Crysomallo, who unclasped a golden latch on the box and opened it. The woman was unable to hide her astonishment. She held up the object within. The small gift. There was a silence.

"Oh, dear," said the Empress of Sarantium softly. "I have lost a wager."

"My lady?" The secretary's brow furrowed. It was not what he'd expected to hear.

"Never mind. Tell the Lady Styliane we are pleased with her gesture and by the . . . celerity with which she chose to send it to us, keeping a hardworking scribe awake so late at night as a messenger. You may go."

That was all. Courtesy, crispness, a dismissal. Crispin was still trying to absorb the fact that the staggeringly opulent pearl necklace he'd seen on Styliane Daleina—the one he'd drawn unwanted attention to—had just been presented to the Empress. The worth of it was past his ability even to imagine. He had a certainty, though—an absolute conviction—that had he not spoken as he had, earlier, this would not have happened.

"Thank you, most gracious lady. I shall hasten to relay your kind words. Had I known I might be interrupting . . ."

"Come, Pertennius. She knew you would interrupt and so did you. You both heard me summon the Rhodian in the throne room."

The man fell silent, his eyes dropped to the floor. He swallowed awkwardly. It was oddly pleasant, Crispin realized, to see someone else being discomfited by Alixana of Sarantium.

"I thought . . . my lady. She thought . . . you might . . ."

"Pertennius, poor man. You'll do better going with Leontes to battlefields and writing about cavalry charges. Go to bed. Tell Styliane I am happy to accept her gift and that the Rhodian was indeed still with me, as she wished him to be, to see her make a gift that outstripped the one he offered her. You may also tell her," added the Empress, "that my hair still reaches the small of my back, unbound." She turned deliberately, as if to let the secretary see, and walked over to the table where the wine flask stood. She picked up the cup Valerius had set down.

Crysomallo opened the door. In the instant before the man named Pertennius—where had he heard that name today?—turned to leave, Crispin saw something flash in his eyes and as quickly disappear as the man repeated his full obeisance and then withdrew.

Alixana did not turn around until the door closed.

"Jad curse you with cataracts and baldness," she said furiously, in that low, utterly magnificent voice.

The Emperor of Sarantium, so addressed by his wife as he came back into the room, was laughing with delight. "I *am* balding," he said. "A wasted curse. And if I develop cataracts you'll have to surrender me to the physicians for treatment, or guide me through life with a tongue to my ear."

Alixana's expression, seen in profile, arrested Crispin for a moment. He was pretty certain it was an unguarded look, something disturbingly intimate. Something caught in his own heart, the past snagging on the present.

"Clever of you, love," Alixana murmured, "to have anticipated this."

Valerius shrugged. "Not really. Our Rhodian shamed her with a generous gift after publicly exposing an error of presumption. She ought not to have worn jewelry exceeding the Empress's and she knew it."

"Of course she knew. But who was going to say so, in that company?"

Both turned, as if cueing each other, to look at Crispin. Both smiled this time.

Crispin cleared his throat. "An ignorant mosaicist from Varena, it seems, who now wishes to ask if he is likely to die for his transgressions."

"Oh, certainly you are. One of these days," said Alixana, still smiling. "We all do. Thank you, though. I owe you for an unexpected gift, and I do extravagantly admire a pearl like this. A weakness. Crysomallo?"

The lady-in-waiting, smiling with pleasure herself, walked over with the box. She withdrew the necklace again, undid the clasp, and moved behind the Empress.

"Not yet," said Valerius, touching the woman's shoulder. "I'd like Gesius to have it looked at before you put it on."

The Empress looked surprised. "What? Really? Petrus, you think . . . ?"

"No, I don't, in fact. But let it be examined. A detail."

"Poison is scarcely a detail, my heart."

Crispin saw Crysomallo blink at that and hurriedly replace the necklace in its box. She wiped her fingers nervously against the fabric of her robe. The Empress seemed more intrigued than anything else, not alarmed at all—so far as he could tell.

"We live with these things," Alixana of Sarantium said quietly. "Do not trouble yourself, Rhodian. As for your own safety . . . you did discomfit a number of people this evening. I would think a guard might be appropriate, Petrus?"

She had turned as she spoke, to the Emperor. Valerius said simply, "It is already in place. I spoke with Gesius before coming here."

Crispin cleared his throat. Things happened swiftly around these two, he was beginning to realize. "I should feel . . . awkward with a guard following me about. Is it permissible to make a suggestion?"

The Emperor inclined his head. Crispin said, "I mentioned the soldier who brought me here. His name is—"

"—Carullus, of the Fourth Sauradian, here to speak with Leontes. Probably about the soldiers' payment. You did mention him. I have named him and his men as your guards."

Crispin swallowed. By rights, the Emperor should not have even recalled the existence let alone the name of an officer mentioned once, in passing. But it was said of this man that he forgot nothing, that he never slept, that—indeed—he held converse, took counsel, with spirits of the half-world, dead predecessors, walking the palace corridors by night.

"I am grateful, my lord," Crispin said, and bowed. "Carullus is by way of being a friend now. His company is a comfort here in the City. I will walk easier for his presence."

"Which is to my advantage, of course," said the Emperor, with a slight smile. "I want your attention on your labors. Would you like to see the new Sanctuary?"

"I am eager to do so, my lord. The first morning when it is possible to be allowed—"

"Why wait? We'll go now."

It was long past the middle of the night. Even the Dykania revels would be ended by now. The bakers at their ovens, the Sleepless Ones at their vigils, street cleaners, city guards, prostitutes of either sex and their clients, these would be the people still awake and abroad. But this was an Emperor who never slept. So the tale ran.

"I *ought* to have expected this," Alixana said, her tone affronted. "I bring a clever man to my rooms for such . . . skills as he may offer me, and you spirit him away." She sniffed elaborately. "I shall take refuge in my bath and my bed, then, my lord."

Valerius grinned suddenly, the boyish look returning. "You lost a wager, my love. Do *not* fall asleep."

With real astonishment, Crispin saw the Empress of Sarantium's color heighten. She sketched a brief, mocking homage, though. "My lord the Emperor commands his subjects in all possible things."

"Of course I do," said Valerius.

"I shall leave you," said his Empress, turning. Crysomallo preceded her through the inner door. Crispin caught a glimpse of another fireplace and a wide bed beyond, frescoes and many-colored fabric hangings on the walls. He realized in that moment that he was about to be alone with the Emperor, after all. His mouth grew dry again with the implications of that.

Alixana turned in the doorway. She paused, as if in thought. Then laid a finger against one cheek and shook her head, as if in self-reproach. "I nearly forgot," she said. "Silly of me. Too distracted by a pearl and the thought of dolphins. Do tell us, Rhodian, your message from the queen of the Antae. What does Gisel say?"

The sensation, after the apprehension of expecting to be private with Valerius to convey exactly this, was very much as if a pit had gaped open beneath his feet, sprung by the lever of that exquisite voice. Crispin's heart lurched; he felt as if he were falling into emptiness.

"Message?" he echoed, wittily.

The Emperor murmured, "My love, you are capricious and cruel and terribly unfair. If Gisel gave Caius Crispus any message at all, it would have been for my ears alone."

Holy Jad, Crispin thought, helplessly. They *were* too quick. They knew too much. It was overwhelming.

"Of course she gave him a message." Alixana's tone was mild, but her eyes remained on Crispin's face, attentive and thoughtful, and there was no amusement in them now, he saw.

He took a steadying breath. He had seen a *zubir* in the Aldwood. He had walked into the forest expecting to die and had come out alive, having encountered something beyond the mortal. Every living moment that followed that time in the mist was a gift. He found he could master fear, remembering that.

He said quietly, "Is that why you asked me here, my lady?"

The Empress's mouth twitched wryly. "That, and the dolphins. I do want them."

Valerius said matter-of-factly, "We have people in Varena, of course. A number of the queen's own guard were killed one night this autumn. Murdered in their sleep. Quite extraordinary. Such a thing only happens when you need a secret kept. Our people in Varena addressed themselves to the matter. It was not difficult for them to learn about the much-talked-about arrival of the courier with our invitation. He conveyed its content publicly, it seems? And for reasons not immediately clear, it was an invitation you took upon yourself, by deception, instead of Martinian. That was of interest. Resources were deployed. You were evidently seen returning home that same night very late, with a royal escort. Meeting someone in the palace? Then came the deaths in the night. Conclusions were plausibly drawn from all of this and posted to us."

It was spoken as calmly, as precisely, as a dictated military report. Crispin thought of Queen Gisel: beset on all sides, struggling to find a path, a space for herself, survival. Brutally overmatched.

If he had a choice, he didn't know what it was. He looked from the Emperor to the Empress of Sarantium, met Alixana's steady gaze this time, and said nothing at all.

It seemed he didn't need to. The Empress said calmly, "She asked you to tell the Emperor that instead of an invasion a wedding might deliver Batiara more surely to him, with less bloodshed on all sides."

There seemed so little point, really, to resisting, but still he would not speak. He lowered his head, but before he did, he saw her sudden, brilliant smile. Heard Valerius cry, "I am accursed! The one night I win a wager she wins a larger one!"

The Empress said, "She did want it relayed only to the Emperor, didn't she?"

Crispin lifted his head, made no reply.

He might die here now, he knew.

"Of course she did. What else could she have done?" Alixana's tone was matter-of-fact, no emotion in it at all. "She would want to avoid an invasion at almost any cost."

"She would. I would," said Crispin finally, as calmly as he could. "Wouldn't any man? Or woman?" He took a breath. "I will say one thing, something I myself believe to be true: Batiara might possibly be taken in war, but it cannot be held. The days of one Empire, east and west, are over. The world is not what it was."

"I believe that," said Alixana, surprising him, again.

"And I do not," said the Emperor flatly. "Else I would not be devising as I am. I will be dead one day and lying in my tomb, and I would have it said of Valerius II that he did two things in his days beneath Jad's sun. Brought peace and splendor to the warring schisms and sanctuaries of the god's faith, and restored Rhodias to the Empire and to glory. I will lie easy with Jad if these two things are so."

"And otherwise?" The Empress had turned to her husband. Crispin had a sense he was party now to a long conversation, oft repeated.

"I do not think in terms of otherwise," said Valerius. "You know that, love. I never have."

"Then marry her," said his wife, very softly.

"I am married," said the Emperor, "and I do not think in terms of otherwise."

"Not even to lie easy with the god after you die?" Dark eyes holding cool gray in a room of candles and gold. Crispin swallowed hard and wished he were elsewhere, anywhere that was not here. He had not spoken a word of Gisel's message, but they seemed to know it all, as if his silence meant nothing. Except to himself.

"Not even for that," said Valerius. "Can you truly doubt?"

After a long moment, she shook her head. "Not truly," said the Empress Alixana. There was a silence. She went on. "In that case, however, we ought to consider inviting her here. If she can survive somehow and get away, her royalty becomes a tool against whoever usurps the Antae throne—and someone surely would—if she were gone."

Valerius smiled then, and Crispin—for reasons he did not immediately grasp—felt a chill, as if the fire had died. The Emperor didn't look boyish now. "An invitation went west some time ago, love. I had Gesius send it to her."

Alixana went very still, then shook her head back and forth, her expression a little odd now. "We are all foolish if we try to stay apace with you, are we not, my lord? Whatever jests or wagers you might enjoy making. Do you weary of being cleverer than anyone?"

Crispin, appalled at what he'd just heard, burst out, "She can't possibly come! They'll kill her if she even mentions it."

"Or let her come east and denounce her as a traitor, using that as an excuse to seize the throne without shedding royal blood. Useful in keeping you Rhodians quiescent, no?" Valerius's gaze was cool, detached, sorting through some gameboard problem late at night. "I wonder if the Antae nobles are clever enough to do it that way. I doubt it, actually." These were real lives, though, Crispin thought, horrified: a young queen, the people of a war-torn, plague-stricken land. His home.

"Are they only pieces of a puzzle, my lord Emperor? All those living in Batiara, your army, your own people exposed in the east if the soldiers go west? What will the King of Kings in Bassania do when he sees your armies leave the border?" Crispin heard his own reckless anger.

Valerius was unruffled. He said, reflectively, "Shirvan and the Bassanids receive four hundred and forty thousand gold solidi a year from our treasury. He needs the money. He's under pressure from the north and south and he's building, too, in Kabadh. Maybe I'll send him a mosaicist."

"Siroes?" the Empress murmured dryly.

Valerius smiled a little. "I might."

"I rather suspect you won't have the chance," Alixana said.

The Emperor looked at her a moment. He turned back to Crispin. "I had an impression in the throne room earlier that you were of the same cast of mind as I am, solving Scortius's challenge. Are your tesserae not . . . pieces of a puzzle, as you put it?"

Crispin shook his head. "They are glass and stone, not mortal souls, my lord."

"True enough," agreed Valerius, "but then, you aren't an Emperor. The pieces change when you rule. Be grateful your craft spares you some decisions."

It was said—had been said quietly for years—that this man had arranged the murder by fire of Flavius Daleinus on the day his uncle was elevated to the Purple. In this moment Crispin could believe it.

He looked at the woman. He was aware that they had played him like a musical instrument between them tonight, but he also sensed that there was no malice in it. There seemed to be a casual amusement even, and a measure of frankness that might reflect trust, or respect for Rhodian heritage . . . or perhaps simply an arrogant indifference to what he thought or felt.

"I," said Alixana decisively, "am going to my bath and bed. Wagers seem to have canceled each other, good my lord. If you return very late, speak with Crysomallo or whoever is awake to ascertain my . . . state." She smiled at her husband, catlike, controlled again, and turned to Crispin. "Fear me not, Rhodian. I owe you for a necklace and some diversion, and one day perhaps will have more of you."

"Dolphins, my lady?" he asked.

She didn't answer. Went through the open inner door and Crysomallo closed it.

"Drink your wine," said the Emperor, after a moment. "You look like you need it. Then I will show you a wonder of the world."

I have seen one, Crispin thought. Her scent lingered.

It occurred to him that he could have safely said it aloud, but he did not. They both drank. Carullus had told him, at some point in their journey here, that there was a judicial edict in the City that no other woman could wear the Empress Alixana's perfume. "What about the men?" Crispin could remember saying carelessly, eliciting the soldier's booming laugh. It seemed a long time ago.

Now, so far enmeshed in intricacies he could not even properly grasp what was happening, Crispin took his cloak again and followed Valerius II of Sarantium out of the Empress's private chambers and down corridors, where he was soon lost. They went outside—though not through the main entranceway—and the Emperor's guards conducted them with torches across a dark garden space and along a stone path with statuary strewn about them, looming and receding in the windy, beclouded night. Crispin could hear the sea.

They came to the wall of the Imperial Precinct and went along it on the path until they came to a chapel, and there they entered.

There was a cleric awake among the burning candles—one of the Sleepless Ones, by his white robes. He showed no surprise at seeing the Emperor at this time of night. He made obeisance, and then—with no words spoken—unhooked a key from his belt and led them to a small, dark door at the back behind the altar of the god and the golden disk of the sun.

The door opened into a short stone corridor, and Crispin, bending to protect his head, realized they were passing through the wall. There was another low door at the end of that brief passage; the cleric unlocked it, too, with the same key, and stood aside.

The soldiers paused as well, and so Crispin followed the Emperor alone into the Sanctuary of Jad's Holy Wisdom in the depths of night.

He straightened up and looked around him. There were lights burning wherever he looked, thousands of them, it seemed, even though this space was not yet consecrated or complete. His gaze went upward and then upward and slowly he apprehended the stupendous, the transcendent, majesty of the dome that had been achieved here. And standing very still where they had stopped, Crispin understood that here was the place where he might achieve his heart's desire, and that *this* was why he had come to Sarantium.

He had collapsed and fallen down in the small roadside chapel in Sauradia, his strength obliterated by the power of the god that had been achieved overhead, stern with judgment and the weight of war. He did not fall here, or feel inclined to do so. He wanted to soar, to be given the glory of flight—Heladikos's fatal gift from his father—that he might fly up past all these burning lights and lay his fingers tenderly upon the vast and holy surface of this dome.

Overmastered by so many things—past, present, swift bright images of what might be—Crispin stood gazing upward as the small door was closed behind them. He felt as if he were being buffeted—a small craft in a storm—by waves of desire and awe. The Emperor remained silent beside him, watching his face in the rippled light of a thousand thousand candles burning beneath the largest dome ever built in all the world.

At length, at great length, Crispin said the first thing that came to his lips among the many whirling thoughts, and he said it in a whisper, not to disturb the purity of that place: "You do not need to take Batiara back, my lord. You, and whoever it was built this for you, have your immortality."

The Sanctuary seemed to stretch forever, so high were the four arches on which the great dome rested, so vast the space defined beneath that dome and the semidomes supporting it, so far did naves and bays recede into darkness and flickering light. Crispin saw green marble like the sea in one direction, defining a chapel, blue-veined white marble elsewhere, pale gray, crimson, black. Brought here from quarries all over the world. He couldn't even conceive of the cost. Two of those towering arches rested on a double ascension of marble pillars with balconies dividing the two courses, and the intricacy of the masons' work on those stone balustrades—even in this first glimpse of them—made Crispin want to weep for the sudden memory of his father and his father's craft.

Above the second tier of pillars the two arches east and west were pierced by a score of windows each, and Crispin could already envisage—standing here at night by candlelight—what the setting and rising sun might do to this Sanctuary, entering through those windows like a sword. And also, more softly, diffused, through the higher windows in the dome itself. For, suspended like an image of Jad's heaven, the dome had at its base a continuous ring of small, delicately arched windows running all around. Crispin saw also that there were chains, descending from the dome into the space below it, holding iron candelabras aflame with their candles.

There would be light here by day and by night, changing and glorious. Whatever the mosaicists could conceive for the dome and semi-domes and arches and walls in this place would be lit as no other surfaces in the world were lit. There was grandeur here beyond description, an airiness, a defining of space that guided the massive pillars and the colossal arch supports into proportion and harmony. The Sanctuary branched off in each direction from the central well beneath the dome—a circle upon a square, Crispin realized, and his heart was stirred even as he tried and failed to grasp how this had been done—and there were recesses and niches and shadowed chapels for privacy and mystery and faith and calm.

One could believe here, he thought, in the holiness of Jad, and of the mortal creatures he had made.

The Emperor had not replied to his whispered words. Crispin wasn't even looking at him. His gaze was still reaching upward—eyes like fingers of the yearning mind—past the suspended candelabras and the ring of round dark windows with night and wind beyond them, toward the flicker and gleam and promise of the dome itself, waiting for him.

At length, Valerius said, "There is more than an enduring name at stake, Rhodian, but I believe I know what you are saying, and I believe I understand. You are pleased with what is on offer here for a mosaicist? You are not sorry you came?"

Crispin rubbed at his bare chin. "I have never seen anything to touch it. There is nothing in Rhodias, nothing on earth, that can . . . I have no idea how the dome was achieved. How did he dare span so large a . . . *who* did this, my lord?" They were still standing near the small doorway that led back through the wall to the rough chapel and the Imperial Precinct.

"He'll wander by, I imagine, when he hears our voices. He's here most nights. That's why I've had the candles lit since summer. They say I do not sleep, you know. It isn't true, though it is useful to have it said. But I believe it *is* true of Artibasos: I think he walks about here examining things, or bends over his drawings, or makes new ones all night long." The Emperor's expression was difficult to read. "You are not . . . afraid of this, Rhodian? It is not too large for you?"

Crispin hesitated, looking at Valerius. "Only a fool would be unafraid of something like this dome. When your architect comes by, ask him if he was afraid of his own design."

"I have. He said he was terrified, that he still is. He said he stays here nights because he has nightmares about it falling, if he sleeps at home." Valerius paused. "What will you make for me on my Sanctuary dome, Caius Crispus?"

Crispin's heart began pounding. He had almost been expecting the question. He shook his head. "You must forgive me. It is too soon, my lord."

It was a lie, as it happened.

He'd known what he wanted to do here before he was ever in this place. A dream, a gift, something carried out from the Aldwood on the Day of the Dead. He'd been granted an image of it today amid the screaming of the Hippodrome. Something of the half-world in that, too.

"*Much* too soon," came a new, querulous voice. Sound carried here. "Who *is* this person, and what happened to Siroes? My lord."

The honorific was belated, perfunctory. A small, rumpled, middle-aged man in an equally rumpled tunic emerged from behind the massed bank of candles to their left. His straw-colored hair stood up in random whorls of disarray. His feet were bare on the ice-cold marble of the floor, Crispin saw. He was carrying his sandals in one hand.

"Artibasos," said the Emperor. Crispin saw him smile. "I must say you look every bit the Master Architect of the Empire. Your hair emulates your dome in aspiring to the heavens."

The other man ran a hand absentmindedly through his hair, achieving further disorder. "I fell asleep," he said. "Then I woke up. And I had a good idea." He lifted his sandals, as if the gesture were an explanation, "I have been walking around."

"Indeed?" said Valerius, with patience.

"Well, yes," said Artibasos. "Obviously. That's why I'm barefoot."

There was a brief silence.

"Obviously," said the Emperor a little repressively. This was a man, Crispin already knew, who did not like being left in the dark. About anything.

"Noting the rough marbles?" Crispin hazarded. "One way to tell them, I suppose. Easier done in a warmer season, I'd have said."

"I woke with the idea," Artibasos said, with a sharp glance at Crispin. "Wanted to see if it worked. It does! I've marked a score of slabs for the masons to polish."

"You expect people to come in here barefoot?" the Emperor asked, his expression bemused.

"Perhaps. Not everyone who wishes to worship will be shod. But that isn't it . . . *I* expect the marble to be perfect, whether anyone knows it or not. My lord." The little architect gazed narrowly up at Crispin. His expression was owlish. "Who *is* this man?"

"A mosaicist," said the Emperor, still with a tolerance that surprised Crispin.

"Obviously," said the architect. "I heard that much."

"From Rhodias," added Valerius.

"Anyone can hear that much," said Artibasos, still glaring up at Crispin.

The Emperor laughed. "Caius Crispus of Varena, this is Artibasos of Sarantium, a man of some minor talents and all the politeness of those born in the City. Why do I indulge you, architect?"

"Because you like things done properly. Obviously." It seemed to be the man's favorite word. "This person will be working with Siroes?"

"He is working *instead* of Siroes. It appears Siroes misled us with regard to his reverse transfer ideas for the dome. Incidentally, had he discussed them with you, Artibasos?"

Mildly phrased, but the architect turned to look at his Emperor before answering and he hesitated, for the first time.

"I am a designer and a builder, my lord. I am making you this Sanctuary. How it is garbed is the province of the Emperor's decorative artisans. I have little interest in that, and no time to attend to it. I do not like Siroes, if that matters, nor his patroness, but that hardly matters either, does it?" He looked at Crispin again. "I doubt I'll like this one. He's too tall and his hair's red."

"They shaved my beard this evening," said Crispin, amused. "Else you'd have been in no doubt at all, I fear. Tell me, had you discussed how you were to prepare the surfaces for the mosaic work?"

The little man sniffed. "Why would I discuss a building detail with a decorator?"

Crispin's smile faded a little. "Perhaps," he said gently, "we might share a flask of wine one day soon and consider another possible approach to that? I'd be grateful."

Artibasos grimaced. "I suppose I ought to be polite. New arrival and suchlike. You are going to have requests about the plaster, aren't you? Obviously. I can tell. Are you the interfering sort who has opinions without knowledge?"

Crispin had worked with men like this before. "I have strong opinions about wine," he said, "but no knowledge of where to find the best in Sarantium. I'll leave the latter issue to you, if you permit me some thoughts on plaster?"

The architect was still for a moment, then he allowed himself a small—a very small—smile. "You are clever at least." He shifted back and forth from one foot to the other on the cold marble floor, struggling to suppress a yawn.

Valerius said, still in his wry, tolerant tone, "Artibasos, I am about to command you. Pay attention. Put on your sandals—you do me no good if you die of a night chill. Find your cloak. Then go home to bed. Home. You do me no good half asleep and worn-out, either. It is most of the way to morning. There is an escort waiting outside the doors for Caius Crispus, or there should be by now. They will take you home as well. Go to sleep. The dome will not fall."

The little architect made a sudden, urgent sign against evil. He seemed about to protest, then appeared—belatedly—to recollect that he was speaking with his Emperor. He closed his mouth and pushed a hand through his hair again, to unfortunate effect.

"A command," repeated Valerius kindly.

"Obviously," said Artibasos of Sarantium.

He stood still, however, while his Emperor reached out and—very gently—smoothed down the sand-colored chaos of his hair, much as a mother might bring some order to the appearance of her child.

Valerius walked them to the main doors—they were silver, and twice the height of a man, Crispin saw—and then out onto the portico in the wind. They both turned there and bowed to him, and Crispin noted that the little man beside him bowed as formally as he himself did. The Emperor went back inside, closed the massive door himself. They heard a heavy lock slide home.

The two men turned and stood together in the wind, looking out at the unlit square before the Sanctuary. The Emperor had assumed Carullus would be here. Crispin didn't see anyone. He was aware, suddenly, of exhaustion. He saw lights a long way across the square, by the Bronze Gates, where the Imperial Guard would be. Heavy clouds blanketed the sky. It was very quiet.

Until a scream tore through the night—a shouted warning—and a figure could then be seen dashing madly across the debris-strewn square straight toward the portico. Whoever it was bounded up, taking three steps as one, landed a bit awkwardly and went right past Artibasos to twist and pull at the bolted door.

The man turned, cursing savagely, a knife in his hand, and Crispin—struggling to comprehend—recognized him.

His jaw dropped. Too many surprises in one night. There were movements and sounds around them now. Turning quickly, Crispin drew a breath of relief to see the familiar figure of Carullus striding up to the steps, drawn sword in hand.

"Scortius of the Blues!" the soldier exclaimed after a moment. "You cost me a fortune this afternoon, you know."

The charioteer, coiled and fierce, snapped something confusing about the Emperor's protection applying to all three of them. Carullus blinked. "You thought we were here to *harm* them?" he asked. His sword was lowered.

The charioteer's dagger drifted down, more slowly. The nature of the misunderstanding finally came home to Crispin. He looked at the lithe figure beside him, then back at his broad-shouldered friend at the bottom of the steps. He performed some evidently necessary introductions.

A moment later, Scortius of Soriyya began to laugh.

Carullus joined him. Even Artibasos permitted himself a small grin.

When the amusement subsided, an invitation was extended. It seemed that, notwithstanding the absurd hour, the Blues' champion was presently expected at the faction compound for a repast in the kitchen. He was, Scortius explained, far too cowardly to cross Strumosus the chef in this—and he happened to be, for no very good reason, hungry.

Artibasos pointed out that he'd had a direct command from the Emperor who had lately left them. He'd been ordered to his bed. Carullus gaped at that, belatedly realizing who it was who had been on the portico while he and the soldiers watched in the shadows. Scortius protested. Crispin looked at the little architect.

"You think he'd hold you to that?" he asked. "Treat it as a genuine command?"

"He could," said Artibasos. "Valerius is not the most predictable of men, and this building is his legacy."

One of them, Crispin thought.

He thought of his home then, and of the young queen whose message had been exposed tonight. He hadn't actually done that himself, he supposed. But alone with Valerius and Alixana he had been made to see that they were so far ahead of anyone else in this game of courts and intrigues that . . . it wasn't really a game at all. Which left him wondering what his place was here, his role. Could he hope to withdraw to his tesserae and this glorious dome? Would he be allowed? There were so many tangled elements in the tale of this night, he wondered if he'd ever unwind the skein, in darkness or at dawn.

Three of Carullus's men were detailed to take the architect home. Carullus and two soldiers stayed with Crispin and Scortius. They angled across the windy square, away from the Bronze Gates and equestrian statue, through the Hippodrome Forum and toward the street that led up to the Blues' compound. Crispin discovered, as they went, that he was drained and overstimulated, in approximately equal measure. He needed to sleep and knew he could not. The mental image of a dome alchemized into that of the Empress, eliding the memory of a queen's touch.

Dolphins, she wanted. He drew a breath, remembering the sallow secretary delivering a necklace, the man's face as he looked from Crispin—alone with the Empress, it would have seemed to him—to the woman herself, with her long dark hair unbound in her intimate rooms. There had been layers to that swiftly veiled expression, Crispin thought. These, too, were beyond him just now.

He thought of the Sanctuary again, and of the man who had taken him there along a low stone tunnel and through a door into glory. In the eye of his mind he still saw that dome and the semidomes around it and the arches supporting them, marble set upon marble, and he saw his own work there, one day to come. The Sanctuary behind them was Artibasos's legacy, he thought, and it might end up being what the Emperor Valerius II was remembered for, and it could be—it *could* be—why the world might one day come to know that the Rhodian mosaicist Caius Crispus, only son of Horius Crispus of Varena and his wife, Avita, had lived once, and done honorable work under Jad's sun and the two moons.

He was thinking that when they were attacked.

He had wondered, moments before, if he might be permitted to withdraw to his tesserae: glass and marble, gold and mother-of-pearl, stone and semiprecious stone, the shaping of a vision on scaffolding in the air, high above the intrigues and wars and desires of men and women.

It didn't appear that would be so, as the night became iron and blood.

STRUMOSUS HAD TOLD HIM once—or, in truth, had told a fishmonger in the market with Kyros standing by—that you could tell much about a man by watching when he first tasted extremely good or very bad food. Kyros had taken to observing Strumosus's occasional guests in the kitchen when he had the chance.

He did tonight. It was so very late and the earlier events had been so extraordinary that an unexpectedly intimate sense of aftermath—of events shared and survived—prevailed in the kitchen.

Outside, the bodies of the attackers had been tossed beyond the gates and the two soldiers of the Fourth Sauradian cavalry who had died defending Scortius and the mosaicist in the first street assault had been brought in with the dead gatekeeper to await proper burial. Nine bodies in all, violently dead. The cheiromancers of the City would be furiously busy today and tomorrow, shaping commissioned curse-tablets to be deposited at the graves. The newly dead had the power of emissaries to the half-world. Astorgus kept two cheiromancers on staff, salaried, preparing counter-spells against those who wished the Blues' charioteers maimed or dead, or besought the same fate for the horses from malign spirits of darkness.

Kyros felt badly about the gatekeeper.

Niester had been playing games of Horse and Fox on one of the boards in the common room after the racing this afternoon. He was a body under a cloth now in the cold of the yard. He had two small children. Astorgus had detailed someone to go to his wife, but had told him to wait until after the dawn prayers. Let the woman sleep through the night. Time enough for grief to come knocking with a black fist.

Astorgus himself, in a grim, choleric mood, had gone off to meet with the Urban Prefect's officers. Kyros would not have wanted to be the man charged with dealing with the Blues' factionarius just now.

The faction's principal surgeon—a brisk, bearded Kindath—had been roused to tend the wounded soldier, whose name was Carullus of the Fourth Sauradian. His wounds turned out to be showy but not dangerous. The man had endured their cleansing and bandaging without expression, drinking wine with his free hand as the surgeon treated his shoulder. He had fought a running battle alone against six men along the dark laneway, allowing Scortius and the Rhodian to reach the faction gates. Carullus was still angry that the attackers had all been slain, Kyros gathered. No easy way to find out who'd hired them now.

Released by the doctor to the dinner table, the tribune of the Fourth Sauradian showed little sign of diminished appetite. Neither wounds nor anger diverted his attention from the bowls and plates in front of him. He had lost two of his soldiers tonight, had killed two men himself, but Kyros guessed that a military man would have to get used to that, and carry on, or he'd go mad. It was those at home who sometimes went mad, as Kyros's mother's sister had three years ago, when her son was killed in the Bassanid siege of Asen, near Eubulus. Kyros's mother remained certain it was grief that had rendered her vulnerable to the plague when it came the next year. His aunt had been one of the first to die. Asen had been returned by the Bassanids the following spring in the treaty that bought peace on the eastern borders, making the siege and the deaths even more pointless. Cities were always being taken and ceded back on both sides of the shifting border.

People didn't come back to life, though, even if a city was returned. You carried on, as this officer was, hungrily sponging up fish soup with a thick crust of bread. What else could one do? Curse the god, tear one's garments, retreat like a Holy Fool to some chapel or a rock in the desert or mountains? That last was possible, Kyros supposed, but he had discovered, since coming to this kitchen, that he had a hunger—a taste, you might say—for the gifts and dangers of the world. He might never be a charioteer, an animal trainer, a soldier—he would drag a bad foot with him through all his days—but there was a life to be lived, nonetheless. A life in the world.

And just now Scortius, First of the Blues, to whose glory a silver statue had been promised tonight for the Hippodrome spina, was glancing up, soup spoon in hand, and murmuring to Strumosus, "What can I say, my friend? The soup is worthy of the banquet hall of the god."

"It is," echoed the red-haired Rhodian beside him. "It is wonderful." His expression was rapt, as revealing as Strumosus had said faces could be at such times.

Strumosus, entirely relaxed now, sitting at the head of the table pouring wine for his three guests, had benignly tilted his head sideways. He said: "Young Kyros over there attended to it. He has the makings of a cook."

Two sentences. Simple words. Kyros feared he might weep for joy and pride. He did not, of course. He wasn't a child, after all. He did blush, unfortunately, and lower his head before all the approving smiles. And then he began waiting ardently for the moment, released to the privacy of his cot in the apprentices' room, when he could reclaim—over and again—that miraculous sequence of words and the expressions that had followed. Scortius had said. Then the Rhodian had added. Then Strumosus had said . . .

Kyros and Rasic were given the next day to themselves: an unexpected holiday, a reward for working all night. Rasic went whistling off to the harbor to buy a woman in a caupona. Kyros used the free time to go to his parents' apartment down in the overcrowded, pungent warrens of the Hippodrome where he'd grown up. He told them, shyly, about what had been said the night before. His father, a man of few words, had touched his son's shoulder with a scarred, bitten hand before going off to feed his beasts. His mother, rather less reserved, had screamed.

Then she had bustled out of their tiny apartment to tell all her friends, before buying and lighting an entire row of thanksgiving candles in the Hippodrome's own chapel. For once, Kyros didn't think she was being excessive.

The makings of a cook.

Strumosus had said that!

THEY DIDN'T END UP going to bed that night. There was food fit for the god's palaces behind the sun and wine to equal it in the blessedly warm, firelit kitchen. They finished with an herbal tea, just before sunrise, that reminded Crispin of the one Zoticus had served him before his journey had begun—which reminded him of Linon, and then home, which made him think, again, of how far away he was. Among strangers, but less so after tonight, it felt. He sipped the hot tea and allowed the faint dizziness of extreme fatigue to wash over him, a sense of distance, of words and movements drifting toward his awareness from far away.

Scortius had gone out to the stables to check on his best horse. Now he came back, rubbing his hands together after the predawn chill of the air, and took the bench next to Crispin again. A calm man, alert and unassuming, for all his wealth and renown. A generous spirit. He'd run madly in the darkness to warn them of danger. That said something.

Crispin looked at Carullus across the stone table. Not a truth to call this man a stranger now, really. Among other things, he knew the big soldier well enough to realize he was hiding discomfort. The wounds weren't dangerous, they'd been assured by the surgeon, but they had to be hurting now, and Carullus would carry new scars from both of them. He had also lost men he'd known a long time tonight. Might even be blaming himself for that; Crispin wasn't sure.

They had no idea who'd paid for the assault. Soldiers on leave were not particularly expensive to hire in the City, it seemed. It required only some determination to arrange an abduction or even a killing. A runner had been sent with a message from Carullus to his surviving men—the ones who had taken the architect home would be expecting them at the inn. It would be a hard message for them to hear, Crispin thought. Carullus, a commander, had lost two men in his charge, but the soldiers would have lost companions. There was a difference.

The Urban Prefect's officer had been polite and formal with Crispin when he'd arrived with the factionarius. They'd spoken privately in the large room where the banquet had taken place. The man had not probed deeply, and Crispin had realized that the officer wasn't certain he *wanted* to know too much about this murder attempt. Intuitively, Crispin had said nothing about the mosaicist dismissed by the Emperor or the aristocratic lady who might have felt herself diminished by this—or embarrassed by a reference to a necklace she wore. Both things had happened in public: the man would learn of them if he wanted to.

Would someone *kill* for such things?

The Emperor had refused to let his wife put on the necklace when it came.

There were threads to be untangled and examined here, but they were not about to reveal themselves when his brain was weary and vague with wine and an overwhelming night.

When the gray rumor of dawn showed in the east, they left the kitchen and went across the courtyard to join the administration and employees of the Blues in chapel for the faction's early-morning invocation. Crispin discovered a genuine gratitude, almost a feeling of piety within himself as he chanted the antiphonal responses: for his life preserved, again; for the dome given to him tonight; for the friend Carullus was, and the friend the charioteer might become; for having survived an entry into court, questions in an Empress's rooms, and swords in the night.

And finally—because the small graces of life really did matter to him—for the taste of a shrimp-stuffed whitefish in a sauce like a waking dream.

Scortius didn't bother going home. He bade them good day outside the chapel and then went off to sleep in a room they reserved for him in the compound. The sun was just coming up. A small party of

Blues escorted Crispin and Carullus to their inn as the bells summoning Sarantines to later morning prayers in other chapels began all around them.

The clouds were gone, swept away south; the day promised to be cold and bright. The City was stirring as they walked, rousing itself to the resumption of the mundane at the end of a festival. There was debris in the streets but less than he'd expected: workers had been busy in the night. Crispin saw men and women walking to chapels, apprentices running errands, a food market noisily opening up, shops and stalls displaying their wares under colonnades. Slaves and children hurried past carrying water and loaves of bread. There were lines of people already outside food stands, snatching the first meal of the day. A gray-bearded Holy Fool in a tattered and stained yellow robe was shuffling barefoot toward what was probably his usual station to harangue those who were not at prayer.

They reached the inn. Their escorts doubled back to the compound. Crispin and Carullus walked in. The common room was open, a fire going, a handful of people eating inside. The two men passed by that doorway and went up the stairs, moving slowly now.

"Speak later?" Carullus mumbled.

"Of course. You're all right?" Crispin asked.

The soldier grunted wearily and unlocked the door to his room.

Crispin nodded his head, though the other man had already closed the door. He took out his key and headed for his own room farther down the hall. It seemed to take an oddly long time to get there. Noises from the street drifted up. Bells still ringing. It was morning, after all. He tried to remember the last time he'd stayed awake an entire night. He fumbled at the lock. It took some concentration but he managed to open the door. The shutters were blessedly closed against the morning, though bands of sunlight penetrated through the slats, stippling the darkness.

He dropped the key on the small table by the door and stumbled toward his bed, half asleep already. Then he realized—too late to check his motion—that there was someone in the room, on the bed, watching him. And then, in the bands of muted light, he saw the naked blade come up.

SOME TIME EARLIER, STILL in the beclouded dark of night, a waiting soldier has handed the Emperor of Sarantium a fur-lined cloak as he emerges into the windy cold from the small chapel and the stone tunnel that leads through the Imperial Precinct walls.

The Emperor, who can remember—though only with an effort now—walking in only a short tunic and torn, sodden boots through a winter the first time he came south from Trakesia, at his uncle's behest, is grateful for the warmth. It is a short enough walk back to the Traversite Palace, but his personal immunity is to fatigue, not cold.

I am growing old, he thinks, not for the first time. He has no heir. Not for want of effort, or medical advice, or invocations of aid from the god and the half-world, both. It would be good to have a son, he thinks, but has been reconciled for some time now to not having one. His uncle passed the throne to him: there is some precedent in the family, at any rate. Unfortunately, his sisters' sons are feckless nonentities and all four of them remain in Trakesia, at his very firm instruction.

Not that they would stir any sort of insurrection. To do such a thing requires courage and initiative and none of them has either. They might serve as figureheads, though, for someone else's ambition—and the god knows there is enough hunger for power in Sarantium. He could have them killed, but he has judged that unnecessary.

The Emperor shivers, crossing the gardens in the night wind. It is only the chill and damp. He is not fearful, at all. He has only been afraid once in his adult life that he can remember: during the rioting two years ago, in the moment he learned that the Blues and Greens had joined together, side by side in the Hippodrome and in the burning streets. That had been too unexpected a development, too far outside the predictable, the *rational*. He was—and is—a man who relies on orderly conduct to ground his existence and his thinking. Something so unlikely as the factions joining with each other had rendered him vulnerable, unmoored, like a ship with an anchor ripped free in a storm.

He had been prepared to follow the advice of his most senior counselors that day. To take a small craft from the little cove below the Precinct and flee the sack of his city. The foolish, illogical rioting over a small increase in taxes and some depravities alleged on the part of the Quaestor of Imperial Revenue had been on the very cusp of bringing down a lifetime's worth of planning and achievement. He had been frightened and enraged. This memory is much more vivid than the one from long ago, the winter trek down to the City.

He reaches the smaller of the two main palaces, ascends the wide steps. Doors are opened for him by the soldiers on duty there. He pauses on the threshold, looking up at the gray-black clouds west over the sea, then he walks into the palace to see if the woman whose words saved them all that day two years ago is still awake, or has—as threatened—gone to sleep.

Gisel—Hildric's daughter, queen of the Antae—is said to be young and even beautiful, though that last hardly matters in the scheme of things. It is distinctly probable she could offer him an heir, though less likely that she would really afford an alternative to the invasion of Batiara. Were she to come east to wed the Emperor of Sarantium it would be seen as an act of treachery by the Antae. A successor would be named, or emerge.

Successors among the Antae tend to follow each other rapidly in any case, he thinks, as swords and poison do their winnowing. It *is* true that Gisel would serve as excuse for Sarantine intervention, lending validity to his armies. Not a trivial thing. The endorsement of the High Patriarch might reasonably be expected in the name of the queen, and that would carry weight among the Rhodians—and many of the Antae—which could turn the balance in a war. The young queen, in other words, is not really wrong in her reading of what she might represent for him. No man who prided himself on his command of logic and capacity to analyze and anticipate could deny that this is so.

Marrying her—if she could be winkled out of Varena alive—would represent a truly dazzling opening up of avenues. And she is indeed young enough to bear, many times. Nor is he so old himself, though he might feel it at times.

The Emperor of Sarantium comes to his wife's chambers by way of the inner corridor he always uses. He sheds the cloak there. A soldier takes it from him. He knocks, himself. He is genuinely uncertain if Aliana will be awake. She values her sleep more than he does—most people do. He hopes she has waited. Tonight has been interesting in unexpected ways, and he is far from tired, keen to talk.

Crysomallo opens the door, admitting him to the innermost of the Empress's rooms. There are four doors here. The architects have made of this wing a maze of women's chambers. He himself doesn't even know where all the corridors lead and branch. The door closes on the soldiers. There are candles burning here, a clue. He turns to her longtime lady-in-waiting, eyebrows lifted in inquiry, but before Crysomallo can speak, the door to the bedchamber itself opens, and Aliana, the Empress Alixana, his life, appears.

He says, "You *are* awake. I am pleased."

She murmurs, mildly, "You look chilled. Go nearer the fire. I have been considering which items of my clothing to pack for the exile to which you are sending me."

Crysomallo smiles, lowering her head quickly in a vain attempt to hide it. She turns, without instruction, and withdraws to another part of the web of rooms. The Emperor waits for the door to close.

"And why," he says, austere and composed, to the woman who remains with him, "do you assume you'll be allowed any of them when you go?"

"Ah," she says, simulating relief, a hand fluttering to her bosom. "That means you don't intend to kill me."

He shakes his head. "Hardly necessary. I can let Styliane do it once you are discarded and powerless."

Her face sinks as she considers this new possibility. "Another necklace?"

"Or chains," he says agreeably. "Poisoned manacles for your cell in exile."

"At least the indignity would be shortened." She sighs. "A cold night?"

"Very cold," he agrees. "Windy for an old man's bones. The clouds will break by morning, though. We'll see the sun."

"Trakesians always know the weather. They just don't understand women. One can't have *all* gifts, I suppose. Which old man were you walking with?" She smiles. So does he. "You will take a cup of wine, my lord?"

He nods. "I'm quite certain there's nothing wrong with the necklace," he adds.

"I know. You wanted the artisan to take a warning about her."

He smiles at that. "You know me too well."

She shakes her head, walking over with the cup. "No one knows you too well. I know some things you are inclined to do. He will be a prize, after tonight, and you wanted to give him some caution."

"He's a cautious man, I think."

"This is a seductive place."

He grins suddenly. He can still look boyish at times. "Very."

She laughs, hands him his wine. "Did he tell us too easily?" She walks over to take a cushioned seat. "About Gisel? Is he weak that way?"

The Emperor also crosses and sits easily—no sign of age in the movement—on the floor by her feet among the pillows. The fire near her low-backed chair has been attentively built up. The room is warm, the wine is very good and watered to his taste. The wind and the world are outside.

Valerius, who was Petrus when she met him and still is when they are private, shakes his head. "He's an intelligent fellow. Very much so, actually. I didn't expect that. He didn't really tell us anything, if you recall. Kept his silence. You were too precise in what you asked and said merely to be hazarding a guess. He drew that conclusion and acted on it. I'd call him observant, not weak. Besides, he'll be in love with you by now." He smiles up at her and sips his wine.

"A well-made man," she murmurs. "Though I'd have hated to see the red beard they say he came with." She shudders delicately. "But, alas, I like my men much younger than that one."

He laughs. "Why *did* you ask him here?"

"I wanted dolphins. You heard."

"I did. You'll get them when we're done with the Sanctuary. What other reasons?"

The Empress lifts one shoulder, a motion of hers he has always loved.

Her dark hair ripples, catching the light. "As you say, he was a prize after discrediting Siroes and solving the charioteer's mystery."

"And the gift to Styliane. Leontes didn't much like that."

"That isn't what he didn't like, Petrus. And *she* will not have liked having to match his generosity, at all."

"He'll have a guard. At least for the first while. Styliane did sponsor the other artisan, after all."

She nods. "I have told you, more than once, that that marriage is a mistake."

The man frowns. Sips his wine. The woman watches him closely, though her manner appears relaxed. "He earned it, Aliana. Against the Bassanids and in the Majriti."

"He earned appropriate honors, yes. Styliane Daleina was not the way to reward him, my love. The Daleinoi hate you enough, as it is."

"I can't imagine why," he murmurs wryly, then adds, "Leontes was the marriage-dream of every woman in the Empire."

"Every woman but two," she says quietly. "The one here with you and the one forced to wed him."

"I can only leave it to him to change her mind, then."

"Or watch her change him?"

He shook his head. "I imagine Leontes knows how to lay a siege of this kind, as well. And he is proof against treachery. He is secure in himself and his image of Jad."

She opens her mouth to say something more, but does not. He notices though, and smiles. "I know," he murmurs. "Pay the soldiers, delay the Sanctuary."

She says, "Among other things. But what does a woman understand of these great affairs?"

"Exactly," he says emphatically. "Stick to your charities and dawn prayers."

They both laugh. The Empress is notorious for mornings abed. There is a silence. He drinks his wine, finishing it. She rises smoothly, takes the cup, fills it again and comes back, sitting as she hands it to him again. He lays a hand on her slippered foot where it rests on a pillow beside him. They watch the fire for a time.

"Gisel of the Antae might bear you children," she says softly.

He continues to gaze into the flames. He nods. "And be much less trouble, one has to assume."

"Shall I resume selecting a wardrobe for exile? May I take the necklace?"

The Emperor continues to look into the tongues of fire. Heladikos's gift, according to the schismatics he has agreed to suppress in the cause of harmony in the faith of Jad. Chieromancers claim they can read futures in flames, see shapes of destiny. They, too, are to be suppressed. All pagans are. He has even—with a reluctance few will know—closed the old pagan Schools. A thousand years of learning. Even Aliana's dolphins are a transgression. There are those who would burn or brand the artisan for crafting them, if he ever does.

The Emperor reads no mystic certainties of any kind in the late-night flames, sitting at the woman's feet, one hand touching her instep and the jeweled slipper. He says, "Never leave me."

"Wherever would I go?" she murmurs after a moment, trying to keep the tone light and just failing.

He looks up. "Never leave me," he says again, the gray eyes on hers this time.

He can do this to her, take breath from chest and throat. A constriction of great need. After all these years.

"Not in life," she replies.

CHAPTER IX

Kasia awakened from a dream at dawn. She lay in bed, confused, half asleep, and only gradually became aware that there were bells pealing outside. There had been no Jaddite bells at home where the gods were found in the black forest or by rivers or in the grainfields; assuaged by blood. These sanctuary bells were a part of city life. She was in Sarantium. Half a million people, Carullus had said. He'd said she'd get used to the crowds, learn to sleep through the bells if she chose.

The dream had been of her waterfall at home, in summer. She'd been sitting on a bank of the pool below the falls, shaded by leafy trees that bent low over the water. There had been a man with her, which had never been so at home, in life.

She couldn't see his face in the dream.

The bells continued, summoning Sarantium to prayer. Jad of the Sun was riding up in his chariot. All who sought the god's protection in life and his intercession after death should be rising with him, making their way, even now, to the chapels and sanctuaries.

Kasia lay very still, thinking about her dream. She felt strange, unsettled; something nagged at her awareness. Then she remembered: the men had not come home last night, or not before she'd fallen asleep. And there had been that disquieting visit from the court mosaicist. An edgy man, afraid. She'd not been able to warn Crispin about him before he was taken off to the court. Carullus had assured her it didn't matter, that the Rhodian could handle himself in the Imperial Precinct, that he'd have protectors there.

Kasia knew that the very idea of a protector meant that there might be someone you needed to be protected *from*, but she hadn't said that. She and Carullus and Vargos had had their dinner together and then come back here through the very wild streets for a quiet glass of wine. Kasia knew the tribune would have greatly enjoyed strolling through the last night of the Dykania with a flask of ale in his hand, that he was staying inside for her. She was grateful for his kindness, his easy way with a story. Several stories. He made her smile and grinned when he did. He had knocked Crispin unconscious with an iron helmet the first moment they met. Vargos had been beaten very badly by his men. Much had changed in a short time.

Later, from the festive chaos outside, a brisk messenger had entered looking for the soldiers: they were to go to the Imperial Precinct, wait by the Bronze Gates—or wherever they were ordered when they got there—and escort the Rhodian mosaicist, Caius Crispus of Varena, home when he was dismissed. It was a command, from the Chancellor.

Carullus had smiled at Kasia across the table. "Told you," he'd said. "Protectors. And he got away with using his own name, too. This is good news, girl." He and five of his men had armed themselves and gone.

Vargos, used to early nights and early mornings, had already gone to bed. Kasia had been alone again. She didn't really have any fears for herself. Or, that wasn't quite true. She had no idea what was to become of her life. That would turn into a fear if she stopped to dwell upon it.

She had left the last of the wine on the table and had gone up to her room, locked the door, undressed, eventually fallen asleep. Had had dreams on and off through the night, awakening at random noises from the streets below, listening for returning footsteps down the hall.

She hadn't heard them.

She rose now, washed her face and upper body at the basin in the room, dressed herself in what she'd worn on the road and since arriving. Crispin had spoken of buying her clothing. The comment had raised in her mind again the uneasy question of her future.

The bells seemed to have stopped. She tugged fingers through her tangled hair and went out into the hall. She hesitated there, then decided it was permissible to look in on him, tell of the other mosaicist who had come, find out what had happened in the night. If it was *not* permitted, best she learn that now, Kasia thought. She was free. A citizen of the Sarantine Empire. Had been a slave less than a year. It did *not* define your life, she told herself.

His door was closed, of course. She lifted a hand to knock and heard voices inside.

Her heart lurched, surprising her greatly, though afterward she would find it less surprising. The words she heard spoken were a shock, however, and so was what Crispin said in reply. Kasia felt herself flush, listening; her lifted hand trembled in the air.

She didn't knock. Turned, in great confusion, to go down.

On the stairs she met two of Carullus's men coming up. They told her about the attack in the night.

Kasia found herself leaning against the wall as she listened. Her legs felt oddly weak. Two of the soldiers had died, the little Soriyyan and Ferix from Amoria: men she had come to know. All six of the attackers had been killed, whoever they had been. Crispin was all right. Carullus had been wounded. The two of them had only just come in, at dawn. They had been seen going up the stairs, hadn't stopped to talk.

No, the soldiers said, there had been no one else with them.

She hadn't heard them in the hallway. Or perhaps she had, and that—not the bells—had drawn her from dream, or had shaped her dream. A faceless man beside a waterfall. Carullus's men, grim and scowling, went past her to their shared room to get their weapons. They would carry them everywhere now, she understood. Deaths altered things.

Kasia paused on the stairway, shaken and uncertain. Vargos would be at chapel by now; there was no one to be with downstairs. It came to her that an enemy might already be upstairs, but Crispin had not sounded . . . alarmed. It occurred to her that she ought to tell someone, or check on him herself, risking embarrassment. Someone had tried to kill him last night. Had killed two men. She took a deep breath. The stone of the wall was rough against her shoulder. He had *not* sounded alarmed. And the other voice had been a woman's.

She turned back and went to Carullus's room. They'd said he'd been wounded. Resolutely, she knocked there. He called out, tiredly. She spoke her name. The door opened.

Small things change a life. Change lives.

CRISPIN TWISTED VIOLENTLY TO one side, away from the leveled knife. He jammed a hand hard against the post at the foot of the bed to stay upright.

"Ah," said the woman in the shuttered half-light of his bedroom. "It *is* you, Rhodian. Good. I feared for my virtue."

She laid down the knife. After, he would remember thinking it was not the weapon she needed to wield. At the time he was speechless.

"So," said Styliane Daleina, sitting at ease upon his bed, "I am told the little actress let down her hair for you in her chambers. Did she go to her knees the way they say she used to onstage, and take you in her mouth?"

She smiled, utterly composed.

Crispin felt himself go white as he stared at her. It took him a moment to find his voice. "You appear to have been misinformed. There were no actresses in the Blues' compound when I arrived there," he said very carefully. He knew what she'd meant. He was *not* going to acknowledge it. "And I was in the kitchen only, no one's private chambers. What are you doing in mine?" He ought to have called her "my lady."

She had changed her clothing. The court garb was gone. She was wearing a dark blue robe with a hood, thrown back now to frame her golden hair, which was still pinned, though without ornament now. She would have had the hood up, he imagined, to pass unknown through the streets, to enter here. Had she bribed someone? She would have had to. Wouldn't she?

She didn't answer his spoken question. Not with words, at any rate. She looked up at him for a long moment from the bed, then stood. A very tall woman, blue-eyed, fair-haired, a scent about her: Crispin thought of flowers, a mountain meadow, an undercurrent of intoxication, poppies. His heart was racing: danger and—rising swiftly and against his will—desire. The expression on her face was thoughtful, appraising. Without hurrying, she lifted one hand and traced a finger along his shaven jaw. She touched his ear, circled it. Then she rose up on tiptoe and kissed him on the mouth.

He didn't move. He could have withdrawn, he thought afterward, could have stepped back. He was no innocent, had known—fatigued as he was—that measuring look in her eyes as she stood up in the shadow and light of the room. He hadn't stepped back. He did refrain from responding, though, as best he could, even when her tongue . . .

She didn't seem to care. Appeared to find it amusing, in fact, that he withheld himself, standing rigid before her. She took her time, quite deliberately, body fitted close against his, tongue brushing his lips, pushing between them, then moving down to his throat. He heard her soft laughter, the breath warm against his skin.

"I do hope she left some life in you," murmured the aristocratic wife of the Supreme Strategos of the Empire, and proceeded to slip a hand down the front of his tunic to his waist—and past it—by way of inquiry.

This time Crispin did step back, breathing hard, but not before she'd touched him through the silk of his garment. He saw her smile, the small, even teeth. She was exquisite, was Styliane Daleina, like pale glass, pale ivory, like one of the knife blades made in the far west of the world, in Esperana, where they crafted such things to be works of beauty as well as agents of death.

"Good," she said, again. She looked at him, assured, amused, daughter of wealth and power, wedded to it. He could taste her, feel where her mouth had been along his throat. She said, musingly, "I will disappoint you, I now fear. How can I compete with the actress in this? It was said in her youth that she lamented holy Jad had granted her an insufficiency of orifices for the acts of love."

"Stop it!" Crispin rasped. "This is a game. Why are you playing it?

Why are you here?" She smiled again. White teeth, hands coming up into her hair, long, wide sleeves of the robe falling back to show bare, slender arms. He said, in anger, fighting desire, "Someone tried to kill me tonight."

"I know," said Styliane Daleina. "Does it excite you? I hope it does."

"You know? What else do you know about it?" Crispin said. Even as he spoke, she began to unpin her golden hair.

She paused. Looked at him, a different expression in her eyes this time. "Rhodian, had I wished you dead, you would be. Why would a Daleinus hire drunks in a caupona? Why would I trouble to kill an artisan?"

"Why would you trouble to come uninvited to his room?" Crispin snapped.

She laughed again at that. Her hands were busy another moment, collecting pins; then she shook her head and the richness of her hair spilled down, falling about her shoulders, filling the hood of her robe.

"Must the actress be allowed *all* the interesting men?" she said.

Crispin shook his head, the familiar anger rising now. He sought refuge in it. "I'll say it again: this is a game you are playing. You are not here because you want to be bedded by a foreign artisan." She hadn't stepped back. There was very little space between them and her scent enveloped them both. A dark redness, heady as poppies, as unmixed wine. Very different from the Empress's. It had to be. Carullus and then the eunuchs had told him that.

Deliberately, Crispin sat down on the wooden chest under the window. He took a deep breath. "I have asked some questions. They seem reasonable in the circumstances. I'm waiting," he said, and then added, "My lady."

"So am I," she murmured, one hand pushing her hair back. But the voice had changed again, responding to his tone. There was a silence in the room. Crispin heard a cart rumble past in the street below. Someone shouted. It was morning. Bands of light and dark fell across her body. The effect, he thought, was quite beautiful.

She said, "You may be inclined to underestimate yourself, Rhodian. You have little concept of what the patterns are at this court. No one is summoned as swiftly as you were. Ambassadors wait *weeks*, artisan. But the Emperor is infatuated with his Sanctuary. In one single night you have been invited to court, given control of the mosaics there, had private counsel with the Empress, and caused the dismissal of the man who was doing the work before you came."

"Your man," Crispin said.

"After a fashion," she said carelessly. "He had done some work for us. I judged it of some use to have Valerius in our debt for finding him a craftsman. Leontes disagreed with that, but had his own reasons for preferring Siroes. He has . . . views on what you and the other artisans should be permitted to do in the sanctuaries."

Crispin blinked. That might need thinking about. Later. "It was Siroes who hired those soldiers, then?" he guessed. "I had no intention of ruining anyone's career."

"You did, however," said the woman. The aristocratic coolness he remembered from before was in her voice again. "Quite completely. But no, I can attest that Siroes was not in a position to hire assassins tonight. Trust me in this."

Crispin swallowed. There was nothing reassuring in her tone, but there was a note of truth. He decided he didn't want to ask *why* she was so certain.

"Who was it, then?"

Styliane Daleina raised her hands, palms out, an elegant, indifferent gesture. "I have no idea. Run down the table of your enemies. Pick a name. Did the actress like my necklace? Did she put it on?"

"The Emperor wouldn't let her," Crispin said, deliberately.

And saw that he'd surprised her. "Valerius was there?"

"He was there. No one went down on her knees."

She was amazingly self-possessed. A lifetime of dealing with intrigue and lesser mortals. She smiled a little. "Not yet," she said, the timbre of her voice lower, the glance direct. It was a game, and he knew it, but entirely against his will, Crispin felt the stirrings of desire again.

As carefully as he could, he said, "I am unused to being offered love-making on so little acquaintance, except by whores. My lady, I am generally disinclined to accept their offers as well."

She gazed at him, and Crispin had a sense that—perhaps for the first time—she was taking the trouble to shape an evaluation of the man in the room with her. She had been standing. Now she sank down onto the end of the bed, not far from the chest where he sat. Her knee brushed his, then withdrew a little.

"Would that please you?" she murmured. "To treat me like a whore, Rhodian? Put my face hard to the pillow, take me from behind? Hold me by the hair as I cry out, as I say shocking, exciting things to you? Shall I tell you what Leontes likes to do? It will surprise you, perhaps. He rather enjoys—"

"No!" Crispin rasped, a little desperately. "What is this *about*? Does it amuse you to play the wanton? Do you wander the streets soliciting lovers? There are other bedrooms in this inn."

Her expression was impossible to read. He hoped his tunic was concealing the evidence of his arousal. He dared not look down to check.

She said, "What is this about, he asks. I have assumed you to be intelligent, Rhodian. You gave some sign of it in the throne room. Are you stupid with exhaustion now? Can you not guess that there might be people in this city who think an invasion of Batiara a destructive folly? Who might assume that you—as a Rhodian—might share that belief and have some desire to save your family and your country the consequences of an invasion?"

The words were knives, sharp and precise, almost military in their directness. She added, in the same tone, "Before you became hopelessly enmeshed in the devices of the actress and her husband, it made some sense to assess you."

Crispin rubbed a hand across his eyes and forehead. She'd given him a partial explanation, after all. A renewal of anger chased fatigue. "You bed all those you recruit?" he said, staring coldly at her.

She shook her head. "You are not a courteous man, Rhodian. I bed where my pleasure leads me." Crispin was unmoved by the reproof. She spoke, he thought, with the untrammeled assurance of one never checked in her wishes. *The actress and her husband.*

"And plot to undermine your Emperor's designs?"

"He killed my father," said Styliane Daleina bluntly, sitting on his bed, pale hair framing the exquisite, patrician face. "Burned him alive with Sarantine Fire."

"An old rumor," Crispin said, but he was shaken, and trying to hide it. "Why are you telling me this?"

She smiled, quite unexpectedly. "To arouse you?"

And he had to laugh. Try as he might to hold back, the effortless shift of tone, the irony of it, was too witty. "Immolation is unexciting for me, I fear. Do I take it the Supreme Strategos shares the view that no war ought to be waged in Batiara? He has sent you here?"

She blinked. "Take no such thing. Leontes will do whatever Valerius tells him. He will invade you as he invaded the Majriti deserts or the northern steppes, or laid siege to Bassanid cities east."

"And all the while his new, beloved bride will be acting to subvert him?"

She hesitated for the first time. "His 'new prize' is the phrase you want, Rhodian. Open your eyes and ears, there are things you ought to learn before Petrus the Trakesian and his little dancer co-opt you to their service."

Contempt lay undisguised in the aristocratic voice. She would have had no choice, Crispin imagined, in the matter of her wedding. The Strategos was young, though, triumphant, celebrated, an undeniably handsome man. Crispin looked at the woman in the room with him and had a sense of having entered black waters, with unimaginably complex currents trying to suck him down. He said, "I am only a mosaicist, my lady. I was brought here to assist with images on sanctuary walls and a dome."

"Tell me," said Styliane Daleina, as if he hadn't spoken, "about the queen of the Antae. Did she offer her body in exchange for your service too? Are you jaded now because of that? Am I too late to be of any appeal? You reject me as lesser goods? Shall I weep?"

The dark waters swirled. This *had* to be a bluff, a guess. That late-night secret encounter could *not* be so widely known. A memory came to Crispin: another hand in his hair as he knelt to kiss an offered foot. A different woman, even younger than this one, as familiar with corridors of power and intrigue. Or perhaps . . . not so. West to the east. Could Varena ever be as subtle as Sarantium? Could any place on earth?

He shook his head. "I am not familiar with the thoughts or the . . . favors of the ruling ones of our world. This encounter is unique in my experience of life, my lady." It was a lie, and yet, as he looked at her through slatted interstices, the lines of shadow and light, it wasn't, at all.

The smile again, assured, unsettling. She seemed able to move, he thought, from the intrigues of empires to those of bedrooms without a pause. "How nice," she said. "I like being unique. You do know it shames a lady, however, to offer herself and be refused? I told you, I lie where pleasure leads me, not need." She paused. "Or rather, where a different sort of need draws me."

Crispin swallowed. He didn't believe her, but her knee within the blue, simple robe lingered a handbreadth from his own. He clung desperately to his anger, a sense of being used. "It shames a man of pride to be seen as a piece in a game."

Her eyebrows arched swiftly and the tone changed—again. "But you *are,* you foolish man. Of course you are. Pride has nothing to do with it. Everyone at this court is proud, everyone is a piece in a game. In many games at once—some of murder and some of desire—though there is only one game that matters, in the end, and all the others are parts of it."

Which was an answer to his thought, he supposed. Her knee touched his. Deliberately. There were no accidental things with this woman, he was sure of it. *Some of desire.*

"Why should you imagine yourself to be different?" Styliane Daleina added, quietly.

"Because I *will* myself to be so," he said, surprising himself.

There was a silence. Then, "You grow interesting, Rhodian, I must concede, but this is almost certainly a self-deception. I suspect the actress has enchanted you already and you don't even know it. I *shall* weep, I suppose." Her expression had changed, but was nowhere near to tears. She stood abruptly, crossed in three strides to the door, turned there.

Crispin also rose. Now that she'd withdrawn he felt a chaos of emotions: apprehension, regret, curiosity, an unnerving measure of desire. He'd been a stranger to that last for so long. As he watched, she drew up her hood again, hiding the spilled gold of her hair.

"I also came to thank you for my gem, of course. It was . . . an interesting gesture. I am not difficult to find, artisan, should you have any thoughts about your home and the prospects of a war. It will become clear to you soon, I believe, that the man who brought you here to make holy images for him also intends to wreak violence upon Batiara for no reason but his own glory."

Crispin cleared his throat. "I am pleased to find my small gift deemed worthy of thanks." He paused. "I am an artisan only, my lady."

She shook her head, the expression cool again. "That is a coward in you, hiding from truths of the world, Rhodian. All men—and women—are more than one thing. Or have you *willed* yourself to be limited in this way? Will you live on a scaffold above all the dying?"

Her intelligence was appalling. Just as the Empress's had been. It crossed his mind that had he not met Alixana first he might indeed have had no defenses against this woman. Styliane Daleina might not be wrong, after all. And then he wondered if the Empress had thought of that. If *that* was why he'd received so immediate a late-night invitation to the Traversite Palace. Could these women be that quick, that subtle? His head was aching.

"I have been here two days only, my lady, and have not slept tonight. You are speaking subversion against the Emperor who invited me to Sarantium, and even against your husband, if I understand you. Am I to be bought with a woman's hair on my pillow for a night, or a morning?" He hesitated. "Even yours?"

The smile returned at that, enigmatic and provoking. "It happens," she murmured. "It is sometimes longer than a night, or the night is . . . longer than an ordinary one. Time moves strangely in some circumstances. Have you never found that, Caius Crispus?"

He dared make no reply. She didn't seem to expect one. She said, "We may continue this another time." She paused. It seemed to him she was wrestling with something. Then she added, "About your images.

The domes and walls? Do not grow . . . too attached to your work there, Rhodian. I say this with goodwill, and probably should not. It is weak of me."

He took a step toward her. She lifted a hand. "No questions."

He stopped. She was an incarnation of icy, remote beauty in his room. But she wasn't remote. Her tongue had touched his, her hand, moving downward . . .

And this woman, too, seemed able to read his very thoughts. The smile came again. "You are excited now? Intrigued? You *like* your women to show weakness, Rhodian? Shall I remember that, and the pillow?"

He flushed, but met her ironic gaze. "I like the people in my life to show some . . . of themselves. The uncalculated. Movements outside the games of which you spoke. That would draw me, yes."

Her turn now to be silent, standing very still by the door. Sunlight, sliding through the shutters, fell in bands of pale morning gold across the wall and floor and the blue of her robe.

"That," she said, finally, "might be too much to expect in Sarantium, I fear." She looked as if she would add something, but then shook her head and murmured only, "Go to sleep, Rhodian."

She opened the door, went out, closed it, was gone, save for her scent and the mild disarray of his bed, and the greater disarrangement of his being.

He fell onto the bed, still clothed. He lay with eyes open, thinking of nothing at first, then of high, majestic walls, with marble columns above marble columns, and the dwarfing, graceful immensity of the dome he'd been given, and then he thought for a long time about certain women, living and dead, and then he closed his eyes and slept.

When he dreamt, though, as the sun rose through the windy, clear autumn morning outside, it was of the *zubir* at first, obliterating time and the world in mist, and then of one woman only.

"LET THERE BE LIGHT for us," Vargos chanted with the others in the small neighborhood chapel as the services came to an end. The cleric in his pale yellow robe made the two-handed gesture of solar benediction

they used in the City, and then people began talking again and milling briskly toward the doors and the morning street.

Vargos went out with them and stood a moment, blinking in the brightness. The night wind had swept away the clouds; it was a crisp, very clear day. A woman balancing a small boy on one hip and a pitcher of water on her shoulder smiled at him as she went by. A one-handed beggar approached through the crowd but veered off when Vargos shook his head. There were enough needy people in Sarantium, no need to give alms to someone who'd had a hand chopped for theft. Vargos felt strongly about such things. A northern sensibility.

He wasn't poor, mind you. His accumulated savings and salary owing had been reluctantly released by the Imperial Postmaster before they left Sauradia, through Carullus's centurion's intervention. Vargos was in a position here to buy a meal, a winter cloak, a woman, a flask of ale or wine.

He was hungry, in fact. He hadn't taken breakfast at the inn before prayers, and the smell from across the road of lamb roasting on skewers at an open-air stand reminded him of that. He crossed, pausing for a cart full of firewood and a giggling cluster of serving women heading for the well at the end of the lane, and he bought a skewer of meat with a copper coin. He ate it, standing there, observing the other customers of the small, wiry vendor—from Soriyya or Amoria, by his coloring—as they snatched a morning bite on their hurried way to wherever they were going. The little man was busy. People moved fast in the City, Vargos had concluded. He didn't like the crowds and noise at all, but he was here by his own choice, and he'd adjusted to more difficult things in his time.

He finished his meat, wiped his chin, dropped the skewer in a pile by the vendor's grill. Then he squared his shoulders, took a deep breath, and strode off toward the harbor to look for a murderer.

Word of the attack had come to the inn from the Blues' compound in the night, while Vargos slept, oblivious. He actually felt guilty about that, though he knew there was no sense to such a feeling. He had learned of the night's events from three of the soldiers when he came down at sunrise, responding to the bells: Crispin attacked, the tribune wounded. Ferix and Sigerus slain. The six attackers killed, by the tribune and by Blue partisans in the faction's compound. No one knew who had ordered the assault. The Urban Prefect's men were investigating, he was told. Men seldom talked freely to them, he was told. Soldiers were too easily hired for something like this. They might not find out anything more—until the next attack came. Carullus's men had armed themselves, Vargos saw.

Crispin and the tribune hadn't come in yet, they'd said. They were both with the Blues, however, and safe. Had spent the night there. The bells were ringing. Vargos had gone to the little chapel down the road—none of the soldiers came with him—and had concentrated on his god, praying for the souls of the two dead soldiers, that they might be sheltered in Light.

Now prayers were done, and Vargos of the Inicii, who had bound himself freely to a Rhodian artisan for an act of courage and compassion and had walked into the Aldwood with him and come out alive, went in search of someone who wanted that man dead. The Inicii made bad enemies, and whoever that someone was had an enemy now.

He had no way of knowing it—and would have been unhappy with the suggestion—but he looked very like his father just then as he strode down the middle of the street. People were quick to give him room as he went. Even a man on a donkey edged hastily out of the way. Vargos didn't even notice. He was thinking.

He wouldn't ever have said he was good at planning things. He tended to react to events, rather than anticipate or initiate them. There hadn't been much need for forethought on the Imperial road in Sauradia, going back and forth for years with a variety of travelers. One needed endurance, equanimity, strength, some skill with carts and animals, an ability to wield a stave, faith in Jad.

Of these, perhaps only the last would be of use in tracing whoever had hired those soldiers. Vargos, for want of a better idea, decided to head for the harbor and spend a few coins in some of the rougher cauponae. He might overhear something, or someone might offer information. The patrons there would be slaves, servants, apprentices, soldiers watching their copper folles. An offered drink or two might be welcome. It did occur to him there might be some danger. It didn't occur to him to alter his plan because of that.

It took him only part of a morning to discover that Sarantium was much the same as the north or the Imperial road in one thing, at least: men in taverns were disinclined to answer questions posed by strangers when the subject was violence and a request for information.

No one in this rough district wanted to be the one to point to someone else, and Vargos wasn't skilled enough with words or subtle enough to steer anyone casually around to the topic of last night's incident in the Blues' compound. Everyone seemed to know about it—armed soldiers entering a faction's quarters and being slaughtered there was an event of note even in a jaded city—but no one was willing to say more than the obvious, and Vargos received black looks and silence when he pushed. The six dead soldiers had been on leave from Calysium: duties along the Bassanid border. They'd been drinking around the City for some days, spending borrowed money. More or less what soldiers always did. That much was commonly known. The issue was who had bought them, and as to that no one knew, or would speak.

The Urban Prefect's men had already begun nosing about the district, Vargos gathered. He began to suspect, after someone deliberately knocked over his ale in one sailor's bar, that they'd learn as little as he was. He wasn't afraid of getting into a fight, but it certainly wouldn't achieve anything if he did. He'd said nothing, paid for the spilled ale and continued on, out into the early-afternoon sunshine.

He was halfway along another narrowing, twisty lane, heading toward the noise of the waterfront, where the masts of ships were leaning in the crisp breeze, when he received an idea, along with a memory from Carullus's army camp.

He would describe it that way, afterward, to himself and to the others. *Receiving* the thought. As if it had been handed to him from without, startling in its suddenness. He would attribute it to the god, and keep to himself a recollection of a grove in the Aldwood.

He asked directions of two apprentices, endured their smirks at his accent, and duly turned toward the landward walls. It was a long walk through a large city, but the boys had been honest with him and not mischievous, and in due course Vargos saw the sign of the Courier's Rest. It made sense that it was near the triple walls: the Imperial riders came in that way.

He'd heard about this inn for years. Had been invited by various couriers to come by if ever he was in the City, to share a flask or three with them. When he'd been younger, he'd understood that a drink with certain of the riders would likely be followed by a trip upstairs for some privacy, which never did hold any appeal for him. As he grew older the invitations lost that nuance and suggested only that he was a useful and easygoing companion to those enduring the steady hardship of the road.

He paused on the threshold before going in, his eyes slowly adjusting to the closed shutters and the loss of light. The first part of his new thought hadn't been especially complicated: after the experiences of the morning it was obvious he had a better chance of learning something from someone who knew him than by continuing to ask questions of sullen strangers near the harbor. Vargos had to admit that he wouldn't have answered any such questions himself. Not from the Urban Prefect's men, not from an inquisitive Inici new to the City.

The deeper idea—the thing given to him on the street—was that he was now looking for someone in particular, and thought he might find him here, or receive word of him.

The Courier's Rest was a good-sized inn, but it wasn't crowded at this hour. Some men were having their midday meal late, scattered among the tables, singly and in pairs. The man behind the stone counter looked up at Vargos and nodded politely. This wasn't a caupona; he was nowhere near the harbor. Civility might be cautiously assumed here.

"Fuck that barbarian up the backside," said someone in the shadows. "What's he think he's doing in here?"

Vargos shivered then, unable to stop himself. Fear, undeniably, but something else as well. He felt in that moment as if the half-world had brushed close to him, forbidden magic, a primitive darkness in the midst of the City, in the crisp, clear day. He would have to pray again, he thought, when this was over.

He knew the voice, remembered it.

"Buying a drink or a meal if he likes, you drunken shit. What are *you* doing here, someone might ask?" The man serving drinks and food glared across the countertop at the shadowed figure.

"What am *I* doing here? Thish's been my inn ever since I *joined* the Post!"

"And now you aren't *in* the Post. Notice I haven't booted you out? I've more than half a mind to. So watch your fucking tongue, Tilliticus."

Vargos had never claimed his thoughts proceeded at any speed. He needed to . . . work things through. Even after he heard the known voice and then the confirming name, he walked to the counter, ordered a cup of wine, watered it, paid for it, took his first sip, before anything coalesced properly in his mind, the recognized voice merging with the summoned recollection from the army camp. He turned. Offered another silent prayer of thanks, before he spoke.

He was quite sure of himself now, as it happened.

"Pronobius Tilliticus?" he said quietly.

"Fuck you, yesh," said the shadowy figure at the corner table.

Some men turned to glance at the other man, distaste in their expressions.

"I remember you," said Vargos. "From Sauradia. You're an Imperial Courier. I used to work the road there."

The other man laughed, too loudly. He was clearly not sober. "You 'n me both, then. I used to work the road, too. On a horse, on a woman. Fading on the road." He laughed again.

Vargos nodded. He could see more clearly now in the muted light. Tilliticus was alone at his table, two flasks in front of him, no food. "You aren't a courier anymore?"

He pretty much knew the answer to this already, with a few other things. Holy Jad had sent him here. Or, he *hoped* it was Jad.

"Dishmished," said Tilliticus. "Five days ago. Last pay, no notice. Dishmished. Like that. Want a drink, barbarian?"

"I have one," Vargos said. He felt something cold in himself now: anger, but a different sort than he was accustomed to. "Why were you dismissed?" He needed to be sure.

"Late with a post, though it's none of anyone's fucking business."

"Everyone fucking *knows*," another man said grimly. "You might mention fraud at the hospice, throwing away posted letters, and spreading disease while you're at it."

"Bugger you," said Pronobius Tilliticus. "As if you never slept with a poxed whore? None of that would've mattered if the Rhodian catamite . . ." He fell silent.

"If the Rhodian hadn't what?" Vargos said quietly.

And now he *was* afraid, because it truly was very difficult to understand why the god might have helped him in this way, and try as he might not to do so he kept thinking and thinking now of the Aldwood and the *zubir* and that leather and metal bird Crispin had carried in around his neck and left behind.

The man at the table in the corner made no reply. It didn't matter. Vargos pushed himself off from the bar and went back out the door. He looked around, squinting in the sunlight, and saw one of the Urban Prefect's men at the end of the street in his brown and black uniform. He went over to him and reported that the person who had hired the soldiers who'd killed three men last night could be found at the table immediately to the right of the door in the Courier's Rest. Vargos identified himself and told the man where he could be found if needed. He watched as the young officer walked into the tavern, and then he headed back through the streets toward the inn.

On the way there he stopped at another chapel—a larger one, with marble and some painted decoration, including the remains of a wall fresco behind the altar of Heladikos aloft, almost entirely rubbed out—and in the dimness and the quiet between services he prayed before the disk and the altar for guidance through and out of the half-world into which he seemed to have walked.

He would not pray to the *zubir*, whatever ancient power of his own people it represented, but within himself Vargos sensed a terrible awareness of it, immense and dark as the forests on the borders of his childhood.

CARULLUS WAS STILL IN his room, evidently sleeping off wounds and treatment, when Crispin came downstairs just past midday. He felt muzzy-headed and disoriented himself, and not only from the wine he'd had last night. In fact, the wine was the least of his afflictions. He tried to put his aching head around some of the things that had happened in the two palaces and the Sanctuary and in the street afterward, and then to come to terms with who had been in his room—on his bed—when he'd stumbled back at dawn. The conjured image of Styliane Daleina, beautiful as an enameled icon, only made him feel more unsettled.

He did what he'd always done at such times as this, back home. He went to the baths.

The innkeeper, eyeing Crispin's unshaven scowl with a knowing expression, was able to offer a suggestion. Crispin looked about for Vargos who was also—unaccountably—absent. He shrugged, ill-tempered and querulous, and went out alone, blinking and squinting, into the irritating brightness of the autumn day.

Or, not really alone. Two of Carullus's soldiers came with him, swords in scabbards. Imperial orders from the night before. He was to have a guard now. Someone wanted him dead. Not the other mosaicist, not the lady, if he could believe her. He *did* believe her, but was aware that he had no very good reason for doing so.

On the way, passing the windowless facade of a holy retreat for women, he thought of Kasia—and then backed away from that as well. Not today. He wasn't deciding anything significant today. She needed clothing, though, he knew that much. Considered sending one of the soldiers to the market to buy her some apparel while he bathed, and his first faint smile of the day came with the image of one of Carullus's men judiciously selecting among women's undergarments in the street market.

He did get a minor, useful idea, however, and at the baths he asked for paper and a stylus. He sent a messenger running to the Imperial Precinct with a note for the eunuchs of the Chancellor's office. The clever men who had shaved and attired him last night would be more than adequate to choosing clothing for a young woman newly arrived in the City. Crispin entreated their aid. On further reflection, he set a budget for the purchases.

LATER THAT AFTERNOON, KASIA—DEALING with some unexpected discoveries of her own—would find herself accosted at the inn by a swirling, scented coterie of eunuchs from the Imperial Precinct and spirited away by them for the surprisingly involved task of acquiring proper garb for life in Sarantium. They were amusing and solicitous, clearly enjoying the exercise and their own wittily obscene disagreements over what was suitable for her. Kasia found herself flushed and even laughing during the escapade. None of them asked what her life in Sarantium was to *be*, which was a relief, because she didn't know.

IN THE BATHS, CRISPIN had himself oiled, massaged, scraped down, and then subsided blissfully into the soothing, fragrant hot pool. There were others there, talking quietly. The familiar drone of murmurous voices almost lulled him back to sleep. He revived with a cool immersion in the adjacent pool, then made his way, wrapped in a white sheet like a spectral figure, toward the steam room, where half a dozen similarly shrouded men could be seen through the mist, lounging on marble benches, when he opened the door.

Someone shifted wordlessly to make room for him. Someone else gestured vaguely, and the naked attendant poured another ewer of water over the hot stones. With a sizzling sound, steam rose up to enclose the small chamber even more densely. Crispin mentally declined the associations with a fogbound morning in Sauradia and leaned back against the wall, closing his eyes.

The conversation around him was sporadic and desultory. Men seldom spoke with much energy amid the enveloping heat of the steam. It was easier to drift, eyes closed, into reverie. He heard bodies shift and rise, others enter and subside as cooler air came briefly in with the opening door and then the heat returned. His body was slick with perspiration, languorous with an indolent calm. Bathhouses such as this, he decided, were among the defining achievements of modern civilization.

In fact, he thought dreamily, the mist here had *nothing* in common with the chill, half-worldly fog of that distant wilderness in Sauradia. He heard the hiss of steam again as someone poured more water, and he smiled to himself. He was in Sarantium, eye of the world, and much had already begun.

"I should be greatly interested to know your views on the indivisibility of the nature of Jad," someone murmured. Crispin didn't even open his eyes. He'd been told about this sort of thing. The Sarantines were said to be passionate about three subjects: the chariots, dances and pantomimes, and an endless debating about religion. Fruit-sellers would harangue him, Carullus had cautioned, regarding the implications of a bearded or a beardless Jad; sandalmakers would propound firm and fierce opinions on the latest Patriarchal Pronouncement about Heladikos; a whore would want his views on the status of icons of the Blessed Victims before deigning to undress.

He wasn't surprised, therefore, to hear well-bred men in a steam room discoursing this way. What did surprise him was his ankle being nudged by a foot and the same voice adding, "It is unwise, actually, to fall asleep in the steam."

Crispin opened his eyes.

He was alone in the swirling mist with one other person. The question about the god had been addressed to him.

The questioner, loosely wrapped in his own white sheet, sat eyeing him with a very blue gaze. He had magnificent golden hair, chiseled features, a scarred and honed body, and he was the Supreme Strategos of the Empire.

Crispin sat up. Very quickly. "My lord!" he exclaimed.

Leontes smiled. "An opportunity to talk," he murmured. He used an edge of the sheet to wipe sweat from his brow.

"Is this a coincidence?" Crispin asked, guardedly.

The other man laughed. "Hardly. The City is rather too large for that. I thought I'd arrange a moment to learn your views on some matters of interest."

His manner was courteous in the extreme. His soldiers loved him, Carullus had said. Would die for him. Had died—on battlefields as far west as the Majriti deserts and north toward Karch and Moskav.

No visible arrogance here at all. Unlike the wife. Even so, the utterly confident control behind this encounter was provoking. There had been at least six men and an attendant slave in the steam a few moments ago . . .

"Matters of interest? Such as my opinion of the Antae and their readiness for invasion?" This was blunt, he knew, and probably unwise. On the other hand, everyone knew his nature at home; they might as well start finding out here.

Leontes merely looked puzzled. "Why would I ask you that? Do you have military training?"

Crispin shook his head.

The Strategos looked at him. "Would you have knowledge of town walls, water sources, road conditions, paths through mountains? Which of their commanders deviate from the usual arraying of forces? How many arrows their archers carry in a quiver? Who commands their navy this year and how much he knows about harbors?"

Leontes smiled suddenly. He had a brilliant smile. "I can't imagine you could help me, actually, even if you wanted to. Even if any such thing as an invasion was being contemplated. No, no, I confess I'm more interested in your faith and your views on images of the god."

A memory clicked into place then, like a key in a lock. Irritation gave way to something else.

"You disapprove of them, might I guess?"

Leontes's handsome face was guileless. "I do. I share the belief that to render the holy in images is to debase the purity of the god."

"And those who honor or worship such images?" Crispin asked. He knew the answer. He had been through this before, though not perspiring in steam and not with a man such as this.

Leontes said, "That is idolatry, of course. A reversion to paganism. What are *your* thoughts?"

"Men need a pathway to their god," Crispin said quietly. "But I confess, I prefer to keep my views to myself on such matters." He forced a smile of his own. "Uncharacteristic as reticence about faith might be in Sarantium. My lord, I am here at the Emperor's behest and will endeavor to please him with my work."

"And the Patriarchs? Pleasing them?"

"One always hopes for the approval of one's betters," Crispin murmured. He passed a corner of his sheet across his streaming face. Through the steam, he thought he saw blue eyes flicker and the mouth quirk a little. Leontes was not without a sense of humor. It came as a relief of sorts. It was very much in his mind that there was no one here with them, and that this man's wife had been in Crispin's bedchamber this morning and had said . . . what she had said. This did not, he decided, represent the most predictable of encounters.

He managed another smile. "If you find me an inappropriate conversationalist on military matters—and I can see why you might—why would you imagine we ought to discuss my work in the Sanctuary? Tesserae and their designs? How much do you know or care to know about tinting glass? Or cutting it? What have you decided about the merits and methods of angling tesserae in the setting bed? Or the composition and layers of the setting bed itself? Have you any firm views on the use of smooth stones for the flesh of human figures?"

The other man was eyeing him gravely, expressionless. Crispin paused, modulated his tone. "We each have our areas of endeavor, my lord. Yours matters rather more, I would say, but mine might . . . last longer. We'd likely do best conversing—should you honor me—about other matters entirely. Were you at the Hippodrome yesterday?"

Leontes shifted a little on his bench; his white sheet settled around his hips. There was a vivid diagonal scar running from his collarbone to his waist in a reddened line like a seam. He leaned over and poured another ewer of water on the stones. Steam cloaked the room for a moment.

"Siroes had no difficulty telling us about his designs and intentions," the Strategos said.

Us, Crispin thought. "Your lady wife was his sponsor, I understand," he murmured. "He also did some private work for you, I believe."

"Trees and flowers in mosaic, yes. For our nuptial chambers. Deer at a stream, boars and hounds, that sort of thing. I have no difficulty at all with such images, of course." His tone was very earnest.

"Of course. Fine work, I'm sure," Crispin said mildly.

There was a little silence.

"I wouldn't know," said Leontes. "I imagine it is competent." His teeth flashed briefly again. "As you say, I could no more judge it than you could appraise a general's tactics."

"You sleep in the room," Crispin replied, perversely abandoning his own argument. "You look at it every night."

"Some nights," said Leontes briefly. "I don't pay much attention to the flowers on the wall."

"But you worry enough about the god in a sanctuary to arrange this encounter?"

The other man nodded. "That is different. *Do* you intend to render an image of Jad on the ceiling?"

"The dome. I rather suspect that is what is expected of me, my lord. In the absence of instruction otherwise from the Emperor, or the Patriarchs, as you say, I should think I have to."

"You don't fear the taint of heresy?"

"I have been rendering the god since I was an apprentice, my lord. If this has formally become heresy instead of a matter of current debate, no one has informed me of the change. Has the army taken to shaping clerical doctrine? Shall we now discuss how to breach enemy walls with chanted Invocations of Jad? Or launch Holy Fools in catapults?"

He'd gone too far, it seemed. Leontes's expression darkened. "You are impertinent, Rhodian."

"I hope not, my lord. I *am* indicating that I find your chosen subject intrusive. I am not a Sarantine, my lord. I am a Rhodian citizen of Batiara, invited here as a guest of the Empire."

Unexpectedly, Leontes smiled again. "True enough. Forgive me. You made a . . . dramatic entry among us last night, and I have to confess I felt easier about the decorations being planned, knowing Siroes was doing them and my wife was privy to his concepts. He was intending a design that did not . . . incorporate the rendered image of Jad."

"I see," said Crispin quietly.

This was unexpected, and solved another part of the puzzle. "I had been told his dismissal might distress your lady wife. I see it is also a matter of concern to you, for different reasons."

Leontes hesitated. "I approach matters of faith with seriousness."

Crispin's anger was gone. He said, "A prudent thing to do, my lord.

We are all children of the god and must do him honor . . . in our own way." He felt a certain weariness now. All he'd come east to do was put pain a little way behind him, seek solace in important work. The tangled complexities of the world here in Sarantium seemed extremely . . . *enveloping.*

On the facing bench, Leontes leaned back, not replying. After a moment he reached over and tapped on the door. At that signal it was pulled open by someone, letting in another rush of air, and then it closed. Only one man seemed to have been waiting to enter. He shuffled, favoring one foot, past the Strategos to take a seat opposite Crispin.

"No attendant?" he growled.

"He's allowed a few moments to cool down," Leontes said politely. "Ought to be back shortly, or a different one will come. Shall I pour for you?"

"Go ahead," the other man said, indifferently.

He was, Crispin realized, evidently unaware who had just volunteered to serve as a bathhouse servant for him. Leontes picked up the ewer, dipped it in the trough, and poured water over the hot stones, once and then again. The steam sizzled and crackled. A wave of moist heat washed over Crispin like something tangible, thick in the chest, blurring sight.

He looked wryly at the Strategos. "A second employment?"

Leontes laughed. "Less dangerous. Less rewarding, mind you. I ought to leave you to your peace. You will come to dine one night, I hope? My wife would enjoy speaking with you. She . . . collects clever people."

"I've never been part of a collection before," Crispin murmured.

The third man sat mute, ignoring them, close-wrapped in his sheet. Leontes glanced over at him briefly, then stood. In this small chamber he seemed even taller than he had in the palace the night before. Other scars showed along his back, and corded ridges of muscle. At the doorway, he turned.

"Weapons are forbidden here," he said gravely. "If you surrender the blade under your foot you will have committed only a minor offense to this point. If you do not, you will lose a hand to the courts, or worse, when tried on my evidence."

Crispin blinked. Then he moved extremely fast.

He had to. The man on the bench opposite had reached down with a snarl and ripped a paper-thin blade free from under the sole of his left foot. He held it deftly, the back of his hand up, and slashed straight at Crispin, without challenge or warning.

Leontes stood motionless by the door, watching with what seemed to be a detached interest.

Crispin lurched to one side, sweeping his sheet from his shoulders, to catch the thrusting blade. The man across from him swore viciously. He ripped the knife upward through the fabric, trying to wrench it free, but Crispin sprang from his bench, wrapping the great sheet in a sweeping movement like a death shroud about the other man's arms and torso. Without thought—or space for thought—but with an enormous, choking fury in his chest, he hammered an elbow viciously into the side of the man's head. He heard a dull grunt. The trammeled blade fell to the floor with a thin sound. Crispin pivoted for leverage, then swung his left arm in a backhanded arc that smashed the side of his fist full into the man's face. He felt teeth shatter like small stones, heard the breaking of bone, and gasped at a surge of pain in his hand.

The other man fell to his knees with a weak, coughing sound. Before he could grapple for the dropped knife, Crispin kicked him twice in the ribs and then, as his assailant slid sideways on the wet floor, in the head. The man lay there and he did not move.

Crispin, breathing raggedly, slumped back naked onto the stone bench. He was dripping wet, slick with perspiration. He closed his eyes then opened them again. His heart was pounding wildly. He looked over at Leontes, who had made no movement at all from his position by the door.

"So kind . . . of you . . . to assist," Crispin gasped. His left hand was already swelling up. He glared at the other man through the eddying mist and the wet heat.

The golden-haired soldier smiled. A light sheen of perspiration glistened all along his perfect body. "It is important for a man to be able to defend himself. And pleasing to know one can. Don't you feel better, having dealt with him yourself?"

Crispin tried to control his breathing. He shook his head angrily. Sweat dripped in his eyes. There was a pool of blood trickling across the stone floor, seeping into the white sheet in which the fallen man lay tangled.

"You should," Leontes said gravely. "It is no small thing to be able to protect your own person and your loved ones."

"Fuck you. Say that to plague sores," Crispin snarled. He felt nauseated, struggling for control.

"Oh dear. You can't talk to me like that," the Strategos said with surprising gentleness. "You know who I am. Besides, I have invited you to my house . . . you *shouldn't* talk to me like that." He made it sound like a social failing, a lapse of civilized protocol. It might have been comical, Crispin thought, had he not been so near to vomiting in the now-stifling wet heat, with a stranger's dark blood continuing to soak into the white sheet at his feet.

"What are you going to do to me?" Crispin rasped through clenched teeth. "Kill me with a hidden blade? Send your wife to poison me?"

Leontes chuckled benignly. "I have no *reason* to kill you. And Styliane's reputation is far worse than her nature. You'll see, when you join us for dinner. In the meantime, you'd best come out of the heat, and take some pride in knowing that this man will quite certainly reveal who it was who hired him. My men will take him to the Urban Prefect's offices. They are extremely good at interrogation there. You have solved last night's mystery yourself, artisan. At the small price of a bruised hand. You ought to be a satisfied man."

Fuck you, Crispin almost said again, but didn't. *Last night's mystery*. It seemed everyone knew about the attack by now. He looked over at the tall commander of all the Sarantine armies. Leontes's blue gaze met his through the eddying of the steam.

"This," said Crispin bitterly, "is the ambit of satisfaction for you? Clubbing someone senseless, killing him? This is what a *man* does to justify his place in Jad's creation?"

Leontes was silent a moment. "You haven't killed him. Jad's creation is a dangerous, tenuous place for mortal men, artisan. Tell me, how lasting have the glories of Rhodias been, since they could not be defended against the Antae?"

They were rubble, of course. Crispin knew it. He had seen the fire-charred ruin of mosaics the world had once journeyed to honor and exalt.

Leontes added, still gently, "I would be a poor creature were I to see value only in bloodshed and war. It is my chosen world, yes, and I would like to leave a proud name behind me, but I would say a man finds honor in serving his city and Emperor and his god, in raising his children and guiding his lady wife toward those same duties."

Crispin thought of Styliane Daleina. *I lie where pleasure leads me, not need.* He pushed the thought away. He said, "And the things of beauty? The things that mark us off from the Inicii with their sacrifices, or the Karchites drinking bear blood and scarring their faces? Or is it just better weapons and tactics that mark us off?" He was too limp, in fact, to summon real anger anymore. It occurred to him that mosaicists—all artisans, really—seemed never to leave behind their names, proud or otherwise. That was for those who swung swords, or axes that could send a man's head flying from his body. He wanted to say that, but didn't.

"Beauty is a luxury, Rhodian. It needs walls, and . . . yes, better weapons and tactics. What you do *depends* on what I do." Leontes paused. "Or on what you just did here with this man who would have killed you. What mosaics would you achieve if dead on a steam room floor? What works here would last if Robazes, commander of the Bassanid armies, conquered us for his King of Kings? Or if the northerners did, made fierce by that bear blood? Or some other force, other faith, some enemy we don't even know of yet?" Leontes wiped sweat from his eyes again. "What we build—even the Emperor's Sanctuary—we hold precariously and must defend."

Crispin looked at him. He didn't really want to hear this. "And the soldiers have been waiting too long for their pay? Because of the Sanctuary? However will the whores of the Empire make a living?" he said bitterly.

Leontes frowned. He returned Crispin's gaze through the mist for a moment. "I should go. My guards will deal with this fellow. I am sorry," he added, "if the plague took people from you. A man moves on from his losses, eventually."

He opened the door and went out before Crispin could offer a reply—to any of what he'd said.

CRISPIN EMERGED FROM THE baths some time later. The attendants in the cold room had winced and clucked over his swollen hand and insisted he immerse it while a doctor was summoned. The physician murmured reassuringly, sucked at his teeth as he manipulated the hand, ascertained that nothing was broken inside. He prescribed some bloodletting from the right thigh to prevent the accumulation of bad blood around the injury, which Crispin declined. The doctor, shaking his head at the ignorance of some patients, left an herbal concoction to be mixed with wine for the pain. Crispin paid him for that.

He decided not to take the concoction, either, but found a seat in the bathhouse's wine room, working his way through a flask of pale wine. He'd more or less decided he had not even a faint hope of sorting through what had just happened. The pain was dull and steady, but manageable. The man he'd pounded so ferociously had been removed, as promised, by the Strategos's personal guard. Carullus's two soldiers had gone ashen-faced when they learned what had occurred, but there was little they could have done unless they'd followed him from pool to pool and into the steam.

In fact, Crispin had to concede, he didn't feel badly, on the whole. There was undeniable relief in having survived another attack, and in the likelihood that the perpetrator would reveal the source of the murderous assaults. It was even true—though this he didn't like admitting—that having dealt with this himself brought a measure of satisfaction.

He rubbed at his chin absently and then did so again, coming to a morose realization. He asked an attendant for directions and, carrying his cup of wine, stoically betook himself to a nearby room. He waited on a bench while two other men were dealt with, then subsided glumly onto the barber's stool for a shave.

The scented sheet tied around his throat felt much like an assassin's cord. He was going to have to do this every day. It was highly probable, Crispin decided, that some barber somewhere in the City was going to slit his throat by accident while regaling the waiting patrons with a choice anecdote. Whoever was paying assassins was simply wasting his money; the deed would be done for him. He did wish this man wouldn't accentuate his flow of wit with a waving blade. Crispin closed his eyes.

He emerged only mildly scathed, however, and having been just quick enough to decline the offered perfume. He felt surprisingly energized, alert, ready to begin addressing the matter of his dome in the Sanctuary. It was already *his* dome in his own thoughts, he realized with some wryness. Styliane Daleina had voiced a warning about that, he remembered, but what artisan worth anything at all could heed such a caution?

He needed to see the Sanctuary again. He decided to head that way before returning to the inn. He wondered if Artibasos would be there, suspected he would. The man practically lived in his building, the Emperor had said. Crispin suspected he might end up doing the same. He wanted to speak with the architect about the setting beds for his mosaics. He'd need to find the Sarantine glassworks, as well, and then see about assessing—and probably reshaping—whatever team of craftsmen and apprentices Siroes had assembled. There would be guild protocols to learn—and work around. And he'd have to start sketching. There was no point having ideas in his head if no one else could see them. Approvals would be needed. Some things he had already decided to leave out of the drawings. No one needed to know *every* idea he had.

There was a great deal to be done. He was here for a reason, after all. He flexed his hand. It was puffy, but that would be all right. He thanked Jad for the instinct that had led him to use his left fist. A mosaicist's good hand was his life.

On the way out he paused by the marble counter in the foyer. On sheerest impulse he asked the attendant there about an address he'd been given a long time ago. It turned out to be close by. For some reason he'd thought it might be. This was a good neighborhood.

Crispin elected to make a call. A duty visit. Get it done with, he told himself, before work began to consume him, the way it always did. Rubbing his smooth chin, he walked out of the baths into the late-afternoon sunshine.

Two grim soldiers striding purposefully behind him, Caius Crispus of Varena followed the given directions toward the house and street name he'd had handed to him on a torn-off piece of parchment in a farmhouse near Varena. Eventually, turning off a handsome square and then into a wide street with well-made stone houses on either side, he ascended the steps of a covered portico and knocked firmly at the door with his good hand.

He hadn't decided what he would—or could—say here. There might be some awkwardness. Waiting for a servant to answer, Crispin looked about. On a marble plinth by the door stood a bust of the Blessed Victim Eladia, guardian of maidens. Given what he had heard before, he suspected it was meant ironically here. The street was quiet; he and the two soldiers were the only figures to be seen, save for a young boy grooming a mare tethered placidly nearby. The row houses here looked cared for and comfortably prosperous. There were torches set in the front walls and on the porticos, promising the security of light after darkfall.

It was possible, standing amid these smooth facades, to envisage an infinitely calmer life in Sarantium than the violent intricacies he had discovered so far. Crispin found himself picturing delicately hued frescoes within proportioned rooms, ivory, alabaster, well-turned wooden stools and chests and benches, good wine, candles in silver holders, perhaps a treasured manuscript of the Ancients to read by a fire in winter or in the peace of a courtyard among summer flowers and droning bees. The accouterments of a civilized life in the city that was the center of the world behind its triple walls and guarded by the sea. The black forests of Sauradia seemed infinitely far away.

The door opened.

He turned, preparing to give his name and have himself announced. He saw the slender figure of a woman dressed in crimson on the threshold, dark-haired, dark-eyed, small-boned. He had just enough time to note this much and realize this was not a servant before the woman cried out and hurled herself into his arms, kissing him with a hungry passion. Her hands clenched in his hair, pulling him down to her. Before he could react in any cogent way at all, while the two soldiers were gaping slack-jawed at them, her mouth moved to his ear. Crispin felt her tongue, then heard her whisper fiercely: "In Jad's name, pretend we are lovers, I beg of you! You will not regret it, I promise!"

"What are you doing?" Crispin heard a stunningly familiar voice say from nowhere he could have placed. His heart lurched. He gasped in shock, then the woman's mouth covered his own again. His good hand came up—obedient or involuntary, he couldn't have said—and held her as she kissed him like a lost love regained.

"Oh, no!" he heard within: a terribly known voice, but a new, lugubrious tone. *"No, no, no! This will never work! You'll get him beaten or killed, whoever he is."*

At which point someone, standing in the front hallway of the house behind the woman in Crispin's arms, cleared his throat.

The woman in the red, knee-length tunic detached herself as if with anguished reluctance, and as she did Crispin received another shock: he realized belatedly that he knew her scent. It was the perfume only one woman in the City was said to be allowed to use. And this woman was not, manifestly, the Empress Alixana.

This woman was—unless he had been led very greatly astray—Shirin of the Greens, their Principal Dancer, celebrated object of the anguished desire of at least one young aristocrat Crispin had met in a tavern yesterday, and very likely a great many other men, young or otherwise. She was also the daughter of Zoticus of Varena.

And the bewailing, anxious inner voice he'd just heard—twice—had been Linon's.

Crispin's head hurt again, suddenly. He found himself wishing he'd never left the baths, or the inn. Or home.

The woman stepped back, her hand trailing lingeringly along the front of his tunic, as if reluctant to let him go, as she turned to the person who had coughed.

And following her gaze, overwhelmed by too many things at once, Crispin found himself struggling suddenly not to laugh aloud like a child or a simple-witted fool.

"Oh!" said the woman, a hand coming up to cover her mouth in astonishment. "I didn't hear you *follow* me! Dear friend, forgive me, but I could not restrain myself. You see, this is—"

"You do seem to insinuate yourself, don't you, Rhodian," said Pertennius of Eubulus, secretary to the Supreme Strategos, whom Crispin had just seen disappearing through steam. And *this* man he had last encountered delivering a pearl to the Empress the night before.

Pertennius was dressed extremely well today, in fine linen, blue and silver, embroidered, with a dark blue cloak and a matching soft hat. The secretary's thin, long-nosed face was pale, and—not surprisingly in the current circumstances—the narrow, observant eyes were not noticeably cordial as they evaluated the tableau in the doorway.

"You . . . know each other?" the woman said, uncertainly. Crispin noted, still struggling to control his amusement, that she had also gone pale now.

"The Rhodian artisan was presented at court last night," Pertennius said. "He has *just* arrived in the City," he added heavily.

The woman bit her lip.

"I warned you! I warned you! You deserve everything that happens now," the patrician voice that had been Linon's said. It sounded distant, but Crispin was hearing it within, as he had before.

It wasn't addressing him.

He forced the implications of this away and, looking at the alchemist's dark-haired daughter, took pity. There was, of course, no way they could pretend to be lovers or even intimate friends, but . . .

"I admit I did not anticipate so generous a welcome," he said easily. "You must love your dear father very much, Shirin." He continued, smiling, giving her time to absorb this. "Good day to you, secretary. We do seem to frequent the same doorways. Curious. I should have looked for you in the baths just now, to share a cup of wine. I did speak with the Strategos, who was good enough to honor me with his company. Are you well, after your late errand last night?"

The secretary's mouth fell open. He looked very like a fish, so. He was courting this woman, of course. It would have been obvious, even if the young Green partisans in The Spina had not said as much yesterday.

"The Strategos?" Pertennius said. "Her *father*?" he said.

"My father!" Shirin repeated in a usefully indeterminate tone.

"Her father," Crispin confirmed agreeably. "Zoticus of Varena, from whom I bring tidings and counsel, as promised by my message earlier." He smiled at the secretary with affable blandness and turned to the woman, who was gazing at him now with unfeigned astonishment. "I do hope I am not intruding upon an appointment?"

"No, no!" she said hastily, coloring a little. "Oh, no. Pertennius simply happened to be in this quarter, he said. He . . . elected to honor me with a visit. He said." She was quick-witted, Crispin realized. "I was about to explain to him . . . when we heard your knock, and in my excitement . . ."

Crispin's smile was all benign understanding. ". . . you offered me an unforgettable greeting. For another such, I'll return all the way back to Varena and come again with further word from Zoticus."

She colored even more. She deserved a little embarrassment, he thought, still amused.

"You do not deserve so much good fortune," he heard inwardly, and then, after a pause, *"No, I will not cook myself in a pot for dinner. I told you not to try such an obviously ridiculous—"*

There was an abrupt silence, as the inward voice was cut off.

Crispin had a good idea what had caused that, having done it himself many times on the road. He had *no* idea what was happening here, however. He should *not* be able to hear this voice.

"You are a Rhodian?" Pertennius's expression, eyeing the slender girl, revealed an avid curiosity. "I didn't *know* that."

"Partly Rhodian," Shirin agreed, regaining her composure. Crispin recalled that it was always easier with the bird silenced. "My father is from Batiara."

"And your mother?" the secretary asked.

Shirin smiled and tossed her head. "Come, scribe, would you plumb *all* of a woman's mysteries?" Her sidelong look was bewitching. Pertennius swallowed and cleared his throat again. The answer, of course, was "yes," but he could hardly say as much, Crispin thought. He himself kept silent, glancing quickly around the entranceway. There was no bird to be seen.

Zoticus's daughter took him by the elbow—a much more formal grip this time, he noted—and walked him into the house a few steps. "Pertennius, *dear* friend, will you allow me the comfort of a visit with this man? It has been *so* long since I've spoken with anyone who's seen my beloved father."

She released Crispin and, turning, took the secretary's arm in the same firm, friendly grip, steering him smoothly the other way toward the still-open doorway. "It was so kind of you to come by just to see if the strains of the Dykania had not wearied me too greatly. You are such a solicitous friend. I am *very* fortunate to have powerful men like you taking a protective interest in my health."

"Not so powerful," the secretary said with an awkward little deprecating movement of his free hand, "but yes, yes, very much, very much *indeed* interested in your well-being. Dear girl." She released his arm. He looked as if he would linger, gazing at her and then past, at Crispin, who stood with hands clasped loosely together, smiling earnestly back.

"We, uh, must dine together, Rhodian," Pertennius said, after a moment.

"We *must,*" Crispin agreed enthusiastically. "Leontes spoke so *highly* of you!"

Leontes's secretary hesitated another moment, his high forehead furrowing. He looked as if there were a great many questions he had a mind to ask, but then he bowed to Shirin and stepped out onto the portico. She closed the door carefully behind him and stood there, resting her head against it, her back to Crispin. Neither of them spoke. They heard a jingle of harness from the street and the muted sound of Pertennius riding off.

"Oh, *Jad*!" said Zoticus's daughter, voice muffled against the heavy door. "What must you think of me?"

"I really don't know," said Crispin carefully. "What should I think of you? That you give friendly greetings? They say the dancers of Sarantium are dangerous and immoral."

She turned at that, leaning back against the door. "I'm not. People would like me to be, but I'm not." She had not adorned herself, or painted her face. Her dark hair was quite short. She looked very young.

He could remember her kiss. A deception, but a practiced one, "Really?"

She flushed again, but nodded. "Truly. You ought to be able to guess why I did what I did. He's been calling almost every day since the end of summer. Half the men in the Imperial Precinct expect a dancer to go on her back and spread her legs if they wave a jewel or a square of silk at her."

Crispin didn't smile. "They said that of the Empress, in her day, didn't they?"

She looked wry; he saw her father, abruptly, in the expression. "In her day it might have been true. When she met Petrus she changed. That's what I understand." She pushed herself off from the door. "I'm being ungracious. Your cleverness just now saved me some real awkwardness. Thank you. Pertennius is harmless, but he tells tales."

Crispin looked at her. He was remembering the secretary's hungry expression last night, eyes passing from the Empress to himself and back to Alixana, with her long hair unbound. "He may not be so harmless. Tale-tellers aren't, you know, especially if they are bitter."

She shrugged. "I'm a dancer. There are always rumors. Will you take wine? Do you really come from my bastard of a so-called father?"

The words were lightly spoken, tossed away.

Crispin blinked. "Yes I will and yes I do. I wouldn't have been able to invent a tale like that," he said, also mildly.

She went past him and he followed her down the corridor. There was a doorway at the end of the hallway, opening to a courtyard with a small fountain and stone benches, but it was too cold to sit outside. Shirin turned in to a handsome room where a fire had been laid. She clapped her hands once, and murmured quiet instructions to the servant who immediately appeared. She seemed to have regained her self-possession.

Crispin found that he was struggling to keep his own.

Lying on a wooden and bronze trunk set against the wall by the fire, on its back as if it were a discarded toy, was a small leather and metal bird.

Shirin turned from the servant and followed his gaze. "That actually *was* a gift from my endlessly doting father." She smiled thinly. "The only thing I've ever received from him in my life. Years ago. I wrote to him that I'd come to Sarantium and been accepted as a dancer by the Greens. I'm not sure why I bothered to tell him, but he did reply. That one time. He told me not to become a prostitute and sent me a child's toy. It sings if you wind it up. He makes them, I gather. A pastime of sorts? Did you ever see any of his birds?"

Crispin swallowed, and nodded his head. He was hearing—could not help but hear—a voice crying in Sauradia.

"I did," he said finally. "When I visited him before leaving Varena." He hesitated, then took the chair she gestured toward, nearest the fire. Courtesy for guests on a cold day. She took the seat opposite, legs demurely together, her dancer's posture impeccable. He went on, "Zoticus, your father . . . is actually a friend of my colleague. Martinian. I'd never met him before, to be honest. I can't actually tell you very much, only report that he seemed well when I saw him. A very learned man. We . . . spent part of an afternoon together. He was kind enough to offer me some guidance for the road."

"He used to travel a great deal, I understand," Shirin said. Her expression grew wry again. "Else I'd not be alive, I suppose."

Crispin hesitated. This woman's history was not something to which he was entitled. But there was the bird, silenced, lying on the trunk. *A pastime of sorts.* "Your mother . . . told you this?"

Shirin nodded. Her short black hair bobbed at her shoulders with the movement. Crispin could see her appeal: a dancer's grace, quick energy, effervescence. The dark eyes were compelling. He could imagine her in the theater, neat-footed and alluring.

She said, "To be just, my mother never said anything bad about him that I can recall. He liked women, she said. He must have been a handsome man, and persuasive. My mother had been intending to withdraw from the world among the Daughters of Jad when he passed through our village."

"And after?" Crispin said, thinking about a gray-bearded pagan alchemist on an isolated farm amid his parchments and artifacts.

"Oh, she did retreat to them. She's there now. I was born and raised among holy women. They taught me my prayers and my letters. I was . . . everyone's daughter, I suppose."

"Then how . . . ?"

"I ran away."

Shirin of the Greens smiled briefly. She might be young, but it was not an innocent smile. The house servant appeared with a tray. Wine, water, a bowl of late-season fruit. Zoticus's daughter dismissed her and mixed the wine herself, bringing his cup across. He caught her scent again, the Empress's.

Shirin sat down once more, looking across the room at him, appraisingly. "Who are you?" she asked, not unreasonably. She tilted her head a little sideways. Her glance went briefly past him, then returned.

"Is this the new regimen? You silence me except when you need my opinion? How gracious. And, yes, really, who is this vulgar-looking person?"

Crispin swallowed. The bird's aristocratic voice was vividly clear now in his mind. They were in the same room. He hesitated, then sent, inwardly, *"Can you hear what I am saying?"*

No response. Shirin watched him, waiting.

He cleared his throat. "My name is Caius Crispus. Of Varena. I'm an artisan. A mosaicist. Invited here to help with the Great Sanctuary."

A hand flew to her mouth. "Oh! You're the one someone tried to kill last night!"

"He is? Wonderful! A splendid fellow to be alone with, I must say."

Crispin tried to ignore that. "Word travels so quickly?"

"In Sarantium it does, especially when it involves the factions." Crispin was abruptly reminded that this woman, as Principal Dancer, was as important to the Greens in her way as Scortius was to the Blues. Seen in that light, there was no surprise in her being well-informed. She leaned back a little, her expression openly curious now, watching Crispin's face.

"You can't be serious? With that hair? Those hands? And look at the left one, he's been in a fight. Attractive? Hah. It must be your time of month!"

Crispin felt himself flushing. He looked down, involuntarily, at his large, scarred hands. The left one was visibly swollen. He felt excruciatingly awkward. He could hear the bird, but not Shirin's replies, and neither of them had any idea he was listening to half their exchanges.

She seemed amused at his sudden color. She said, "You dislike being talked about? It can be useful, you know. Especially if you are new to the City."

Crispin took a needed drink of wine. "It depends what . . . people are saying, I suppose."

She smiled. She had a very good smile. "I suppose. I do hope you weren't injured?"

"Is it the Rhodian accent? Is that it? Keep your legs closed, girl. We know nothing about this man."

Crispin began to wish Shirin would silence the bird, or that he had a way to do so. He shook his head, trying to concentrate. "Not injured, no, thank you. Though two of my companions died, and a young man at the gates to the Blues' compound. I have no idea who hired those soldiers." They would know, soon enough, he thought. He had battered a man senseless just now.

"You must be a terribly dangerous mosaicist?" Shirin's dark eyes flashed. There was a teasing irony in the tone. The report of deaths seemed not to disturb her. This was Sarantium, he reminded himself.

"Oh, gods! Why not just undress right here and lie down? You could save the long walk all the way to the bed—"

Crispin breathed a sigh of relief as the bird was silenced again. He looked down at his wine cup, drained it. Shirin rose smoothly, took the cup. She used less water this time filling it, he saw.

"I didn't think I was dangerous at all," he said as she brought it to him and sat down again.

Her smile was teasing again. "Your wife doesn't think so?"

He was glad the bird was silent. "My wife died two summers ago, and my daughters."

Her expression changed. "Plague?"

He nodded.

"I'm sorry." She looked at him a moment. "Is that why you came?"

Jad's bones. Another too-clever Sarantine woman. Crispin said, honestly, "It is almost why I didn't come. People urged me to do so. The invitation was really for Martinian, my partner. I passed myself off as him, on the road."

Her eyebrows arched. "You presented yourself at the Imperial Court under a false name? And lived? Oh, you *are* a dangerous man, Rhodian."

He drank again. "Not exactly. I did give my own name." Something occurred to him. "In fact, the herald who announced me may also have lost his position because of that."

"Also?"

This was becoming complex, suddenly. After the wine at the baths, and now here, his head wasn't as clear as it needed to be. "The . . . previous mosaicist for the Sanctuary was dismissed by the Emperor last night."

Shirin of the Greens eyed him closely. There was a brief silence. A log crackled on the fire. She said, thoughtfully, "No shortage of people who might have hired soldiers, then. It isn't difficult, you know."

He sighed. "So I am learning."

There was more, of course, but he decided not to mention Styliane Daleina or a hidden blade in the steam. He looked around the room, saw the bird again. Linon's voice—the same patrician accent all the alchemist's birds had—but a character entirely other. Not a surprise. He knew, now, what these birds were, or once had been. He was quite certain this woman didn't. He had no idea what to do.

Shirin said, "And so, before someone appears to attack you in my house for some good reason or other, what message did a loving father have for his daughter?"

Crispin shook his head. "None, I fear. He gave me your name in case I should need assistance."

She tried to hide it, but he saw the disappointment. Children, absent parents. Inward burdens carried in the world. "Did he say anything *about* me, at least?"

She's a prostitute, Crispin remembered the alchemist murmuring with a straight face, before amending that description slightly. He cleared his throat again. "He said you were a dancer. He didn't have any details, actually."

She reddened angrily. "Of course he has details. He *knows* I'm First of the Greens. I wrote him that when they named me. He never replied." She tossed her head. "Of course, he has so *many* children scattered all over. From his travels. I suppose we all write letters and he just answers the favored ones."

Crispin shook his head. "He did say his children didn't write to him. I couldn't tell if he was serious."

"He never replies," Shirin snapped. "Two letters and one bird, that is all I have ever had from my father." She picked up her own wine cup. "I suppose he sent birds to all of us."

Crispin suddenly remembered something. "I don't . . . believe so."

"Oh? And how would you know?" Anger in her voice.

"He told me he'd only ever given away one of his birds."

She grew still. "He said that?"

Crispin nodded.

"But why? I mean . . . ?"

He had a guess, actually. He said, "Are any of your . . . siblings here in the City?"

She shook her head. "Not any I know of."

"That might be why. He did say he'd always planned to journey to Sarantium and never had. That it was a disappointment. Perhaps your being here . . . ?"

Shirin looked over at her bird, then back to Crispin. Something seemed to occur to her. She said, with an indifferent shrug, "Well, why sending a mechanical toy would be so important to him, I have no idea."

Crispin looked away. She was dissembling, but she had to do that. So was he, for that matter. He was going to need time, he thought, to sort this through as well. Every encounter he had in this city seemed to be raising challenges of one sort or another. He sternly reminded himself that he was here to work. On a dome. A transcendent dome high above all the world, a gift to him from the Emperor and the god. He was *not* going to let himself become trammeled in the intrigues of this city.

He rose on that thought, resolutely. He'd intended to go to the Sanctuary this afternoon. This visit was to have been a minor interlude, a dutiful call. "I ought not to outstay your welcome to an uninvited stranger."

She stood up quickly, her first awkward motion. It made her seem younger.

He approached, became aware of her perfume again. And had to ask, against his own better judgment. "I . . . was given to understand earlier that only the Empress Alixana was allowed that particular . . . scent. Is it indiscreet to ask . . . ?"

Shirin smiled suddenly, visibly pleased. "You noticed? She saw me dance in the spring. Sent a private message with a note and a flask. It was made public that, in appreciation of my dancing, the Empress had permitted me to use the scent that was otherwise hers alone. Even though she's known to favor the Blues."

Crispin looked down at her. A small, quick, dark-eyed woman, quite young. "A great honor." He hesitated. "It suits you as much as it does her."

She looked ironic. She would be used to compliments, he realized. "The association with power *is* attractive, isn't it?" she murmured dryly.

Crispin laughed aloud. "Jad's blood! If all the women in Sarantium are as clever as the ones I've already met . . ."

"Yes?" she said, looking up at him slantwise. "What follows, Caius Crispus?" Her tone was deliberately arch, teasing again. It was effective, he had to concede.

He couldn't think of a reply. She laughed. "You'll have to tell me about the others, of course. One must know one's rivals in this city."

Crispin looked at her. He could imagine what her bird would have said to that. He was grateful it was silent. Otherwise—

"Oh, gods! You are a disgrace! You bring shame upon . . . everything!"

Crispin winced, covering it with a quick hand to his mouth. Not silenced, obviously. It was evident that Zoticus's daughter had her own methods of controlling her bird. She'd been toying with both of them, he thought. Shirin turned, smiling privately to herself, and led the way back down the corridor to the front door.

"I'll call again," Crispin murmured, turning there. "If I may?"

"Of course. You must. I'll assemble a small dinner party for you. Where are you staying?"

He named the inn. "I'll be looking for a house, though. I believe the Chancellor's officials are to find me one."

"Gesius? Really? And Leontes met with you at the baths? You have powerful friends, Rhodian. My father was wrong. You couldn't possibly need someone like me for . . . anything." She smiled again, the clever expression belying the words. "Come and see me dance. The chariots are finished, it is theater season now."

He nodded. She opened the door and stood back to let him pass.

"Thank you again for the greeting," he said. He wasn't sure *why* he'd said that. Teasing. Mostly. She'd done enough of it, herself.

"Oh, dear," Shirin of the Greens murmured. "I'm not to be allowed to forget that, am I? My beloved father would be so ashamed. It isn't how he raised me, of course. Good day, Caius Crispus," she added, keeping a small but discernible distance this time. After her own gibes at him, he was pleased to see that she had reacted a little, however.

"Don't kiss him! Don't! Is the door open?"

A brief pause, then, *"No I do not know that, Shirin! With you I am never certain."* Another silence, as Shirin said whatever she said, and then in a very different tone Crispin heard the bird say, *"Very well. Yes, dear. Yes, I know. I do know that."*

There was a tenderness there that took him straight back to the Aldwood. Linon. *Remember me.*

Crispin bowed, feeling a sudden wave of grief pass over him. Zoticus's daughter smiled and the door closed. He stood on the portico thinking, though not very coherently. Carullus's soldiers waited, watching him, eyeing the street . . . which was empty now. A wind blew. It was cold, the late-afternoon sun hidden by the roofs of houses west.

Crispin took a deep breath, then he knocked on the door again.

A moment later it swung open. Shirin's eyes were wide. She opened her mouth but, seeing his expression, said nothing at all. Crispin stepped inside. He himself closed the door on the street.

She looked up at him.

"Shirin, I'm sorry, but I can hear your bird," he said. "We have a few things to talk about."

THE URBAN PREFECTURE IN the reign of the Emperor Valerius II fell under the auspices of Faustinus the Master of Offices, as did all of the civil service and, accordingly, it was run with his well-known efficiency and attention to detail.

These traits were much in evidence when the former courier and suspected assassin, Pronobius Tilliticus, was brought to questioning in the notorious, windowless building near the Mezaros Forum. The new legal protocols established by Valerius's Quaestor of the Judiciary, Marcellinus, were painstakingly followed: a scribe and a notary were both present as the Questioner set out his array of implements.

In the event, none of the hanging weights or metal probes or the more elaborate contrivances proved necessary. The man Tilliticus offered a complete and detailed confession as soon as the Questioner, gauging his subject with an experienced eye, elected to suddenly clutch and shear off a hank of the man's hair with a curved, serrated blade. As his locks fell to the stone floor, Tilliticus screamed as if he'd been pierced by the jagged blade. Then he began to babble forth far more than they needed to hear. The secretary recorded; the notary witnessed and affixed his seal when it was done. The Questioner, showing no signs of disappointment, withdrew. There were other subjects waiting in other chambers.

The detailed revelations made it unnecessary to interrogate formally the soldier from Amoria who had been interrupted and personally halted by the Supreme Strategos while apparently attempting a further assault on the Rhodian artisan in a public bathhouse.

In accordance with the new protocols, a member of the judiciary was requested to attend immediately at the Urban Prefecture. Upon arrival, the judge was presented with the onetime courier's confession and such further details as had been assembled regarding the events of the night before and that afternoon.

The judge had some latitude under Marcellinus's new Code of Laws. The death penalty had been largely eliminated as contrary to the spirit of Jad's creation and as a benign Imperial gesture in the aftermath of the Victory Riots, but the possible fines, dismemberments, mutilations, and terms of exile or incarceration were wide-ranging.

The judge on duty that evening happened to be a Green supporter. The deaths of two common soldiers and a Blue partisan was a grave matter, to be sure, but the Rhodian involved—the only *important* figure in the story, it seemed—had been unharmed, and the courier had confessed his crimes freely. Six perpetrators had been killed. The judge had barely divested himself of his heavy cloak and sipped once or twice from the wine cup they brought him before ruling that the gouging of one eye and a slit nose, to label Tilliticus as a punished criminal, would be a proper and sufficient judicial response. Along with a lifetime's exile, of course. Such a figure could not possibly be allowed to remain in the City. He might corrupt the pious inhabitants.

The Amorianite soldier was routinely branded on the forehead with a hot iron as a would-be assassin and—of course—thereby forfeited his place in the army and his pension. He too was exiled.

It all unfolded with satisfying efficiency, and the judge even had time to finish his wine and exchange some salacious gossip with the notary about a young pantomime actor and a very prominent Senator. He was home in time for his evening meal.

That same evening, a surgeon on contract to the Urban Prefecture was called in and Pronobius Tilliticus lost his left eye and had his nose carved open with a heated blade. He would lie in the Prefecture's infirmary for that night and the next and then be taken in chains across the harbor to Deapolis port and released there, to make his one-eyed, marked way in exile through the god's world and the Empire—or wherever he chose to go beyond it.

He went, in fact, as most of the god's world would come to know one day, south through Amoria into Soriyya. He quickly exhausted the meager sum his father had been able to put together for him on short notice and was reduced to begging for scraps at chapel doors with the other maimed and mutilated, the orphans, and the women too old to sell their bodies for sustenance.

From these depths he was rescued the next autumn—as the story was to tell—by a virtuous cleric in a village near the desert wastes of Ammuz. Smitten with divine illumination, Pronobius Tilliticus went forth a distance alone into the desert the next spring carrying only a sun disk, and found a precipitate tooth of rock to climb. It was a difficult ascent, but he did it only once.

He lived there forty years in all, sustained at first by supplies sent out by the humble cleric who had brought him to Jad, and later by the pilgrims who began to seek out his needlelike crag in the sands, bearing baskets of food and wine which were hauled up on a rope-and-pulley arrangement and then lowered—empty—by the one-eyed hermit with his long, filthy beard and rotting clothes.

A number of people, carried out to the site in litters, unable to walk or gravely ill, and not a few women afflicted with barren wombs, were afterward to claim in carefully witnessed testaments that their conditions had been cured when they ate of the half-masticated pieces of food the Jad-possessed anchorite was wont to hurl down from his precarious perch. Besought by the people below for prophecies and holy instruction, Pronobius Tilliticus would declaim terse parables and grim, strident warnings of dire futures.

He was, of course, correct in large measure, achieving his immortality by being the first holy man slain by the heathen fanatics of the sands when they swept out of the south into Soriyya following their own star-enraptured visionary and his ascetic new teachings.

When a vanguard of this desert army reached the stiletto of rock upon which the hermit—an old man by then, incoherent in his convictions and fierce rhetoric—still perched, seemingly impervious to the winds and the broiling sun, they listened to him fulminate for a time, amused. When he began coarsely spitting food down upon them, their amusement faded. Archers filled him with arrows like some grotesque, spiny animal. He fell from his perch, a long way. After routinely cutting off his genitalia they left him in the sand for the scavengers.

He would be formally declared holy and among the Blessed Victims gathered to Immortal Light, a performer of attested miracles and a sage, two generations later by the great Patriarch Eumedius.

In the official *Life* commissioned by the Patriarch it was chronicled how Tilliticus had spent hard and courageous years in the Imperial Post, loyally serving his Emperor, before hearing and heeding the summons of a far greater power. Movingly, the tale was told of how the holy man lost his eye to a wild lion of the desert while saving a lost child in peril.

"One sees Holy Jad within, not with the eyes of this world," he was reported to have said to the weeping child and her mother, whose own garment, stained by the blood that dripped from the sage's wounds, came to be included among the sacred treasures of the Great Sanctuary in Sarantium itself.

At the time the *Life of the Blessed Tilliticus* was written, it was either forgotten or deemed inconsequential by the recording clerics what role a minor Rhodian artisan might have played in the journey of the holy man to the god's eternal Light. Military slang also comes and goes, changes and evolves. No coarse, ribald associations at all would attach to the name of Jad's dearly beloved Pronobius by then.

CHAPTER X

On the same day that the mosaicist Caius Crispus of Varena survived two attempts on his life, first saw the domed Sanctuary of Jad's Holy Wisdom in Sarantium, and met the men and women who would shape and define his living days to come under the god's sun, far to the west a ceremony took place outside the walls of his hometown in the much smaller sanctuary he had been commissioned with his partner and their craftsmen and apprentices to decorate.

Amid the forests of Sauradia the people of the Antae had—along with the Vrachae and Inicii and the other pagan tribes in that wild land—honored their ancestors on the Day of the Dead with rites of blood. But after forcing their way west and south into Batiara as the Rhodian Empire crumbled inward, they had adopted the faith of Jad and many of the customs and rituals of those they conquered. King Hildric, in particular, during a long and shrewd reign, had made considerable strides toward consolidating his people in the peninsula and achieving a measure of harmony with the subjugated but still haughty Rhodians.

It was considered unfortunate in the extreme that Hildric the Great had left no surviving heir save a daughter.

The Antae might worship Jad and gallant Heladikos now, might carry sun disks, build and restore chapels, attend at bathhouses and even theaters, treat with the mighty Sarantine Empire as a sovereign state and not a gathering of tribes . . . but they remained a people known for the precarious tenure of their leaders and utterly unaccustomed to a woman's rule. It was a matter of ongoing surprise in certain quarters that Queen Gisel hadn't been forced to marry or been murdered before now.

In the judgment of thoughtful observers, only the tenuous balance of power among rival factions had caused a clearly unacceptable condition to endure until the long-awaited consecration of Hildric's memorial outside the walls of Varena.

The ceremony took place late in the autumn, immediately after the three days of Dykania ended, when the Rhodians were accustomed to honor their own ancestors. Theirs was a civilized faith and society: candles were lit, prayers articulated, no blood was shed.

A significant number of those close-packed in the expanded and impressively decorated sanctuary did feel sufficiently unwell in the aftermath of Dykania's excesses to half wish that they themselves were dead, however. Among the many Rhodian festivals and holy days that dotted the round of the year, Dykania's inebriate debaucheries had been adopted by the Antae with an entirely predictable enthusiasm.

In the wan light of a sunless dawn, the fur-cloaked court of Varena and those of the Antae nobility who had traveled from afar now gathered, mingling with Rhodians of repute and a quantity of clerics, greater and lesser. There were a small number of places set aside for the ordinary folk of Varena and its countryside, and many of these had lined up since the night before to be present today. Most had been turned away, of course, but they lingered outside in the chill, talking, buying hot food and spiced wine and trinkets from quickly erected booths in the grassy spaces around the sanctuary.

The still-bare mound of earth that covered the dead of the last plague was an oppressive, inescapable presence in the north of the yard. A few men and women could be seen walking over there at intervals to stand silently in the hard wind.

There had been a persistent rumor that the High Patriarch himself might make the trip north from Rhodias to honor the memory of King Hildric, but this had not come to pass. The talk, both within and without the sanctuary, was clear as to why.

The mosaicists—a celebrated pair, native to Varena—obedient to the will of the young queen, had put Heladikos on the dome.

Athan, the High Patriarch, who had signed—under duress from the east, it was generally believed—a Joint Pronouncement forbidding representations of Jad's mortal son, could hardly attend at a sanctuary that so boldly flouted his will. On the other hand, in the reality of the Batiaran peninsula as it was under the Antae, neither could he ignore a ceremony such as this. The Antae had come to the faith of Jad for the son as much as the father, and they were not about to leave Heladikos behind them, whatever the two Patriarchs might say. It was a . . . difficulty.

In the expected, equivocal resolution, half a dozen senior clerics had made the muddy trip from Rhodias, arriving two days before, in the midst of Dykania.

They sat now with grim, unhappy faces at the front of the sanctuary before the altar and the sun disk, taking care not to look up at the dome, where an image of golden Jad and an equally vivid, forbidden rendering of his son carrying a torch of fire in his falling chariot could be seen.

The mosaics had already been judged very fine by those who understood such things, though some had disparaged the quality of the glass pieces used. Perhaps more important, the new images overhead had caused the pious folk of Varena, who had waited longest and been rewarded with places at the back, to murmur in genuine wonder and awe. Shimmering in the light of the candles the queen had ordered lit for her mighty father, the torch of Heladikos seemed to flicker and glow with a light of its own as the shining god and his doomed child looked down on those gathered below.

Afterward, rather too obvious analogies were made by a great many and complex, competing morals drawn from the ferocious events of a morning that began in cold, windy grayness, moved into a consecrated space of candlelight and prayers, and ended with blood on the altar and the sun disk beyond.

PARDOS HAD ALREADY DECIDED that this was the most important day of his life. He had even half decided, frightening himself a little with the immensity of the thought, that it might *always* be the most important day of his life. That nothing would or could ever match this morning.

With Radulph and Couvry and the others, he sat—they were *sitting*, not standing!—in the section allocated to the artisans: carpenters, masons, bricklayers, metal workers, fresco painters, glaziers, mosaicists, all the others.

Laborers, on instructions from the court, had brought in and carefully placed wooden benches all through the sanctuary over the past few days. The sensation was odd, to be seated in a place of worship. Clad in the new brown tunics and belts Martinian had bought them for this morning, Pardos struggled furiously to both appear calm and mature *and* see every single thing that happened in each moment that passed.

Pardos knew he had to try to seem poised: he wasn't an apprentice any more. Martinian had signed the papers for him and Radulph and Couvry yesterday afternoon. They were formally attested craftsmen now, could serve any mosaicist who would hire them, or even—though that would be foolish—seek commissions on their own. Radulph was returning home to Baiana; he'd always said he would. There would be plenty of work to be found in that summer resort. He was Rhodian, his family knew people. Pardos was Antae and knew no one outside Varena. He and Couvry were staying on with Martinian—and with Crispin, if and when he ever returned from the glories and terrors of the east. Pardos hadn't expected to miss so acutely a man who had routinely threatened him with maimings and dismemberments, but the fact was, he did.

Martinian had taught them patience, discipline, order, the balance between the imagined and the possible. Crispin had been teaching Pardos to *see*.

He was trying to apply those lessons now, observing the colors worn by the burly Antae leaders and those of the well-born Rhodians who were present here, men and women both. Martinian's wife, beside him, had a shawl of a wonderfully deep red color over her dark gray robe. It looked like summer wine. Crispin's mother, on Martinian's other side, wore a long blue cloak so dark it made her white hair seem to gleam in the candlelight. Avita Crispina was a small woman, composed and straight-backed, with a scent of lavender about her. She had greeted Pardos and Radulph and Couvry by name and offered them felicitations as they walked in together: they'd had no idea, any of them, that she'd even known they existed.

To the left of the raised altar, close to where the clerics would chant the rites of the day and of Hildric's memorial service, the most important members of the court were seated beside and behind the queen. The men were bearded, unsmiling, clad soberly in browns and russets and dark greens—hunting colors, Pardos thought. He recognized Eudric, yellow-haired and battle-scarred—handsome for all that—once commander of the northern cohorts that did battle with the Inicii, now Chancellor of the Antae realm. Most of the others he didn't know. He thought some of the men looked distinctly uncomfortable without their swords. Weapons were forbidden in the chapel, of course, and Pardos saw hands straying restlessly to gold and silver belts and finding nothing there.

The queen herself sat on an elevated seat set among the first row of the new wooden benches on that side. She was exquisite and a little frightening in the white robes of mourning with a white silk veil hiding her face. Only the almost-throne itself and a single band of dark purple in the soft hat that held the veil in place marked her as royalty today. Wives and mothers and daughters had always worn the veil, Martinian had told them, in the glory days of Rhodias when a man was buried or at his memorial. The queen, so garbed and hidden, raised above everyone else, seemed to Pardos to be a figure out of history or from the tales of other, fantastic worlds, told around night fires.

Martinian, of course, was the only one of them who'd ever spoken to her in the palace, when he and Crispin were commissioned to the work, and afterward as he requested funds and reported progress.

Radulph had seen her once, up close, as she rode back through the city from a royal hunt beyond the walls. Pardos never had. She was beautiful, Radulph had said.

In the strangest way, you could almost tell that now, even if you couldn't see her face, Pardos thought. It occurred to him that dressing in white amid those clad in deeper autumn colors was an effective way to draw the eye. He considered that, how it might be used, and thought of Crispin as he did.

There was a rustling sound and he turned quickly to the front. The three clerics who would conduct the rites—the celebrated Sybard of Varena from the court, and two from this sanctuary—stepped forward from behind the sun disk and paused, in yellow, in blue, in yellow, until the murmurous sounds grew slowly quieter and then stopped. In the flicker of candle and olive oil lamp, under the god and his son on the small dome, they raised their hands, six palms held outward in the blessing of Jad.

What followed was not holy.

Afterward, Pardos understood that the clerics' gestures had been chosen as a prearranged signal. Some device for coordinating actions had been needed, and everyone knew how this ceremony would begin.

The brown-bearded, big-shouldered man who stood up, just as the clerics were about to start the rites, was Agila, the Master of Horse, though Pardos knew that only later. The burly Antae took two heavy-booted strides toward the altar from beside the queen and threw back his fur-lined cloak in the full view of all those assembled.

He was perspiring heavily, his color was high, and he was wearing a sword.

The clerics' hands remained in the air like six forgotten appendages as they faltered into silence. Four other men, Pardos saw, his heart now beginning to pound, also stood up from the back of the royal section and moved into the aisles between the rows of benches. Their cloaks were also withdrawn; four swords were revealed, and then unsheathed. This was heresy, a violation. It was worse.

"What are you doing?" the court cleric cried sharply, his voice shrill

with outrage. Gisel the queen did not move, Pardos saw. The big, bearded man stood almost directly in front of her, but facing the body of the sanctuary.

He heard Martinian say softly under his breath, "Jad shelter us. Her guards are outside. Of course."

Of course. Pardos knew the rumors and the fears and the threats—everyone did. He knew the young queen never took food or drink that had not been prepared by her own people and tasted first by them, that she never ventured forth, even within the palace, without a cadre of armed guards. Except here. In the sanctuary: veiled in mourning on her father's memorial day, in the sight of her people both high and low and of the holy clerics and the watching god, in a consecrated space where arms were forbidden, where she could assume she would be safe.

Except she couldn't.

"What," rasped the muscular, sweating man in front of the queen, ignoring the cleric, "does Batiara say about treason? What do the Antae do to rulers who betray them?" The words rang harshly in the holy space, ascended to the dome.

"What are you saying? How dare you come armed into a sanctuary?" The same cleric as before. A brave man, Pardos thought. It was said Sybard had challenged the Emperor of Sarantium on a question of faith, in writing. He would not be afraid here, Pardos thought. His own hands were trembling.

The bearded Antae reached into his cloak and pulled out a bunched-together sheaf of parchments. "I have papers!" he cried. "Papers that prove this false queen, false daughter, false whore, has been preparing to surrender us all to the Inicii!"

"That," said Sybard the cleric with astonishing composure, as a shocked swell of sound ran through the sanctuary, "is undoubtedly a lie. And even if it were not so, this is *not* the place or time to deal with it."

"Be silent, you gelded lapdog of a whore! It is Antae warriors who decide when and where a lying bitch dog meets her fate!"

Pardos swallowed hard. He felt stunned. The words were savage, unthinkable. This was the *queen* he was describing in that way.

Two things happened very quickly then, almost in the same moment. The bearded man drew his sword, and an even bigger, shaven-headed man behind the queen stood up and moved forward, placing himself directly in front of her. His face was expressionless.

"Stand aside, mute, or you will be slain," said the man with the sword. Throughout the sanctuary people had risen and now began pushing toward the doors. There was a scraping of benches, a babble of sound.

The other man made no movement, shielding the queen with only his body. He was weaponless.

"Put down your sword!" cried the cleric again from the altar. "This is madness in a holy place!"

"Kill her, already!" Pardos heard then, a flat, low tone, but quite distinct, from among the Antae seats near Gisel.

Someone screamed then. The movement of retreating bodies made the candles flicker. The mosaics overhead seemed to shift and alter in the eddies of light.

The queen of the Antae stood up.

Her back straight as a spearshaft, she lifted her two hands and drew back her veil, and then removed the soft hat with the emblem of royalty around it and laid it gently down on the raised chair so that every man and woman there could see her face.

It was not the queen.

The queen was youthful, golden-haired. Everyone knew. This woman was no longer young, and her hair was a dark brown with gray in it. There was a cold, regal fury in her eyes, though, as she said to the man before her, beyond the intervening mute, "You are unmasked, Agila, in treachery. Submit yourself to judgment."

Pardos was watching the perspiring man named Agila as he lost what remained of his self-control. He could see it happen—the dropping jaw, the gaping, astonished eyes, then the foul, obscene cry of rage.

The unarmed mute was the first to die, being nearest. Agila's sword swept in a vicious backhand that took the man at an angle across the upper chest, biting deeply into his neck. Agila tore the blade back and free as the man fell, soundlessly, and Pardos saw blood fly through holy space to spatter the clerics, the altar, the holy disk. Agila stepped right over the toppled body and plunged his sword straight into the heart of the woman who had impersonated the queen, balking him.

She screamed as she died, taken by agony, twisting and falling backward onto the bench beside her chair. One hand clutched at the blade in her breast as if pulling it to herself. Pardos saw Agila rip it back, savagely, slicing her palm open.

There was screaming everywhere by then. The movement to the doors became a frenzied press, near to madness. Pardos saw an apprentice he knew stumble and fall and disappear. He saw Martinian gripping his own wife and Crispin's mother tightly by the elbows as they entered the frantic press, steering toward the exits with everyone else. Couvry and Radulph were right behind them. Then Couvry moved up, even as Pardos watched, and took Avita Crispina's other arm, shielding her.

Pardos stayed where he was, on his feet but motionless.

He could never afterward say exactly why, only that he was watching, that someone *had* to watch.

And observing in this way—quite close, in fact, a still point amid swirling chaos—Pardos saw the Chancellor, Eudric Goldenhair, step forward from his place near the fallen woman and say in a voice that resonated, "Put up your sword, Agila, or it will be taken from you. What you have done is unholy and it is treachery and you will not be allowed to flee, or to live."

His manner was amazingly calm, Pardos thought. He watched as Agila wheeled swiftly toward the other man. A space had cleared, people were fleeing the sanctuary.

"Fuck yourself with your dagger, Eudric! You horse-buggered offal! We did this together and you will *not* disclaim it now. Only a dice roll chose which of us would stand up here. Surrender my sword? Fool! Shall I call in my soldiers to deal with you now?"

"Call them, liar," said the other man. His tone was level, almost grave. The two of them stood less than five paces apart. "There will be no reply when you do. My own men have dealt with yours already—in the woods where you thought to post them secretly."

"What? You treacherous bastard!"

"What an amusing thing for you to say, in the circumstances," said Eudric. Then he took a quick step backward and added: *"Vincelas!"* extremely urgently, as Agila, eyes maddened, clove through the space between them.

There was a walkway overhead, not especially high: a place for musicians to play unseen, or for clerics' meditation and quiet pacing on days when winter or autumn rains made the outdoors bitter. The arrow that killed Agila, Master of the Antae Horse, came from there. He toppled like a tree, sword clattering on the floor, at the feet of Eudric.

Pardos looked up. There were half a dozen archers on the walkway. As he watched, the four men with drawn swords—Agila's men—slowly lowered and then dropped their weapons.

They died that way, surrendering, as six more arrows sang.

Pardos realized he was standing quite alone now, in the section reserved for the artisans. He felt utterly exposed. He didn't leave, but he did sit down. His palms were wet, his legs felt weak.

"I do apologize," said Eudric smoothly, looking up from the dead men to the three clerics still standing before the altar. Their faces were the color of buttermilk, Pardos thought. Eudric paused to adjust the collar of his tunic and then the heavy golden necklace he wore. "We should be able to restore order quickly enough now, calm the people, bring them back in. This is a political matter, a most unfortunate one. Not your concern at all. You will carry on with the ceremony, of course."

"What? We will not!" said the court cleric, Sybard, his jaw set. "The very suggestion is an impious disgrace. *Where is the queen?* What has been done to her?"

"I can assure you I am far more anxious to know the answer to that than you are," said Eudric Goldenhair. Pardos, watching intently, had Agila's words still ringing in his head: *We did this together*.

"One ventures to guess," added Eudric smoothly, to no one and to all of them left in the sanctuary, "that she must have had some word of Agila's vile plot and elected to save herself rather than be present at the holy rites for her father. Hard to *blame* a woman for that. It does raise some . . . questions, naturally." He smiled.

Pardos would remember that smile. Eudric went on, after a pause, "I propose to restore order here and then establish it in the palace—in the queen's name, of course—while we ascertain exactly where she is.

Then," said the yellow-haired Chancellor, "we shall have to determine how next to proceed here in Varena, and indeed in all of Batiara. In the meantime," he said, in a voice suddenly cold that did not admit of contradiction, "you are under a misapprehension of your own, good cleric. Hear me: I did not ask you to do something, I *told* you to do it. The three of you will proceed with the ceremony of consecration and of mourning, or your own deaths will follow upon those you have seen. Believe it, Sybard. I have no quarrel with you, but you can die here, or live to achieve what goals you have set for yourself and our people. Holy places have been sanctified with blood before today."

Sybard of Varena, long-shanked and long-necked, looked at him a moment. "There are no goals I could properly pursue," he said, "were I to do as you say. I have offices to perform for those slain here and comfort to offer their families. Kill me if you will." And he walked from the raised place before the altar and out the side door. Eudric's eyes narrowed to slits, Pardos saw, but he said nothing. A smaller Antae nobleman, smooth-chinned but with a long brown mustache, stood beside him now, and Pardos saw this man lay a steadying hand on the Chancellor's arm as Sybard passed right by them.

Eudric stared straight ahead, breathing deeply. It was the smaller man who now gave crisp commands. Guards began mopping with their own cloaks at the blood where the woman and the mute had died. There was a great deal. They carried their bodies out through the side exit, and then those of Agila and his slain men.

Other soldiers went out into the yard, where frightened people could still be heard milling about. They were instructed to order the crowd back in. To report that the ceremony was to proceed.

It amazed Pardos, thinking of it after, but most of those who had rushed out, trampling each other in terror, did come back. He didn't know what that said about people, what it meant about the world in which they lived. Couvry came back, Radulph did. Martinian and the two women did not. Pardos realized that he was glad of that.

He stayed where he was. His gaze went back and forth from Eudric and the man beside him to the two remaining clerics before the altar. One of the clerics turned to look back at the sun disk, and then he walked over to it and, using the corner of his own robe, wiped at the blood there and then at the blood on the altar. When he turned around and came back, Pardos saw the smeared blood dark on his yellow robe and saw that the man was weeping.

Eudric and the one beside him took their seats, exactly as before. The two clerics glanced nervously over at them and then raised their hands once more, four palms outward, and then they spoke, in perfect ritual unison.

"Holy Jad," they said, "let there be Light for all your children gathered here, now and in days to come." And the people in the sanctuary spoke the response, raggedly at first and then more clearly. Then the clerics spoke again, and the response came again.

Pardos rose quietly then as the rites began, and he moved past Couvry and Radulph and those sitting beyond them toward the eastern aisle and then he walked past all the people gathered there beneath the mosaic of Jad and Heladikos with his gift of fire, and he went out the doors into the cold of the yard and down the path and through the gate and away from there.

AT THE MOMENT A man and a woman she had loved since childhood were dying in her father's sanctuary, the queen of the Antae was standing furcloaked and hooded at the stern railing of a ship sailing east from Mylasia through choppy seas. She was gazing back west and north to land, to where Varena would be, far beyond the intervening fields and forests. There were no tears in her eyes. There had been earlier, but she was not alone here and visible grief, for a queen, required privacy.

Overhead, on the mainmast of the sleek, burnished ship, whipped by the stiff breeze, flew a crimson lion and a sun disk on a blue field: the banner of the Sarantine Empire.

The handful of Imperial passengers—couriers, military officers, taxation officials, engineers—would disembark at Megarium, giving thanks for a safe journey through wind and white waves. It was late to be sailing, even for the short run across the bay.

Gisel would not be among those leaving the ship. She was going farther. She was sailing to Sarantium.

Almost everyone else on board had been present as a screen, a mask, to deceive the Antae port officials in Mylasia. If this ship had not been in the harbor, the other passengers would have ridden the Imperial road north and east to Sauradia and then back down south to Megarium. Or they might have taken another, less trim craft than this royal one, had the seas been judged safe for a fast trip across the bay.

This ship, expertly manned, had been riding at anchor in Mylasia waiting for one passenger only, should she decide to come.

Valerius II, Jad's Holy Emperor of Sarantium, had extended an extremely private invitation to the queen of the Antae in Batiara, suggesting she visit his great City, seat of Empire, glory of the world, to be feted and honored there, and perhaps hold converse upon matters of moment for both Batiara and Sarantium in Jad's world as it was in that year. The queen had had conveyed to the ship's captain in Mylasia harbor—discreetly—her acceptance six days ago.

She had been about to be killed, otherwise.

She was likely to die in any case, Gisel thought, looking back over the white-capped sea at the receding coastline of her home, wiping at tears that were caused by the wind at the stern, but only by the wind. Her heart ached as with a wound, and a grim, hard-eyed image of her father was in her mind, for she knew what he would have thought and said of this flight. It was a grief. It was a grief, among all the others of her life.

Her hood blew back in a swirling of the salt wind, exposing her face to the elements and men's eyes, sending her hair streaming. It didn't matter. Those on board knew who she was. The need for uttermost care had ended when the ship slipped anchor on the dawn tide carrying her from her throne, her people, her life.

Was there a way to return? A course to sail between the rocks of violent rebellion at home and those of the east, where an army was almost certainly being readied to reclaim Rhodias? And if there *was* such a course, if it existed in the god's world, was she wise enough to find it? And would they let her live so long?

She heard a footfall on the deck behind her. Her women were below, both of them violently unwell at sea. She had six of her own guards here.

Only six to go so far, and not Pharos, the silent one she'd so dearly wanted by her side—but he was *always* by her side, and the deception would have failed had he not remained in the palace.

It wasn't one of the guards who approached now, nor the ship's captain, who was being courteous and deferential in exactly proper measure. It was the other man, the one she had summoned to the palace to help her achieve this flight, the one who had said why Pharos would have to remain in Varena. She remembered weeping then.

She turned her head and looked at him. Middling height, long gray-white hair and beard, the rugged features and deep-set blue eyes, the ash-wood staff he carried. He was a pagan. He would have to be, she thought, to be what else he was.

"The breeze is a good one, they tell me," said Zoticus the alchemist. He had a deep, slow voice. "It will carry us swiftly to Megarium, my lady."

"And you will leave me there?"

Blunt, but she had little choice. She had needs, desperate ones; could not make traveler's talk just now. Everything, everyone who *might* be a tool needed to be *made* a tool, if she could manage it.

The craggy-faced alchemist came to the rail, standing a diffident distance apart from her. He shivered and wrapped himself in his cloak before nodding his head. "I am sorry, my lady. As I said at the outset, I have matters that must be attended to in Sauradia. I am grateful for this passage. Unless the wind gets wilder, in which case my gratitude will be tempered by my stomach." He smiled at her.

She did not return it. She could have her soldiers bind him, deny him departure at Megarium; she doubted the Emperor's seamen would interfere. But what was the point of doing that? She could bind the man with ropes, but not his heart and mind to her, and that was what she needed from him. From someone.

"Not so grateful as to stay by your queen who needs you?" She did not veil her reproach. He had been a man inclined to women in his youth, she remembered learning once. She wondered if she might think of something yet, to keep him. Would her maidenhead be a lure? He might have bedded virgins but would never have slept with a queen before, she thought bitterly. There was a pain in her, watching the gray coastline recede and merge into the gray sea. They would be in the sanctuary by now, back home, beginning her father's rites under the candles and the lanterns.

The alchemist did not avert his eyes, though her own gaze was icy cold. Was this the first of the prices she was paying, and would continue to pay, Gisel thought . . . that a queen adrift on another ruler's boat, with only a handful of soldiers by her and her throne left behind for others to claim, could not compel proper homage or duty anymore?

Or was it just the man? There was no disrespect in him, to be fair, only a frank directness. He said gravely, "I have served you, Majesty, in all ways I can here. I am an old man, Sarantium is very far. I have no powers that would aid you there."

"You have wisdom, secret arts, and loyalty . . . I still believe."

"And are right to believe that last. I have as little desire as you, my lady, to see Batiara plunged into war again."

She pushed at a whipping strand of hair. The wind was raw on her face. She ignored it. "You understand that is why I am here? Not my own escape? This is no . . . escape."

"I understand," said Zoticus.

"It isn't simply a question of who rules in Varena among us, it is Sarantium that matters. None of them in the palace has the least understanding of that."

"I know it," said Zoticus. "They will destroy each other and lie open to the east." He hesitated. "May I ask what you hope to achieve in Sarantium? You spoke of returning home . . . How would you, without an army?"

A hard question. She didn't know the answer. She said, "There are armies and . . . armies. There are different levels of subjugation. You know what Rhodias is now. You know what . . . we did to it when we conquered. It is possible I can act so that Varena and the rest of the peninsula is not ruined the same way." She hesitated. "I might even stop them from coming. Somehow."

He did not smile, or dismiss that. He said only, "Somehow. But then you would not return either, would you?"

She had thought of that, too. "Perhaps. I would pay that price, I suppose. Alchemist, if I knew all paths to what will be, I'd not have asked for counsel. Stay by me. You know what I am trying to save."

He bowed then, but ignored the renewed request. "I do know, my lady. I was honored, and remain so, that you summoned me."

Ten days ago, that had been. She'd had him brought to her on the easy pretext that he was once more to offer his spells of the half-world to help ease the souls of the dead in the plague mound—and her father's spirit, too, with the memorial day approaching. He had first come to the palace more than a year before, when the mound was raised.

She remembered him from that time: a man not young but measured and observant, a manner that reassured. No boasting, no promised miracles. His paganism meant little to her. The Antae had been pagans themselves, not so long ago, in the dark forests of Sauradia and the blood-sown fields beside.

It was said that Zoticus spoke with the spirits of the dead. That was why she had summoned him two summers ago. It had been a time of universal fear and pain: plague, a savage Inici incursion in the wake of it, a brief, bloody civil war when her father died. Healing had been desperately needed, and comfort wherever it could be found.

Gisel had invoked every form of aid she could those first days on the throne, to quiet the living and the dead. She had ordered this man to add his voice to those that were to calm the spirits in the burial mound behind the sanctuary. He had joined the cheiromancers, with their tall, inscribed hats and chicken entrails, in the yard one sundown after the clerics had spoken their prayers and had gone piously within. She didn't know what he had done or said there, but it had been reported that he was the last to leave the yard under the risen moons.

She had thought of him again ten days ago, after Pharos had brought her tidings that were terrifying but not, in truth, entirely unexpected. The alchemist came, was admitted, bowed formally, stood leaning on his staff. They had been alone, save for Pharos.

She had worn her crown, which she rarely did in private. It had seemed important somehow. She was the queen. She was still the queen. She could remember her own first words; imagined, on the deck of the ship, that he could as well.

"They are to kill me in the sanctuary," she had said, "on the day after Dykania, when we honor my father there. It is decided, by Eudric and Agila and Kerdas, the snake. All of them together, after all. I never thought they would join. They are to rule as a triumvirate, I am told, once I am gone. They will say I have been treating with the Inicii."

"A poor lie," Zoticus had said. He had been very calm, the blue eyes mild and alert above the gray beard. It could surprise no one in Varena, she knew, that there were threats on her life.

"It is meant to be weak. A pretext, no more. You understand what will follow?"

"You want me to hazard a guess? I'd say Eudric will have the others out of the way within a year."

She shrugged. "Possibly. Don't underestimate Kerdas, but it hardly matters."

"Ah," he had said then, softly. A shrewd man. "Valerius?"

"Of course, Valerius. Valerius and Sarantium. With our people divided and brutalizing each other in civil war, what will stop him, think you?"

"A few things might," he'd said gravely, "eventually. But not at first, no. The Strategos, whatever his name is, would be here by summer."

"Leontes. Yes. By summer. I must live, must stop this. I do not want Batiara to fall, I do not want it drenched in blood again."

"No man or woman could want that last, Majesty."

"Then you will help me," she'd said. She was being dangerously frank, had already decided she had next to no choice. "There is no one in this court I trust. I cannot arrest all three of them, they each walk with a small army wherever they go. If I name any one of them my betrothed, the others will be in open revolt the next day."

"And you would be negated, rendered nothing at all, the moment you declared it. They would kill each other in the streets of every city and in the fields outside all walls."

She had looked at him, heartsick and afraid, trying not to hope too much. "You understand this, then?"

"Of course I do," he had said, and smiled at her. "You should have been a man, my lady, the king we need . . . though making us all the poorer in another way, of course."

It was flattery. A man with a woman. She had no time for it. "How do I get away?" she'd said bluntly. "I must get away and survive the leaving so I can return. Help me."

He had bowed, again. "I am honored," he'd said, had to say. And then: "Where, my lady?"

"Sarantium," she had said baldly. "There is a ship."

And she'd seen that she'd surprised him after all. Had felt some small pleasure then, amid the bone-deep anxiety that walked with her and within her as a shadow or half-world spirit through all the nights and days.

She'd asked if he could kill people for her. Had asked it once before, when they had raised the plague mound. It had been a casual question then, for information. It wasn't this time, but his answer had been much the same.

"With a blade, of course, though I have little skill. With poisons, but no more readily than many people you might summon. Alchemy transmutes things, my lady, it does not pretend to the powers the charlatans and false cheiromancers claim."

"Death," she had said, "is a transmutation of life, is it not?"

She remembered his smile, the blue eyes resting on her face, unexpectedly tender. He would have been a handsome man once, she thought; indeed, he still was. It came to her that the alchemist was troubled in his own right, bearing some burden. She could see it but had no room to acknowledge the fact in any way. Who lived in Jad's world without griefs?

He'd said, "It may be seen that way, or otherwise, my lady. It may be seen as the same journey in a different cloak. You need," he had murmured, changing tone, "at least a day and a night away from these walls before they discover you are gone, if you are to reach Mylasia safely. My lady, that requires that someone you trust pretend to be the queen on the day of the ceremony."

He was clever. She needed him to be. He went on. She listened.

She would be able to leave the city in a disguise on the second night of Dykania when the gates were open for the festival. The queen could wear the heavily veiled white of full Rhodian mourning in the sanctuary, which would allow someone to take her place. She could declare an intention to withdraw from public view into her private chambers the day before the consecration, to pray for her father's soul. Her guards—a select, small number of them—could wait outside the walls and meet her on the road. One or two of her women could wait with them, he said. Indeed, she would need ladies-in-waiting with her, would she not? Two other guards could, in festival guise themselves, pass out through the walls with her amid the night chaos of Dykania and join the others in the countryside. They could even meet, he said, at his own farmhouse, if that was acceptable to her. Then they would have to ride like fury for Mylasia. It could be done in a night and a day and an evening. Half a dozen guards would keep her safe on the road. Could she ride like that, he asked?

She could. She was Antae. Had been in the saddle since girlhood.

Not so long ago.

She made him repeat the plan, adding details, going step by step. She changed some things, interpolated others. Had to, he couldn't know the palace routines well enough. She added a female complaint as a further excuse for her withdrawal before the consecration. There were ancient fears about a woman's blood among the Antae. No one would intrude.

She had Pharos pour wine for the alchemist and let him sit while she considered, finally, who might pose as herself. A terrible question. Who could do it? Who would? Neither she nor the gray-bearded man sipping at his wine said so, but each of them knew it was almost certain that woman would die.

There was only one name, really, in the end. Gisel had thought she might weep, then, thinking of Anissa, who had nursed her, but she did not. Then Zoticus, looking at Pharos, had murmured, "He, too, will have to stay behind, to guard the woman disguised as you. Even I know he never leaves you."

It was Pharos who had reported the triple-headed plot to her. He looked at the other man now from by the doorway, shook his head once, decisively, and moved to stand next to Gisel. The shelter at her side. Shield. All her life. She looked up at him, turned back to the alchemist, opened her mouth to protest, and then closed it, as around a pain, without speaking.

It was true, what the old man said. It was agonizingly true. Pharos *never* left her, or the doorway to her chambers if she was within. He had to be seen in the palace and then the sanctuary while she fled, in order that she *could* flee. She lifted one hand then and laid it upon the muscled forearm of the mute, shaven-haired giant who had killed for her and would die for her, would let his soul be lost for her, if need be. Tears did come then, but she turned her head aside, wiped them away. A luxury, not allowed.

She had not been, it seemed, born into the world for peace or joy or any sure power—or even to keep those very few who loved her by her side.

AND SO IT WAS that the queen of the Antae was nearly alone when she walked forth in disguise on the second night of Dykania, out from the palace and through her city, past bonfires in the squares and moving torchlight and out the open gates amid a riotous, drunken crowd and then, two mornings later, under gray skies with a threat of rain, leaving behind the only land she had ever known for the seas of late autumn and the world, sailing east.

The alchemist who had come to her summons and had devised her escape had been waiting in Mylasia. Before leaving her chambers ten days ago he had requested passage to Sauradia on the Imperial ship. Transactions of his own, he had explained. Business left unfinished long ago.

HE DOUBTED SHE WOULD ever know how deeply she had touched him.

Child-queen, alone and preternaturally serious, mistrustful of shadows, of words, of the very wind. And what man could blame her for it? Besieged and threatened on all sides, wagers taken openly in her city as to the season of her death. And yet wise enough—alone of all in that palace, it seemed—to understand how the Antae's tribal feuds *had* to be altered now in a greater world or they would revert to being only a tribe again, driven from the peninsula they'd claimed, hacking each other to pieces, scrabbling for forage space among the other barbarian federations. He stood now on a slip in the harbor of Megarium, cloaked against the slant, cold rain, and watched the Sarantine ship move back out through the water, bearing the queen of the Antae to a world that would—some truths were hard—almost certainly prove too dangerous and duplicitous even for her own fierce intelligence.

She would get there, he thought; he had taken the measure of that ship and its captain. He had traveled in his day, knew roads and the sea. A commercial ship, wide, clumsy, deep-bellied, would have been at gravest risk this late in the year. A commercial ship would not have sailed. But this was a craft sent especially for a queen.

She would reach Sarantium, he judged—see the City, as he himself never had—but he could see no joy in her doing so. There had been only death waiting at home, though, the certainty of it, and she was young enough—she was terribly young enough—to cling to life, and whatever hope it might offer in the face of the waiting dark, or the light of her god that might follow.

His gods were different. He was so much older. The long darkness was not always to be feared, he thought. Living on was not an absolute good. There were balances, harmonies to be sought. Things had their season. The same journey in a different cloak, he thought. It was autumn now, in more ways than the one.

There had been a moment on board, watching Batiara disappear in grayness off the stern, when he had seen her weighing whether or not to try seducing him. It had wrung his heart. For Gisel in that moment, for this young queen of a people not his own, he might even have surmounted all the inward matters of his own, truths apprehended in his soul, and sailed on to Sarantium.

But there were powers greater than royalty in the world, and he was traveling to meet one now in a place he knew. His affairs were in order. Martinian and a notary had the necessary papers. His heart had quailed at times once the decision had come to him—only a fool, vainglorious, would have denied that—but there was no least shadow of doubt in him as to what he had to do.

He had heard an inward cry earlier this autumn, a known voice from the distant east, unimaginably far. And then, some time after, a letter had arrived from Martinian's friend, the artisan to whom he had given a bird. Linon. And reading the careful words, discerning the meaning beneath their ambiguous, veiled phrasing, he had understood the cry. Linon. First one, little one. It *had* been a farewell, and more than that.

No sleep had come to him the night that letter came. He had moved from bed to high-backed chair to farmhouse doorway, where he stood wrapped in a blanket looking out upon the mingled autumn moonlight and the stars in a clear night. All things in the shaped world—his rooms, his garden, the orchard beyond, the stone wall, the fields and forests across the ribbon of road, the two moons rising higher and then setting as he stood in his open doorway, the pale sunrise when it came at last—all things had seemed to him to be almost unbearably precious then, numinous and transcendent, awash in the glory of the gods and goddesses that were, that still were.

By dawn he had made his decision, or, more properly, realized it had been made for him. He would have to go, would fill his old traveling pack again—the worn, stained canvas, Esperanan leather strap, bought thirty years since—with gear for the road and with the other things he would have to carry, and begin the long walk to Sauradia for the first time in almost twenty years.

But that very same morning—in the way the unseen powers of the half-world sometimes had of showing a man when he had arrived at the correct place, the proper understanding—a messenger had come from Varena, from the palace, from the young queen, and he had gone to her.

He had listened to what she told him, unsurprised, then briefly surprised. Had taken thought as carefully as he could for Gisel—younger than his never-seen daughters and sons, but also older than any of them might ever have to be, he mused—and pitying her, mastering his own grave meditations and fear, his growing awareness of what it was he had done long ago and was now to do, he gave her, as a kind of gift, the plan for her escape.

Then he asked if he might sail with her, as far as Megarium.

AND HERE, NOW, HE was, the watched ship heeling already away to the south across the line of the wind and the white waves, the driven rain cold in his face. He kept the pack between his feet on the stone jetty, wise to the ways of harbors. He wasn't a young man; waterfronts were hard places everywhere. He didn't feel afraid, though; not of the world.

The world was all around him even in autumn rain: seamen, seabirds, food vendors, uniformed customs officers, beggars, morning whores sheltering on the porticos, men dropping lines by the jetty for octopus, wharf children tying ship ropes for a tossed coin. In summer they would dive. It was too cold now. He had been here before, many times. Had been a different man then. Young, proud, chasing immortality in mysteries and secrets that might be opened like an oyster for its pearl.

It occurred to him that he almost certainly had children living here. It did not occur to him to look for them. No point, not now. That would be a failure of integrity, he thought. Rank sentimentality. Aged father on last long journey, come to embrace his dear children.

Not him. Never that sort of man. It was the half-world he had embraced, instead.

"Is it gone?" Tiresa said, from inside the pack. All seven of them were in there, unseeing but not silenced. He never silenced them.

"The ship? Yes, it is gone. Away south."

"And we?" Tiresa usually spoke for the others when they were being orderly: falcon's privilege.

"We are away as well, my dears. We are, even now."

"In the rain?"

"We have walked in rain before."

He bent and shouldered the pack, the smooth, supple leather strap sitting easily across his shoulder. It didn't feel heavy, even with his years. It shouldn't, he thought. He had one change of clothing in it, some food and drink, a knife, one book, and the birds. All the birds, all the claimed and crafted birdsouls of his life's bright courage and dark achievement.

There was a boy, perhaps eight years old, sitting on a post, watching him watch the ship. Zoticus smiled and, reaching into the purse at his belt, tossed him a silver piece. The boy caught it deftly, then noted the silver, eyes wide.

"Why?" he asked.

"For luck. Light a candle for me, child."

He strode off, swinging his staff as he walked through the rain, head high, back straight, northeast through the city to pick up the spur of the Imperial road at the landward gate as he had so many times long and long ago, but here now to do something very different: to end the thirty years' tale, a life's untellable story, to carry the birds home that their called and gathered souls might be released.

That cry in the distance had been a message sent. He had thought, when he was young, reading in the Ancients, shaping a prodigious, terrifying exercise of alchemy, that the *sacrifice* in the Sauradian wood was what mattered there, the act of homage to the power they worshipped in the forest. That the souls of those given to the wood god might be dross, unimportant, free to be claimed, if dark craft and art were equal to that.

Not so. It was otherwise. He had indeed discovered he possessed that knowledge, the appalling and then exhilarating capacity to achieve a transference of souls, but earlier this autumn, standing in his own farmyard of a morning, he had heard a voice in his mind cry out from the Aldwood. Linon, in her own woman's voice—that he had heard only once, from hiding, when they killed her in the wood—and he had understood, an old man now, wherein he had been wrong, long ago.

Whatever it was that was in the forest had laid claim to the souls, after all. They were not for the having.

A sleepless night had followed then, too, and a burgeoning awareness like a slow sunrise. He was no longer young. Who knew how many seasons or years the blessed gods would have him see? And with the letter, after, had come certainty. He knew what was asked of him, and he would not go down into whatever traveling followed the dropped cloak of mortal life with these wrongly taken souls charged against his name.

One was still gone from him; one—his first—had been given back.

The others were in his pack now as he walked in rain, carrying them home.

What lay waiting for *him* among the trees he did not know, though he had taken something not meant for him, and balancings and redress were embedded at the core of his own art and the teachings he had studied. Only a fool denied his fear. What was, would be. Time was running, it was always running. The gift of foretelling was not a part of his craft. There were powers greater than royalty in the world.

He thought of the young queen, sailing. He thought of Linon: that very first time, bowel-gripping terror, and power and awe. So long ago. The cold rain on his face now was a leash that tethered him to the world. He passed through Megarium and reached the walls and saw the road ahead of him through the open gates, and had his first glimpse of the Aldwood in the gray distance beyond.

He paused then, just for a moment, looking, felt the hard, mortal banging of his heart. Someone bumped him from behind, swore in Sarantine, moved on.

"What is it?" Tiresa asked. Quick one. A falcon.

"Nothing, love. A memory."

"Why is a memory nothing?"

Why, indeed? He made no reply, went on, staff in hand, through the gates. He waited by the ditch for a company of horsed merchants to pass, and their laden mules, and then began walking again. So many autumn mornings here, remembered in a blur, striding alone in search of fame, of knowledge, the hidden secrets of the world. Of the half-world.

By midday he was on the main road, running due east, and the great wood marched with him, north and very near.

It remained there through the days of walking that followed, in rain, in pale, brief sunlight, the leaves wet and heavy, almost all fallen, many-colored, smoke rising from charcoal pits, a distant sound of axes, a stream heard but not seen, sheep and goats to the south, a solitary shepherd. A wild boar ran from the woods once, and then—astonished in the sudden light as a cloud unsheathed the sun—darted back into dark and disappeared.

The forest remained there in the nights, too, beyond shuttered windows in inns where he was remembered by no one in the common rooms and recognized no one after so long, where he ate and drank alone and took no girls upstairs as once he had, and was walking again with the day's first eastward breaking.

And it was there, a boy's stonethrow from the road, toward evening of a last day, when an afternoon drizzle had passed and the westering sun lay red and low behind him, throwing his own long shadow forward as he went through a hamlet he remembered—shuttered at day's end now in the cold, no one at all in the single street—and came, not far beyond, his shadow leading him, to the inn where he had always stayed before going out in the dark before sunrise to do what he did on the Day of the Dead.

He stopped on the road outside the inn, irresolute. He could hear sounds from the enclosed yard. Horses, the creak of a cart being shifted, a hammering in the smithy, stablehands. A dog barked. Someone laughed. The foothills of the mountains that barred access to the coast and the sea rose up behind the inn, goats dotting the twilit meadow. The wind had died. He looked back behind him at the red sun and the reddened clouds along the horizon. A better day tomorrow, they promised. There would be fires lit inside the inn, mulled wine for warmth.

"We are afraid," he heard.

Not Tiresa. Mirelle, who never spoke. He had made her a robin, copper-chested, small as Linon. The same voice all of them had, the wry, patrician tones of the jurist by whose new-laid grave he had done his dark, defining ceremony. An unexpected irony there . . . that nine souls of Sauradian girls sacrificed in an Aldwood grove should all sound, when claimed, like an arrogant judge from Rhodias, killed by too much drink. Same voice, but he knew the timbre of each spirit as he knew his own.

"Oh, my dears," he said gently, *"do not be fearful."*

"Not for us." Tiresa now. Hint of impatience. *"We know where we are. We are afraid for you."*

He hadn't expected that. Found he could think of nothing to say. He looked back along the road again, and then east, ahead. No one riding, no one walking. All sane mortals drawing themselves now within walls at day's end, barred windows, roofs, fires against the cold and nearly fallen dark. His shadow lay on the Imperial road, the shadow of his staff. A hare startled in the field and broke, zigzagging, caught by the long light, down into the wet ditch by the road. The sun and the western clouds above it red as fire, as the last of a fire.

There was no reason, really, to wait for morning, fair as it might prove to be.

He walked on, alone on the road, leaving the lights of the inn behind, and after no very great distance more came to a small, flat bridge across the northern roadside ditch and knew the place and crossed there as he had years ago and years ago, and went through the wet, dark autumn grass of that field, and when he came to the black edgings of the wood he did not pause but entered into the weighted, waiting darkness of those ancient trees, with seven souls and his own.

Behind him, in the world, the sun went down.

DARKNESS LASTED IN THE Aldwood, night a deepening of it not a bringing forth. Morning was a distant, intuited thing, not an altering of space or light. The moons were usually known by pull, not by shining, though sometimes they might be glimpsed, and sometimes a star would appear between black branches, moving leaves, above a lifting of mist.

In the glade where blood was shed each autumn by masked priests of a rite so old no one knew how it had begun, these truths were altered—a very little. The trees here gave way enough for light to fall when the tendrils of fog were not hovering. The noontide sun might make the leaves show green in spring or summer, red-gold as they were claimed by autumn frosts. The white moon could make a cold, spare beauty of the black branches in midwinter, the blue one draw them back into strangeness, the half-world. Things could be seen.

Such as the crushed grass and fallen leaves and the sod where a hoofed tread that ought to have been too massive for the earth had fallen, just now, and had gone back among the trees. Such as seven birds lying on the hard ground, crafted birds, artifices. Such as the man near them. What was left, more truly, of what had been a man. His face was untouched. The expression, by the moonlight which was blue just then, serene, accepting, a quiet laid upon it.

He had returned of his own will: some weight had been given to that, allowance made, dispensation. The body below was ripped apart, bloodily, from groin to breastbone. Blood and matter lay exposed, trailed along the grass away, where the hoofprints went.

An old, worn traveler's pack lay on the ground a little distance away. It had a wide leather strap, Esperanan, worn soft.

It was silent in the glade. Time ran. The blue moon slipped through empty spaces overhead and passed away from what it saw below. No wind, no sound in the bare branches, no stirring of fallen leaves. No owl called in the Aldwood, or nightingale, no rumbling tread of beast, or god returning. Not now. That had been and had passed. Would be again, and again, but not tonight.

Then, into such stillness in the cold night, came speech. The birds on the grass, and yet not them. Voices of women were heard in the air, in the darkness, soft as leaves, women who had died here, long ago.

Do you hate him?

Now? Look what has been done to him.

Not only now. Ever. Before. I never did.

A quiet again, for a time. Time meant little here, was hard to compass, unless by the stars slipping from sight as they moved, when they could be seen.

Nor I.

Nor I. Should we have?

How so?

Truly. How so?

And only look, said Linon then, her first words, who had been first of them to be claimed and to return, *look how he has paid.*

He wasn't afraid, though, was he? Tiresa.

Yes, he was, said Linon. A breath in the stillness. *He isn't, anymore.*

Where is he? Mirelle.

No one answered that.

Where are we to go? asked Mirelle.

Ah. That I do know. We are there already: We are gone. Only say goodbye and we are gone, said Linon.

Goodbye, then, said Tiresa. Falcon.

Goodbye, whispered Mirelle.

One by one they bade farewell to each other, rustling words in the dark air as the souls took leave. At the end, Linon was alone, who had been first of all, and in the quiet of the grove she said the last words to the man lying beside her in the grass, though he could not hear her now, and then she spoke something more in the dark, more tender than a farewell, and then at last her bound soul accepted its release, so long denied.

And so that hidden knowledge and those transmuted souls passed from the created world where men and women lived and died, and the birds of Zoticus the alchemist were not seen or known again under sun or moons. Except for one.

When autumn came round again, in a mortal world greatly changed by then, those coming at dawn on the Day of the Dead to perform the ancient, forbidden rites found no dead man, no crafted birds in the grass. There was a staff, and an empty pack with a leather strap, and they wondered at those. One man took the staff, another the pack, when they were done with what they had come there to do.

Those two, as it happened, were to know good fortune all their days, afterward, and then their children did, who took the staff and the pack when they died, and then their children's children.

There were powers greater than royalty in the world.

"I SHOULD BE EXCEEDINGLY grateful," said the cleric Maximius, principal adviser to the Eastern Patriarch, "if someone would explain to us why a cow so absurdly large is to be placed on the dome of the Sanctuary of Jad's Holy Wisdom. What *does* this Rhodian think he is about?"

There was a brief silence, worthy of the arch, acidic tones in which the comment had been made.

"I believe," said the architect Artibasos gravely, after a glance at the Emperor, "that the animal might be a bull, in fact."

Maximius sniffed. "I am, of course, entirely happy to defer to your knowledge of the farmyard. The question remains, however."

The Patriarch, in a cushioned seat with a back, allowed himself a small smile behind his white beard. The Emperor remained expressionless.

"Deference becomes you," said Artibasos, mildly enough. "It might be worth cultivating. It is customary—except perhaps among clerics—to have opinions preceded by knowledge."

This time it was Valerius who smiled. It was late at night. Everyone knew the Emperor's hours, and Zakarios, the Eastern Patriarch, had long since made his adjustments to them. The two men had negotiated a relationship built around an unexpected personal affection and the real tension between their offices and roles. The latter tended to play itself out in the actions and statements of their associates. This, too, had evolved over the years. Both men were aware of it.

Excepting the servants and two yawning Imperial secretaries standing by in the shadows, there were five men in the room—a chamber in the smaller Traversite Palace—and they had each, at some point, spent a measure of time examining the drawings that had brought them here. The mosaicist was not here. It was not proper that he be present for this. The fifth man, Pertennius of Eubulus, secretary to the Supreme Strategos, had been making notes as he studied the sketches. Not a surprise: the historian's mandate here was to chronicle the Emperor's building projects, and the Great Sanctuary was the crown jewel among them.

Which made the preliminary drawings for the proposed dome mosaics of extreme significance, both aesthetic and theological.

Zakarios, behind his thick, short, steepled fingers, shook his head as a servant offered wine. "Bull or cow," he said, "it is unusual . . . much of the design is unusual. You will agree, my lord?" He adjusted the ear flap of his cap. He was aware that the unusual headgear with its dangling chin strings did no favors to his appearance, but he was past the age when such things mattered and was rather more concerned with the fact that it was not yet winter and he was already cold all the time, even indoors.

"One could hardly fail to agree," Valerius murmured. He was clad in a dark blue wool tunic and the new style of trousers, belted, tucked into black boots. Working garb, no crown, no jewels. Of all those in the room, he was the only one who seemed oblivious to the hour. The blue moon was well over to the west, above the sea by now. "Would we have preferred a more 'usual' design for this Sanctuary?"

"This dome serves a holy purpose," the Patriarch said firmly. "The images thereon—at the very summit of the Sanctuary—are to inspire the devout to pious thoughts. This is not a mortal palace, my lord, it is an evocation of the palace of Jad."

"And you feel," said Valerius, "that the proposal of the Rhodian is deficient in this regard? Really?" The question was pointed.

The Patriarch hesitated. The Emperor had an unsettling habit of posing such blunt queries, cutting past detail to the larger issue. The fact was, the charcoal sketches of the proposed mosaic were astonishing. There really was no other simple word for it, or none that came to the Patriarch's mind at this late hour.

Well, one other word: humbling.

That was *good*, he thought. Wasn't it? The dome crowned a sanctuary—a house—meant to honor the god, as a palace housed and exalted a mortal ruler. The god's exaltation ought to be greater, for the Emperor was merely his Regent upon earth. Jad's messenger was the last voice they heard when they died: *Uncrown, the lord of Emperors awaits you now.*

For worshippers to feel awe, sweep, immense power above them . . .

"The design is remarkable," Zakarios said frankly—it was risky to be less than direct with Valerius. He settled his fingers in his lap. "It is also . . . disturbing. Do we want the faithful to be uneasy in the god's house?"

"I don't even know where I *am* when I look at this," Maximius said plaintively, striding over to the broad table surface where Pertennius of Eubulus was standing over the drawings.

"You are in the Traversite Palace," said the little architect, Artibasos, helpfully. Maximius flashed him a glance etched in rancor.

"What do you mean?" Zakarios asked. His principal adviser was an officious, bristling, literal-minded man, but good at what he did.

"Well, look," said Maximius. "We are to imagine ourselves standing beneath this dome, within the Sanctuary. But lying along the . . . I suppose the eastern rim, the Rhodian is showing what is obviously the City . . . and he is showing the Sanctuary itself, seen from a distance . . ."

"As if from the sea, yes," said Valerius quietly.

". . . and so we will be *inside* the Sanctuary but must imagine ourselves to be *looking* at it from a distance. It . . . it gives me a headache," concluded Maximius firmly. He touched his brow, as if to emphasize the pain. Pertennius gave him a sidelong glance.

There was a little silence again. The Emperor looked at Artibasos. The architect said, with unexpected patience, "He is showing us the City within a larger meaning. Sarantium, Queen of Cities, glory of the world, and in such an image the Sanctuary is present, as it must be, along with the Hippodrome, the Precinct palaces, the landward walls, the harbor, the boats in the harbor . . ."

"But," said Maximius, a finger stabbing upward, "with all respect to our glorious Emperor, Sarantium is the glory of *this* world, whereas the house of the god honors the worlds above the world . . . or should." He looked back at the Patriarch, as if for approval.

"What is above it?" the Emperor asked softly.

Maximius turned quickly. "My lord? I beg your . . . above?"

"Above the City, cleric. What is there?"

Maximius swallowed.

"Jad is, my lord Emperor," said Pertennius the historian, answering. The secretary's tone was detached, the Patriarch thought, as if he'd really rather not be forced to participate in any of this. Only to chronicle it. Nonetheless, what he had said was true.

Zakarios could see the drawings from where he sat. The god was indeed above Sarantium, magnificent and majestic in his solar chariot, riding up like sunrise, straight on, unimpeachably bearded in the eastern fashion. Zakarios had half expected to protest a prettily golden western image here, but the Rhodian had not done that. Jad on this dome was dark and stern, as the eastern worshippers knew him, filling one side of the dome, nearly to the crown of it. It would be a glory if it could be achieved.

"Jad is, indeed," said Valerius the Emperor. "The Rhodian shows our City in majesty—the New Rhodias, as Saranios named it in the beginning and intended it to be—and above it, where he must be and always is, the artisan gives us the god." He turned to Zakarios. "My lord Patriarch, what confusing message is there in this? What will a weaver or a shoemaker or a soldier beneath this image take to his heart, gazing up?"

"There is more, my lord," added Artibasos quietly. "Look to the western rim of the dome, where he shows us Rhodias in ruins—a reminder of how fragile the achievements of mortal men must be. And see how all along the northern curve we will have the world the god has made in all its splendor and variety: men and women, farms, roads, small children, animals of all kinds, birds, hills, forests. Imagine these sketched trees as an autumn forest, my lords, as the notes suggest. Imagine the leaves in color overhead, lit by lanterns or the sun. That bull is a part of that, a part of what Jad has made, just as is the sea sweeping along the southern side of the dome toward the City. My lord Emperor, my lord Patriarch, the Rhodian is proposing to offer us, in mosaic, upon my dome, a rendering of so much of the world, the god's world, that I am . . . I find it overwhelming, I confess."

His voice trailed away. Pertennius, the historian, gave him a curious look. No one spoke immediately. Even Maximius was still. Zakarios drew a hand through his beard and looked across at the Emperor. They had known each other a long time.

"Overwhelming," the Patriarch echoed, claiming the word for himself. "Is it *too* ambitious?"

And saw he'd hit a sore point. Valerius looked directly at him a moment, then shrugged. "He has sketched it, undertakes to achieve it if we give him the men and material." He shrugged. "I can cut off his hands and blind him if he fails."

Pertennius glanced over at that, his thin features betraying no expression, then back to the sketches, which he'd been continuing to study.

"A question, if I may?" he murmured. "Is it . . . unbalanced, my lords? The god is always at the *center* of a dome. But here, Jad and the City are to the east, the god mounting up that side toward the apex . . .

but there is nothing to match him to the west. It is almost as if the design . . . *requires* a figure on the other side."

"He will give us a sky," said Artibasos, walking over. "Earth, sea, and sky. The notes describe a sunset, west, over Rhodias. Imagine that, with colors."

"Even so, I see a difficulty," said Leontes's long-faced scribe. He laid a manicured finger on the charcoal sketch. "With respect, my lords, you might suggest he put something *here*. More, um, well . . . *something*. Balance. For as we all know, balance is everything to the virtuous man." He looked pious, briefly, pursing his thin lips together.

Some pagan philosopher or other had probably said that, Zakarios thought sourly. He didn't like the historian. The man seemed to be always present, watching, giving nothing away.

"That," said Maximius, a little too petulantly, "might be so, but it does nothing to ease my headache, I can tell you that."

"And we are all very grateful," said the Emperor softly, "to be told that, cleric."

Maximius flushed beneath his black beard and then, seeing Valerius's icy expression, which did not sort with his mild tone, went pale. It was too easy to forget, sometimes, with the easy manners and open nature the Emperor displayed, Zakarios thought, sympathizing with his aide, how Valerius had brought his uncle to the throne and how he had kept it, himself.

The Patriarch intervened. "I am prepared to say that I am content. We find no heresies here. The god is honored and the City's earthly glory is properly shown to lie beneath Jad's protection. If the Emperor and his advisers are pleased we will approve this design on behalf of the god's clergy and bless the doing and the completing of it."

"Thank you," said Valerius. His nod was brief, formal. "We had relied upon you to say as much. This is a vision worthy of the Sanctuary, we judge."

"If it can be done," said Zakarios.

"There is always that," said Valerius. "Much that men strive to achieve fails in the doing. Will you take more wine?"

It was really very late. It was later still when the two clerics and the architect and historian took their leave, to be escorted from the Precinct by Excubitors. As they left the room, Zakarios saw Valerius signaling one of his secretaries. The man stumbled forward from the shadows along the wall. The Emperor had begun dictating to him, even before the door was closed.

Zakarios was to remember that image, and also the sensation he had, in the depths of the same night, waking from a dream.

He seldom dreamed, but in this one he was standing under the dome the Rhodian had made. It was done, achieved, and looking up by the blazing of suspended chandeliers and oil lamps and the massed candles, Zakarios had understood it wholly, as one thing, and had grasped what was happening on the western side, where nothing but a sunset lay opposite the god.

A sunset, while Jad was rising? Opposite the god? There *was* a heresy, he thought, sitting suddenly up in his bed, awake and disoriented. But he couldn't remember what *sort* it was, and he fell fitfully asleep again. By morning he had forgotten all but the moment, bolt upright in darkness, a dream of candlelit mosaics gone from him in the night like water in a rushing stream, like falling summer stars, like the touch of loved ones who have died and gone away.

IT CAME DOWN TO *seeing*, Martinian had always said, and Crispin had taught the same thing to all their apprentices over the years, believing it with passion. You saw in the eye of your mind, you looked with fierce attention at the world and what it showed you, you chose carefully among the tesserae and the stones and—if they were on offer—the semiprecious gems you were given. You stood or sat in the palace chamber or chapel or the bedroom or dining hall you were to work within, and you watched what happened through a day as the light changed, and then again at night, lighting candles or lanterns, paying for them yourself if you had to.

You went up close to the surface where you would work, touching it—as he was doing now, on a scaffold dizzyingly high above the polished marble floors of Artibasos's Sanctuary in Sarantium—and you ran your eyes and your fingers over and across the surface that had been given to you. No wall would ever be utterly smooth, no arc of a dome could attain perfection. Jad's children were not made for perfection. But you could *use* imperfections. You could compensate for them, and even turn them into strengths . . . if you knew them, and where they were.

Crispin intended to have the curve of this dome memorized, sight and touch, before he allowed even the bottom layer of rough plaster to be laid down. He'd won his first argument with Artibasos already, with unexpected support from the head of the bricklayers' guild. Moisture was the enemy of mosaic. They were to spread a shielding coat of resin over all the bricks, beginning it as soon as he was done with this traverse. Then the team of carpenters would hammer thousands of flat-headed nails through that coat and between the bricks, leaving the heads protruding slightly, to help the first coarse layer of plaster—rough-textured sand and pounded brick—adhere. It was almost always done in Batiara, virtually unknown here in the east, and Crispin had been vehement in his assurance that the nails would go a long way to helping the plaster bind firmly, especially on the curves of the dome. He was going to have them do it on the walls, too, though he hadn't told Artibasos or the carpenters yet. He had some further ideas for the walls as well. He hadn't talked about those yet, either.

There would be two more layers of plaster after the first, they had agreed, fine and then finer yet. And on the last of these he would do his work, with the craftsmen and apprentices he chose, following the design he had submitted and which had now been approved by court and clerics. And in the doing would seek to render here as much of the world as he knew and could compass in one work. No less than that.

For the truth was, he and Martinian had been wrong all these years, or not wholly right.

This was one of the hard things Crispin had learned on his journey, leaving home in bitterness and arriving in another state he could not yet define. Seeing was indeed at the heart of this craft of light and color—it had to be—but it was not all. One had to look, but also to have a *desire*, a need, a vision at the base of that seeing. If he was ever to achieve anything even approaching the unforgettable image of Jad he'd seen in that small chapel on the road, he would have to find within himself a depth of feeling that came—somehow—near to what had been felt by the unknown, fervently pious men who had rendered the god there.

He would never have their pure, unwavering certainty, but it seemed to him that something that might be equal to it was within him now, miraculously. He had come out from behind city walls in the fading west, carrying three dead souls in his walled heart and a birdsoul about his neck, and had journeyed to greater walls here in the east. From a city to the City, passing through wilderness and mist and into a wood that terrified—that could not but terrify—and out alive. Granted life, or—more truly, perhaps—with his life and Vargos's and Kasia's bought by Linon's soul left there on the grass at her own command.

He had seen a creature in the Aldwood he would have in him all his days. Just as Ilandra would be with him, and the heartbreak of his girls. You moved through time and things were left behind and yet stayed with you. The nature of how men lived. He had thought to avoid that, to hide from it, after they'd died. It could not be done.

"You do not honor them by living as if you, too, have died," Martinian had said to him, eliciting an anger near to rage. Crispin felt a deep rush of affection for his distant friend. Just now, high above the chaos of Sarantium, it seemed as if there were so many things he wanted to honor or exalt—or take to task, if it came to that, for there was no *need* for, no justice in, children dying of plague, or young girls being cut into pieces in the forest, or sold in grief for winter grain.

If this was the world as the god—or gods—had made it, then mortal man, *this* mortal man, could acknowledge that and honor the power and infinite majesty that lay within it, but he would *not* say it was right, or bow down as if he were only dust or a brittle leaf blown from an autumn tree, helpless in the wind.

He might be, all men and women might be as helpless as that leaf, but he would not admit it, and he would do something here on the dome that said—or aspired to say—these things, and more.

He had journeyed here to do this. Had done his sailing and was still sailing, perhaps, and would put into the mosaics of this Sanctuary as much of the living journey and what lay within it and behind it as his craft and desire could encompass.

He would even have—though he knew they might maim or blind him for it—Heladikos here. Even if only veiled, hinted at, in a sunset shaft of light and an absence. Someone looking up, someone tuned to images in a certain way, could place Jad's son himself where the design demanded he be, falling into the fallen west, a torch in his hand. The torch *would* be there, a spear of light from the low sunset clouds shooting up into the sky, or from heaven descending to earth where mortals dwelled.

He would have Ilandra here, and the girls, his mother, faces of his life, for there was room to place such images and they belonged, they were part of the sailing, his own and all men's journey. The figures of men's lives were the essence of those lives. What you found, loved, left behind, had taken away from you.

His Jad would be the bearded eastern god of that chapel in Sauradia, but the pagan *zubir* would be here on the dome, an animal hidden among the other animals he would render. And yet not quite so: only this one would be done in black and white stone, after the old Rhodian fashion of the first mosaics. And Crispin knew—if those approving his charcoal drawing could not—how that image of a Sauradian bison would show amid all the colors he was using here. And Linon, shining jewels for her eyes, would lie in the grass nearby—and let men wonder at it. Let them call the *zubir* a bull if they would, let them puzzle at a bird on the grass. Wonder and mystery were a part of faith, were they not? He would say that, if asked.

On the scaffold, he stood alone and apart, eyes to the brickwork, running his hands across and across like someone blind—and aware of that irony, as ever when he did this—gesturing below at intervals for the apprentices to wheel the scaffold for him. It swayed when it moved, he had to grip the railing, but he had spent much of his working life on platforms such as this and had no fear of the height. It was a refuge, in fact. High above the world, above the living and the dying, the intrigues of courts and men and women, of nations and tribes and factions and the human heart trapped in time and yearning for more than it was allowed, Crispin strove not to be drawn back down into the confusing fury of those things, desiring now to live—as Martinian had urged him—but *away* from the blurring strife, to achieve this vision of a world on a dome. All else was transitory, ephemeral. He was a mosaicist, as he had told people and told people, and this distanced elevation was his haven and his source and destination, all in one. And with fortune and the god's blessing he might do something here that could last, and leave a name.

So he thought, was thinking, in the moment he glanced down from so far above the world to check if the apprentices had locked the scaffold wheels again, and saw a woman come through the silver doors into the sanctuary.

She moved forward, walking over the gleaming marble stones, graceful, even as seen from so high, and she stopped under the dome and looked up.

She looked up for him and, without a word spoken or a gesture made, Crispin felt a tugging back of the world as something fierce and physical, imperative, commanding, making a mockery of illusions of remote asceticism. He was not made to live his life like a holy man in an untouchable place. Best he acknowledge it now. Perfection, he had just been thinking, was not attainable by men. Imperfections could be turned into strengths. Perhaps.

Standing on the scaffold, he laid both hands flat for a moment more against the cold bricks of the dome and closed his eyes. It was extremely quiet this high up, serene, solitary. A world to himself, a creation to enact. It ought to have been enough. Why was it not? He let his hands fall to his sides. Then he shrugged—a gesture his mother knew, and his friends, and his dead wife—and motioning for those below to hold the platform steady, he began the long climb down.

He was in the world, neither above it nor walled off from it anymore. If he had sailed to anything, it was to that truth. He would do this work or would fail in it as a man living in his time, among friends, enemies, perhaps lovers, and perhaps with love, in Varena under the Antae or here in Sarantium, City of Cities, eye of the world, in the reign of the great and glorious, thrice-exalted Emperor Valerius II, Jad's Regent upon earth, and the Empress Alixana.

It was a long, slow descent, hand and foot, the familiar movements, over and again. Out of careful habit he emptied his mind as he came down: men died if they were careless here, and this dome was higher than any he had known. He felt the pull, though, even as he moved: the world drawing him back down to itself.

He reached the wooden base of the rolling platform, set on wheels upon the marble floor. He swung around and stood on the base a moment, that little distance yet above the ground. Then he nodded his head to the woman standing there, who had neither spoken nor gestured but who had come here and had claimed him for them all. He wondered if, somehow, she had known she was doing that. She might have. It would sort with what he knew about her, already.

He drew a breath and stepped down off the scaffolding. She smiled.

AUTHOR PHOTO BY BETH GWINN

Guy Gavriel Kay is an international bestselling author. He has been awarded the International Goliardos Prize for his work in the literature of the fantastic, is a two-time winner of the Aurora Award, and has won the 2008 World Fantasy Award for *Ysabel*. His works have been translated into twenty-five languages. Visit his authorized Web site at www.brightweavings.com.